Maria Josepha Stanley, Jane H. Adeane

The Girlhood of Maria Josepha Holroyd

Maria Josepha Stanley, Jane H. Adeane

The Girlhood of Maria Josepha Holroyd

ISBN/EAN: 9783337367435

Printed in Europe, USA, Canada, Australia, Japan

Cover: Foto ©Andreas Hilbeck / pixelio.de

More available books at **www.hansebooks.com**

THE GIRLHOOD OF MARIA
JOSEPHA HOLROYD [LADY
STANLEY OF ALDERLEY]. RECORDED
IN LETTERS OF A HUNDRED
YEARS AGO: FROM 1776
TO 1796. EDITED BY
J. H. ADEANE

SHEFFIELD PLACE, 1791

'Lord Sheffield's eldest daughter is indeed a most extraordinary young woman'—GIBBON to his Stepmother, 1791

LONGMANS, GREEN, AND CO.
LONDON, NEW YORK, AND BOMBAY
1896

TO MY SISTER

CONSTANCE MARIA JOSEPHA

GRANDCHILD, GODCHILD, AND NAMESAKE

OF THE MARIA JOSEPHA

WHOSE EARLY LIFE IS HERE DEPICTED

PREFACE

THE early letters of MARIA JOSEPHA HOLROYD were considered by her contemporaries to be of unusual merit and worthy of careful preservation. Her acquaintance with many of the actors in the stirring scenes amid which her youth was spent furnished her with subjects of more than passing interest. 'Were you to keep a journal,' Gibbon writes to her, 'of all the authentic facts which the French exiles relate, it would be an agreeable exercise at present, and a future source of interest and instruction.' What Gibbon thought too of her style the following extracts from his letters to her father, Lord Sheffield, show : 'I must have from the very excellent pen of the Maria the tragedy of the Archbishop of Arles, and the longer the better ; ' and again, 'The five incomparable letters of Maria.'

For more, however, than style or energy of description were they valued. Serena Holroyd writes to her niece, 'Your remarks on the present state of literature are so strikingly just on all sides that I should almost like to publish them. As I think it is likely some of your younger children may be poor, if your letters are collected they might make one of them rich ! ' Now that this suggestion, after the lapse of a hundred years, is being in part fulfilled, it may not be too much to hope that the letters, which then gave so much pleasure, will not have lost their charm, but will interest others besides the grand-daughter to whose care they were entrusted, and to whom the arrangement and editing of them has been so great a delight.

J. H. A.

October 11, 1896.   *The Centenary of Maria Josepha's wedding-day.*

CONTENTS

---◦◦◦---

CHAPTER I.

EARLY DAYS.

1777-1787.

CHAPTER II.

FIRST FLIGHTS.

JANUARY, 1788—JUNE, 1791.

CHAPTER III.

CRAZY PARIS.

JUNE TO AUGUST, 1791.

CONTENTS. xi

CHAPTER VIII.

EVIL DAYS. THE PITY OF IT.

1792.

CHAPTER IX.

THE PRIESTS' TALE

AUGUST TO DECEMBER, 1792.

CHAPTER X.

DEATH OF ABIGAIL, LADY SHEFFIELD.

1793.

CHAPTER XI.

MARIA JOSEPHA AS CHÂTELAINE.

1793.

CHAPTER XII.

THE HISTORIAN'S LAST PAGE.

JANUARY TO JULY, 1794.

CHAPTER XIII.

OLD FRIENDS AND NEW TIES.

JULY TO DECEMBER, 1794.

CHAPTER XIV.

LUCY, LADY SHEFFIELD, 'THE DEAR LADY.'

1795.

CHAPTER XV.

'THAT SOMETHING MAY COME OF SOMETHING.'

JANUARY TO APRIL, 1796.

CHAPTER XVI.

THE WORD 'OBEY' IS SAID.

MAY TO OCTOBER, 1796.

Errata.

Page 29, line 5, *for* ' polisettes ' *read* ' jolisettes.'
 „ 239, lines 3 and 4 from bottom, *for* Castaux *read* Carteaux.
 „ 336, line 10, *for* Puisaye *read* Puisaye.
Pages 351, 352, 354, *for* Bromerton *read* Bomerton.

LIST OF PLATES.

The figures of Gibbon and Lord Sheffield, on the cover, are reproductions of silhouettes taken in 1791, and preserved by Maria Josepha Holroyd, among her souvenirs of the visit to Lausanne.

INTRODUCTION.

MARIA JOSEPHA HOLROYD was born January 3, 1771. Her father, John Baker Holroyd, was created Baron Sheffield of Dunamore, Co. Meath, in 1781, given an English peerage in 1802, and advanced to the Earldom of Sheffield, in the Peerage of Ireland, in 1816.

Lord Sheffield was a man of cultivated literary taste, an authority on questions of Finance, Commerce, and Agriculture, and an industrious Member of Parliament. He was a weighty speaker; a writer on Political Economy, and an energetic and enlightened County Magistrate. He represented Coventry and Bristol in the House of Commons; was a Lord of Trade, and later, President of the Board of Agriculture, and a member of the Privy Council. He especially interested himself in the Government of Ireland, and in the commercial relations between England and America.

Lord Sheffield's first wife was Abigail, daughter of Lewis Way, of Old Court, Richmond, by his third wife, Abigail, daughter and heiress of Edward Lockey, of Denham Place, Bucks, which became their home in 1730, and was the birthplace of their daughter.

Abigail, Lady Sheffield, was a refined and beautiful woman, whose grace and charm of manner endeared her to her husband's friends.

a

Gibbon's appreciation of her was shown by his expressions when writing of his intended visit to England, 'Lord Sheffield and yourself will be the loadstone that attracts me,' and again to Lord Sheffield, 'Insinuate to your silent Consort that separate letters require separate answers.'

The fatigue and hardships of their foreign tour in 1791 seem to have been too much for Lady Sheffield's fragile health and nervous temperament, and from that time many of her duties devolved on her bright and capable daughter Maria Josepha.

It is a pathetic fact and worthy of record that Lady Sheffield died from a chill caught on Good Friday 1793, while ministering to the comfort of French refugees lying ill at Guy's Hospital, of which Institution her father and brother were Presidents in succession.

At his house in Downing Street and in the 'hospitable retreat' as Gibbon found it, of Sheffield Place, in Sussex, Lord Sheffield entertained the leading spirits of his day. Men of mark in politics, science, literature, and art met at his home and shone in its congenial atmosphere. Lord Sheffield's lifelong friendship with Gibbon dated from the time they were together at Lausanne in 1764, when the historian wrote of him as 'a friend whose activity in the ardour of youth was always prompted by a benevolent heart and directed by a strong understanding.'

During the social upheaval in France, distinguished Emigrés such as Comte de Lally Tollendal, Prince de Poix, M. Malouet, fugitive princesses, exiled savants, and shipwrecked priests, found under Lord Sheffield's roof the kindest welcome and the most efficient aid. In such varied society Maria Josepha and her sister Louisa spent their girlhood.

Maria's keen intellect was early stimulated by the conversation around her ; and she entered eagerly, while yet a child, into all her father's interests. She had de-cided views of people and things, and formed her own opinions on every sort of subject, social, political, and religious, and was accustomed to read and criticise the best books, English and foreign. She early acquired a love of botany from Sir Joseph Banks, and delighted in gardening and country pursuits. Nor were domestic concerns beneath her notice. A new stitch in needle-work, a good pattern for her father's shirt, or a house-hold recipe (even for feeding nightingales), were equally welcome to her.

At seven years old Maria Josepha was already con-sidered a delightful companion by her grandfather, Mr. Isaac Holroyd, and by his daughter Sarah Martha, better known as 'Serena,' a name perhaps suggested by a sweet-ness of disposition as great as that of Hayley's 'Serena' in his once popular poem of 'The Triumphs of Temper.' At the age of twelve she was writing on easy terms of equality to her older relations ; indeed, when her father was too busy, and her mother too tired to write, they depended entirely on Maria to transmit tidings of the family, which she never failed to do.

To her Aunt 'Serena' most of Maria's letters are addressed. Another correspondent was Miss Ann Firth, long a member of the household circle at Sheffield Place, and tenderly cared for by successive generations up to her hundredth year.

This family correspondence, interspersed with occa-

sional letters from friends, foreign and English, gives
pictures of Society in London and in Bath ; of a journey
across France in the early days of the French Revolution, of the state of Paris, and of one of the most
fantastic incidents of that strange time, the Apotheosis
of Voltaire.

A visit to Mr. Gibbon's home at Lausanne is also
described, together with the return journey of the
travellers through Germany, when all Europe was
beginning to arm. Later, there are allusions to the
threatened invasion of England by the French, the life
of the French Emigrés, the trial of Warren Hastings,
and the serious condition of the agricultural classes in
England.

The home life of Maria Josepha is brought vividly
before us, her mother's sudden death, her father's second
marriage, and the growth of that friendship with Mr.
Stanley which determined the whole course of her
after life.

These letters cover the period of twenty years of
Maria Josepha's eventful youth—ending in 1796.

The first letter was written to her when she was a
child of six by Serena Holroyd. The last letter is
written by herself as a bride to her old friend Miss Firth,
dated from her new home, in the first happy days of her
marriage to Mr. Stanley, afterwards first Lord Stanley
of Alderley.

THE GIRLHOOD

OF

MARIA JOSEPHA HOLROYD

CHAPTER I.

EARLY DAYS.

1777–1787.

Letter from Serena—Going to the play—The Polish dwarf—An éloge—
First mention of Gibbon—Original story—Serena's advice as to deport-
ment—Mrs. Siddons—Lord Sheffield an author—Varied reading—
Daily occupations—Duchess of Portland's museums—Improvements at
Sheffield Place—First Sunday School at Bath—Industrial Schools—
Gibbon's expected visit—Sir Joseph Banks.

Serena to her Niece Maria Josepha.

Bath : January, 1777.

THOUGH I have been prevented from answering my
dearest Maria's letter sooner, I thought it a very pretty
one, and it gave great pleasure both to Grandpapa and me.
We are very happy whenever we hear that our dear little
Maria is well and deserves to be loved. We remembered
your Birthday[1] and drank your health, and wished you
many happy years, and longed to give you sweet kisses.
We hoped you would live to be the joy of Papa and
Mama, and by your affection and goodness make them a
return for their care and tenderness, and then you will be
as happy as we wish. You are now, I daresay, entertaining dear Grandmama and comforting her for their absence.

[1] January 3, Maria's birthday, an anniversary always observed in the
family.

B

You are her little nurse and companion, and she loves you
for it and so do we. . . . We wish to see Dr. Foster, who
is coming to Bath, because he will give us a particular
account of you, and I hope will tell us that you grow every
day more pleasing, and that you are gentle, good and
obliging to everybody.   Girls that are not so always pass
for vulgar, ill-bred children, and are despised and unhappy.
You will remember this I am sure, and will try to gain
hearts by the sweetness of your temper.   Your Grandpapa
sends love to you, and if he was able, would go two
hundred miles to see you. . . . I hope, some time, we
shall have this pleasure.   Remember us, as kindly as
possible, to dear Gran, who we hope is better than usual.
Say everything kind for us to Miss Firth, whom we all
love.   Mrs. Gibbon [1] never forgets you, but presents compliments.   I should write more, but that I have written a
long letter to mama, and don't know anything that would
entertain you.   Think of us often, my dear little Maria,
and believe that I love you with my whole heart, and shall
be ever, your sincerely affectionate Aunt,

S. HOLROYD.

Maria Josepha to Serena.

Sheffield Place : Sunday, July ye 7, 1782.

Your letter quite delighted me ; they are always so
entertaining that (except papa and mama) I had rather
have one letter from my dear Serena, than ten from anybody else. . . . As I have not wrote to you for some time,
I must tell you a few things about London, tho' we have
been in the country a month next Wednesday.   About
three weeks or a month before we went out of town, we
went to Sadler's Wells ; Louisa [2] went for the first time of

[1] Stepmother to the historian.
[2] Her younger sister, afterwards Lady Louisa Clinton.

her going into those sort of places; it was very well
bestowed upon her, for she was as delighted as ever she
could be. Have you ever been there? and how do you
like it? For my part I liked it very much, but not to
come up to a Play. Then we went to see the Polish
Dwarf and the Irish Giant, I do not know whether you
may have heard talk of them; the first is exactly three
foot high, and the last eight foot, two Inches. What a
difference! I beg you will never make what you call an
apology for not writing; you write when you please, and I
write when I please without any set time. . . . I will
allow you to moralise as much as you please, for the more
you do, the more agreeable are your letters. The Lessons
you mention as having received from my dear Grandfather
are excellent; and, pray God! I may profit by them as
you have. You showed me when you was in Downing
Street an éloge on him, I think in French, made by yourself, may I beg a copy of it from you. I will keep it as
the virtues of one who is now no more, and as a proof of
my dearest Serena's talents. You say you felt like a
young woman again when you was drinking tea out of
doors at Miss Cooper's. Pray how long is it since you
was an old one? I could have romped with you very
well just as I do at home. You think I do not regret
London. I should not if the year was equally divided;
but we are only five months in town, and seven in the
country. I do not give you any settled time to write in,
but be assured that my Serena's letters will always be
acceptable to her most affectionate,

MARIA JOSEPHA HOLROYD.

[The following copy of the 'Eloge' shows that Serena
complied with the request. It was found carefully preserved among Maria's treasures.]

Cinq mois après la mort de mon Père. October. 1778.

C'était l'âme la plus sensible qui fut jamais ; l'exacte vérité, l'équite délicate, l'inviolable fidélité, la tendre et bienfaisante humanité résidoient dans son cœur. Elles y étoient nées et s'y maintenoient sans effort. Cette chaleur vivifiante qui donne de la grâce à tout, (même aux défauts) ornoit ses vertus et le rendoit aussi aimable qu'il étoit estimable. Mais ce que plus que tout le reste lui attachoit ses amis, c'est qu'on trouvoit en lui la vraie et parfaite amitié, si souvent soupçonnée de n'être qu'une vaine Idée. La confiance qu'il savoit inspirer, c'etoit celle qu'on a pour soi-même, et volontiers on lui eût dit ce qu'on auroit eu peine à s'avouer. Le tendre intérêt dont on le voyoit pénétré et sa vive attention à ce qu'on lui disoit, alloit jusqu'au fond du cœur et en développoit les replis les plus cachés.

Voilà le vrai Portrait du cher Père que j'ai perdu.

Est-ce qu'il me faut le pleurer ?

Peut-on l'oublier ?

Il est mort Mai 11me, 1778.

S. HOLROYD.

Serena to Maria Josepha.

Bath : August 8, 1782.

How happy my dearest Maria makes me in telling me that our correspondence is a pleasure to her ! I could scarce flatter myself it would be so, though I did not doubt that you would comply with the request to oblige me. . . . If I told you all that I think of your letters it would seem like flattery, and might prevent the liberty and ease of your stile, which is the very thing I like best, and what I have scarce met in a young beginner. I can hardly persuade myself that a dear girl between eleven and twelve, writes to an Aunt past 40, as if it were to her friend of her own age; and yet it is doubly pleasant, because it is a sure proof of affection, and that you don't think that same Aunt a formal, cross creature. Believe me, my dear Maria, she will ever love you most sincerely and hopes to be ever dear to you. . . . I fear these heavy rains must be bad for the corn. I wonder how 'Farmer Sheffield' escapes. . . . Adieu now, my dearest Maria. I may tire you as well as myself; though we shall not be tired of loving one another, we may be tired of too long writing.

I am, most sincerely and affectionately yours,

S. HOLROYD.

Serena to Maria Josepha.

Bath: November 30, 1782.

. . . . I drank tea with the Duchess of Ancaster, and Lady Mary Bertie asked very obligingly for you, and said she liked you so much she wished you were better acquainted. She said you were very sprightly and polite. . . . I hope you will see the little Polish Count, who had a sister only 17 inches high; a perfectly proportioned beautiful creature, eighteen years old, who died of the small pox. I enclose the real measure of the Count's sole of his shoe. My shoemaker made him a pair. I have not seen him and you will think me very dull; but to say truth I have no pleasure in those sort of objects, though everybody says he is so lively and entertaining, that he is a very pleasing companion. Mr. Gibbon liked him so much that he will give you the best account, and had I been here, when Mr. Gibbon was at Bath, I should have seen the Count to great advantage in his company, as he entertained him particularly well.

Maria Josepha to Serena.

London: Monday, February 16, 1783.

If I knew not how fully your time is employed, I should be indignant at your long silence; but the Length and Agreeableness of your Letters when you do write, take from me all possibility of complaining.

You desire to have a Journal of my London life. You forget who you are writing to. I am no Rake. However, for me, I have been one. Last Thursday Papa, Mama, my Aunt Way, Mrs. Foster and myself went to the Opera. I was very much entertained; but what is an Opera compared with Mrs. Siddons and a Play? Have you got 'Les Annales de la Vertu,' or have you only heard of it? I have not got it. Did I not tell you some time ago I had seen the little Baron? If not, I do now. I saw him last year. You have lost a very curious sight by not seeing him. I likewise saw the Irish Giant: since I saw them, the little Baron has been prevailed upon to visit the Giant. They measured: and the Baron came up to the second knee Button! I did not see them together, but had this account from Mr. Gibbon, (who is now laid up with a fit of the Gout).

I am writing on the Duchess of C—— though slowly; but my time is so taken up with different affairs such as Dancing, Music, Geography, Work, &c., &c., that I have scarce any time to write, but on a Sunday. I am very much afraid you have forgot the beginning of the story; however, this I dare say you will remember,[1] that

---

[1] This is a sarcastic allusion to *The Duchesse de C.*, an original story by Maria, in which the heroine meets with a tragic fate at the hands of her jealous husband.

the Duke is a Good-tempered, Agreeable, Affectionate, kind husband. If ever you marry, I hope you will meet with full as good a one. . . .

I am, my dear Serena's most affectionate
MARIA JOSEPHA HOLROYD.

Maria Josepha to Serena.

Sheffield Place : September 12, 1783.

Indeed, my dearest Serena, I think it a great condescension on my part to write to you, since you have not wrote to me from April 12. But as the last sheet of the Duchess of C—— left her in the Dungeon, I thought you would be glad to know how she liked her situation, and I thought likewise that I might as well write, if it was only for the pleasure of finding fault with you.

I have got ' Les Annales de la Vertu.' I like them very much. . . . I think all Madame de Genlis' works that I have seen very pretty ; but I prefer ' Adèle and Theodore ' as yet, for I have but begun ' Les Annales.' . . .

I expect a letter very soon, or I shall be no longer my dearest Serena's affectionate
MARIA JOSEPHA HOLROYD.

Serena to Maria Josepha.

Brighton : Sunday, September 15, 1783.

Last night I received the dear Maria's letter, and, to make amends for past omissions, don't delay a post sending a thousand thanks. You know I delight in your letters. . . . However, I allow it to be condescending in you not to drop such a correspondent as this same Serena, and if she is not very ungrateful, I think your manner of correcting her for her faults must have a good effect upon her.

I am very much obliged to you for introducing me again to the poor Duchesse de C——. I began to think it cruel to make no inquiry about her in such a situation and for such a time. Her misfortunes so interest me, and still more as a certain little pen that writes them will be so dear to me, that I shall keep the whole when finished to look at in future days, and perhaps show you some twenty years hence. When your husband treats you as the Duchesse de C——, which is probable, I flatter myself you will have the same patience, fortitude, and resignation ! . . .

I saw Lady Rothes yesterday, and asked her the question mama desired—of the year in which the same sort of meteor, as we have lately seen, made its appearance, and she says it was in 1716.

Lady Rothes heard that Mr. Gibbon was nominated to succeed Mr. Maddison, as Secretary to the Embassy; but I want faith, and don't think he would accept it. I want to hear more of him.

I hope Mrs. Porten [1] arrived safe and well at Sheffield Place.

Ever, dear Maria's affectionate
S. H.

Serena to Maria Josepha.

Bath : January 19, 1784.

I have been so much taken up with my Bath friends after a long absence from them, that I have never had time to write to my dearest Maria, though I have often sent my love to her. I have never, however, had you out

---

[1] Gibbon's favourite aunt, of whom he writes to Lord Sheffield, ' You have obliged me beyond expression by your kindness to Aunt Kitty. . . . *Apropos*, I think Aunt Kitty has a secret wish to sleep in my room ; if it is not occupied, she might be indulged.'

of my thoughts, nor ever forgot the pleasure I had when at Sheffield Place, in observing not only the prettiest, kindest attention to myself, and many sweet marks of your affection, but also in your whole stile and manner to everybody. . . . Beauty in a woman is of no consequence, but a good carriage, a strait shape, and genteel person, mark the well-educated, and seem to me as necessary for a woman of any fashion as to know how to spell. We have got an Air-Balloon in Bath, but I don't go to see it, as I saw it in London ; nor have I gone to a Play or a Ball. I am quite the Dowager, but my beauty, embonpoint, and bloom are much admired in a quiet way. I hear that you don't allow me to be a ' cat ' ! Mama was so good to tell me so, and I was delighted with your clearing me from such vile aspersions. . . .

Maria Josepha to Serena.

Downing Street : March, 1784.

I have seen Mrs. Siddons ; she was not ill this time. My Aunt Gregory Way had the two front Rows of a Front Box, and offered Mama two places. The Play was ' Isabella,' which, on Mama's account, I was sorry for, as she had seen it twice. I myself had no objection to it. Mrs. S—— fully answered my expectations. She left out that dreadful Shriek I have heard she gave on seeing Biron. Her dress was very pretty, particularly the white. Her voice was so low that in many parts I could scarce hear her. I think her very pretty. . . .

As for the Duchess de C——, you must not expect to hear anything of her till I go into the Country; but I think we left her very properly ; for, as she was uncertain of her fate for nine years, is it not fair that you should be so for at least as many weeks ? We have got a Seat in Duke Street Chapel. I should have preferred a Church with an Organ in it.   Mr. Catton has given [Louisa] an Air-Balloon work bag; it is made of pink silk.   Everything now is Air-Balloons: there are Balloon Hats, Balloon Cakes, Work Bags, and even Balloon Noses. . . .

Serena to Maria Josepha.

Bath : May 2, 1784.

. . . I am not reconciled to the loss of franks.[1]   I love the liberty of enclosing letters and of scribbling as much as I please, but I shall not allow it to deprive me of my dear Girl's letters.   It would be a bad compliment to say I only valued them at fourpence, therefore I flatter myself it will never stop you from writing, when you have time and inclination.

Maria Josepha to Serena.

Sheffield Place: December 22, 1784.

. . . Papa returned on Sunday; he is writing hard about Ireland; he has abundance of papers on the subject.   He thinks Mr. Pitt knows very little about it; he is trying to learn it, but has nobody about him that knows anything of the matter better than he; however, Papa's opinions are not concealed.   Ireland is pretty quiet just now, but it is thought the Patriots will be troublesome in the House.   M. Caplin[2] is come, and says Mr. Gibbon was never better in health, not having had the gout since he was at Lausanne, and, we are sorry to hear, never happier.   Mr. Corry, an active member of the Irish Parliament, and Mr. Tarleton, the very warm admirer of the Author (my Papa), are to be here on Friday next. We have no hopes that he will now ever be better than

---

[1] Lord Sheffield had just lost his seat for Coventry.
[2] Mr. Gibbon's English valet.

an Author. If he must be one I wish he was a Poet ; it
would be pleasanter to me when I speak to him that he
should utter some sublime verses, than let it appear he
was attending only to the Herring Fishery or the Woolen
Manufacture. I am occasionally employed to read some
horrid and almost illegible Manuscripts on these Subjects ;
dear Mama does not doat upon these pursuits more than
Louisa or I ; Louisa calls it ' nasty commerce,' but Miss
Firth has more reason to complain, as she has the tremendous business of making out Tables of Figures. A
Scotch Author called on Papa last week in London, and
told him he might come in for any place in Scotland if
there was a vacancy, and Mr. Tarleton says that some
great Frenchman, talking of Papa's work, said, ' If he
should live to see a French Nobleman write thus on
Commerce, he should be quite content and satisfied.' . . .

I am, my dear Serena's most affectionate
MARIA J. HOLROYD.

Maria Josepha to Serena.

Downing Street : February 13, 1786.

You wish to know my Studies. In the first place I
am reading ' Les Œuvres de Dieu,' for which I cannot
thank you enough. I never read anything of the sort
that was at the same time so amusing and instructive,
and where everything is turned to a Religious Purpose.
' Sully's Memoirs ' and ' Plutarch's Lives ' I am also
reading. I like very much separate lives of Great Men ;
these, you know, are ancient, but I have read, too, John-
son's ' Lives of the Poets,' which entertained me very
much. . . . Did you ever read Destouche's ' Plays ' in
French ? Ten very small Duodecimos, and are, I think,
very good plays ; but my favourite plays are Le Mercier.'s,

who wrote the 'Tableau de Paris.' His are mostly serious, and the 'Deserter' is one from which that charming Dance was taken, performed for two Seasons at the Opera House. . . . You have heard, I daresay, of Mrs. Jordan, who is all the fashion here. I hope to see her soon, and I will then give you my opinion of her. I do not wish to see Miss Brunton, for I am so delighted with Mrs. Siddons that I would not be put out of conceit with her.

Papa has put me this year upon my allowance, and gives me forty pounds a year for everything. . . . I think Sheffield Place is much preferable to this place, at least at present; for putting together my rides, my dining and supping down stairs, I feel myself more of a Woman there; but however, that is to come even in Town some time or other, and then, perhaps, I may change my opinion.

Maria Josepha to Serena.

Sheffield Place : March 1, 1786.

I used formerly to be a greater Friend to London than Sheffield; but since I have begun to ride upon Pearl, she and my riding habit, add great charms to the country. I look forward with pleasure to July, when I hope to renew my farming rides with the Author, for Mama does not take as much pleasure as I do, in Ploughed Fields and Dirty Lanes. I hope you will come to Sheffield this summer to ride with me. I do not know whether you are fond of what we call Expeditions, but if I can persuade you to come I will give them up to ride Serene-ly and Sober-ly.

I went last Thursday to my first Play at the Haymarket Theatre with Mama, Mrs. Porten, and Mr. Lascelles. Papa was too busy Importing and Exporting to think of such a thing.

Serena to Maria Josepha.

Bath: March 5, 1786.

. . . I am glad your hair is turned up, because I think you will look neater and better for it. Neatness is elegance, and in that your Mama sets you the very best example. Might I advise, if she does not disapprove of it, that you should learn to dress your hair a little yourself? I do not mean that you should not have a hairdresser as often as you please; but I mean that you should know how to do it when occasion may require, for you cannot imagine how inconvenient it is to be totally helpless sometimes. . . . I know girls of the very first fashion who are taught to dress themselves entirely—to pack up even, and take care of all their cloaths. I dwell upon these subjects, my dear Maria, because this is your only time. It will be too late when you are in the world. . . .

Maria Josepha to Serena.

Sheffield Place: April, 1786.

May I entreat you, my dear Serena, to intercede for me with my *Aunt*; it is true I do not deserve forgiveness and my reasons for not writing are pretty near the same as Madame de Sévignè's. 'La raison pourquoi je n'ai pas écrit, c'est que j'ai eu le tems de vous écrire, j'aime beaucoup à vous écrire, et je sais bien qu'il y a long-temps que je devois vous écrire.' Some such words she says to M. de Coulanges; but I forget where. This is exactly my case. As I hear from her through Mama every week, she cannot accuse me of indifference towards her—for my part, I shall not dare to write to her till I hear from you. . . . As I flatter myself you, (through my Aunt,) have some little regard for me, I will give an

account of one day and then you will see every day. I
get up at 8, I walk from 9 to 10; we then breakfast;
about 11, I play on the Harpsichord or I draw. 1, I
translate, and, 2, walk out again, 3, I generally read, and,
4, we go to dine, after Dinner we play at Backgammon;
we drink Tea at 7, and I work or play on the Piano
till 10, when we have our little bit of Supper and, 11, we
go to Bed. . . . I am to have Miss Firth's room nicely
done up for me, and I think I have very near carried
another point, which is to breakfast down stairs.

Pray give my kindest love to my Aunt and believe me,
dear Serena's

Most affectionate

MARIA HOLROYD.

Maria Josepha to Serena.

Downing Street: April 25, 1786.

I am reading the Peruvian Letters, which I like
very much; there is so much Nature in them. Zilia's
thoughts in the Ship and on first coming to France
entertained me very much. Do you remember her describing the French as 'escaped out of their Maker's
Hand when they were only composed of Fire and Air!'

Since I last wrote I have been to the Duchess of
Portland's Museums; the time of Exhibition was only
9 Days; but there was such variety and numbers that
a Month's looking would not have been enough to see
them entirely, especially the Shells, of which there were
some beautiful ones. The famous Vase of Alexander
Severus did not please me so much as some of the other
curiosities. Queen Elizabeth's Prayer Book, composed
and written, as they say, by herself, with the pictures of
the Duke D'Alençon and herself; the Miniature Portraits
of Madame de Sévigné, Madame de la Vallière, and

Milton and his Mother, I think are much more agreeable to see, because as they lived in later Times, I know more about them.

I have learnt the Fillagree work this winter, and have done a Box in purple, green and gold for Mama. It is dirty work, the dye of the paper comes off when wet with Gum.

Maria Josepha to Serena.

Sheffield Place: September 1, 1786.

. . . I trust you will not spend another Summer without coming to give a look at Sheffield Place and its Inhabitants; how many new things there will be to amuse you! Fletching alone will take up a great deal of your attention; the Lodge, in which will reside a Serjeant of Papa's Regiment,[1] sent for on purpose out of Scotland, who is to open the Gate for you in his Helmet and Regimentals; his broad Sword and Musquet to hang over the Chimney; the Mausoleum in which we shall one day reside ourselves, and last, though not least, an Oven, (now building at the Griffin,) large enough to bake for the whole county of Sussex. To come nearer the House, there are four young Swans, upon the Pond before the Windows, now entirely grey, which supposing they neither die, or fly away, will be very pretty objects from your Room; then the Deer are new since you was here. . . . I have just begun to work myself a Gown in Spots, which is a very great undertaking; but I do not despair of finishing it in a year or two, and I hope the Fashions will have the complaisance to wait for me; and that Spotted Muslin will not go out.

Pray are you as tired of Margaret Nicholson as we

---

[1] Lord Sheffield commanded a regiment of light dragoons, which he raised himself, and which was disbanded in 1783.

are ? our Papers have not done with her yet, but I
suppose now the King of Prussia will take her place.
My family desires compliments to your family, especially
the Bullfinch, who is now singing, which I interpret to
be fine speeches to you and yours.   I am, dear Aunt,

Yr most affectionate and dutiful

MARIA J. HOLROYD.

Maria Josepha to Serena.

Sheffield Place : December 31, 1786.

As it is necessary, I suppose, to mention something
on the subject of the New Year at the end of the old one,
if I do not say as much as I ought, I hope you will
understand it as meant.   However, this I think, is the
usual form : I wish you a Merry Christmas and a Happy
New Year and good health to enjoy many of them ; and
in addition to this, entirely out of my own head, I assure
you, I hope and trust 1787 will not pass over 'till you
have paid us a visit at Sheffield Place, and likewise a
promise not to be gone 'till we are tired of you, particularly if we do not go to Town as Papa threatens us.
You gave us some hopes of your coming when you was
last in Town ; I hope you have not forgot it entirely.

Maria Josepha to Serena.

Sheffield Place : July ye 21, 1787.

Pray give my love to Cousin Brunette and tell her
when she comes to Sheffield, she will find a new Cousin
and a very pretty one too in Tuft,[1] who begs his love
also.   To give you an Account of my Family, I have
got a young Bullfinch, so tame that it will sit upon my
shoulder and hand while I work, and pick the Thread out
of my Needle, and is the dearest little Creature.

[1] Lady Sheffield's lapdog.

Serena to Maria Josepha.

Bath: August 4, 1787.

I won't allow, my dearest Maria, that your letter was dull. . . . One affectionate line from you gives me more pleasure than all the entertainment you could possibly send me, were you even a Madame de Sévigny. . . . Papa and Mama both tell me how much you are improved. I only hear of a certain bad carriage and walk, with a little too fast speaking, which I intend should be quite got rid of before Winter, as you will now in a Manner begin the world, and make your first appearance as being no longer a child. Lord Chesterfield, you will find, reckons speaking fast as totally inconsistent with grace or dignity even in the female, who is allowed the privilege of being less solemn than a man ; but it is like a pert chambermaid rather than a woman of fashion, to chatter fast, and it is a common observation that few sensible women do so. . . . You can hardly imagine how often I think of you. I never see anything I like but I wish you to enjoy it. Last Sunday, for example, I particularly wished to have had you witness to a scene that struck me beyond description.

It was at our Cathedral, which we call the Abbey. I daresay you have heard of Sunday Schools. It is but lately we have had that institution here, and at first it went on slowly ; but by joining it to a School of Industry, they now all crowd to the other, which is a necessary step to that of industry. There is a clergyman employed for this Sunday evening service for the children alone, after the other common service is over, and it is in the great Isle where you must suppose nine hundred children in perfect order, placed on benches in long rows, so quiet that you could hardly have heard a pin drop while the Clergyman was reading. Reflect how very extraordinary

C

this circumstance alone! when you recollect that most of them were taken out of the streets, untaught and actually almost savage, cursing, swearing, and fighting in the streets all day, and many without a home at night. Two girls, I myself know, slept in the street. Most of them not only ragged and starving, but without a chance of being put in the way to earn their bread. Yet here I saw them, not only in such order, but so well instructed as to have most of the service by heart; for though they had books, I observed they scarce looked at them, and yet repeated the responses perfectly, aloud. At one instant also, without direction to do so, the nine hundred dropped on their knees and rose again, which showed they knew what they were about; their little hands lifted up and joined together, looking with such innocent devotion. They sang the Psalms, all in time with the organ by heart, and notwithstanding the number, the sound was neither too loud nor too harsh, but, on the contrary, soft and affecting beyond measure. I confess, though I am no enthusiast, it drew tears from me. . . . I will only remark how much this order and decency must civilise these children, and what a great step this is towards reformation of Morals. But go with me also into the School of Industry. There see the poor little creatures who had been starving and without a home, many of them Orphans without a chance of earning their living. They are taken in here, and according to their age and capacity, taught to work, and in a few months have completely clothed themselves. They spun the woollen coats they wear, as well as their linnen, which they also made up; and they knit their stockings and sell besides. In one room you see thirty girls spinning. In another room so many boys and girls with reels to wind. In another, a loom where a man weaves the children's work. In another, thirty or forty little things knitting. They begin to knit garters at three years old.   In another room, girls making their chemises, &c.   Here I often go with great pleasure, and would have carried you.

I am, dear Brattikins, affectionately,

SERENA.

Maria Josepha to Serena.

Sheffield Place : August 12, 1787.

A Thousand and a thousand thanks to my dear Serena for her kind and long letter. . . . I am better pleased when there is a little of your kind advice in your letters ; for you have such a pleasant way of mentioning faults that it can never fail of having its effect. . . .

Papa is going to Town this morning to meet Mr. Gibbon, who we expect here the end of this week, after an absence of four years.   He will find us much altered, for the better, I hope ; be that as it may, I shall be very glad to see him.   Having thanked you for your letter altogether, I must in particular mention your account of the Sunday Schools, &c., which pleased me very much ; but your manner of describing would make every, the most trifling thing, entertaining.   I hope the Sunday Schools will be more generally adopted, as I think they may be of great use.   I wish Papa would set up one here, but we Sussex people are so obstinate and fond of what we have been used to, that I don't know if they would approve of it if ever so much use. . . .   We are all turned Botanists since Sir Joseph Banks came here ; as for Louisa, I believe she was born a Botanist, for she has been fond of gathering and examining flowers ever since she could distinguish one from another.   I am very fond of it, but have only been wild about it since Sir J. was here. . . .

CHAPTER II.

FIRST FLIGHTS.

JANUARY, 1788—JUNE, 1791.

Invitation from Gibbon to Serena—Portrait of Lord Sheffield by Sir Joshua
Reynolds—Trial of Warren Hastings—Study of Botany—Sir G. and
Lady Webster—The Sloop ' Maria '—Dress—Performance of the
' Messiah '—Lord Sheffield's Reception at Bristol—Lady Sheffield's
Pets—Exeter Change—Lady Bristol's Assembly—The Drawing Room
and Ball—Projected Visit to Gibbon at Lausanne—Preparations for the
Journey—Serena's Fears.

Serena to Maria Josepha.

Bath : January 3, 1788.

My Own Dear Precious Child,—Can I let this day pass
without sending you the thousand blessings my heart
wishes you ?   Since you are not here to receive them, you
shall at least know that I am thinking of you.   That all
the family, even ' Mrs. Tompot,' shall get tipsy drinking
your health.   Indeed, I can hardly tell you how this little
visit has endeared you to me. . . . I do not think you and
my dear Sheff have been a moment out of my thoughts
since we parted, nor shall I ever forget this happy fortnight.   I wander about the house and it looks empty, as
if all the furniture was gone.   I miss the dear mad Girl's
happy spirits.   I even wish for the riot upstairs at night,
and want Brunette to bark.   I do assure you she goes to
the door and wags her tail and looks for you when I call
' Maria.'   I distributed Sheff's bounty to the servants,
and had one of William's lowest bows.   As for Betty,
cook, she directly bought a gown with her half-guinea

and called it her Sheffield gown. . . . I had a note yesterday from Mr. Gibbon as follows:

'Would it not be civil and kind and decorous if you
were to drink tea this evening with Mrs. G. and the gouty
historian to deplore our common losses? Should you be
restrained by the iron fetters of pre-engagement, I should
like in the room of this evening to propose next Friday.'

I wrote a gracious note and chose next Friday. He
gains ground every day, and walks about his room. The
papers come daily, and I sent them to him to keep for
Sheff. . . .

Serena to Maria Josepha.

Bath: January 6, 1788.

Tho' it will be but a bit of a letter, yet as I can save
the half-way postage by means of the Historian conveying
it to Town, I will write three words to say how delightful
it was to get the precious Maria's sweet scrib from London. . . . I had your letter just as I was going to dine at
Mrs. Gibbon's; she having converted my evening visit
into a dining one, *en trio.* Mr. Gib.'s first dinner abroad.
I staid till nine, and nothing could be pleasanter than the
said Gib., tho' he had been two hours in the morn at the
feet of his Adorable. She being his deity, he did but right
to pay her homage the first moment of emerging. I only
think how he could be afterwards so agreeable to us poor
souls! . . .

Serena to Maria Josepha.

Bath: March 6, 1788.

. . . I hope Sir Joshua will make a good likeness as
well as a fine picture of our dear Sheff. Pray tell Mr.
Gibbon, that, contrary to my nature, I do very seriously
envy him for obtaining what I have been for years wishing and begging. Tell him, however, that I will forgive,

and thank him also, if he will leave it to me as a legacy, in case I should survive him, and that I will promise to leave it you at my death.   In the meantime you may assure Mr. Gibbon that I am so fond of precedence, that much as I wish for the picture, I do most certainly wish much more to go to Heaven, and therefore do not insist on his going before me, particularly as he may like this world as well.   You quite astonish me in your account of Mrs. Siddons' voice and figure; but all agree in the incomparable dulness of Mrs. Cowley's Play.

Maria Josepha to Serena.

Downing Street : May 28, 1788.

My Dearest Aunt . . . The Summer is now advancing and I do not see any chance of having you at Sheffield; you cannot think what pleasure it would give me, if it had been possible for you to come to Town to the Trial.[1]   I think you ought to have done it.   We are waiting to hear Sheridan, or we should have gone out of Town next Sunday.   There is such wonderful expectation of this famous speech, that I think it impossible he can answer it; it must be, in my opinion, a disagreeable situation for him to speak in, as he must in a degree feel awkward, and in wishing to surpass all expectation, it is not unlikely but he may fail, for everybody of every sort is looking forward to that day, as superior to anything that has been for a long time past.   I have not been there yet, being ill at the time Mr. Fox spoke.

Maria Josepha to Serena.

Sheffield Place : August 24, 1788.

My Dearest Aunt,— . . . We have been quite alone for some time, so that I really have no events to com-

---

[1] That of Warren Hastings.

municate. We have not had a single creature here to
stay since we lost Mr. Gibbon. Mama would say with
Mark Anthony, 'Oh, what a loss was there, my countrymen!' I am reconciled to my fate. How I wish it had
been possible to have had you this summer! I would
have made a Botanist of you. Sir Joseph Banks' Company was the greatest Treat that I could possibly have in
that way, and with his assistance I have made a tolerable
proficiency in the Study. My collection is a pretty considerable one; I have above 250 plants all gathered by
my own hands, within five miles of this place. I have
another collection on hand, viz., Seals, which I must beg
your assistance in; I shall be so obliged if you will save
for me all the seals that come to you, and if they are
Arms, to write the name of the owner on the back. . . .

I am, my dearest Aunt's most affectionate

M. J. HOLROYD.

Here is a very good Charade in return for one I cannot
find out, and which suits the end of a letter very well.
'Mon premier est le premier de son espèce. Mon second
est sans second. Mais, hélas! comment vous dire mon
tout? *A-dieu.*'

Maria Josepha to Serena.

Sheffield Place: 1788.

Behold! my dear Aunt, a Haunch of Venison, and,
what is a greater wonder, my handwriting! I am now
writing in the Library just before Supper, surrounded with
divers Tongues, and a great deal of use made of them, and
I own my Ideas are not very clear.

Sir G. Webster is here, and has brought a Fidler (who
attends upon his lady [1]), which is very agreeable, as he
accompanies one on the Pianoforte every evening. I have

---

[1] Afterwards Lady Holland.

no doubt but that in former Letters Mama has mentioned Lady W—— in no very favourable light. If so, it is but justice to say, three years never made a greater alteration for the better in anybody as they have made in her. If it must be as long before we meet, I wish you may find as great a one in me.

Serena to Maria Josepha.

Bath : November 27, 1789.

. . . I had a letter from Mrs. Carter yesterday, in which she mentions the ' Lord Sheffield ' being launched at Ipswich on the Wednesday before, a remarkable fine and beautiful Ship. The General, Sir Henry Clinton, K.B., sent a Haunch of Venison and a brace of Hares to the captain. I reckon this a real honour to our Papa, because it is the consequence of his Commercial Merits, I suppose. I shall mark it down in my book of Events, that in the year 1789, not only the ' Lord Sheffield,' but also his dear little Sloop ' Maria ' was launched upon the uncertain Ocean of the world,[1] where she escaped the ' Rocks of Folly,' and gently steered aright to the ' Harbour of Peace,' without loss or damage, in full enjoyment of all her best tackle. May her Voyage through Life be equally happy !

Lady Sheffield to Maria Josepha.

London: January 25, 1790.

Mem.—Spotted Muslin Dress.

The Body of the spotted Muslin to be lined with white Persian, and white silk Sleeves with Circassian Sleeves of the Muslin, if either long or short, (long ones most fashionable) ; lace or plaited ribbon down the sides ; the forebody much sloped off to meet at top, and worn with two

---

[1] Letter from Gibbon, Lausanne, May 1790. ' How has Maria, since her launch, supported a quiet winter in Sussex ? '

large Buckles, no Sash to go round, to be tied up and fixed under the Buckle of the left side ; the Stomacher silk, colour of the Sleeves ; the bottom strap the colour of the Sash ; the Petticoat, with a narrow flounce and deep head, which gives the appearance of a double flounce, might be worn without Trimming. No capes or frill of any kind worn.

Mem.—Silver-sprigged Muslin.

The Body to be lined with white ; white Lute-string Petticoat with a Tiffany over it, the flounce edged with silver coxcomb or lace, as likewise the Circassian Sleeve and down the sides.

· As to the Crape Dress, till it is washed and .the best selected, it cannot be settled in what form to remake it, but it shall be done in the smartest manner and at the least expense.

The above is the cream of a very lengthy confab this morning with Mrs. Jones ; she thinks the spangled body so soiled and cockled, that it will make the silver muslin look like an old thing. I agree with her. I forget whether you have a spotted petticoat, or only my quondam apron ; but, if wanted, I should propose borrowing Louisa's spotted breadth, and assisting her to work another. . . . I think each of the above will look very elegant.

The ' Messiah ' never was more incomparably performed by all the performers, vocal and instrumental, than it was yesterday. I could, with the greatest pleasure, have heard a repetition of the whole at one sitting. My Sister[1] and Bella were equally charmed ; we sat in the second row of the Director's Box, a very superior place for hearing and for commanding the glorious Orchestra ; there were one thousand and thirty-six Performers. We got in and away from the Abbey without the smallest

[1] Mrs. Way.

trouble. Lord S—— and I dined in Chandos Street. It would have given me great delight to have had you with me yesterday to examine the odious heads of all sorts. The Fashions are fearfull indeed, and disguise ninety-nine out of a hundred. Lord S—— left me in Chandos Street at nine ; went to Lord North's ; never said he should not return, though he knew I had no conveyance home, and that Thomas was not ordered. When the Clock struck twelve I thought it full time to go my way, and set off as soon as a Hack could be procured, solo with my brother's footman. Lord S—— had walked home at twelve from Lord North's, and totally forgot I was in being ! . . . His lordship was snug in Bed !

Miss Grove . . . looked very pretty, on her way just now to dinner, in as tiny a bonnet as you could wish— white, with a pretty painted border. I sent Maynard this morn. to examine Mrs. Coxe's Regiment of Caps, but they are all so fashionable—they were totally useless to me ; but I have picked up a decent Cap at one of Mrs. Coxe's millinery friends, that must do ; it is the most fashionable sort of undress Cap, but I shall look a scare-crow !

Lord Sheffield to Maria Josepha.

Chandos Street : Wed., May 26, 1790.

My Dear Girl . . . tell Fletcher if the Weather should prove too Wet for ploughing that he should take the opportunity, while the roads are cool, to send the oxen every second day from Stone to Forest Row ; but that he should forward the cabbages and Turnips as much as possible. I hope he is now planting cabbages with as many hands as can be employed. The Weather is very favourable for it. Tell him also to take care the Masons do not make use of any improper stone. . . . The Duke of Cumberland, instead of dying, attended the Abbey

this morning. It is true that the Duchess of Devon
has produced a Marquess of Hartington. . . . I have the
honour to be yours and Loll, and Dear Nancy, and Tuft's,
and all the Family's

S.

Maria Josepha to Serena.

Sheffield Place: Sunday, June 20, 1790.

. . . Papa says he wrote to you on Monday. Nothing
remarkable or new has occurred, except his public Éntry
on Tuesday [into Bristol], met by the Whigs in Cavalcade
two miles from the City, placed in a Phæton and four (I
wish I could have seen him) ; horses dismissed from the
Carriages, and dragged to the Council Chamber, where he
was received by Personages in their Canonicals. Went to
the Exchange to make a Speech, which he says, thank
God ! could not be heard. Dined with a large party
at the Bush Tavern, and finally, in my opinion the
pleasantest part of the ceremony, conducted by Mr. Ames
to his house at Clifton, where he found a very pleasing
and genteel wife and family. I imagine Papa informed
you of his extravagance at Reading, notwithstanding that
he had the fear of Miss Firth before his eyes. His Bill
came to 7s. 6d., and he left a whole Guinea with the
Waiters. . . . It seems likely to be a very stupid General
Election. One hears of no disturbance anywhere. Even
Westminster is quiet, and Horne Tooke continues to
stand the Poll, though he never can exhibit more than
two figures against Fox and Hood's three. . . . Lewes
has turned out as expected—Mr. Pelham 154, Mr. Kemp
145. The poll finished in one day. I am selfish enough
to wish you was here, though you are in the midst of so
many pleasant friends and pleasant things, for we are in
high Beauty. Our Oaks are uneat by Insects, and their
Foliage is more beautiful than I have seen it for some

years past. Mama and Louisa desire a million (you see how diminutive a figure your 10,000 make) of loves to you. . . . Mama has got an addition to her family in a large green Parrot, because her Birds, Beasts, and Children did not make noise enough. I daresay, if I should ever marry or any other accident befall me, Mama would get a Monkey. Till then, she thinks she has no need of one.

Your ever most affectionate,

M. J. H.

Lady Sheffield to Maria Josepha.

Tuesday Evening—The Day of Days—April 26, 1791.

Ben and William Way came from the Powis Ball at two o'clock; about Eighty People—a very nice Ball and Supper; but William says he did not like it one half so well as our Ball, though there were a great many beautiful powdered ladies. The only unpowdered Miss, was Miss Neville, and only two unpowdered beaux.

I have been charmed with the Birds and Beasts at Exeter Change,[1] (where Lewis and William accompanied us,) and also the Spectres; but my heart failed me, and I did not look at the Dagger. I felt fagged with standing and talking at Exeter Change first, and I thought I would look at terrifick objects when I felt quite stout. Louisa was quite stout and not in the least frightened. The Pictures I did see were surprising indeed.

Lady Sheffield to Maria Josepha.

Downing Street : Saturday Morning, April 30, 1791.

Most welcome our daily food from S. P.; it gives us a relish to our breakfast, and does us more good than ten

---

[1] Exeter Change was in the Strand, and used partly as a museum and partly as a menagerie. It was built in 1620, and demolished in 1829, to make room for the Strand improvements. The birds and beasts were removed first to the King's Mews, and afterwards to the Surrey Zoological Gardens.

breakfasts. . . . Last night to Lady Bristol's . . . by
Eleven o'clock. There seemed everything of fashion, from
the Prince of Wales to all and every body, English and
foreign, that one ever sees or hears of at Assemblies. I
arrived at half-past nine. After 'polisettes,' most tender
ones, from Lady Bristol, she ushered me in the inward
Room, composed of Lady Mary Cooke (the odd Cap lady),
Duchess of Bedford, Lady Payne, Lord Stormont, and a
few more such-like. I should have felt a *few unked* [1] (ask
Papa to explain that word) had not Mr. Hervey flown to
me as soon as he discovered me, and sat by me a considerable time. . . . Lady K. Douglas sat by me an hour
and a half, and told me who all and everybody were, and
I could not have had a better Historian. Lord Sackville
talked a great deal to her, and all the other young men of
Ton. Mr. Douglas and Lady K. and Miss Mercer were
going to sup at Lady Malmesbury's at one o'clock.
Lady K. Douglas asked Lord Sackville if he was going.
He said ' No, he hated French and the French People;
she might say he was sick; he did not like such company,
as all the great foreigners were to be there.' (N.B. A
very large importation just arrived.) We had the Queen
of the *French's* Musick Master, three Miss Chitteres,
Lady Louisa Hervey, and Lady Caroline Creighton, and
three or four other Lady and Gentlemen Performers. Lady
Charlotte Bruce has been sitting here an hour, entertaining me much with an account of the Eardley Ball
and of her party at Buckingham House last Thursday—
the three younger Princesses, Miss Goldworthy, and the
Duke of Clarence; he came at seven to his sisters and
staid till Eleven. They play eighteen-penny ' Commerce.'
He said he never played higher, he could not afford it;
the Princesses made Lady Charlotte play Country Dances
to them; the Duke of Clarence sung and seemed all

[1] Sussex dialect.

delight with his company, and said he did not know how
to leave them at eleven, their hour for retiring. An invitation from the Duchess of Portland to us all for Cards,
the 20th of May. Love and kisses to all.

Your most affectionate,

A. SHEFFIELD.

Maria Josepha to Serena.

Downing Street : June 6, 1791.

I think, except you have a great deal of time upon
your hands, I should have deferred writing till you should
have fewer Letters from other People ; but as I do not
know when that is likely to happen, I had better run the
risk of fatiguing than of disappointing you. Mama is
gone to sit for her Picture to Plimer [1] for the Angel. She
had a letter from her this morning, which Tom,[2] in a fit
of Absence, or Love, dated the 6th, tho' it was written and
put in the Post the 5th. Great Souls overlook such
Trifles ! Now for the Drawing-Room. It was exceedingly
crowded, and we were an hour and a half hunting the
King before we could catch him. I never felt the heat
equalled by anything except the Ball-room at Night, which
was much hotter. Mr. Bernard conducted the Lady
Mayoress and us thro' Byeways to his House at five
o'clock, and gave us an excellent dinner a little after six.
Sir James Wright, Mr. Smith, and Col. Boyd dined there,
and, unfortunately, Sir J. Wright is a famous Gardener
and has a famous Garden, consequently the one subject of
Conversation was, as may be supposed, Gardening. The
only observations worthy of communicating that I heard
during Dinner and an hour after were, that when the
King could not afford to buy Peaches from the Scarcity
and Dearness of them, Sir J. Wright sent him sixty that

---

[1] Miniature painter.
[2] Thomas, eldest son of second Lord Pelham.

weighed half a Pound a piece, and some, ' I assure you,
ma'am, half a pound and half an ounce ; ' that Lady
Wright had cured him of an Ague for which he had taken
innumerable infallible Remedies, that the Lady Mayoress
eat her dinner in white Gloves, and took up Peas with a
knife.

We went to the Ball-room a little after Eight, as the
Queen had ordered the Ball to begin at half past eight on
account of Saturday night. We got a very comfortable
Seat opposite the King and Queen, Lady Dumfries and
her Daughter just behind us, Lady Fludyer and Mrs.
Beadon before us. Princess Mary made her first appearance at Court, and is really very handsome. I believe you
saw her at the Abbey. Prince William of Gloucester,
who the Newspapers are so obliging as to compliment with
the appellation of a 'Modest Youth,' danced his first
Minuet at Court. . . The Duke of Clarence was so lively
that he would certainly have danced as steady a Minuet
on Quarter Deck in a storm, and when he turned his Back
to the King he put out his Tongue quite to the Bottom of
his Chin, to the great Dismay and astonishment of the
Princess Mary, his Partner. I must say in excuse, that
he, with his Papa, had been drinking the healths of all
the family, and he said he never saw the King so good
humoured and agreeable in his life. The Prince of Wales
danced the most graceful Minuet possible, and was most
magnificently dressed. The Duke of Bedford had the
most superb Carriage and Coat at Court, so much so that
when he arrived the Guard stood to arms, taking him for
the Prince of Wales. The Lady Colyears both danced
Minuets, and were very handsomely dressed in Silver
Crapes and silver Fringes. The Miss Coutts, of whom
one has heard so much, wore very remarkable Dresses ;
Purple Gauze Trains and Petticoats, Caps and everything
the same, spangled in stars, so that they would have

represented a fine Starlight night extremely well, and
have made up a Country Dance with the Sun and Moon.
We left the Ball-room after one Country Dance at half
past eleven, got a comfortable supper at Mr. Bernard's,
and came home a little before one, most happy to find
ourselves there. . . .

Yours ever and ever,
M. J. HOLROYD.

[1791. In June of this year, Lord and Lady Sheffield
and their two daughters, Maria Josepha and Louisa,
yielded to Mr. Gibbon's pressing entreaties that they
would visit him at Lausanne.

Maria's letters to Serena and some extracts from her
diary tell the story of their travels, while an occasional
reply from Serena and other friends in England keeps her
in touch with events occurring at home.]

Maria Josepha to Serena.

Sheffield Place : June, 1791.

There has hardly been time enough since the receipt
of your Letter to hear what Papa's intentions are ; but I
believe, at all events, to go as we intended ; but whether
to travel as fast as he can to Lausanne, which is my wish,
or whether to aim at Paris, I cannot tell.   It is a great
satisfaction to me that there is no Post to-morrow, that
is, no letters come from London, because People are so
troublesomely kind that they would frighten us out of
our Wits, and perhaps put an end to our Journey, which,
as it has proceeded so far, I should be very sorry for.   I
only hope you will not be in a fidget, as I am sure Papa
will not run any risks with his whole family about him,
and, indeed, it would be unkind to you, as, if we were all
exterminated you must marry immediately. . . . May I
beg you will insist on your husband's changing his name
to Holroyd ? for if you change your's, marrying will

answer no purpose. How glad I shall be to write to you from the Lake of Geneva! for I am afraid your mind will not be quite at rest till then; but if you do not promise to be as quiet as you can, and make yourself agreeable to Mrs. Garrick, or anybody else who may have the misfortune of your company, till we are safely lodged at Lausanne, I will not promise to write to you as often as it is in my power. However, hoping you will behave well, I will venture to say before I have your promise, that without any regard for your purse I will write every other day if possible during our journey. But then, another thing, you must not amuse yourself with being frightened if you do not hear from me, because you must remember that you depend upon the Winds and the Waves to bring my letters over, who perhaps will not be sensible of the precious Cargo they are intrusted with. I would write of something else if I could, but I can think of nothing else, and I always write my thoughts to you.

Adieu. Now don't make yourself uneasy, and depend on hearing from me whenever I can; and when you don't hear take it for granted we are safe and well.

Your ever affectionate

M. J. H.

Papa is quite undecided. He talks of staying a week longer, but I pin my faith on Mr. Pelham, who encourages us to go on and prosper. Once more, do not be disagreeable. Mama is as eager to go as possible, and has not a fear belonging to her. Miss Firth thinks she already sees us all adorning the Lanthorns—if I may judge by the *effroi* painted in her countenance. The Neaves were in and about Paris during all the troublesome time of the destruction of the Bastille, etc., and were never the least incommoded. Lady C. Bruce the same. Adieu.

D

Serena to Maria Josepha.

Windsor : June 8, 1791.

. . . It is very ridiculous to say that your going abroad makes some difference with me, and that I felt a weight I cannot describe when the door shut you all out, and when, lastly, my Sheff disappeared.   In the meantime, I do assure you, I sincerely rejoice in the scheme as being good for you all ; and I shall delight in the three pounds worth of Letters I am to have. . . . This evening we go to Herschel's to walk into his Telescope. . . .

Sarah Martha Holroyd,
"Serena"
n. 1739   ob. 18??

CHAPTER III.

CRAZY PARIS.

1791.

Departure from Sheffield Place—Flight of Louis XVI. and Marie Antoi-
nette—Arrival at Dieppe—Rouen—Château de Navarre—Paris in 1791
—Debate on King and Constitution—Royal Prisoners at the Tuileries
—Dinner at Roberts'—Apotheosis of Voltaire—Visit to the National
Assembly—Noailles—Palmerston—Extracts from Maria's Diary—Fon-
tainebleau—Discomfort—Dijon—The Hospital—Letter from Serena.

Extract from Maria Josepha's Diary.

June 27, 1791.

LEFT Sheffield Place and in three hours got to the Castle
at Brighthelmstone. Slept there. On Sunday (26th), Mr.
Pelham wrote word of the escape of the King and Queen
of France. They went from Paris the night of the 21st.
It was not discovered till the morning, when curiosity
brought everybody into the streets, and the whole City was
much alarmed, but quiet. The 22nd they returned to
their different occupations, as if nothing had happened.
The King and Queen, the Dauphin, Monsieur and
Madame, Madame Elizabeth and the young Princess
went in two coaches and six. They were discovered at
Varennes by the Post-Master, who stopped them, and the
National Assembly sent guards to bring them back. The
three Couriers who went with them were brought in Chains
on the top of the King's carriage; the Queen fainted
twice when brought to the Tuilleries. A Guard is now
constantly in her room Day and Night.

June 28.

Dined at Sir R. Heron's; went into the boat to go to

* D 2

the Packet at half-past eight. Sailed at nine in the
'Princess Royal,' Captain Chapman; wind S.E. and
calm, storm of thunder and lightning from eleven to one
at night.

Maria Josepha to Miss Ann Firth.

10 o'clock, morning. Dieppe: June 30, 1791.
Hôtel de Londres.

So far we are safe, and everybody says we shall be so to
the end of our Journey tho' I hope the rest will not be
so tedious.   We have been thirty-seven hours from setting our foot into the boat at Brighton, to setting it on
shore at Dieppe.   But that we might not be fatigued by
sameness, we have been treated with great vicissitudes in
this life.   Calms, contrary winds, Thunders, Lightning,
Rain, by turns, have contributed to our Amusement.   Upon
the whole, we have come off better than I expected.
Mama has been very sick at times, but not constantly as
poor Mrs. Maynard[1] has.   I have been quite pert, except
for about five minutes.   Papa quite well, and Louisa very
tolerable.   There were several Passengers, most of them
French.   One Englishman, a Governor Morris,[2] was a
very pleasant, sensible man, and helped to pass the time
better than a mere family party.   At least, Papa, I
believe, got some conversation with him.   Here we are in

---

[1] Lady Sheffield's maid.

[2] Gouverneur Morris, in his *Diary and Letters*, thus speaks of this
meeting with Lord Sheffield: ' The King and Queen of France have made
their escape, but we do not yet know whether they are out of the kingdom.
This event makes me very anxious to get back to Paris, for I think the
confusion will work favourably for the sale of American lands.   Eleven at
night: Intelligence is received that the royal fugitives are intercepted near
Metz.' On receipt of this news, Morris set off at once for Paris.   Crossing
the Channel, he says: ' I find Lord Sheffield with his family are my fellow
passengers, with whom I make acquaintance.   His Lordship, who supposes
me to be an Englishman, gives free scope to his sentiment respecting
America, as all other countries.   I promised to see them at Paris.'

a very clean room, and much amused by the odd figures passing before the windows. All the French in the Packet assured us we should be as safe as possible. I believe we shall go on to Rouen to-day, where we shall get a letter from Mr. Pelham with further particulars. The King and Queen were brought back to Paris last Saturday, and it is not true that Montmarin is murdered. . . . The woman of the House, a beautiful little Brunette, has just brought us some National Cockades, and assures us of the necessity of buying them, because the People have leave to whip all the ladies who have not one. We perfectly agree with her, that it is very necessary. She talks English nicely.

Maria Josepha to Serena.

Chateau de Navarre.

I have left the Descendant of the great Turenne [1] in order to tell you my history, as in the hurry of our journey delays are dangerous, and I fear, if I get to Paris without beginning a letter, I shall not have it in my power to say as much as I should like. Whenever I think of it, I am vexed to the last degree at the length of time that must have elapsed before you could hear of our safety; but the first Packet that sailed was the one we went in, and that did not sail till Saturday; so that a week must have passed before it reached you. . . . I will go back to Rouen and trace our adventures since; a full account I must leave for our meeting. The day I wrote to you we went to the Abbaye of St. Ouen, a Benedictine monastery. The Monks were turned out into the wide world only last Easter; at present the Regiment de Bourgogne is lodged there; the officers have taken possession of the Cells, three Monks only remaining. The Horses are

[1] Duc de Bouillon.

put up in the Cloisters; the foot of the Staircase serves the Officers of the Regiment for a Coach-house.

The Church is the finest Gothic architecture you can imagine; and the lofty Arches and painted windows strike one amazingly, particularly if Mass is performing, which does not prevent Gapers in the least. I cannot say their devotion was warm enough to prevent their gaping in return; we had the pleasure of attracting universal admiration of some kind or other. The Arms upon the carriage caused much speculation, but have not been any inconvenience, as they all see immediately it is an English Carriage; indeed, it is impossible they can mistake, for I never could have figured anything so awkward as their Carriages of all kinds are, so heavy, dirty and low.

In the Church of St. Ouen there are two Flags hung up, one dedicated 'Au Mânes de Mirabeau,' the other, a National Flag, with the words 'Force, Union, Liberté,' and the inscription 'Fait et donné par les Dames Blanchisseuses et Lavandières de Rouen. 1791.'

We visited the Cathedral, which I did not like so well as the Church of St. Ouen. The Monuments are mostly of English; the heart of Richard I., the bodies of Henry 2nd, John, Duke of Bedford and many others; there is a monument of Louis de Brun, Sieur de Maulevrier, Seneschal of Normandy, with the Virgin on one side, and the famous Diane de Poitiers on the other, a curious contrast. The painted glass in the windows is beautiful. There is a National Flag in memory of the Confederation in the Cathedral, and I understand there is one in every Church in the Kingdom. We did not go up to the great Bell; the number of steps being 164, we thought it would tire us more than the sight would pay us for. We then went to the Hill of St. Catherine, walked over the Camp of Henri 4th, which commands a view of the town, and two villages,

Darnebul and Subville, which appear to join. From the latter, Louis 14th always had his cream and butter; consequently you may suppose it is famous for being remarkably good. The Seine winds beautifully through the Valley, covered with considerable islands well wooded. It is the most winding river I ever saw. The road from Rouen to Louviers runs close by the side of it, and the country is most romantic; there are no large Trees, but much small, which at a distance does as well. They cut up their Trees just as they do about London, which disfigures the woods very much—in short, Nature seems quite in disgrace in the part of France I have yet seen.

We left Rouen yesterday morning; dined at Louviers and went to the Woollen Manufactory, which is reckoned the best in France, and Decretôt's is the best at Louviers. I wished Miss Firth had been there; she would have been so well amused, and would have understood it so well. He has three thousand people constantly at work, so you may imagine, though I did not understand what I saw, the extent of the place, and the number of people employed was a great amusement. Decretôt was gone to the National Assembly; but his Partner, Monsr. Pieton, was there, and did the honours very graciously.

We were told at Rouen that the Château de Navarre was the most magnificent place in France, and that the Prince de Bouillon was remarkably fond of the English, and would be very ready to let us see it. We thought it a desirable thing to see a French Country House inhabited; but did not know to what a degree Hospitality was carried in his Château. We arrived here at 8 o'clock last night, and sent in to know if it was *permis* to see the House. We were announced to the Duke, and he came out to us, and insisted on our coming in, though we would have made our retreat, on finding he was in his Salon with a great deal of company. Figure to yourself the dismay we were in, at being shewn into the room, introduced to Madame de Bouillon, and obliged to figure across with every body standing up, and in our travelling dresses. The Duke is a fine, venerable, old man, who for his sins has been married two years to a very pretty young Woman, who is now only 16. It is January and May to the life. Her Mother lives in the house and takes the lead.

The Duke insisted on our staying all night; he lives in a princely stile—indeed he is a Prince; but that is not always the rule. The Forêt d'Evreux, close to his house, belongs to him, and contains 80,000 acres, and is the finest wood I have seen yet: we drove about in it to-day for three hours. There was, before the Revolution, great plenty of game of all kinds, which, since the Nation has become free, have been all destroyed by the common People. Even the swans upon the water before the house have been killed; much wood in the forest cut down, and a great many trees have the bark cut round, out of pure malice, and are entirely dead. Evreux belongs to the Duke; it was given in exchange for Sédan. He has but one son, and he is an Imbécile, so he has adopted one of a distant branch of his family, le Comte D'Auvergne. He is a compleat Englishman, and is in the English Service. It is impossible to be more hospitable than the Duke is, and he is universally beloved all round the country. I have not time to enter into the detail of their manner of living, the only very striking difference from English Manners is the Breakfast; roast Fowls, Beef-steaks, Spinage and Soup. This was our Breakfast, and though we poor English were allowed Tea, the smell of the hot victuals was intolerable. We dined at 4 o'clock —23 people at dinner, 24 footmen and 10 men cooks. Servants take veils and have no wages.

Maria Josepha to Serena.

Paris: July 5, 1791.

I brought this letter with me, meaning to tell you of our safe arrival, and send it to the Post; but am much disappointed to find no Post goes to England till Thursday, so if I am not as good as my promise, my ignorance and not my indolence is in fault. I have some hopes of sending it by the messenger if he goes to England tomorrow.

. . . We left the Château de Navarre yesterday morning, much pleased with our reception. The Duke's manners are quite of the *Vieille Cour* and very engaging. We were taken out on Sunday morning to the Forest, which has Rides cut in it of several leagues in length, in two Carriages that they call ' Une Calèche,' open all round, covered at top, and drawn by six of the most beautiful Black Horses I ever saw, one Set with long tails, the other without. We left Navarre at 9 o'clock, dined at Mantes, drank Tea at St. Germains, and arrived at Paris at 9. The road is chiefly on the banks of the Seine, which, from its winding so much, we frequently crossed ; it is not very broad, but the number of Islands in it, and from Mantes to Paris, the hills on the opposite side, covered with the most beautiful villas, trees and Vineyards, form the most pleasing scene I could have imagined. We walked round the Palace of St. Germain and went to the Terrace ; but as we wished to enter Paris by daylight, we did not go into the Palace ; it is a fine old building. We met Mr. Pelham in the street, just come from the Play, and we are magnificently lodged in the Hôtel de l'Université, Faubourg St. Germain. They are not the rooms Lady Webster had. I believe Prince Hamilton has them on the ground floor. Ours are up one pair of stairs ; we have a suite of eight rooms, furnished very elegantly and perfectly clean, which is the first instance of the kind I have seen since I entered this Land of Liberty.   My Bed chamber, from which I am writing to you, is furnished with yellow damask, Bed, chairs and window curtains.   Mr. Dundas, a son of Sir F. Dundas, is with Mr. Pelham; they supped with us last night.   They saw the King enter Paris; it was a perfect Triumph.   The two men who stopped him, were drawn into the town in a *Calèche* hung with Laurels, 30,000 National Guards preceding the Carriage.   You never saw any thing like the joy, that all the common People we have spoke to, express at the King's being taken.   Papa asked one of the Girls at the Inn where we dined yesterday, where the King was? and what they had done to him ? by way of seeing what she would say—she said ' Oh! Mon Dieu, on l'a bien enfermé, il n'échappera plus ! ' with such pleasure you cannot think. He is indeed ' bien enfermé '—a Garde is constantly in his room and the Queen's, night and day.   Nobody is permitted to enter the Tuilleries Gardens, and we shall not be able to see them while we stay.

The Apotheosis of Voltaire is put off to the beginning of next week.   We do not say how long we mean to stay, but I believe certainly above a week.   We have had very little trouble on our journey as to Passports ; Papa got one at Dieppe, which had some additions made to it at Rouen and Louviers, to say we passed such a day.   We did not know it was necessary to have anything done at Louviers, and were stopped in the street for twenty minutes, till the right ceremony was gone through, at the Hôtel de Ville.   We have had excellent horses, and, in short, we have reason to be quite disappointed that we have met with no adventures on the road.   Mr. Anderson, for whom Mr. Colquhoun gave us a letter, tells us Paris is divided into four parties—' L'Aristocrate enragé,' for

Passive Obedience to a despotic Monarch ; ' L'Aristocrate,' for a King with limited Authority ; ' Le Démocrate,' for the present Constitution ; and ' Le Démocrate enragé,' for a Republic.

Tuesday evening.—We have been taken by that jewel of a man, Tom, all over Paris in a Carosse de Remise, which Papa takes by the day. We have walked over the ruins of the Bastille, seen the Lanterne upon which poor Foulon was hung, paid our respects to Henri IV. upon the Pont Neuf, and walked in the gardens of the Palais Royal. It is the prettiest scene in the World, very like the Pantiles at Tunbridge Wells, only that the shops are very handsome, that the view from the open side is a garden, and that the walk is a great length.

I think all the French women look alike ; the great objection I have to make against the beauty of the ladies is, that they have no ' shape,' as they never wear stays ; they are an immense size, and a little French woman is quite as broad as she is long.

We are going to-night to the Comédie Françoise, ' Athalie,' the last night of its being represented. By this account you will guess I have not much time on my hands, and I hope you will excuse me if I have, as I suspect, repeated the same thing, or made a great many mistakes. I hope you will be able to read this criss-cross writing, but the paper is not half large enough for all I have to say. Sir Godfrey left Paris in a violent hurry at last, though he had intended to stay some time longer. He and Mr. Wyndham had been compleat Husbands all the time—in English, very perverse ; what cause they had I cannot pretend to say, but Mr. Pelham says they were perfectly disagreeable the whole time.

Adieu. I will write by Monday's post ; it only goes Mondays and Thursdays.

Yours ever,
Maria J. Holroyd.

Maria Josepha to Serena.

Hôtel de l'Université, Paris: July 11, 1791.

It is quite melancholy to write, and not to hear whether you have received the letters, whether you think we are murdered, etc., etc. A line from you when we are settled in Mr. Gibbon's 'Mansion of Peace' will be a real delight to me. It is very pleasant and curious to be here just now in the midst, or at least, at the eve of an important crisis for this Country ; and though I think, from what I hear, that the minds of the common People are in that state, that a trifle would blow them into a flame, yet the Chiefs are desirous of taking reasonable measures, but are afraid of declaring themselves openly, on account of the lower order. It was agreed, at a meeting of the Chiefs, on Wednesday night, that the person of the King is inviolable, and that he must be restored to his former functions. Lazowski, a very sensible pleasing man, who lives with the Duc de Liancourt, Son to the Duc de Rochefoucault, and for whom Arthur Young gave Papa a letter, told us that they were compleating the Charter of the Constitution as fast as possible, till when, the King was to be confined ; but when it was finished, it was to be carried to him. He was to be allowed his own counsellors, and some time to consider of it, and if he pointed out anything he wished altered, they would correct it ; but when finally compleated, he must swear to observe it, or leave the Kingdom. The Dauphin to be left, with a Regency appointed by the National Assembly, and the Queen, to intimidate the Emperor. In the meantime, they are compleat Prisoners. Only yesterday I saw the three doors of the Tuilleries, looking towards the river, bricking up, because it was thought possible the King might escape that way. Lazowski told us he was amazed Bouillé did not re-take the King, for that four determined men might have carried him out of France, even after he had been taken a great way back towards Paris. Every sign on which are the words 'Roi,' 'Reine,' or 'Royal,' have been painted over or effaced; for instance, 'L'Hôtel Royal' is now 'l'Hôtel' of nothing; 'La Loterie Royale,' the same. In short, the people are neither more nor less than mad.

Nothing can pass pleasanter than our time does, under the direction of Mr. Pelham. He lays out a plan for our mornings, goes to the Play and sups with us. He is so pleasant that I hardly remember the Mr. Pelham that was. Tom is quite a different man, and the most agreeable I ever saw. . . .

He goes with us to Besançon; from thence he goes to Les Eaux de Bourbon, to see his brother, and then to Lausanne. How odd it is that the Post should only go to England twice a week! I begin writing two days before it can go. Last Thursday, we went to the National Assembly. It was expected to be a great day, but nothing of consequence was debated. We sat in a very good place, just behind the President with his dust bell, and opposite the speakers. No place can exceed the noise, except the 'Société de Jacobins,' where we were last night. You will now understand I am writing in the greatest of all possible hurries.

Monday morning, 9 *o'clock.*—I can only give you the heads of our adventures. After the National Assembly, we went to see the Hôtel des Invalides, the finest church I have seen, and in the Council Chamber are all the pictures of my old Friends, Louis XIV.'s ministers. After dinner we walked in the Champs Elysées, the Kensington Gardens of Paris, where Mr. P. met us and took us to Les Italiens, like an Opera in English, pretty, lively musick, and good acting. Friday, Dr. Anderson and

Broussonet breakfasted with us. The first, is Provost of something in Scotland, and a very sensible, prosy, deaf, good-humoured Scotchman. The second, tired me very much, as he is a manufacturer, and instead of attending upon or to the ladies, carried off Papa and Mr. P. to some Mills and Farms, &c., &c., and kept Mama and us waiting in the Carriage at the King's Garden, (where they had appointed to meet us) an hour and a half.

We walked over the Gardens and Hothouses—much inferior to the Gardens at Kew, and indeed not to be named in the same line. The Cabinet d'Histoire Naturelle is very curious, and everything is classed and arranged exceedingly well; but we had not time to examine it thoroughly. Went to the Church de St. Geneviève, now building, where Mirabeau is buried, and where Voltaire, who some years ago was privately stole into a Churchyard by night, as hardly deserving of Christian burial, is to-day to be deposited with every possible mark of respect and veneration. In the Front, in large gold letters, is this inscription, put there since Mirabeau was buried :—

' Aux grands hommes ! la patrie reconnoissante ! '

We dined with Mr. Pelham at a Tavern, the most famous one in Paris, and in the Palais Royal, which, if you understood the humours of this place, you would be surprised at. We sat as long as the gentlemen, and then went to the Opera. I have stated it thus to oblige Mr. Pelham, who desired me when I wrote to the gravest of my Friends, to elevate and surprise them with this account; but I am afraid you will not be sufficiently surprised. The explanation is, that Mr. Pelham was desirous we should see an entirely French dinner, dressed in the best style, and for that reason gave us a dinner at

Roberts', the best *Traiteur* here. You may perceive I am under the hands of the Hairdresser, and by my writing that I receive a good many Concussions. As to sitting as long as the Gentlemen, they never stay a moment after the dessert is over, during which the servants always wait; but to make up for that, the dinner is eternal. *Entremets* after *entremets* without end, and never more than a dish at a time.[1] Colonel Tarleton surprised us by walking into the room just after the opera. He is come to see what mischief is going on.

Saturday, we went to St. Cloud, Sèvres, Versailles, and Trianon, and returned by moonlight at eleven o'clock. We were much amused; but it was a melancholy sight to see at St. Cloud, in the Queen's private apartments, her Pianoforte, the Dauphin's little chair, and many other things of the same kind; the apartments fitted up in the most superb, yet comfortable, style; and to think she might probably never see them again. To add to the insults she receives, La Fayette has placed three Tents in the garden just under her windows, merely, one would think, to remind her at every moment of the day that she is a Prisoner, or else could they suppose she would jump out

---

[1] Bill of Fare at Roberts' in the Palais Royal, July 8, 1791 :—

Potage au Cresie.
Turbeau.
Petits Pâtés à la Béchamele.
Ris de Veau glacé à la Chicorée.
Filets de Lapreau au Pois.
Filets de Poulets au Suprême.
Petits Pigeons en Macédoine.
Côtelettes d'Agneau à l'Epigramme.
Buisson d'Ecrevisse.
Dindonneau.
Caille.
Artichaux.
Haricots Verts.
Choufleurs.
Salade à la Piédmontoise.
Pâtisserie.
Crème.

of a two-pair-of-stairs window? or, if she would, how
could she, when a guard is constantly in her own Bed-
chamber? All the reasonable people are much shocked
with it. The Vicomte de Noailles, a great friend of Mr.
P——'s, and a very sensible man, though a Democrat, is
very indignant. He has been very civil to us, which is a
great favour, since his time is so much taken up that he
never hardly goes into women's company. You must
distinguish between a 'Democrate' and a 'Democrate
enragé.' The last are for a Republic; the first are only
for a King with a good constitution; though both agree
in one thing, that there is no dependance on the present
King, and that he is a 'méprisable' Being.

Sunday morning, Mama, Dr. Anderson, and us went to
Nôtre Dame, and saw the Archbishop of Paris in his
Pontifical robes, say Mass; went up all the steps to the
Tower of Nôtre Dame, near 400 steps. The view of Paris
from the top is very fine. (Papa and Broussonet were
gone to see a farm in the neighbourhood.) Afterwards
we walked in the Palais Royal, and came home to dress, to
dine at the English Ambassador's.

Lady Sutherland charmed me; her manner is the
most engaging I ever saw.

I shall be too late for the post. Adieu.

Pray write to Sheffield and say what we are about.
I have not time. It rains very hard, and Voltaire's bury-
ing is put off to-morrow. We were at the Jacobins last
night.

Diary, July 6.—Lazowski came after breakfast. Mr.
Young gave a letter for him. He said if the Queen had
spoken to the Housards in German and given them any
encouragement, they would all have followed her anywhere; that the Great Majority of the National Assembly
would, at the time the King went away, have agreed to

any terms. The Viscomte de Noailles had promised to take us to the Jacobins, but a warm debate about the King, being expected, which took place, he declined going, as he wished not to be under the necessity of speaking, as he must have done had he been present. The Royal Family·are allowed to dine together, but a Guard constantly stands behind their chairs.

Maria Josepha to Serena.

Paris : Monday, July 11, 9 o'clock, 1791.

My Morning and Evening song will contradict one another a little, but it is not my fault ; it is the fault of the Aristocrats, it is the fault of the weather. The Aristocrats put up papers in different parts of the Town this morning, saying the Fête of Voltaire was put off. As it rained very hard, this was easily credited, and Decretôt, who was to have taken us, sent us word at nine o'clock, just as we had dressed ourselves for the occasion. So here we were upon the wide world, without a plan for the Morning. Papa was going out manufacture-hunting, Mr. P—— was engaged somewhere else, and we were in great tribulation. We had hardly made up our minds to the disappointment, and taken off our dresses that we might be fit to see sights, instead of being shown for a sight, and just setting off upon an expedition with Our Jewel of a Guide, who put off his engagement to go with us, when we were informed that the ' Convoi étoit en Marche.' Frightened out of our wits, for fear we should be too late, we hurried away to dress, and went to our destination at one o'clock. And now, being for the first evening since I arrived here, quietly seated at my writing desk, you shall have a full and true account, as far as I can recollect, of the Events of the Day.

Madame de Villette, Voltaire's niece, who he·used to

E

call ' Belle et Bonne,' lives on the Quai de Voltaire, nearly
opposite the Pont Royal, and ' à deux pas de nous.' Le
très aimable Monsieur Decretôt nous a procuré l'entrée de
sa maison. La Maison de Paris la plus à désirer, pre-
mièrement, parce que c'est la Maison où Voltaire mourut ;
secondement, parce que le Convoi s'arrêtoit and chantoit
des Hymnes à l'honneur du Saint Voltaire, devant cette
Maison ; troisièmement, parce que la Maison étoit plein
d'Enragés et d'Enragées très curieux à voir ; et 4ᵉᵐᵉ, parce
que Madame de Villette devoit joindre le Convoi avec une
suite de 18 femmes.' Our dress, as we were instructed
beforehand, was white, with a blue sash,[1] beautifully
engraved with Voltaire on a Car, Fame crowning him
with Laurel, and the Church of St. Geneviéve, where he
was to be deposited ; a wreath of roses in the hair ; Mama
wore hers in a Cap, which was not correct. From one to
four, every National Guard, every lady was supposed to be
Voltaire, or part of his train, at which hour we were told
that the Procession set out so late, owing to the rain, that
it would be three hours before it would arrive. Our alarm
and hunger, which had been pretty considerable for some
time, now increased to an alarming degree, and, after a
little consultation, it was agreed that we should return
home to dinner and come again at six o'clock, which we
did, and at a quarter before seven the Procession passed
the house. Never did I see, and I could never have
imagined, such a piece of folly as the whole ceremony
was. They set off from the ruins of the Bastille, on

---

[1] The following memorandum in the original, and the blue sash itself,
have been preserved to this day :—

> ' Costumes de femmes :
> Ceinture bleue à la Voltaire, gravée
> Chez Arthur.   Sur le Boulevard, vis à vis
> Le pavillon D'hanovre,
> Robe blanche,
> Couronne de Roses dans les cheveux.'

which they sang a hymn to Liberty. The Procession began by some Dragoons, which were followed by part of a Regiment of Boys, none above sixteen years of age, which has been lately raised, that ' Démon-crates' may never be wanting in this mad nation.

These were followed by Deputations from the Academies, &c. ; then came a bust of Mirabeau, carved out of a stone of the Bastille, between four Banners, on which were the heads of Voltaire, Rousseau, Mirabeau, and another friend of Liberty, whose name I have forgot. I forgot to mention two or three flags with the cap of Liberty; La Fayette, bare headed, on a beautiful white horse, after the infantine regiment. Garlands of Roses, oak leaves, &c., were thrown on the figure of Mirabeau as it passed, and women, as well as men, clapped and bravoed enough to deafen anybody who had not the spirit of Democracy as perfect as themselves. Then a plan and model of the Bastille; pieces of the Bastille, cut into the form of, and painted to look like Books, and old pieces of armour and cannon balls, which were found in the Bastille when it was taken and destroyed ; flags were carried with sentences out of Voltaire's works in favour of Liberty ; after these, a gilt figure of Voltaire, seated on a Chair, was brought and placed before the House. A Man placed a crown of roses on his head and kissed him. Madame de Villette took off the crown and placed one of Bay leaves in the place of it, prostrated herself at his feet, seemed to weep, kissed him, and returned to her place, in a temporary erection before the House where we were. Her child, a girl about five years old, was raised up to go through the same ceremony, and the Statue moved on. Then followed a Case with Voltaire's Works, very richly-bound; National Guards ; Deputies from the Municipality, Theatres, and Académies de Musique et de Danse. Some of the Poissardes who distinguished them-

selves most in the famous Revolution, marched in the
Procession in a most ludicrous dress, perfectly amphibious,
for they were neither man nor woman.   They had a petticoat on, which gave one reason to suppose they were
females, while the Coat and Epaulette appeared as much
the contrary ; but the best information I could get, said
they were Women.   I really supposed they had been men
in Women's clothes.

After these and some other sets of worthy Patriots,
came a magnificent Car drawn by twelve beautiful grey
Horses, some belonging to the Queen, some to Madame,
and some to Beaumarchais ; they had each a blue mantle
with gold stars thrown over their back ; were four abreast,
and led by people from the Theatres, dressed like Eastern
slaves.   Several Actresses, in fancy dresses, preceded the
car, upon which was a gilt Statue of Voltaire, which
was crowned and halted before the house, while a Hymn
or two in honour of the Hero of the day was sung, accompanied by the Band from the Opera House, inferior to the
most indifferent Band of the most indifferent regiment in
England.   The Opera band is good because of the number
of violins, but, as they were omitted, the remainder was
very moderate.   Madame de Villette, with about eighteen
ladies, (among whom were the widow and two daughters
of Calas [1]), followed the Car.   Madame de Villette is a very
pretty woman, and an elegant figure.   She was dressed
in a Crape chemise, with the sash of the day, only in black
and white, a Coronet of roses on her head, and the ribbon
that Voltaire was crowned with, by the People of Paris
twelve years ago, which she had preserved.   At the back
of her head was a long veil of black Tiffany, put on with a
great deal of taste, and altogether she had a very graceful

[1] Jean Calas. Protestant accused at Toulouse of having murdered his
son, and executed 1762. Voltaire established his innocence, 1768.

appearance. Her followers were all dressed alike in white, with wreaths of roses on their heads, except the Calas, who were in mourning. The Procession was closed by twenty-four of the Deputies and a regiment of Veterans, who wear the dress of Henri Quatre, the Scarf and Hat turned up on one side with white feathers. What is extraordinary in them is, that tho' they are the old race, who might be supposed to be attached to their former principles, they are more violent for the Revolution than any body. There was a great deal of rain in the course of the day, but it luckily was fair just while the Procession passed, but the Streets were excessively dirty. You cannot imagine anything like the eagerness with which the ladies flung garlands of Oak leaves and flowers upon La Fayette, the statues of Voltaire, Mirabeau, etc. It was a very curious sight, and what I could hardly have believed if I had not seen it; there was so much childishness in the whole, and, if I was not afraid you might think I was giving myself airs of Wisdom and Goodness, I would say it was more than childishness; for while they were singing Hymns, and crowning such a man as Voltaire, it appeared to me as little less than an insult to Heaven.

It is very extraordinary to see how the Clergy, who have hitherto had the lead in this country, are sunk into nothing; even more, they hardly dare walk the streets; those who do, are obliged to wear the National Cockades and tie their hair behind. At the beginning of the Revolution, the people put on National cockades upon the Virgins and Jesuses at the corners of the streets. All the statues of Henri IV., Louis XIV., etc., have cockades. Women do not wear them at all.

It was no bad idea of somebody, when the King and Queen were brought into Paris, who tied a handkerchief over the eyes of Louis XV. in the Place Louis XV. while the King passed, and, when he was gone, took it off and

wiped his eyes with it, as if he had wept at the disgrace
his Grandchild suffered.

Maria Josepha to Serena.

Paris: July, 1791.

Wednesday morning.—Here I am again. Tuesday
morning we went to the National Assembly in the President's Box, but were very unlucky. Once a year all the
Deputies are called over, and this was the day; an hour
and a half we waited with infinite patience, to hear names
called over and letters of excuse read, but at last human
nature could hold out no longer and we decamped. We
should not have stayed so long, but that Decretôt had
got the Box for us, which is the best in the Assembly, and
as we have an awkward trick of shaking him off when we
can get a better Beau, we stayed, not to appear to slight
his offer; but were much better amused the rest of the
morning, sight-seeing with our *Elégant*, which I have
learnt is the French word for a lady's Beau.

We went to the Sorbonne, where we saw the famous
Monument of the Cardinal de Richelieu, and to the
Carmelites, to see the Picture of Madame de la Vallière.
It is the most lovely thing I ever saw, and no print or
copy can give an idea of it. She has flung her Casket of
jewels on the ground, and is tearing off her robes, while
her eyes, swelled with weeping, are cast up to Heaven;
the expression of them is delightful—it needs no explanation to tell one she is a Magdalen. They now say it is
not Madame de la Vallière's picture, but that as it was
painted at the time of her conversion, the Painter gave it
her name. We then went to l'Eglise de St. Sulpice,
walked through the gardens of the Luxembourg belonging to Monsieur, and to the Gobelin Manufactory, where
we saw the Weavers at work, and some pieces of Tapestry
finished, but none so well done as three copies of Pictures

we saw at Versailles, Louis XV., Joseph, the Queen's Brother and his Mama; they were in the Queen's apartments and were quite equal to fine Paintings; they were of the Gobelin Manufacture. We wound up our Expedition by visiting the Hôtel de Bouillon. The good old Duke wrote to his Steward to show us the House, and I suppose told him not to take anything, for he refused two crowns which Papa offered him, over and over again. The Duke has not been in Paris for several years, but part of his family sometimes comes there. He has several fine pictures, and some very rare: Agnès Sorel, the only original picture of her, painted after her death. She would not suffer herself to be painted during her lifetime. An original of the great Turenne, which the Duke will not allow to be moved, two fine Claude Lorraines, and some Teniers. They showed us the cup that Henri IV. used to drink the health of 'La belle Gabrielle' out of, a set of breakfast china belonging to Madame de Pompadour, and two China cups set in silver, given to Louis XIV. by the Senate of Venice, and that Madame de Pompadour begged of him. After her death, Bouillon's Father bought them of her heirs. We went to the Italian Opera in the evening. 'L'Italiana in Londra,' the Théâtre de Monsieur. The principal Woman Singer has a charming voice. I longed to propose to her to come and try her Fortune in London. This Morning we went to the National Assembly at 8 o'clock. The question of whether the King might or ought to be tried was to be debated, and a crowd was expected.

Noailles, the pleasantest, most animated man, if I may use the expression, I ever saw, got an order for us to go to the best places just opposite the President, but when we went, every part of the House was full. However, by having several friends at Court, we got placed, or rather squeezed, into a Corner, where we remained till 4 o'clock, of which time more than two-thirds was spent in reading a Report, of which I could not hear a syllable, but which is to be printed and will be very curious. An account of the King's escape, how and what it was, and stating all his Crimes and Misdemeanours. It is not determined whether he is to be tried or not, the question is to be decided to-morrow.

The greatest part of the National Assembly are in favour of him, but the People violently against. It is thought the National Assembly will soon be unpopular. Bouillé, and the officers who assisted him in his Flight, are all to be tried for High Treason. We are not decided whether we go to the National Assembly or to the Confederation to-morrow ; the latter will not be so considerable a thing as last year's Ceremony, but as we did not see that, this little one will be better than nothing. Friday, I believe, we shall certainly remove ourselves from this mad city.

I had not time in my last letter, to tell you any particulars of the proceedings at the Jacobins. I heard a famous Speech, which I daresay will soon reach England ; the question was the same as at the National Assembly to-day, and Brissot spoke most furiously against the King, ending with a motion that whoever mentioned any fear of foreign Countries, (something of that sort having been said), should be voted ' Indigne du nom de François, indigne de cette Société, et que le roi peut et doit être jugé.' The extravagant applause at this speech is beyond all imagination. The men clapped, and threw their hats in the air, and the women their pocket-handkerchiefs, for above ten minutes, and a more compleat set of Bedlamites could not be seen. All the reasonable Democrats are much displeased with the Speech ; but there were not many at the Société de Jacobins. It was voted and carried, that the Speech should be printed, and Copies sent to every Deputy, all the Regiments, and all the Municipalities.

Will you send this letter to Sheffield? they may like to see some account of our proceedings, and I really have not time to write to them. I intended to finish this and write to them last night, after the Play, which is the only time I have; but Noailles and Pelham came, and if the welfare of the whole Kingdom of France had depended on my writing, I must have gone to listen to them. My best love to the amiable Trio, and if they knew how pleasant these People are, they would forgive me.

My last I wrote to you while my hair was dressing. Lord Palmerston, Lazowski and Pelham are now in the next room; but as Noailles is not there, I have been able to get through my letter. Mama tells me I have missed a very entertaining account by Lazowski of the K. and Q. I don't say this to make a merit of writing, but as an excuse to the Sheffieldites. Every moment is so precious.

[A few extracts from Maria's Diary during her stay in Paris give some incidents not mentioned in her letters.]

'*July* 13.—Went to the National Assembly, at eight o'clock in the morning; had tickets for the Bar, but found every place full, so sat in a Box opposite that of the Rédacteurs de la "Moniteur." Report read of the state of the Frontiers—of the escape of the King. Question whether the King should be tried or not. Robespierre, d'André, and Pétion spoke. Returned home at four.

'*July* 14.—-The Confederation went as far as the gate of the Champ de Mars. Saw the National Guards march in. Papa went afterwards to the National Assembly. Mob very riotous. Women tried to force their way into the Assembly. Deputies insulted coming out. M. Decretôt has given Papa a medal struck in commemoration of the 14th July, 1790, one of which was given to each Deputy.

'*July* 15.—Papa went to the National Assembly. Decree in favour of the King that he cannot be tried. De Salle made very fine speeches in favour of the King.

'Décrets de l'Assemblée Nationale :—

'1ᵉʳ. Un roi qui quitte son poste, pour se mettre à la tête d'une armée ennemie contre la nation, est censé d'abdiquer le trône.

'2ᵐᵉ. Un roi qui, après avoir prêté le serment, se rétractera, sera déchu de la couronne.

'3ᵐᵉ. Un roi qui aura abdiqué reviendra simple citoyen, et pourra être accusé pour les actes subséquens à son abdication.

Twenty thousand persons assembled in the Champ de Mars, but dispersed at night very quietly. . . Duc de Liancourt took Papa to introduce him to La Fayette.

Maria Josepha to Serena.

Dijon : July 19, 1791.

I hope you have received the letter I wrote last Thursday, giving an account of Voltaire's Fête. Notwithstanding all I said, I wrote a long letter to Sheffield, owing to a delay in sending which gave me more time ; but I did not say a word the same as in your letter ; I do not mean that I contradicted in one what I said in the other, but that I treated of different matters. We left Paris on Saturday morning at eleven, and got to Fontainebleau at five. We waited dinner for Mr. Pelham till seven, and in the meantime explored the Country. The Queen's apartments at the Palace were all new fitted up in the year 1786, and are most elegant. Her Boudoir is a Chef d'œuvre of taste and elegance; the ground is gold ; the compartments painted in the style of the

Loggia del Vaticano, upon a silver ground. All the
ornaments are in the lightest style possible. Most of the
old Pictures are removed. The Carp in the Pond are the
largest I ever saw, and some are quite white. The story
is that they grow grey from age ; but that cannot be true,
as there are a great number of little white ones.

We left Fontainebleau the next morning. Papa went
with Mr. Pelham in his Cabriolet, which reduced us to
the number four, which is rather more agreeable in the
month of July than the number five ; but this good fortune did not last long, for Mr. Pelham in the most
barbarous manner left us at Sens. He had unfortunately
been very busy looking at the maps, and had discovered
that if he went on to Besançon with us, it would be three
days' journey out of his way, as Bourbonne les Bains is on
the borders of Champagne and Franche Comté. We got
to Auxerre at nine, where we slept, in comparison of
the night before, in Paradise, for since the Revolution,
there is so little company comes to Fontainebleau, that
the Bugs were very sharp set, and were so delighted to
meet with me, that, as the least evil of the two, I slept in
a chair all night not in the most comfortable manner.

Yesterday morning at seven o'clock, we left Auxerre,
and did not arrive at Dijon till twelve at night, with only
a rest of one hour at Vitteaux to eat a little bit. You
may imagine how tired we were on one of the hottest
days possible, and Louisa and Tuft very fidgetty. The
Carriage has met with an accident, which I am afraid will
keep us here another day, or else we were to go on to
Besançon tomorrow, and get to Lausanne on Friday ;
but I thought you would not like to wait till then, to hear
that we were safe out of Paris. Pray write to Sheffield
and tell them, in spite of my terrific accounts, everything
went on very quietly in the Champ de Mars. I suppose
you have heard that the Decree in the National Assembly

passed in favour of the King; but he must mind his behaviour another time, or he will not escape so well. The People are violent against him; 20,000 assembled in the Champ de Mars the day the decree passed, (on Friday), vowing they would have no King; but spent themselves in going round to all the Theatres and ordering them to shut up, which they very quietly did.'

Adieu. Yours ever,

M. J. H.

Extract from Maria Josepha's Diary.

'*July* 19, 1791.—Went to the Monastery of the Chartreuse on the road from Dijon to Paris, about half a mile from Dijon. The Monks all left it about two months ago. Went into one of the Cells. Every Monk had three small rooms, a garden, a little court, a well and a cellar. There were twenty-two. Could not go into the Church where the Dukes of Burgundy are buried, because "La Nation" had put their Seal on the Door; there being some Pictures not yet disposed of. The Entrance to this Town from Paris is through a long handsome Gateway. It was begun before the Revolution, but not finished till lately. Over the gate "A la Liberté"—on each side are tablets with "Les Droits de l'homme" upon them. Above, figures holding shields, upon which is inscribed :' "La Nation, la Loi et le Roy."

'*20th.*—Went to the Hospital and into one of the rooms. Beds white and very clean. Ladies of the Town attend the sick. Before the Revolution, Nuns attended them, but their Priests refused to take the Oath, and as they did not choose to have other Priests, they left the Hospital. Beds for five hundred. Left Dijon at a quarter before two.'

Serena to Maria Josepha.

Bath: August 1, 1791.

It is utterly impossible to fill such a Patagonian Paper; but it will show my disposition to make the only return in my power, to the dear precious Maria, for her delightful attention to me, and her folios of interesting history. . . . I have received one from Dijon and Dôle. I must particularly, however, thank you for not waiting till you got to Lausanne; for I may confess that I should have been very uneasy if you had not kindly written on. the road, as I heard of fresh disturbances, and as I suppose dear Sheff full as likely to be led by curiosity to see the Manœuvres of the Mob, as to see a Farm, a Manufactory, or a Regiment, without the least idea of his being concerned in Riots, and to say truth, I know no Monster I so much dread as a savage Mob. Thank God! I may now suppose you, according to your Phrase, in Mr. Gibbon's ' Mansion of Peace,' where I hope you found him well, and also that you received a letter addressed to ' Myladi' Maria. And now that my pannicks are at an end, I am really glad you have been at Paris, at a Period so very extraordinary, which must always be curious to you to recollect, though I must confess it was at some hazard and required courage. . . . I hope my Sister will soon recover her fatigues and be able to enjoy being in Mr. Gibbon's charming House. . . .

CHAPTER IV.

1791.

WITH GIBBON AT LAUSANNE.

Arrival at Lausanne—Gibbon's Home—The Severy Family—M. and
Madame Necker—Madame de Staël—Excursion to Chamounix—Lady
Webster—Geneva—Marriage of the Duke of York—Society at Lausanne
—Comte de Lally Tollendal—Scenery—Sufferings of the Exiles—Letters
from England.

Maria Josepha to Serena.

[THIS letter is dated on the outside in Serena's hand,
'First from Lausanne.']

July 23.—Arrived at Lausanne at nine. . . . Nothing
can exceed Mr. Gibbon's attentions and wishes to make
our residence here pleasant and comfortable to us.   Mama
has a Bed-chamber, Dressing-room and Boudoir; we
have two Rooms and two Beds, and the rooms below
stairs are entirely at Mama's service to receive her company in.

We breakfast in a room he has lately built at the end
of his Terrace, which commands a delightful view of the
Lake and Mountains.   Much as I have heard of the beauty
of this Country, it far exceeds my expectations.   As to the
Severy family, they have also.   Our Severy is quite a
different creature to what he was in England; so much
pleasanter; the Father is a very friendly, good kind of
man; but a little *ennuyeux* ; Madame very pleasing and
elegant in her appearance and manner, and Mdlle. very
handsome, sensible and lively.   If one met upon more
equal terms, that is, understood one another's language

better, I think we should like each other very much. She does not understand a word of English.

I own my surprise is very great, that Mr. Gibbon should chuse to spend his days here in preference to England, for there does not appear to me anybody with whom he can converse on equal terms, or who is worthy to hear him; but it is a proof how much pleasure Flattery gives the most sensible people. This is the only advantage this place can have over England for him. However, he is so much attached to the Place and the People, that he cannot bear the slightest joke about them. He has given me a 'scouting' several times.

There is a very pleasant set of French here, with whom Lady Webster is very intimate; but we live entirely with the Severys and Mr. G.'s set, which is certainly not equally pleasant. The French and Swiss do not take to one another at all. There are here : the Princesse de Bouillon, daughter-in-law to our friend of Navarre; Madame de Biron, Madame de Guiche, daughter to Madame de Polignac; Madame de Caylus, Madame de Guigne, La Maréchale de Castres, La Duchesse de Castres, Le Duc de Guignes, Le Prince de Salms, and Madame de Grammont. Mr. Pelham arrived yesterday. Mr. Trevor is here, Lord Molineux, Mr. and Mrs. Harrison and some others, whose names I do not recollect. The Balfours[1] are expected here soon, and Madame Cerjat told us that George Coxe was going to travel with Mr. Balfour. Is it true?

We went to Coppet on Thursday to see M. Necker, and slept there. I never saw anything so broken-hearted as he appears to be. He speaks very little. Papa got a little conversation upon Politicks with him, while we were walking; but he does not join at all in general conversation. Madame Necker is very learned, as you know, and

---

[1] Of Townley Hall, co. Louth.

talked a great deal with Mr. Gibbon upon subjects of
literature. She is rather a fine woman ; much painted,
and, when she is not painted, very yellow, but upon the
whole better looking than I expected. Necker is a very
vulgar-looking man, very like the Print of him in 'The
Importance of Religious Opinions.' Madame de Staël
was there ; she is uglier than Lady K. Douglas ; but so
lively and entertaining, that you would totally forget in
five minutes whether she was handsome or ugly. They
seem to be very fond of one another. Madame de Staël
is perfectly wild, and must keep up her Papa and Mama's
spirits very much. She is soon to leave them, and then
Coppet will be a very dull lamentable place. The House is
a very good one, and the Garden pleasant.

On Monday, we set out for Chamouny and the Glaciers.
It will be a true Party of Pleasure ; in other words, the
most unpleasant thing in the world. The Party consists
of Sir G. and Lady Webster, Severy, and us. Sir G. is
more cross than you can imagine ; in short, he has just
discovered that he is married, and that Mr. P. has a great
regard for his Lady. I really believe that he need not
have the least fear about him, and that he had much
better let her quietly like a Man of Honour, than one who
might be less scrupulous ; and like Somebody, she must.
She lives entirely with the French ; the Swiss do not like
her much, and she returns the compliment very thoroughly.
We are to be about a week on our Expedition. What
innumerable misfortunes Mama will discover during that
time ! You are not likely to hear from her, for she has
not been able to persuade herself to write a single line
since She left England. Such as I am you must take me,
for better for worse in the Epistolary way ; I promise to
be more agreeable next time I write. Don't think twice
about what I have said.

Maria Josepha to Serena.

Valley of Chamouny: August 11, 1791.

I write to you from this place for an infinity of reasons. In the first place it rains, and then I think it is the first and probably the last time that you will receive a letter dated from this place, and if I do not give an account of what I see and do, *à mesure* of what I see and do, I shall probably forget half.

Monday morning, after more delays than would have been necessary for the National Assembly to have decided the most consequential article in their constitution, we left Lausanne at eight o'clock. And if anybody ever offends you so grievously that you do not recollect any punishment bad enough for them, only wish them on a Party of Pleasure with Lady Webster! The ceremony began with irresolution in the extreme whether they should go or not! How and which way they should go? and everything that was proposed she decidedly determined on a contrary scheme, and as regularly altered her mind in a few hours.

However, Monday morning saw us on our route with the French Cook; the first, I daresay, who has been brought to the peaceful Valley of Chamouny. The party consisted of Sir G. and Lady Webster, and the French Cook, Lord and Lady Sheffield and Misses, Mrs. Maynard and the two servants. Recollect the evening when you enjoyed the amusing Society of Tom and Betty [1] in Downing Street, and you have a lively image of our fine Lady, and a perfect idea of the pleasure we must derive from her company! I think I have given words enough to this subject and will dismiss her Ladyship from my thoughts, when I have told you that the day we stayed at Geneva she passed in

[1] Mr. Pelham and Lady Webster.

her Bed, *à la Française*, surrounded by her Beaux, the
cause, Fatigue, in consequence of a Thunder Storm at
Lausanne the day before.

I always expected the only amusement in our party
that would fall to my share would proceed from Severy,
who Mr. Gibbon had always promised should accompany
us, prophesying that Betty would employ every Beau she
could in her service, so particularly recommended Severy
to me, as he does not admire her as much as he ought,
owing to her chief *Passe-temps* being abuse of the Swiss,
or at best Sovereign Contempt for them and their manners.
The day before we departed, Severy gave for his reasons
to decline accompanying us on our Tour, his Mother's ill-
health and some business he had to do in the course of the
week.   These were the ostensible reasons ; but I believe
there were some hidden causes which had some weight
with him, viz., a sneaking kindness for Madame de * * *.
who soon leaves Lausanne ; secondly, a shrewd guess at
the irresolution attending our movements ; and thirdly, a
due portion of Swiss Tranquillity in his Composition,
which has the effect of keeping him in one place, without
any roving ideas in his head.   In his place, Mr. Gibbon
provided us with the Person who arranged his Library, to
arrange our Expedition.   M. Levade is a very sensible
man, and has made the same Tour with several people.
He went with Henry Dawkins, of whom he speaks with
great regard.   If I had written to you from Geneva I
should not have done him justice, my indignation being at
its height from the loss of Severy.   I certainly possess
greatness of mind beyond what I had any idea of, because
I acknowledge candidly when I change my mind, and here
I declare that this aforesaid Swiss Gentleman, Severy, is
now a great Favourite, whereas in England I took rather
a dislike to him ; but this I must say in my justification,
that the Severy of Uckfield was as different from the

Lausanne Severy, as the Paris Pelham from the Pelham
in the Glaciers; I retract—I will have nothing to say to
him, at least during Lady W.'s lifetime! for his heart
seems incapable of receiving two at a time, and his tongue
of speaking to two at a time, for he has scarce spoken to
the inferior race of Beings in our Caravan since we set off.
I am very angry with myself; here I am scribbling all
the nonsense that comes into my head without coming to
the point, viz., an account of our adventures, and without
reflecting that a Letter from the Valley of Chamouny,
should contain things of greater importance than have
employed a page and a half of this letter.

Well—I suppose you looking at the Leman Lake in a
map—the first place we reached was Morges, a very
pretty little Town on the banks of the Lake; then Rolle,
where we stopped a little while to rest the horses; dined
at Nyon; passed through a little bit of the Land of
Liberty at Var; passed through Coppet, where Necker
lives in the Château which the Duke of Gloucester had;
and finally alighted at Secheron, an Inn about half a mile
without the Town of Geneva, close to the Lake. We
found here, on their passage to or from the Glaciers,
Lord and Lady Somers and Miss Cocks, Sir F., Lady,
Mr., and Miss Sykes, and Sir J. Macpherson. The Duc
de Guignes came to flirt with the Lady W. Lord and
Miss Cravens were in the house to stay; Lord C. is in a
bad state of health.

Tuesday morning, Sir John Shelley came to breakfast.
He is much grown and very thin. He likes Geneva very
much, which is a very good thing for him. Young Campion [1] dined with us. There is quite a Colony of English
at Geneva. In the evening we went to a Country House
near, the Terrace of which commands a beautiful view of
the conflux of the Arve and the Rhone and the Town

---

[1] Of Danny, Sussex.

of Geneva, which is a very handsome one, built of Stone,
the whole bounded by the magnificent Mountains of
Savoy. This House belongs to Count Apraxin, a great
Russian nobleman. He was upon his Terrace when we
went, and was very civil, inviting us to drink Tea with
him. He asked Papa if he knew the Lord Sheffield who
had written the 'Voyage en Amerique.' Another ridiculous
mistake was a Prince, at Lausanne, asking if he was the
Lord Chesterfield ' qui a fait pendre son Précepteur ' ?

We went to the Town of Geneva, and saw the rapid
Rhone in great beauty. I never saw water of such a
beautiful colour or so transparent. Just under the Bridge
it is very deep, above twenty feet, and yet we saw the
Stones at the bottom as clear as if it had been a foot
deep. When I saw the amazing rapidity with which it
rushes along, Madame de Sévigné's alarms for Madame
de Grignan came into my thoughts. If it is as furious all
the way, I think her fears were not without foundation.

On Wednesday morning we were on the road a little
after five, the disposition of our troops as follows : the
Websters, Tom, and Mama in one carriage, Papa, the
young ladies, Levade, and Mrs. Maynard in another.
We breakfasted at Bonneville and dined at Salenches,
from which place the road is impassable for Coaches.
The Carriage that is made use of in this Country is called
a *Char-à-banc*. The name is very descriptive. It is a
very low four-wheeled Carriage, with a Bench that holds
three people, without sides, and with a board to support
our feet. The road from Salenches to Chamouny is
beautiful ; many torrents to pass, some so rapid that we
were carried over and the *Char-à-bancs* were held up by
six or seven people. The ' Torrent Noir ' is very terrific.
For Lady Webster's amusement there came a Thunder-
Storm, attended with violent rain ; which last was the
most inconvenient part of the story, as the only covering

to the *Char-à-bancs* is an Awning of Sail-cloth, which is soon penetrated by the rain. At Servoz we stopped to see a bas-relief of Mont Blanc, which was very well executed, and the worst part of the Storm was while we were there, but it continued raining all the evening. One of the Torrents we arrived at after it was dark, and the rain had increased it so much that the people told us it was not safe to pass it. It was a tremendous scene ; the darkness relieved by frequent flashes of lightning, the roaring of the Torrent, and nearly fifty of the country people assembled round us, all talking at once, some magnifying the danger, others assuring us there was none at all. You cannot think how well Mama bore it. Lady W. thought hysterics becoming. We and our *Char-à-bancs* were carried safely over in the space of three-quarters of an hour, and we arrived at Chamouny at half-past nine, wet through. A dram of Brandy was administered to us, and we none of us found any bad effects from our adventures.

Thursday we went to the Glacier des Bois and the Source of the Arviron. Rode upon mules. Friday, after many different opinions and resolutions on the subject, Mama, Lady W., and Louisa agreed to let us go to the top of Montanvert without them, as everybody said the fatigue was very great. Sir John Macpherson and Mr. Hawkins, the Son of an Irish Bishop, are at Chamouny, and went with us. They are very pleasant, lively men, and made the expedition much pleasanter. We were four hours ascending the Mountain, through Woods of Fir trees, with frequent views through the Trees of the beautiful valley and the mountains on the opposite side. Most of the way was so steep we were obliged to walk. From the top of the Montanvert we went upon the Glacier des Bois, from its size called the ' Mer de Glace.'

It is a beautiful scene, and such as no description can

give an idea of. The Glacier takes a fine turn among the
Mountains, and has exactly the appearance of a very
rough Sea. We carried a cold dinner and Champagne
with us, and drank the Prince of Wales's health in
Blair's Cabbin, built by an Englishman of that name.
The descent was very steep, and rendered worse by heavy
showers of rain, which made it very slippery. We did
not go back the same way, as we wished to see the source
of the Arviron again, which bursts out of a beautiful
Cave of blue Ice at the foot of the 'Mer de Glace.' We
arrived at the Inn at six o'clock like *drowned Rats*, with
some reason to be fatigued, as we had walked the whole
time, an hour and a half excepted, when we rode upon
Mules.

Saturday morning it was agreed that Sir G. and Lady
Webster and Mama and Mr. Pelham should return by
Geneva, and that we should pursue our journey over
the 'Col de Balme,' attended by Sir J. Macpherson,
Mr. Hawkins and Levade. The whole day's journey,
having to be performed on Mules or on foot, the married
Ladies thought would be too much fatigue for them. This
and the next day I enjoyed the Scenes and myself
thoroughly; the country was beautiful beyond all expression; every body was in good humour, and we knew
from one five minutes to another what we meant to do—
a state of happiness we had not arrived at since leaving
Lausanne.

We left Chamouny at half past six, and from that time
to half past six at night were either walking or riding, à
la Françoise, upon mules, up and down almost perpendicular Mountains, with the most delightful view all
round us. We dined in a compleat rural style seated
upon our Portmanteaux, with our cold dinner spread on
the ground before us.

At Martigny in the Vallais we found our Carriage and

good Roads again and arrived at Bex where we slept, at half past nine. The next day, Sunday, we arrived at Lausanne, seeing on our Way the Salt works at Aigle, and the Castle of Chillon, and passing by Clarens, the scene of Rousseau's 'Eloïse,' which would interest anybody who had read the work. As I have not, I did not feel the *raptures* that those would who have. The road from Vevay, where we dined, to Lausanne is close to the Lake. The evening was uncommonly fine, and the setting Sun, followed by the full Moon, made it the pleasantest Evening and the most delightful Scene I ever saw. Papa went to wait upon P. Augustus, who resides at Vevay. He told Papa of the Duke of York's marriage with the Princess Royal of Prussia. Mama returned last night as much pleased with what she had seen as we were; but a little cooled in her violent affection for Lady W. We met Mr. Giffard at Vevay. He was going to Milan; in coming through France the carriage was overturned and he and his Servant broke their Shoulders. One of the people sitting on the top of the Coach was killed, and likewise an Abbé. They were in one of the French Diligences, which are loaded beyond anything you have any Idea of.

I have written such a long letter to Sheffield that I am quite tired. I am a little disappointed at not hearing again from you; pray don't spare my money; a letter from you is my greatest pleasure here. I should have told you that we are none of us in the least fatigued by the difficulties and dangers in our Tour. Louisa is quite well. Mama is still the same as to her spirits, but bore the journey very well. Papa continues not to have a moment to spare to write to any body. The weather is intolerably hot.

Adieu. Your ever and ever affec.

M. J. H.

Miss Moss [1] *to Maria Josepha (Chez M. Gibbon*
à Lausanne).

August 25, 1791.

. . . Although you are much nearer the Court of
Prussia than we are, you may not hear of its Motions so
soon as do the English : therefore I inform you that the
King does not chuse his Daughter should marry, till
there is a proper settlement made for her; and as that
cannot be till the Parliament meets, His Highness of
York must remain a Bachelor some months longer. This
he does not altogether like, and therefore it has been
resolved to trust to the Honour of the British Senate, rely-
ing on their Generosity in order to enable them to marry
immediately. The Princess is to have the sum of Three
Hundred Thousand Pounds for her Fortune ; Cumberland
House is to be the Residence of their Royal Highnesses
and is in future to be called York House. The Queen is
to assist her son of Clarence in the purchase of the Duke
of York's House at Whitehall, which is to be the Residence
of the Royal Sailor. . . . The only Country news I can
offer is, that 'Lord Sheffield is taken up as a Spy, that he
is put into Prison, that Lady S. and Miss Louisa are
coming home in a violent hurry, and that Miss Holroyd
remains to console her father during his imprisonment; '
it has gained great credit with the Work People, for Mr.
Poole went on Tuesday to examine the Navigation at
Sheffield Bridge, and on asking some of the Men if they
had heard anything of his Lordship? was answer'd, ' O
Lord ! Sir, his Lordship is clapped up.'

[1] Miss C. Moss, a friend and frequent visitor at Sheffield Place.

Maria Josepha to Serena (*incomplete*).

Lausanne : Sept. 3rd, 1791.

Madame —— and Madme. de Silva, a Portuguese lady, were to have given two balls this week, but the Bailiff would not give leave. This is what they call 'la Semaine Sainte;' there is a Communion four times a year, two Sundays together, and the week between no dancing is allowed, which is quite ridiculous, as Card Parties go on just the same and the Bailiff never refuses leave to dance on Sundays. We go to a Party generally every evening ; they begin at half past six and break up at nine or half past nine. Some are very pleasant, some very dull. It is a continual scene of eating. At their Goûter, which is the first ceremony in the Evening parties, they eat very heartily of hot puddings and pies, fruit, etc., and continue eating Ice and drinking Lemonade during the whole time the party lasts. Mr. Gibbon dislikes the French very much, which is nothing but Swiss prejudice, of which he has imbibed a large quantity. The French and Swiss do not agree in the least. They mix very little. Most of them are going very soon. The Websters live much with the French and like them very much. She has not ingratiated herself with Mr. Gibbon or the Natives, and is considerably out of favour even with Mama. That is saying a great deal.

I believe I told you Lord Craven and his daughters were at Secheron when we were there. Miss Cravens have been on a Tour round the Lake with Lord Molineux and Mr. Nott by themselves. Some gentlemen who were on the same tour found them all fast asleep on the top of the Col de Balme. They say Lord Molyneux is to marry one of them : but it appears rather odd they should go without any Woman as a chaperon on such a party.

We are going with Sir J. Legard in his Boat across

the Lake to Meilleraie on Monday. If the weather is
fine, it will be a very pleasant party; another Excursion
is talked of to the Lac de Joux, but not settled. We
went yesterday morning to a beautiful Place belonging
to Mr. Weston, about two miles from Lausanne. There
is a very fine Wood with walks cut in it, and Seats placed
wherever there are any beautiful Views. The greatest
part of the Trees are Firs on the sides of two hills, with
a beautiful Valley between, and Cascades. There is a
rustic Building commanding a fine view of the Lake
where a large party dined, Lady W, the Duchesse de
Guiche, their Lords and Masters, Mr. Pelham, Sir J.
Shelley, etc. We did not belong to them, to my great
satisfaction.

I hope you will have fine weather for your Tour. I
am sorry your Dog does not satisfy you; the sooner you
get quit of him the better, or you will grow fond of him
whether you will or no. Tuft is in very good health, but
I cannot say in high preservation, as great part of his
Coat was rubbed off in the journey, and he does not enjoy
this Country as much as he ought, as he does not get
much exercise. .

We regretted Sheffield and the dance in the Laundry
on Thursday very much.

We had the honour and pleasure of dining and spend-
ing the evening at Mons. de Severy's. Madame de Severy
is called Mont Blanc, and I cannot give you a better Idea
of her. I feel more inclination to admire and respect
that family than to love them. There is a great deal of
dignity and frigidity in their composition, which is much
increased by Mr. Gibbon's attentions. He dotes upon
them. They are called 'Gibbon's adopted.'—Adieu.
Pray, Pray write often, it is such a pleasure to me.

Your ever affectionate

M. J. H.

Maria Josepha to Serena.

Lausanne: September 9, 1791.

Do not start! I dare say I shall not fill every side; but as I have often found at the end of my Letters that I have still much to say, I have determined to take a sheet of Paper that shall make that an Impossibility, and when you have read one side you may lay by the rest till the next Post day, and imagine it a new Letter. My disappointment this morning was very great at not receiving a Letter from you; but, on enquiry, I found the Post was not yet come in, so that I have still hopes which I trust will not be disappointed.

This week has been a very pleasant one. On Tuesday we crossed the Lake to Meilleraie. Sir John Legard lives at a Country house close to the Lake, about a mile from Lausanne. He is a great Navigator, and has the best Vessel on the Lake. Lady Legard is sister to the famous Mrs. Hodges and the no less famous Harvey Aston, and a pleasing sensible woman. Sir John is Guardian to the Miss Grimstones, who, with their Mother, live with him and make a very agreeable party. Our Water party was Sir John and Lady Legard, Mrs. and three Miss Grimstones, Sir J. Macpherson, a Swiss Gentleman Monsieur Seigneux, and ourselves.

We set off at half past eight, and as they rowed all the way, were three hours and a half crossing over. We landed while dinner was preparing, and had a delightful walk in a grove of Walnut Trees—we dined just opposite to les Rochers de Meilleraie, which Rousseau has made classic ground. The Coast is beautiful, much more so than this side of the Lake. Steep hills, covered with fine Walnut Trees, sometimes varied by Pines, seem to rise immediately out of the Lake. Picturesque old Towers and Steeples peep out above the Trees, so happily, that it

is doubtful whether they would be equally well placed if
much Art and Taste had been employed to beautify the
spot, supposing it a Pleasure ground.   The Pays de Vaud
had a very shabby appearance from the Coast of Savoy,
as it has neither Mountain or Woods to compare with
those about Meilleraie.   The day was uniformly beautiful,
and we returned home at eight o'clock, better pleased
and satisfied than I ever knew so many people with a
party of pleasure, particularly a water party, the amusement of which depends upon wind and weather, as well
as Tempers.   Mr. Gibbon had some thoughts of going
with us, but his heart failed him.   Luckily, Lady Webster
is so much afraid of the water that we had not even the
alarm of her Company.   She is going with Sir G., Pelham ·
and Mr. Trevor, who is just arrived here, to Turin the
end of this month, and she is to pass the Winter at Nice
by herself ; the two Gentlemen return to England—this
is the present plan, but perhaps before the end of the
week she will have determined upon going to Constantinople ! I wonder that idea never struck her, as she is fond
of doing uncommon things.

The Comte Lally Tollendal came with Mr. Trevor
last Monday.   He is lately married to a Scotch lady and
is going to England to reconcile her to her Friends—
she having committed a little indiscretion, viz : of having
a little Girl of six years old although she has not been
married above six weeks ; but that is Lally's affair and
nobody has a right to object if he does not.   He acknowledges the young lady as his daughter.   It is very rare
that anything, and particularly any Person, of whom one
has heard much answers one's expectations—but Lally
surpasses mine.   He is a Favourite of Mrs. Trevor's and
we were invited on Thursday to her house to hear him
read his Tragedy, and I was never more entertained at any
Tragedy though Mrs. Siddons were the Heroine.   It was

'Le Comte de Strafford.' In general, when a Foreigner attempts an English story, they make many Blunders; but he has been perfectly correct. The characters are very well supported; but he has been too good to Charles, who, instead of tamely giving up Strafford to the Parliament, supports him to the last as his firm Friend. He has made a very interesting Scene by bringing Charles into his Prison, and Strafford being torn from his arms by the Chiefs of the Parliament. There are many very fine passages and interesting scenes in the Tragedy. He read it remarkably well; and as he chooses to make poor Charles go mad, the exertion was very great.

Mr. Gibbon had a large dinner yesterday, where Lally was the principal Actor, and, contrary to the Swiss custom, the company stayed all the evening, and I never passed one more pleasantly. Sir G. and Lady Webster, Mr. and Mrs. Trevor, Mr. Pelham, Mr. Wallace, the late Attorney-General's son, Mr. Ellis, Sir J. Macpherson and Lally dined here. Monsieur and Madame de Silva, her 'Cavaliere Servente,' and Schomberg came in the evening, and did not go till ten o'clock; a late hour in this good sort of country. Lally is always in very high spirits or very low ones: we were very lucky yesterday; he amused us without ceasing, introducing a great many Stories and productions of his own, and did not seem in the least alarmed at engrossing the whole Conversation; indeed we all listened to him as we would to an Actor on the Stage, and thought as little of interrupting him. He is a Companion that would not suit Mr. Gibbon constantly, as he does not much like playing a second part. Vive les Suisses for that! who, when the 'King of the Place,' as he is called, opens his mouth, (which you know he generally does sometime before he has arranged his sentence), all wait in awful and respectful silence for what shall follow, and look up to it as an Oracle!

To-day we are to go to the Cerjats first, and then sup at Madame de Severy's, where Lally is to be. At a Party that Mr. Gibbon had last week, I saw the fellow-fugitive of Lally, Mounier; if I had not heard the one speak, and heard of the other, I should have set them both down as very stupid men; so little skill have I in Physiognomy, and Lally has a very heavy Countenance till it is animated by Conversation, and Mounier looks insignificant, if you can form an Idea of that look. The time of our Departure is not fixed; but as many Plans are talked of as to our Route, I suppose it will take place early in the next Month. I believe and hope that we shall go through Germany, down the Rhine, to Brussels, and sail from Calais. We shall go to Berne and Basle and see that part of Switzerland, and also go to Coblentz, where are the Princes and their Army. It will be a satisfaction in a few months—when we hear of one Prince being beheaded, another hanged, and a third torn in pieces by the Monarchs of Paris, etc.—that we saw them first. Most of the Aristocrats here are gone to join them. The Duc de Guiche has been here and is now gone to Coblentz, the Duchess to Vienna, where her Mother is. The Duc de Guiche and his Brother the Comte de Grammont are very pleasing young men; the former was Captain of the Garde du Corps, and behaved with great Courage on the famous 6th of October.

The Constitution has been offered to the King. I am very impatient to know what answer he will give, but I suppose he will accept anything. He is so far restored to Liberty that the Gardens of the Tuileries are open, and to amuse him the amiable 'Parisians' come in and cry 'Vive la Nation!' under his Windows, but in reality he is no more at Liberty to accept or refuse than before. The uncertain State of the finances of the Aristocrats is quite melancholy to think of, and nothing but the fear of not having Bread to eat by the end of next Year would reconcile them to their present condition. Madame de Guiche, who might be called the second Woman in France three years ago, the Queen's favourite, caressed by everybody, was in a very shabby Lodging here, without a *Femme de Chambre*, and obliged to her Mother-in-law, Madame de Grammont, for her dinner every day. Monsieur de Schomberg was a Lieut.-Colonel and of rank sufficient to be Field Marshal. He lives at Ouchy, and all weathers is obliged to walk to Lausanne, and sometimes beyond it, to pay Visits, as he cannot afford to keep a Carriage, and he is between sixty and seventy. All the Bishops, but four, refused to take the Oath, and there are two or three here reduced from 5,000 a year to 500, and that 500 very precarious.

I should have been much surprised and rather incredulous if anybody had told me last Winter that in six months I should be in Company with 'La petite Blot,' so celebrated in Lord Chesterfield's Letter, and yet I have, frequently. She has no remains of Beauty, but the manners of a Woman of fashion. I do not wonder that the Swiss are not partial to the French, for they certainly cannot stand the comparison. It is not a fair one without doubt, as the French we have here are the flower of the French Court, and very elegant and pleasing they are. Of the Swiss there seems to be but one opinion; they certainly do not possess 'Les Graces.' I wish I could transport their country, at least this part of it, the Lake and its environs, to England; they are not worthy of it, for they are satisfied with vegetating in the Place where they are born, without any curiosity about those Beauties that lay at the distance of a day's journey from them. Very few that I have met with have seen the beautiful Valley of Chamouny. There is nothing like seeing with one's own eyes, for when I had seen that delightful

valley, the Glaciers, etc., I had not patience with Mr.
Coxe. His descriptions were so cold and imperfect. It
did not seem possible to me to speak or write about them
without raptures, and yet he merely says he 'passed over
the Col de Balme' on such a day, in such a year. I see,
large or small Paper, it is just the same thing. I do not
tire as soon as I am afraid my Reader will.

Yours ever and ever,

M. J. H.

Maria Josepha to Serena.

Lausanne : September 17, 1791.

. . . When we came into this Country from France, we
imagined we were amongst a happy People who had just
sense enough to be satisfied and to have nothing to wish
for; but I find we were mistaken, and that the Spirit
of Freedom is dispersed over more countries than one.
Things are beginning to wear a very serious aspect in this
Town. I told you in my last that two Gentlemen of this
place were taken up and confined in the Castle of Chillon.
Several have removed themselves for fear of the same
habitation being provided for them, and one of them has
been summoned to appear before the Commission from
Berne, under penalty of Confiscation and outlawry. The
Army, consisting of 2,500 men, which was first encamped
at Berne and afterwards at Payerne and Moudon, arrived
here last Friday with a Train of Artillery, and has spread
terror in the Town ; as, except the Cerjats, Severys, and
two or three more of the principal Families, everybody
here is more or less inclined to Democracy. The Commission of Rolle, consisting of some of the Members of
the ' Deux cents,' are to arrive here on Monday, and it is
expected more ' criminals ' will be taken up and tried ;
but very little is known except what is seen, for the

crimes of the two Gentlemen in the Castle of Chillon are not well known. A Correspondence with the Club of the Jacobins is talked of.

By-the-bye, the arrival of the Commission has been very inconvenient to the Balfours, and therefore, out of compliment to them, it is necessary you should be a Democrate. They had taken a house in a very pleasant situation in Lausanne, and the Bailiff sent his compliments and informed them they must give it up—it was wanted for the Gentlemen of the Commission. They are still at Morges ; we have not seen them yet. They called, but we were not at home. The Troops are quartered in the churches, in the Manège, and in all the private Houses ; particular notice is taken of the Democratic Inhabitants by favouring them with a double portion of visitors, whose whiskers make them look a little tremendous, and, according to the idea of a Soldier I have been brought up with, they have not the least appearance of that animal. An army of Sussex smugglers, provided they were not afraid of holding a gun, would make as respectable an appearance. Nobody knows how long they will stay or what they are to do, but it is supposed to support some vigorous measure. An order was given out this morning to forbid the singing of 'Ça ira' in the streets. You know that is a Democratical song, very much the fashion, every verse ending with ' Ça ira ! Ça ira ! les Aristocrates à la Lanterne ! ' It was sung to us at every great Town through France, and at our arrival here, the arms upon the Coach giving some cause for it. It has done much mischief here by inflaming the minds of the people.

Prince Augustus came on Thursday, and Papa and Mr. G. dined with him at M. Cerjat's house. Sir J. Macpherson gave him a Breakfast yesterday morning, and we danced till two o'clock. There was a large Party of English ; the number here is amazing. The Cravens, Harrisons, Grimstones, Mrs. Trevor, Miss Crawfurd, Lord Montacute, Mr. Sawbridge, Mr. Wallace and Mr. Ellis, two pleasant young men who brought a letter of recommendation to Mr. G. from Sir R. Payne, and several others were at the Breakfast.

Sir G. and Lady Webster set off the day before yesterday on a Tour through Switzerland. An Express was sent after them entreating their return to the Breakfast, but it either did not reach them in time, or it had no effect, for they did not come. Mr. Gibbon is desperately in love with Madame de Silva, a pretty Portuguese, who has been some time in England. He courts her at a great rate, and pays her great attention.

We begin to talk of returning, but no time has been mentioned. However, I suppose the first week in October we shall move, and our present intention is to join the army at Coblentz. Everybody agrees that it is very disagreeable going through France at present ; the Soldiers are following their own inventions. We hear the King has accepted the Constitution, but we do not know whether there is any foundation for the report.

I won't be unreasonable and expect long letters, but I hope there are some on the road, be they ever so short. We have been here two months, and I have only three letters, but I will be honest and say that if it had been three dozen, I should have thought them too few. Pray give our united good wishes to the Foster Family, and
Believe me, yours ever and ever,
M. J. HOLROYD.

Serena to Maria Josepha.
Bath : September 19, 1791.

. . . I so much like the accounts you give of the Lausanne stile of life and Society, that I think you had better look out for a little Villa for me there, that, when I can shake off a foolish sort of affection I have for friends here, I may go and end my days in those sublime scenes and that simplicity of life, so near perfection as to serve for half way to Heaven.

Mr. Gibbon's must be an absolute Palace to afford such apartments of two or three rooms apiece for his guests.

From Miss Moss to Maria Josepha (*chez M. Gibbon, Lausanne*).

Stanmer: September 21, 1791.

Très Chère et Bienaimée Joséphine— . . . According to my calculation, your return to England will be preparing about the time you receive this Letter, and therefore I must rummage up every anecdote and intelligence I can to fill a Sheet of Paper. . . . To do all in order, I begin with the Marriages, thus : Lord Mulgrave, to Miss Lawrence ; the Duke of Athol, to a Lady Macleod, a very pretty woman ; Lord Blandford, to Lady Susan Stewart ; . . . Miss Cumberland, to a Mr. Badcock. The manner by which Miss Cumberland's match was brought about is rather curious. A very pretty Work Box was raffled for at Tunbridge, and Mr. Badcock was the fortunate winner. Miss Thrale happening to be in the Shop at the time, Mr. B. offered it to her ; but as the Gentleman was an entire Stranger to her, she declined accepting it. She, however, related the Circumstance to Miss Cumberland, whom she met soon after, and who replied, ' Good Lord ! How could you be so silly ? I am sure if he had offered to me I would have accepted it ! ' This was told to Mr. B., who thought it probable if the Lady was so willing to receive the Box, she might perhaps do him the Honour to accept his Hand. He accordingly offered it directly, and She accepted it most graciously.

The wedding took place immediately. The Lady is Thirty ; the Gentleman just Nineteen. ' Dix ans de plus, dix ans de moins,' you know, is nothing. Now for Births . . . Accidents, and Deaths. . . . Madame la Comtesse de la Motte is dead, in consequence of her having broke both her Thighs and a few Ribs, by jumping out of a Two pair of Stairs' Window at her Lodgings at Lambeth, to avoid being taken by the Bailiffs, who were pursuing her Ladyship. I think her Remains should be conveyed to Paris, that so famous a Character might be honoured by a Voltairian Procession, the Cardinal de Rohan walking first with a Diamond Necklace hanging from a Pole !

. . . I hear we are to have a Madame la Marquise de Coigny to dine here to-day. She is daughter to Monsieur de Conflans, who came over a few years ago with the Duke of Orleans. Her family are just now unpleasantly distributed, for it is thought she favour'd the Queen's Escape, and therefore she has flown to England. I give you leave to re-visit Paris before you return to us, that you may have a chance of seeing their French Majesties, and any other curiosity you may have hitherto over-looked. . . .

Maria Josepha to Serena.

Lausanne : October 1, 1791.

Tuesday, is the day fixed upon for leaving a place which I am just reconciled to enough to wish to prolong my stay. Indeed, now I am accustomed to dirt and nastiness, and got a little more acquainted with the People here, it is impossible to spend one's time more pleasantly. . . .

I must tell you that I am more indignant than you can possibly imagine, at the long intervals of time between your letters ; a few lines once a week would have been such a treat to me. Now it will be impossible for me to hear of or from you till I am quietly settled at Sheffield Place, thinking of the Dream I am just waked from, for such it will appear to me : some part pleasing, and some much the contrary. However, this I am sure of, that the last three months will have furnished me with a stock of conversation and amusement for a great while to come. How impatient shall I be to meet and talk everything over with you ! Our return home is fixed through Germany, which will be a very pleasant tour. We shall go first to Berne, from thence to Basle, Strasburg, Mayence, Coblentz, Cologne, Brussels, Ostende, and Calais. At Coblentz we shall see the Princes and several of the Aristocrats we have made acquaintance with here, who will introduce Papa to their Royal Highnesses. Part of the way we are to go by water down the Rhine ; but I suppose you will expect to hear from me during my Journey, and it is better to tell you what I have done than what we talk of doing. The troops are to leave Lausanne on Monday. Yesterday the Magistrates of Lausanne, and Deputies from twelve of the principal Towns in the Pays de Vaud, took an Oath of Allegiance before the Bailiff and the Commissioners ; and those who had misbehaved received a severe reprimand. The first alarm that was given to the Government of Berne, was the Feasting and rejoicing that took place here on the 14th of July. Many democratical toasts were drunk, and a Boat on the Lake displayed the National colours of France ; at present everything is quiet. The Commission stays till the middle of November to try the Prisoners at Chillon.

One of the officers of the Berne Troops brought twenty of his men here one evening last week, some Wrestlers, and others, to sing Helvetic Songs. Their Songs were some of them very pleasing. ' La Rance des Vaches,' the air which is forbid to be played before the Swiss Troops in the service of France, did not answer my expectations; but I was told it was not well sung. One of the Wrestlers gave a proof of great good humour and fortitude : by an unfair turn in Wrestling his Adversary put out his Shoulder ; the Man knew, if it was known, it would vex the Captain, who was present, and that the rest of his Companions would probably be very violent with the Man, who had been the cause of the accident. He had presence of mind enough to say nothing about it and join in the singing all the evening, as if nothing was the matter with him. This is for the honour of Berne whiskers.

Lausanne empties itself of Foreigners very fast. The Harrisons and Trevors are gone to Geneva. The Websters are going to Nice next week. Lord Craven died last Monday ; poor Girls ! I pity them very much ; their brother was expected last night from Vienna.

I will certainly write to you on the road. I do not promise a very lively letter for the next, as I shall be rather melancholic at leaving this place and some few in it.

Adieu, my dearest Aunt,

Ever yours most affectionately,

M. J. HOLROYD.

Serena to Maria Josepha.

From my own Château, Queen's Parade, Bath : October 6, 1791.

My best of little dear Correspondents. . . . From a letter of Sheff's to Miss Firth I find I am to direct this to Brussels. . . . I very much approve of your intended Tour home, as I think you will then have seen the best you could, and it is perhaps the safest ; but I confess I now begin to have the 'fidgets,' and shall rejoice when you are once more on dear English ground, escaped from all the mad regions you have gone through. Perhaps, indeed, there never was a period which would have afforded you such curious, interesting Scenes ; but scarce any less safe. The present state of Lausanne seems very extraordinary, and your account is wonderfully clear, &c. At the moment when the Constitution of Paris is supposed settled, it appears to be most likely to be the contrary, for I am told the number of Emigrants to join the Princes has been so great since all that was settled, that the Nation—or the Legislation—have drawn a line round to keep them at home. This looks unpleasant, and I do wish my dear Sheffs in their own beautiful, happy, peaceful Château at S. P. When I hear it, I will illuminate for joy.

CHAPTER V.

1791.

ACROSS PERTURBED EUROPE.

Homeward journey—Berne—Basle—Strasburg—Arrest of officers—The new National Assembly—Adventures on the road—Mannheim— Embarkation on board the Rhine boat—Disasters—The Aristocrats— Through Belgium—Departure from Calais—Trials *en voyage*—Joyful home-coming—Lady Webster's letter from Nice—Gibbon to Maria Josepha—' Old Nick's ' letter—Lady Craven—The Orleans Princesses— Madame de Genlis—Pamela—Lavater's remarks on Lord Sheffield's picture—His nose—' Caroline de Lichfield.'

Maria Josepha to Serena.

Strasburg : Oct. 12, 1791.

DOES not the Idea that we are actually on the road to England give you a sensation as if we were to meet in a short time ? And yet, in fact, where is the difference whether the distance is 600 or 100 miles, if any distance at all exists between us ?

I was very much disappointed indeed, and not a little anxious at not hearing from you before I left Lausanne, which I did last Tuesday se'ennight, at the time with great reluctance ; I say at the time, for I should be quite indignant if any body suspected me of a fixed reluctance to return to my own, dear native Country, like which I have seen nothing ; but can one leave Friends possibly one may never see again, and who have shown one great and uniform attention, without a little regret ? The Severy family improved upon me every day.

We have not come the direct road from Lausanne to Strasburg ; but made several delightful excursions. We

stayed two days at Berne, from whence we made a very
pleasant expedition to the Lac de Thun. The country from
Berne there, is one continued Pleasure ground, laid out with
the greatest taste by that excellent Gardener, Nature.
How can I have patience with the Fir Grove, after the
magnificent Forests of Pines I have been accustomed to !

The Conseiller Fischer, who is at the head of the
Commission at Lausanne, gave Papa a letter of introduction to his wife. She was at a Country house, on the
banks of the Lac de Thun. It is in a delightful situation ;
the snowy Mountains of Switzerland appear quite close,
though above seventy miles distant.

M. Fischer gave Papa several letters for people at
Berne. You cannot think what great friends they were at
Lausanne. One of the gentlemen we saw at Berne was a
Mr. Friedenreich, who is very well acquainted with Mr.
Bowdler. I do not recollect whether you correspond
with Mr. Coxe ? If you do, pray tell him how much I
am obliged to him for two things, introducing us to Mr.
Wyttenbach, and sending us into the Valley of Munster.
Mr. W. has given me near one hundred Alpine plants,
and promised to send me more, when he has time to look
over his 'Herbier.' We had a great deal of botanical
conversation, and he has given me a great deal of information on the subject. I have myself collected several
plants on my journey. Mr. W. is as obliging as Sir
Joseph Banks. Can I say more ?

But this has broken the thread of my narrative.
Berne is the handsomest Town I have seen, and the
Houses are all of Stone, built upon Arcades which are
very pleasant to walk under.[1] From Berne we went to
Bienne and to the Isle of Pierre. It is a very pretty spot ;

---

[1] 'Walked on the ramparts. Four Bears, two old ones and two young
ones, kept in the ditch. The two old ones very large.'—*Extract from
Maria's Diary.*

but its greatest merit is having been the residence of
Rousseau ; without that, it certainly would not be so
much celebrated.

The Environs of the Lake are very poor in comparison
to the Lake of Geneva. We wrote our names in Rousseau's Bed-Chamber—a miserable little room without furniture. From Bienne we came to Basle in two days,
sleeping at Moutier in the valley of Munster, a more
beautiful spot than which I have not seen, not even in
our Tour to the valley of Chamouny. I imagined myself
a thousand miles from any habitation, so wild and
romantic is the road the whole way through the valley.
The road is very excellent, but put Mama's fortitude to
a trial, as there is but just room for it between the Rocks
and the Precipice, at the foot of which is a very rapid
river. We walked great part of the way, which I was
very glad of, as it gave me an opportunity of Plant
hunting. A number of Castles, some very perfect, others
quite in ruins, are placed on almost perpendicular Rocks
on each side of the road, between the valley of Munster
and Basle ; I counted eight. We stayed at Basle a
whole day, which we employed in visiting the Library and
the Gardens of Arlesheim. We were at ' Les trois Rois,'
which you may have heard mentioned because of the
Gallery which is open to the Rhine. It is an excellent
Inn. Lord Craven and his sisters, attended by Lord
Molyneux and Mr. Nott, came there the day after us, on
their way home to England. From Basle we came to
Strasburg, on the French side the River, without any
difficulty. They are much quieter here than in the other
part of France. We walked over the Fort of Huningue,
near Basle, on our way here. From this place we go by
land to Mayence, and then go down the Rhine to
Cologne, staying two or three days at Coblentz with the
Princes and their Army of Officers, for I believe their

number of Soldiers is very small. At Cologne we shall find our Friend the Maréchal de Castries and his family; but I shall write before we get there, so that I need not inform you of what we shall do, but of what we have done. The greatest part of the Officers here are Aristocrats, and the Sunday before we came, at the Play of ' Richard, Cœur de Lion,' there was a great disturbance in the Theatre, during the famous Song which began the Riots at Versailles at the beginning of the Revolution, ' O Richard! O mon Roi!' They are suspected of having placed people in the Pit, who applauded the Song before it was finished, which displeased the good Patriots, and a disturbance followed which was ended by sending ten of the Aristocrat applauders to Prison.

On Tuesday, three officers were taken up, who are suspected to belong to the Army on the other side the river. They were at the Play wrapped up in great Coats, their hats flapped over their faces and their hair cut short, which is the fashion among the Princes' officers, and they seemed to avoid observation. The account they give of themselves is, that they belong to one of the Regiments at Besançon, but that they have left the Garrison without leave from the commanding officers. They are in confinement till an answer is had from Besançon about them. If they are what they are suspected to be, I should not be fond of being in their situation.

Three of the Citizens of this place, whose affairs carried them across the Rhine, have been ill used by the Aristocrats, and the danger is, they should make reprisals. We are not likely to be at a loss for amusement in the Political way in France. The new National Assembly have debated and passed a decree, to take away the title of ' Majesty' from the King, as only belonging to the People; but they were obliged to reverse this next day, as the National Guards, jealous of the new Assembly, said they made the Revolution, and would make a Counter Revolution if any innovations were attempted. There were many turbulent but clever people in the old N. A., who no doubt will make it their business to inflame the minds of the people against the new one, 'pour passer le Temps;' being too much accustomed to make and break laws and customs, to sit down contented with 'La belle Constitution' they have formed.

Mama regrets that She is not able to write to you. I assure you it is not for want of inclination. As to Papa, you may imagine that his desire for Information takes up every moment of his time.

I have so much pleasure in writing to you, that the Task falls most naturally upon me.

Ever yours,
M. J. H.

Maria Josepha to Serena.

Bonn: October 23, 1791.

I hope you have received a letter I wrote from Strasburg, with our history up to that time. The sequel will furnish more Adventures. Your dear long letter came to Lausanne after we left it, but was sent after us to Coblentz: a thousand thanks for it. . . .

I do not know if I mentioned that Papa was introduced at Strasburg to the Comte de Paravicini, a Grisons officer, who is married to an English woman, Miss Byron. What could tempt a native of England to leave that country to bury herself in the Grisons, or go from one Garrison to another, I cannot guess; it supposes great merit in her choice. He is a Gentlemanlike man, and was very civil to us in shewing us the Town, and did the honours of the Troops, Artillery, and all that kind of thing, to Papa, who was very much pleased with dining with the

Colonel of a Regiment of Carabineers. You would be astonished to hear how well he has brushed up his French, which has lain dormant for a quarter of a century.

We left Strasburg October 15, and continued on the French side of the river, as we were told all the Inns on the German side were full of 'Fuyards.' However, we repented, as we found the roads very bad, the Country flat and insipid, and when we arrived at the place where we were to sleep, only one room to be had in the Inn; and we all, including Papa, slept in three beds, and by the help of Curtains and putting out the Candles, our delicacy did not suffer.

I should tell you that we passed through a very large Forest above ten miles in width; it rained incessantly, the roads were very bad, and it was late in the evening. It appeared to us as if the Postilions did not know the way; in short, you may imagine Mama's consternation. I believe we have the merit of having visited an unknown, or at least unfrequented country, for judging from the astonishment and admiration with which the People at Germersheim (near Spires, where we slept) viewed us, I should think we are the first family who have been so unfortunate as to travel that road. When we got into the Inn, everybody crowded from every corner to look at us, and the room where we sat for some time was quite full of Spectators. We bore it with great patience, as we hoped some abatement would be made in the bill, as it was very hard to be shewn for nothing; but the exorbitance of the account next morning undeceived us. The 16th we breakfasted at Spires, a very ugly Town, which has never recovered being destroyed when the Palatinate was laid waste by Louis XIV. My indignation was raised to see the ruins of many fine Buildings, and several Monuments in the Cathedral quite

broken and destroyed by Civilised People, and it is the
same in several other Towns we passed through.

We arrived at Mannheim at two o'clock, and went to
the Elector's Palace.   He has a very fine Gallery of Pictures, and a magnificent Library, containing one hundred
thousand volumes, and many curious Manuscripts.   The
Church of the Jesuits is a very handsome Church.   Papa
went to the Theatre in the evening.   Mannheim is a very
handsome Town, and, as well as all the German Towns we
have seen, has the appearance of a French Garrison from
the numbers of officers dispersed everywhere.   The 17th
we breakfasted at Worms, where the Prince de Condé and
his Family reside in the Episcopal Palace, and arrived at
Mayence in the Evening, quite out of humour with German
Post Horses and Post Masters.   We could not get a good
Boat at Mannheim.   In the Morning of the 18th we hired
a Boat, and saw the World while our Baggage was loading.
The Elector's Palace is very handsomely furnished ; there
is a small Cabinet furnished entirely with Looking-Glasses,
and an oval Glass in the centre of the Ceiling that has a
very pretty effect.   The Library is very small compared
to the Elector Palatine's, but for elegance of furniture I
have seen nothing equal to the House belonging to the
Grand Prévôt.   Those good Priests take excellent care of
themselves.   Most of the rooms receive light from the
top, which will not perhaps give you an idea of comfort
to live in ; but to see only, it had a very good effect, as in
all the places where there should have been windows in
the Recesses, were Sofas and large Plate Glasses behind.
The quantity of Glass in all the Houses abroad is one
great superiority over English houses.   In every thing
else, comfort particularly, how inferior !   Every part of
the Prévôt's was furnished with the greatest taste and
elegance.

We went to a Summer Residence of the Elector's near

the Town, and two or three Churches, and left Mayence
about two. Our Boat has one room with Benches round
it and a Table in the middle, a place for the Coach, and
when the weather is fine we can go out upon the Top ;
but we have been very unlucky in the weather, as it
has rained almost incessantly for the last week or ten
days. We went as far as Bingen that day, and the day
after, the 19th, got to Coblentz, delighted with all we had
seen in the course of the voyage. The banks of the Rhine
are romantic and wild to the greatest degree, and a fine
Ruin or a picturesque village presented itself every half
mile.

Now for our Disasters. When we arrived at Coblentz
we stayed in the Boat till we knew where we could procure Lodgings. After the Servants had inquired at
every Inn in the Town, and at many private Houses, we
could only have one miserable room without a bit of
Furniture, and only one Bed, without Curtains. This was
just better than Nothing, and we four women adjusted
ourselves as well as we could on Mattresses upon the
Ground ; Mama occupying the Bed, which broke down as
soon as she got in. Papa slept in the Boat, as there was
no place for him to dress and undress in, the House was
so full. The next day, with great difficulty, we procured
three Garrets, literally without a Table or Chair, but with
this acquisition we thought ourselves very happy, though
still obliged to sleep on the ground. In this Palace we slept
three nights, and I cannot undertake a description of the
disagreeable time I passed there. It is easier imagined
or felt than described ; you may guess it was not the bad
accommodations I objected to. . . .

I was very glad Papa had an opportunity of seeing all
the Aristocrats. He was acquainted with the Duc de
Guiche at Lausanne, who introduced him at Court to
the Elector, Monsieur, Madame, the Comte d'Artois, the

Prince of Condé, the Marshal Broglie, and many other considerable People.   There are near one thousand of the Garde de Corps now at Coblentz, and between two and three thousand Officers.   The Empress of Russia has sent Count Romanzow with credentials, and a supply of money to the Princes.   It is said that much Jealousy and many divisions reign in the Council of Coblentz, and that the Queen is more afraid of the Comte d'Artois than of the National Assembly.   I think we shall soon see some more Events, Comical or Tragical in France.   The people do not like the new N. A.   They are more wild than the old, a thousand times.   Many of them have got an idea of an agrarian law, and they talk of removing themselves to some other place, and of a Bankruptcy. We left Coblentz yesterday, and came as far as this place, the residence of the Elector of Cologne.   To-day we go to Cologne ; we shall be in England about the end of the first week in November.

If I take you at your word and write oftener than you like, you must take the Punishment of telling Stories, and not make me so vain another time.

I am sorry to say I have not so much merit in writing as I should like to have ; it is my greatest Amusement of an evening, and prevents me from thinking.

Adieu, believe me ever, most sincerely yours affectionately,

M. J. H.

Maria Josepha to Serena.

Brussels : October 29, 1791.

I believe I wrote from Bonn, but as I have written several Letters on the road, if I should recapitulate or make a chasm you must not be angry.

Sunday, 23rd, we left Bonn, first going to see the Elector of Cologne's Palace.   We went the night before, but had not time to see it thoroughly. He has a good Library and a Cabinet of Natural History, very well arranged. There are two very fine rooms : one, the Concert room, 184 ft. by 50, and a very handsome Gallery, 270 by 36. The latter has eighteen windows on each side, the other twelve, commanding a fine view of the Country, which is very beautiful. The Town is very handsome from the River, but the streets are narrow and dirty. We travelled to Cologne the same day before one o'clock, and went to see the Cathedral, St. Ursula and her 11,000 Virgins, and other curiosities of the Town, of which there are not many. It is the dirtiest, ugliest, and most dismal-looking Town I have seen.

Papa was in hopes of meeting with the Maréchal de Castries, but he was gone to Brussels, so we left Cologne, Monday 24th, and slept at Juliers. Tuesday, we passed through Aix-la-Chapelle, and slept at Liège, which is a very large and handsome Town. Wednesday, we went to Louvain, and Thursday, came to Brussels. The Town is so full of Strangers that we were not able to get lodgings in the best Hotels—that is, those in the pleasantest situations ; but we were very lucky in arriving at this Hotel, ' l'Impératrice,' just as the Princesse de Salms was going, so we have her Suite of Rooms, which are excellent ones, and certainly, had we been an hour later, would have been let. Brussels is a beautiful Town, not only in comparison with what we have seen lately, but even with Paris. My prejudices will not suffer me to say, equal to London ; but, indeed, impartially speaking, I have seen no Town to compare with London for the width of the Streets and the uniformity of the Houses, though there are many separate buildings in most of the principal Towns, that one may acknowledge very handsome. The Archduchess and her Spouse have a delightful Palace about a league from Brussels, which we went to see yesterday. It is fitted up

H

with more taste than any Palace we have seen, and compleatly comfortable, which all Palaces are not.   We have
not lost a moment's time since we have been here, but
have seen a great deal.   I was much delighted, and felt a
strong temptation to steal at the Arsenal, where we saw
the armour of Charles V., the Duke of Alva, Alexander
Farnese, Prince of Parma, and the sword of Francis I.
when taken Prisoner at the battle of Pavia.   I longed to
bring away some Relick of these great Men.   I was very
desirous of returning through Flanders, as it is an interesting Country, from having been the scene of many
Battles, &c.   How much more entertainment I shall find
in History than ever I did before, from having seen the
very places I read of!   We leave Brussels to-morrow,
go to Malines, Antwerp, Ghent, Ostende, Dunkirk, and
Calais, at which last place we shall probably arrive next
Thursday.   The Sunday after, we shall, I hope, reach
Sheffield.   I feel nothing but Delight and Pleasure in the
idea of returning home.   I should only wish for the
return of Mama's spirits; so much I feel the loss of them,
that it seems as if there was nothing beyond to wish for;
and yet—was I of that opinion when she was quite well?
There are no two things I am so much convinced of as
that, one point gained, another (in Idea) as necessary for
one's happiness remains to be wished for, and that one
knows the value of few things till they are gone for ever.

I should not laugh at moralizing now.   I am quite in
the humour for it.   Adieu, my dear Aunt, and Believe me
ever in the humour to love you sincerely, though I may
have raised doubts in your mind sometimes on that head.
I shall not write again till I tell you we are on English
ground.

When you write to Mrs. Carter, will you give my love
to her, and tell her I thought of her at Cologne.   Once
on a time, when I did not think it likely I should go

there, she desired me to get some Eau de Cologne if I
went. I went! I saw! I bought! Latinize that, and it
will be a good pendant for Cæsar's motto.

Serena to Maria Josepha.

Bath: November 2, 1791.

. . . There must be a letter to meet my best of all
sweet correspondents, to thank her a thousand times for
the delight she has given me by her accounts, so pleasant
in all respects and so very interesting to me in particular.
I long for a line on English ground. . . . Thank my dear
Sheff for his Letter of Politics, notwithstanding the
affronts in it, which I bear with great philosophy.

Maria Josepha to Serena.

Calais: November 4, 1791.

This is to inform you that we hope to arrive safe at
Dover sometime to-morrow; but, seriously, I think it is
better to write from this place if you wish to see more
than four lines, and have an account of our Life and
adventures since I wrote last; so you will please to conclude when you receive this, that we are happily returned
to our native shore; and if you receive a Frank with half
the pleasure I write from the sea-shore, hoping every
hour to sail for England, you will be very happy, and I
shall be still more delighted to add a word or two at
Dover, giving an account of Sickness Past. At present
the wind is against us, but we live in hopes of its
changing. We go with Captain Sampson of the 'British
Fair.' His vessel is reckoned an excellent Sailer, and he
is very careful and civil. We left Brussels October 30th,
and went to Antwerp, where I have been more amused

H 2

than at any place in the Journey, from the number of fine
Collections of Pictures and the excellent Paintings in the
Churches by Reubens and Vandyke.   We arrived there at
one o'clock, and left it the next day at the same hour,
during which time we saw a great deal.   31st. we went to
Ghent, and saw some more Churches and Pictures the
next Morning before we set off for Ostende.   It was a
great Fête, and at Bruges, where we stopped in our way
to Ostende, we saw the Bishop in all his Glory, saying
Mass : Crozier and Mitre into the Bargain, which I did not
know was ever worn but in a Picture.   It was All Saints'
Day, which is, I believe, the greatest Day with the Roman
Catholics.   All the Churches we went into were quite full.
All the Chapels even open, and the People seemed quite
alive.   Last Wednesday we went to Furnes ; we intended
to have gone to Dunkirk, but the Gates shut early, and
we could not arrive in time.   Yesterday we came here,
and here ends the history of my Travels, which I conclude
with infinite pleasure.   The recollection of what I have
seen will give me much pleasure and amusement, and yet
I have had enough not to wish to prolong my stay abroad.
Indeed, all the Pleasure must be in Recollection, for there
has been but little in Actual Enjoyment.   Pray write to
me immediately, that I may see a Letter from you directed
to Sheffield.   We were much concerned to see by the
papers the 'Aquilon's' Voyage is delayed.   I hope the
Fosters were not much alarmed ; as Newspapers love
exaggeration, possibly the danger was not so great as they
represent it.   The account said the Vessel was at Plymouth to refit.   I am afraid it has vexed you.   I cannot
write a longer letter.   I can only ask myself, ' Is it possible
we are returned to England ? '   I have often enquired of
this same person, ' How was it possible any one of the
party could ever think of coming abroad ? '   Particularly
the one who was most anxious for it, and has been most

dissatisfied with it. I am in such an Agitation of Pleasure and a hundred Ideas that I can hardly write legibly or spell intelligibly.

Adieu, I hope soon to add an account of our Passage.

Ever most affly. yours,

M. J. HOLROYD.

Maria Josepha to Serena.

Dover : Nov. 7, 1791.

The night of the 6th October was a memorable one to the King and Queen, and that of the 6th November will be equally so to us. I cannot do justice to the scene, but if I state particulars you may set your Imagination to work. We sailed yesterday morning at 9 o'clock, after waiting three days for a favourable wind, and owing to a perfect calm were 24 hours on the passage. This was the least of our Disasters. 2dly, Mrs. Maynard was brought to bed last night of a fine girl at 9 o'clock in the Packet Boat. 3dly, We shall probably dine with you on Wednesday ; and 4thly, Believe me ever affectionately yours, and out of my wits for joy to be so near home,

M. J. H.

Serena to Maria Josepha.

Bath : November, 1791.

Oh ! the delight of seeing dear Sheff's frank again. It is this instant arrived. . . . Once more God bless you, and believe that of all fatigues I shall least tire of loving you.   S. H.

Lady Webster, (afterwards Lady Holland), to Maria Josepha.

Nice : November 8, 1791.

My Dear Maria,—To prove to you that you have not wasted your time upon one who is not capable of Esti-

mating its value, I instantly return you my Sincerest
Thanks for having employed it so, and you will admit it
is not lost when it has made me so happy—particularly
from hearing that Lady Sheffield is well and courageous.
So, little thing, have done with Sneers. I am glad you
are amused with your Journey, indeed you must have
been as obstinately bent on being dissatisfied as you
were about disliking Lausanne, not to have admired the
Country; but as we are a variable Sex, even if you had
Resolution to Dislike it, the Resolution would not have
held you stronger than a Certain Determination, which
I trust you will allow proved Futile at last. So much
for dear Lausanne—excepting, by the bye, to tell you that I
did not stay a week after you, not much more than 48 hours,
in which period I did not see Gibbon, as I stayed at home.
Severy said many kind things about you all, and supped
with us, and my parting from the poor Duc de Guisnes
affected me very much, as he really had Endeared himself
to me from his pleasing, engaging attention. . . . Pelham set off for Paris, but hearing on his route that there
were disturbances where we were going, he returned and
joined us at Pont St. Esprit.

Our Journey here was fatiguing and dangerous; the
Mountains are Infested by Robbers who commit Depredations upon the unwary Travellers, but we did not come
under that Description, as we had two Maréchaussée
'armés jusqu'aux Dents,' So, came very safe. This place
is vastly pretty, the Town handsome and the comble of
my Climax is the Glorious Climate, which is beyond everything, and I am convinced Medea's Kettle had no Charm
but the transporting of a Poor Mortal from a foggy Hole
(for instance like Sheffield or Battle) into this Invigorating
air. . . . I beg you will tell me how Lady Sheffield's
spirits are and whether hearing from me will Fatigue her:
but at all Events unless you are Cruel, I shall not Re-

linquish you as a Correspondent and I am a very punctual one, so in that Case you must Recollect that Letters are 3 weeks coming, so don't delay your answers.

Edward Gibbon to Maria Josepha.

Lausanne: Nov. 9, 1791.

Gulliver is made to say in presenting his interpreter, ' My tongue is in the mouth of my friend.' Allow me to say with proper expressions and excuses ' my pen is in the hand of my friend; ' and the aforesaid friend begs leave thus to continue.[1]

I remember to have read somewhere in Rousseau of a lover quitting very often his mistress, to have the pleasure of corresponding with her. Though not absolutely your lover, I am very much your admirer, and should be extremely tempted to follow the same example. The spirit and reason which prevail in your Conversation appear to great advantage in your letters. The three which I have received from Berne, Coblentz, and Brussels, have given me much real pleasure ; first, as a proof that you are always thinking of me ; secondly, as an evidence that you are capable of keeping a resolution ; and thirdly, from their own intrinsic merit and entertainment. The style, without any allowance for haste or hurry, is perfectly correct; the manner is neither too light nor too grave ; the dimensions neither too long nor too short : they are such, in a word, as I should like to receive from the daughter of my best friend. I attend your lively Journal through bad roads and worse inns. Your description of men and manners conveys very satisfactory information, and I am particularly delighted with your remark concerning the irregular behaviour of the Rhine. But the Rhine, alas ! after some temporary

---

[1] The remainder of the letter was dictated by Mr. Gibbon, and written by M. Wilh. de Severy.

wanderings, will be content to flow in his old channel, while man—man is the greatest fool of the whole creation.

I direct this letter to Sheffield Place, where I suppose you arrived in health and safety. I congratulate my lady on her quiet establishment by her fireside; and hope you will be able, after all your excursions, to support the Climate and manners of old England.

Before this epistle reaches you, I hope to have received the two promised letters from Dover and Sheffield Place. If they should not meet with a proper return, you will pity and forgive me. I have not yet heard from Lord Sheffield, who seems to have devolved on his daughter the task which she has so gloriously executed. I shall probably not write to him till I have received his first letter of business from England; but with regard to my lady I have most excellent intentions.

I never could understand how two persons of such superior merit as Miss Holroyd and Miss Lausanne could have so little relish for one another as they appeared to have in the beginning; and it was with great delight that I observed the degrees of their growing intimacy, and the mutual regret of their separation. Whatever you may imagine, your friends at Lausanne have been thinking as frequently of yourself and Company as you could possibly think of them; and you will be very ungrateful if you do not seriously resolve to make them a second visit, under such name or title as you may judge most agreeable. None of the Severy family, except perhaps my secretary, are inclined to forget you; and I am continually asked for some account of your health, motions, and amusements. Since your departure no great events have occurred. I have made a short excursion to Geneva and Coppet, and found Mr. Necker in much better spirits than when you saw him. They pressed me to pass some weeks this winter in their house at Geneva; and I may possibly comply, at least in part, with their invitation.

The aspect of Lausanne is peaceful and placid; and you have no hopes of a revolution driving me out of the Country. We hear nothing of the proceedings of the Commission,[1] except by playing at cards every evening with Monsieur Fischer, who often speaks of Lord Sheffield with estime and respect. There is no appearance of Rosset and La Motte being brought to a speedy trial, and they still remain in the Castle of Chillon, which (according to the geography of the National Assembly) is washed by the Sea. Our winter begins with great severity; and we shall probably have many balls, which, as you may imagine, I lament much. Angletine does not consider two French words as a letter. Montrond sighs and blushes whenever Louisa's name is mentioned; Philippine wishes to converse with her on men and manners.

The French ladies are settled in town for the winter, and they form, with Mrs. Trevor, a very agreable addition to our Society. It is now enlivened by a visit of the Chevalier de Boufflers, one of the most accomplished men in the *cy-devant* kingdom of France. As Mrs. Wood[2] is about to leave us, I must either cure or die; and, upon the whole, I believe the former will be most expedient. You will see her in London with dear Corea next winter. My rival magnificently presents me with an hogshead of

[1] This Commission, at the head of which was Monsieur Fischer, was sent for the purpose of examining into some attempts to introduce the French revolutionary principles into the Pays de Vaud. Several persons were seized; the greater part were released. The examination was secret, but Rosset and La Motte were confined in the Castle of Chillon; and being afterwards condemned for correspondence with the French to a long imprisonment, were transferred to the Castle of Arbourg, from whence they escaped.

[2] Madame de Silva, his great friend.

Madeira, so that in honour I could not supplant him; yet I do assure you, from my heart, that another departure is much more painful to me.

The apartment below [1] is shut up, and I know not when I shall again visit it with pleasure.   Adieu.

Believe me, one and all, most affectionately yours,

E. GIBBON.

From Rev. N. Nichols [2] to Maria Josepha.

Blundeston Parsonage : November 9, 1791.

Detesting as much as any sin that of Ingratitude, I take the first week, as I conjecture, of your arrival at Sheffield Place, to thank you sincerely for the Entertainment and Satisfaction your obliging, lively, and well-written letter afforded me.   In the first place it relieved me from the anxiety I had for some time felt, on account of the profound silence from Lausanne.   The subject of your Letter is highly interesting to me.   I am almost jealous of the Manner in which you talk of Mountains. It is true that, added to the magnificent and awful spectacle they afford and the unavoidable impression of it, there is something, as you say, in the feel of the air that produces a mechanical effect, and gives one a new, a better existence.   No work of Art ever pleased me like the Alps. I am not surprised that a fine Lady should find herself out of her element in such a country!   You seem to have seen a very curious part of that curious and delightful country, with your usual spirit and indefatigability. . . . It is certainly better than dreaming and loitering away one's life in the same insipid round of amusements, in

---

[1] The apartment principally inhabited during the residence of Lord Sheffield's family at Lausanne.

[2] Rev. N. Nichols, vicar of Blundeston, Norfolk, frequently alluded to by Maria as ' Old Nick.'

which one suffers oneself to be engaged for want of knowing what else to do. I knew the Duc de Bouillon in England. He used to dine frequently at the *Petit Couvert* of old Lady Jerningham, in Grosvenor Square, and drink willingly a quart of her Ladyship's bad port wine after dinner. You give me a very good idea of the President and his National Assembly, which has been confirm'd by a speech I read in the 'Moniteur' lately, of some nameless member, who, after having demanded with great eagerness, but in vain, the '*Question préalable*,' cries out again, '*Question préalable, êtes-vous sourd, Monsieur le Président?*' At Blickling I asked our friend Harry Hobart, if he did not suppose that Black Rod would take charge of any Member of his House who should venture to put such a question to the Speaker. I really cannot bear this Apotheosis of Voltaire. Why give honours that carry an idea of immortality with them, to a man who laugh'd at such childish superstitions! . . . Your account of Necker is a melancholy lesson to Ambition. In spite of my Aristocratical friends at Richmond, who would persuade me that he is Beelzebub, the Prince of the Devils, I cannot persuade myself that he had bad intentions, nor, indeed! that he had not good ones. I am reading, and have read ninety pages of his account of his administration, and I think he makes no contemptible defence.

I have received a letter from Monsieur de Bonstetten, who regrets very much that he miss'd seeing you. He gives me nearly the same account that you do, of the fears of the Government of Berne, and an armament of 4,000 men in consequence, but thinks that all will subside, without its being necessary to use this Military force. I begin to be of opinion that France itself will settle by degrees, though I cannot conceive how, without a foreign war. . . . Now, if by chance anybody should have the curiosity to inquire what I have been doing this summer and autumn, it is told in a moment—Nothing.

My Mother and I came here the first week in July. We have had at Lowestoft your acquaintance, Lord and Lady Cadogan and all their family. Sir John and Lady Wilson, the Judge, and which is best of all because it is something from Sheffield Place, and is, besides, intrinsically good, Mrs. Carter, Miss Clinton, Mr. Calcraft, and Mr. Clinton. I returned last Saturday from visits at Holkham and Raynham. Mr. Coke is doing wonders in planting and improvement. Mrs. Coke all good nature and civility. Lady Townshend, you know, casts a radiance over Raynham. We had, besides, Lady Elizabeth Loftus, Mr. and Miss Orme, nephew and niece of Lord T.—she a beauty, Sir George Montgomery, brother to Lady T., a good humoured, lively, brogue-speaking Paddy, and poor blind Colonel Barré. This, with the two young Lords and Lady Ann made a charming Society. I hope some body will be so good as to let me hear soon, and that you will always believe me your most obliged friend and Humble Servant,

N. N.

Serena to Maria Josepha.

Bath: November 23, 1791.

. . . I was told that Lady Craven, on hearing of her Lord's death, put on deep mourning that very day, Wept, and went thro' the whole Ceremony of a Widow. The next morn she wiped her tears, Threw off her weeds, Put on bridal trappings, and was married to the Margrave! I hope it is certain that one of her poor Daughters is to marry Lord Molineux. . . . My room is pretty; a dear convex Mirror opposite the window, which wanted something, My Sheff and my looking-glass *vis à vis* as before. I now see him twice in the same room by these glasses. My beauteous carpet compleats the whole.

Serena to Maria Josepha.

Bath : November 29, 1791.

. . . Madame de Genlis, Sillery (or what you please) is much talked of. If you have not seen her, you have only lost seeing an ordinary-looking French woman. Her children—one in particular is beautiful—dance *en l'air* with the greatest grace. How happy the state of a country where there is no distinction between the Blood royal and the children of a Madame de Genlis! When the Master of the Ceremonies proposed putting the little Mademoiselle d'Orleans above Pamela, Madame de Genlis interposed and said, ' Non, Non, tous sont Egaux.' Another trait of her's will, I think, amuse you. There is here a Mr. Southwell, an active, busy sort of man, who is always ready to show the Lions, etc. He happened to procure her lodgings, and she in return invited him to .tea. He went, and one of her first questions was, if he could recommend her a good *avocât*. He started with concern, that she should be in any embarrassment which required a lawyer's assistance, but she soon put an end to his concern by telling him it was no such thing, but that she wished to learn the English Law and should like instructions from the best Master. Mr. S., not a little surprized, gently ventured to observe that it was a knowledge which the cleverest men could scarcely obtain perfectly in sixteen or seventeen years, and he understood Madame only meant to stay here six months. It was all the same to her ; she returned to her point and desired to know the best Lawyer, upon which Jefferies, the Town Clerk was sent to her, and on being told her design, he

gave her as an introductory Grammar ' Coke upon Lyttel-
ton,' which she has seriously begun to read.   This is a
real fact, and would be fine fun for those who laugh at
Women's Knowledge ; while I confess I think it only
another proof to the many we have already, of the Incon-
sistency of the human mind, be it male or female, for
tho' Madame de Genlis' writings may not be faultless,
yet surely they mark something besides Genius, and yet,
in this Instance, she is absolutely childish.   I must not
write any more, for it begins to fidget me.   Give my dear
love to Sheff, to Mam, and to the Louisa, and I permit
you to think what you please for yourself, from your
affectionate

S. H.

The Rev. N. Nichols to Maria Josepha.

Blundeston: November 27, 1791.

Tho' I have not the least inclination to wear your
patience out in return for the great Entertainment you
have afforded me, and tho' I am perfectly aware that I
am paying you in ' assignats ' for your Bank Notes, yet it
is impossible for me not to thank you for your last excellent and obliging letter.   You do me justice in supposing that the news of your safe arrival would be welcome
to me.

You deserve the advantages of travelling, because you
feel them and know how to make use of them.   I am
glad you are satisfied with Mr. Wyttenbach, he is a Man
of Merit and a good Botanist.   Did he not talk to you of
our Alpine journey, the horrors of Grimsel, and the sufferings of the Upper Vallais ; of the Baths of Leuk, where
we were taken for Magicians, and the Ball we gave to
Madame la Grande Chatelaine D'Albematten ?   I feel
myself unworthy, but shall be very glad to see your

Alpine plants. I, too, have some if they are yet unde-
voured by insects. My Glaciers, I believe, still bow before
yours, which I still hope to see. The Lac de Thun is
surely fine ; I never shall forget its perpendicular rocks
lifting their forests of pine to the Sky. . . .

There is a Revolution, you see, in French Manners as
well as Government, or you would not have been suffered
to sleep on the ground at Coblentz !

Lord Sheffield's night passed in the Boat was recorded
in all the Newspapers, but of the Ladies not a word. . . .
I am delighted that you are pleased with Lee ; it is
indeed a Monument of Art and Genius, and will do honour
to our friend Wyatt, as long as its frail materials permit.
. . . On the 2nd January we shall leave this place for the
winter. . . . A Suffolk Turkey will be directed to Downing Street at Christmas, and I hope find its 'way from
there to Sheffield Place. My kindest compliments, if you
please, to all there. How foolish it is that Suffolk and
Sussex should be placed on such distant coasts.

Your sincere friend,

N. N.

Caractère de Lord Sheffield par Lavater.

La Physionomie d'un Inconnu, qui m'a été présenté
par Mr le Chevalier Macpherson, m'a frappé d'abord
comme une des plus décisives que j'aye jamais vû. C'est
une Tête foncièrement bien organisée, plein d'une mémoire
immense, le Coup d'œil grand et juste, un jugement ferme
et profond. Les yeux ne sont pas aussi bien exprimés
comme le front le demandoit, mais assez décisifs pour une
pénétration tout à fait singulière. Le Nez seul vaut une
centaine de Nés ordinaires. J'en suis sûr, comme de
mon existence, quand il est vrai, comme je le crois, c'est
le Nez d'un homme 'prudentissime.' La bouche est plus

juste que bon.   Je ne voudrois comparoître devant lui, après avoir fait du mal.

LAVATER.

Zurich, le 25 Octobre, 1791.

Après avoir écrit cela, le Chevalier Macpherson me disoit que c'est le portrait de Milord Sheffield.

Maria Josepha to Serena.

[Enclosing Lavater's Character of Lord Sheffield.]

Does this satisfy you ?

All my Grief is that I do not think the Print like Papa. If Lavater could have seen the Original, I should have been better pleased.   Levade, who I believe you are acquainted with, from my writings, asked Papa for one of his Prints, to send to Zurich by Sir J. Macpherson who was going there.   He cut off the Arms and the Name, and Sir J. was to shew it to Lavater, as a Person about whom he was not at all interested.   My cousin Bell [1] writes me word that there has been a Paragraph in the Papers, to say that Lavater fell on his Knees to beg for Mama's Physiognomy.   I assure you there is no foundation for the Report.   The only Impediment being that we did not see him while we were in Switzerland.   Now for the Vindication of Injured Innocence.   Lady E. is not with the Duke, notwithstanding Newspaper Evidence.   She arrived at Dover while Mrs. Maynard was there, with Caroline and one of the Duchess's children, and only waited for a wind to go over to France.   What a curious story of Madame de Sillery !   The Law Learning entertained us very much, and put me in mind of Miss Holman's learning ' Religion in Three Weeks.'

Mademoiselle D'Orléans I saw at the National Assembly,

<hr>

[1] Isabella Way.

John Baker Holroyd
Lord Sheffield
n 1735.   ob 1821

with one of her Brothers, and Madame la Metz, the then President's wife. Madame de Sillery I did not see. Where is the Duchess of Orleans? I pity her very much. She is a most amiable woman and very fond of her Children. She has been very contemptuously treated by Madame de Sillery, and is now judged an improper person to have the care of her Children, being convicted of the Crime of Aristocracy. We are not at a loss for Conversation, for we are come home flaming Aristocrats, and the three Maidens are as furious Democrats.

Liberty is a fine word, and till one has been an Eyewitness of the bad Effect of it I do not wonder at the admiration it meets with. I am living in daily fear that the Princes will go sneaking home again, and yet am almost afraid it is the only thing left for them to do. They have no Troops. The Emperor is contented to believe the King's Letters and protestations, and at present the National Troops are united and actuated by one spirit.

Serena to Maria Josepha.

December 6, 1791.

I looked and read, and looked again. Still thinking it was not the beginning of the dear Maria's letter, and yet I am sure I had reason to be satisfied, which are the first words in it. As Lavater is the subject I will answer it in order—*id est* first. It is a real curiosity, even if we were not interested in it, and says more of Lavater's skill than anything I have read in his works. At least it is to me more, for I observe that what does not exactly suit my brother's character in this Description, is precisely the difference between him and his Print. All the beginning exactly true except a little strongly marked. I do not think *prudentissimo*, which I suppose means either cautious or frugal, belongs entirely to my brother, and yet in some

I

senses it certainly does. What is said of the mouth
would not be said of my brother, tho' very right as to the
print. Lavater certainly means to say that the expression
is that of one who would judge severely and just, rather
than be merciful and good. Such I am sure is the French
phrase ending in ' Bon.' He says, you know, that he
would not willingly appear before him if he had been
doing anything wicked. He means this both in respect
to Sheff's penetration and severity. Now there is in his
real countenance an uncommon sweetness for so animated
and sensible a face, therefore this last part of Lavater's
observation is owing to the fault of likeness in the print.
Let me know if you think my criticism right ? Now
would I give Twenty guineas for Lavater's observations on
your Phyz, and yet I do not want it to read your character,
and what is still more I do really think you read it yourself more justly than I ever knew any one capable of
doing their own. . . . I went this day se'en night to the
Play, ' The Wild Oats.' I was very fortunate in having
Madame de Sillery and all the French children in the
Box with me, so that I had full room for observation, and
I saw tears flow from Pamela's fine eyes. I saw them all
affected at parts so refined that it marked not only their
feeling, but their perfect knowledge of our language.
They laughed and clapped their hands at other parts.
Once more, Dieu vous bénisse.

Yours ever,

S. H.

Maria Josepha to Serena.

Sheffield Place : December 9, 1791.

How can I think your Criticism on Lavater otherwise
than right, when it is precisely my own opinion ? I was
not quite satisfied with that nasty cross Print going as
Papa's likeness. If Lavater writes another volume, his

stern Visage will be handed down to Posterity with a
Character just suited to Rhadamanthus or Minos, the
Judges of the Infernal Regions. I would have given a
good deal to have shown his Lordship's own face, in a
good humour, to the penetrating Eye of the Physiognomist.
. . . . 'I am very glad you did not suffer by sowing
your wild Oats.' His Lordship's observation, (with an
epithet!) when he heard you were going to the Play,
though not quite pert. I hope a second and a third
Trial, if not too frequently repeated, will find you stronger
and stronger.

I conclude that as Pamela has fine eyes she must
be handsome, but I want more Description of her and the
French Princess. How came you to be in the Box with
them? Are you acquainted? If you are, I shall envy
you an Acquaintance with the Authoress of 'Adèle and
Théodore,' though she does study the English Law. I
do not know whether I mentioned that I saw Mdlle. de
Montolieu at Lausanne—the author, or at least first
mover of 'Caroline de Lichfield,' my favourite of all
favourite books of that species. Mr. Deyverdun and Mr.
Gibbon gave a finishing stroke to the Novel, which sets it
so infinitely above the rest of the family of Novels.
Madame de Montolieu has the most piercing Eyes I ever
saw, and a most sensible Countenance; but neither young
nor handsome, as I expected the Woman to be who had
put Mr. Gibbon's liberty in danger ; for he acknowledges
there was a time when he had a narrow Escape. It never
occurs to him that she might have refused him, and if it
was mentioned to him, I dare say he would sooner believe
a Miracle, than the possibility of a sensible Woman's
shewing such a want of Taste. There is a Portuguese
Lady who has been in England, Madame da Silva, who
possessed Mr. Gibbon's tender heart for some weeks
before we came away from Lausanne. I have been

amused to the greatest degree by his waddling across the
room, whenever she appeared, and sitting by her and
looking at her, till his round Eyes run down with Water.
Not Tears of Love—for, poor man, he could not help it, as
they are not of the strongest and if you fix the Sun, you
will weep in spite of yourself.   She is attended by her
Husband, a quiet kind of Man, who sits peaceably behind
the Door, and her Cicisbeo, who did not half like Mr.
Gibbon's being so constantly at her Elbow.   This last
Gentleman is a Man of great property and possesses half
the Island of Madeira.   In a letter I have had from Mr.
Gibbon since our return, he says, his Rival has presented
him with a Hogshead of Madeira, so he cannot supplant
him.   They are coming to England next spring.

Papa went to Beckenham on Tuesday and was to go
to the Levée on Wednesday and to the Drawing Room
yesterday.   He is quite a Courtier.

Serena to Maria Josepha.

Bath : December 14, 1791.

That you may not absolutely hate me out of Envy, I
will tell you I am not acquainted with Madame de Sillery.
It was entirely to chance I owed the sitting in the same
Box.   Pamela has a beautiful face and countenance, and
the very prettiest manner possible.   The little Princesses
are less handsome, and still one of them called Adèle, has
very pretty features in miniature, and particularly such
a nose as none but *the* nose can equal; most elegant
little forms, and dancing like airy Beings, all soft and light
and graceful.   I am told Madame had a little Abbé
who wrote most of what she published, but I do not
believe it.   First, because a Man could not have imagined
some parts of it.   Secondly, that I hate to have my old
ideas deranged.   I am like Mdme. de Grignan, who so

drolly laments the recovery of her friend's child, because all her thoughts were thrown away.

Lady Webster to Maria Josepha.

Nice : December 12, 1791.

. . . You know my Enthusiasm about this Climate ; it ought to Compensate for the absolute Deprivation of every other Earthly Blessing, as one might imagine the Genius of Nice ' Swore, nor should his.Vow be vain, that he till Death, Nice Dulness would Maintain,' and if a Monotony of Stupid Things can Establish it, the promise has not been nugatory . . . From this you may suppose that our Society is limited both as to Members and Talents.   After this florid description, it would hardly be fair to name a Soul. . . . The Devonshires are expected every day, but they cannot stay, as there is literally not a House for them.

Faithfully yours,

E. WEBSTER.

CHAPTER VI.

1792.

JANUARY TO MAY.

THE TRAVELLERS AT HOME.

First visit of Comte de Lally Tollendal to Sheffield Place—French enigma
—Foreign politics—Pamela introduces a Red Cap—Louisa Holroyd sent
to live with ' Aunt Serena '—Letters to her sister—Lady Webster cor-
responds with Maria Josepha—Miss Moss at Geneva—Her adventures
at Gray.

Maria Josepha to Serena.

Sheffield Place : January 6, 1792.

THOUGH I cannot return your good wishes for my
improvement, as that would be a little superfluous, yet I
return every one and a thousand more for your enjoying
health and happiness for many, many years. The Servants
are to have the satisfaction of getting tipsy to night in
your honour—and now for the event of the week, that is,
since I wrote.

On Friday evening arrived the Comte de Lally Tollendal,[1] in great spirits, and has ever since furnished us full
amusement ; and a few months ago, we should not have
suspected that this Man, who made so considerable a figure

---

[1] Comte de Lally was one of the early Reformers, and as a leading
' Anglomaniac Constitutionalist,' exercised a moderating influence on the
Committee of National Safety. He had good cause to hate the Ancien
Régime, under which his Father, Commander-in-Chief in India, had been
barbarously executed for the surrender of Pondicherry, 1766.

Carlyle thus refers to Father and Son :—' Behold him, that hapless
Lally,—his wild dark soul looking through his wild dark face ; trailed on the
ignominious death hurdle ; the voice of his despair choked by a wooden gag !

in the beginning of the French Revolution, would spend the Xmas of '91 with us at Sheffield Place; that he would read his Tragedy to us; repeat his Verses, or justify himself to us for quitting the National Assembly. Much less, after having seen the man, would you have supposed that he would dance with the greatest good humour with me to the Musick of a Fletching Fidler. His spirits are always low in the morning; he gets up late, and we see nothing of him till Dinner time, from which time till three in the morning (if we were disposed to *Veiller*), he would amuse us without ceasing. He has answered a part of Burke's second letter to a member of the National Assembly, in which he and Mounier are blamed for quitting their Posts. It is not yet published; but is to be, and he read it to us, and fully satisfied all our objections to his Conduct.

He has translated great part of the Tragedy of ' Cato ' into French verse, which shows he understands the Language thoroughly—the Speech of ' Plato, thou reason'st well ' is a very close translation, though it preserves all the spirit of the original. This Tragedy we heard at Lausanne, and I did not like it so well now as then, though there are many Beauties. It would act and read heavily by anyone but the Author.

On Tuesday Mr.[1] and Mrs. Woodward, Mr. Barr,[2] and M. Menet, a Genevan, who is learning English at Mr. Woodward's, dined with us. We played at cards as usual in the evening, supped at eleven, and a little before twelve Mama proposed sending for one of the Fidlers out of the Laundry; this Motion was promptly seconded, and we danced for above an hour in the Eating Parlour.

The wild-fire soul that has known only peril and toil; and, for threescore years, has buffetted against Fate . . . faithfully enduring and endeavouring. . . . The dying Lally bequeathed his memory to his boy; a young Lally has arisen, demanding redress in the name of God and Man.'

[1] The clergyman.   [2] The family doctor.

Lally and I; Mama and Francillon; Papa and Mrs. Woodward; Mr. W. and Miss Moss; Louisa and M. Menet, and the two Miss Firths. No eloquence could move Mr. Barr. He was Spectator. Lally, though a large Man, danced very light and in excellent good time, and altogether we had a pleasantish Dance. After our Ball, Lally sung till two o'clock, when we went to Bed and to sleep.

Pleasantish, was involuntarily written, but it is true I do not enjoy anything of that kind as much as I did and as I hope I shall, having made a discovery within these few months which I could have excused, viz., that I have nerves which I had flattered myself were sinews, and the poor things were a good deal tired abroad and since, and have not quite recovered their original firmness. I am every day more and more astonished, that we ever for a moment thought of transporting a John Bull family to foreign parts.

Serena to Maria Josepha.

Bath: January, 1792.

. . . You cannot think how I enjoyed your brilliant History of your Christmas gambols. Your calling a fidler out of the Laundry was in the Collon stile [Lord Oriel's place in Ireland]. I should have delighted in such a party more than in a ball, and I should enjoy your Comte Lally.

I shall write tomorrow to Mrs. Moss for the large size watch with Chiffres Arabes. The present opportunity would make it less expensive, as a dozen guineas would get what in England would be double. If Pap will pay it, Louisa and I will both make him low curtsies. If not I know the worst. I pay for it and go to Jail. . . .

To the Honourable Unique Maria.

```
feu                                              feu

                    əuoɹ⊥

        Gloire        France        Justice

                    La Religion

feu                                              feu
```

1792.

Throne	.	.	.	.	Overthrown.
Religion	.	.	.	.	Cast down.
Glory	.	.	.	.	Effaced.
Justice	.	.	.	.	Put on one side.

Flame in every quarter.

Serena to Maria Josepha.

January, 1792.

To be sure it must be the present state of France.

The Throne	.	.	.	.	Renversée
Religion	.	.	.	.	Cast down
Glory	.	.	.	.	Effaced

and all quarters of the Kingdom in Flames; but I confess I can go no further. I cannot make out what Justice has to say to the business unless you suppose it to revenge Despotism, or as Justice in French means punishment sometimes. This is all my own dear brain, and very possibly none of it right; but as I have done my best, I am now to have your explanation. Was it an Enigma of M. Le Comte de Lally?

Maria Josepha to Serena.

Count Lally goes out in the evening; whether it rains or not is a matter of indifference to him. For my part I do not like his walks, and am always glad to see him return, for his Behaviour is sometimes so wild and his expressions so remarkable, that I should never be surprized were I to hear he had walked into the Pond. One evening when he returned from one of his rambles, Papa said in a joking way that he thought he had been very snug in the Pond. He answered : ' Mon Dieu ! ne me parlez pas de ça ; j'ai des idées assez noires.' He frequently talks of Lord Clive and asks particulars of his end. The Maids who sleep over his Room, say that he walks about greatest part of the night, and groans, stamps, and sighs most horribly. He has written a Letter to the King, asking to be made an Irish Peer, and promising to give up his own country for ever and be one of His Majesty's most faithful subjects. I hope Lord Loughborough will be able to persuade him against sending it, as it would only make him ridiculous ; but pray do not mention this again, as he may not like to have it talked of. When you see Miss Benson pray tell her our Packet adventure. Mrs. Maynard lived with her, and in the winter we often laughed at the possibility of such an event taking place. Tell her that Mrs. M. has called three times at her house in Town to show her the little Nymph, who is a little Beauty, and that I call My Child. It has a peculiar claim upon us, for probably Mama will never more assist in the Birth of a little Christian, and I shall never either contribute my Flannel Petticoat, or serve as Pillow for the Mother, which I did for the rest of the night that we were in that disastrous situation. Mama has had a Letter from Lady Webster. Sir G. has left her and is coming to

England by Turin when he goes to see Mr. Trevor. She says poor Foster[1] is very ill indeed, that the Physicians say he cannot live. She lays Plans for a good deal of Decorum and good Behaviour, which I hope she will persevere in.

You have guessed my Enigma like an angel of a Conjuror—except 'La Justice,' which you will see is 'à côté.' Lally is not the Author. His Letters received from Paris, say that both sides are very desirous of War, and that the Princes will not listen to any accommodation whatever. Poor France must see much more distress and much greater calamities before things are restored to any order. The Emperor, it is said, will certainly attack France in the spring; but he will not suffer a Frenchman in his Army, least the Contagion should infect his Troops; neither does he chuse to appear to assist Rebels, as it would be a bad example to his seditious Subjects in Brabant. The Elector of Trêves has ordered all the Emigrants to leave Coblentz: the few that remain are forbid to wear regimentals. The Princes are at present with the Margrave of Baden, or with the Cardinal de Rohan, who has a small Territory on the opposite side of the Rhine to Strasbourg. It is said they mean to go to the King of Prussia. Many of the Emigrants are gone into the Principality of Nassau. They were all obliged to decamp in the midst of Snow, and the roads were almost impassable. Rochambeau and Luckner are made Maréchals of France, and their Army, at least the part that will do most Execution, is of an extraordinary kind ; three hundred Pamphlet Writers from the most violent of the Clubs at Strasbourg, who are to inflame the minds of people and inculcate the doctrine of 'Les Aristocrates à la Lanterne !' These are to be the Pioneers of the National Army, and to prepare the Way before them. . . .

[1] Married to Lady Eliz., afterwards Duchess of Devonshire.

I am glad you are reading 'Zeluco;'[1] it is a great favourite of mine, and much above any Novel I have read. The scene between Buchanan and Targe always entertains me, though I have read it over and over again. We made Papa undergo attending to it all through: we read it to him after supper. Perhaps I am beyond the bounds of Truth when I say he attended to it.

Serena to Maria Josepha.

Bath: January 18, 1792.

. . . I called yesterday at the Wells on Miss Boswell. They told me the Margrave and Margravine of Anspach were all the amusement there. The Master of the Ceremonies' Ball was filled by the curiosity they occasioned. Only think of her dancing a minuet and country dance. Sir Walter and Lady Jane James, and Lady Mary Hume are the party. . . . Even a common coachman at Bristol said 'par distinction,' 'The Prince who married Lady Craven.' He is an insignificant looking Man, and undoubtedly he must be a poor, mean silly fellow to leave his country, &c. for such a purpose. . . . General Coxe wants to coax me to pay him a fortnight's visit at Bemerton to meet Lady Rivers and promises me a Gala. . . . He was lately at Stourhead, Sir R. Hoare's, to meet Madame de Genlis and her party, and he was much pleased with her, and scouts all the nonsense of her not being supposed to have written the works published in her name. He also much admired Adèle, the little Orleans.

Serena to Maria Josepha.

Bath: January 31, 1792.

. . . Last night also I was a rake, (*id est*) till near eleven at the Sister Mores, where I read a number of the

---

[1] By Dr. John Moore, b. at Stirling 1729. Buchanan, a Whig from West of Scotland; Duncan Targe, a hot Highlander, two Scotch servants.

most natural lively letters from Horace Walpole to Hannah. He is a wonderful old man. One letter deplores his being no longer H. W. It was a delightful letter. So unlike the studied stile of Pope.

Serena to Maria Josepha.

Bath : Monday, February 11, 1792.

. . . The Lally work is wonderfully well written and most interesting. . . . What do you think of decreeing a Civic Fête once a week instead of a Sunday, and of the prohibition of religion only in the Education of youth ? And such people shall prosper ! Surely not a moment longer than as tools for some design of Providence. I do not like the idea of a war with Savages, because one does not know how they will act, as they are without the bounds usual to civilized people. I dread their sending some millions here to do mischief. To them the loss would be nothing, and humanity is out of the question. . . . I hope they will not find ships quickly to bring them here. It all appears like a dream, and I ask myself is it possible in so few years such amazing revolution? . . . I might say months. And may not the next Generation live to see France return to a state of total Ignorance and Barbarity? . . . .

Mary Balfour tells me they are in Town, but that her brother is made Sheriff of the County (Louth), and must remain at Townley Hall, also to defend their Castle ; as the Rioters swear vengeance for his activity against them ; and since they have not admittance to the house to take arms and what they please out of it, they threaten to destroy and burn all they can. . . . Lady Edward Fitzgerald, *alias* Pamela, has introduced a red cap for the Ladies to represent the Cap of Liberty, and they are Fools enough many of them to wear it. . . . Is it true that the P—— W—— sent to Mr. Pitt to say his

father's friends and his should in future be the same?
I am disposed both to wish and believe it.

Serena to Maria Josepha.

Bath : February, 1792.

Nobody so admired at the Ball as Mrs. Holroyd and
her petticoat. It is right you should guess at the gown,
ergo I enclose an inch of it which in the whole lot looks
genteel, though but 4*s*. the yard. . . . If no trouble to
Mrs. Moss, beg the favour of her to bring me a pound of
ten shilling green tea from Mr. Smith & Co. warehouse
in Pall Mall. . . .

Serena to Maria Josepha.

Bath : Thursday, February, 1792.

. . . I do not know anything I have felt more than
the History of our Guards. A mixture of pleasure and
pain. The horror of the storm kept me compleatly
awake, not certain of their safety, and I now feel as if
the Devil might lend Dumouriez and all his army, wings
to fly into Holland to do his work. I never felt so much
a Coward and yet Reason tells me we have every hope on
our side. The state of Paris, and France in General
seems compleat ruin and anarchy. I wish Fox, Sheridan
and their little party were settled there as being best
suited to their wisdom and merit. . . .

[Early in 1792 Louisa Holroyd went to Bath to stay
with her Aunt Serena.]

Louisa to Maria Josepha.

Bath : Friday, March 9, 1792.

How most sincerely does one sympathize with the
distresses of others when it is ordained by the Fates that
we should undergo the same hardships ! How little did
I feel for the sufferings of the Learned Pig who was

harrassed from morning till night by his Introductions!
'Sir, this is my Pig.' 'A very wonderful Pig, Madam.'
'He has very extraordinary abilities, Miss;' till finding
myself in the same predicament it has greatly excited
my fellow feeling. 'May I take the liberty of introducing my niece to you.' 'I am extremely happy to
have the pleasure of seeing you.' 'I hope you left Lord
and Lady Sheffield well and Miss Holroyd.' 'Very well,
Ma'am I am much obliged to you '—this is from Aurora
to Somnus. Heaven knows when this said niece will
have been shewn to every one. We walked up Lansdown
Hill, very hard work in my opinion, particularly in Pattens,
things perfectly new to me, went to Mrs. Gibbon's and
Mrs. Humphrey's and to the Milliner's and left names
at divers places. We drank Tea at Mrs. Denison's, and
spent an exceedingly pleasant evening. Our party consisted of Mrs. Pointz, the Dutchess of Devonshire's great
friend, Mrs. Dolben, an old Maid, sister of Sir W. Dolben,
bearing a perfect resemblance to one of the figures in the
Dance of Death; very good-natured, well informed and
pleasant, equally pleased to talk of Henri Quatre, Mountains, dying a gown, making a pudding, Sully's Memoirs,
Vineyards, the French Constitution, good singing, chess,
cards, or anything else you can possibly think of. Mrs.
Dolben and I talked till she was wanted for Cards, and
the rest of the evening Miss Coxe and I worked at one
corner of the Table. I could almost fancy myself at a
Lausanne party for more than one reason. You would
call these parties rather sober, but for a poor creeping
Christian like me, they do very well; go at a little
after 6 or 7 and return at 9, have in the mean time
abundance of tea, wine, bread and butter, milk punch,
cake buttered and plum cake, etc. etc. I fear I have
many more introductions to come, before I have got
through all the acquaintance. To be sure what I have

seen are chiefly composed of the halt, the lame, and the blind, though they are all the very best creatures in the world. We went this morning to see some Antiques. They have been found within this year or two as they were digging the foundations of some houses, and are collected together; they are thought to belong to a Temple of Minerva from an Owl's Head being on one of the stones. There are a great many stones very well carved, a Medusa's Head in excellent preservation, a Jupiter and Juno, Diana's Head with her Crescent, parts of pillars etc. etc.; skulls of Greyhounds, heifers, etc. that were sacrificed to the Deities. The Circus and the Crescent are very handsome, but I cannot but be of opinion, that Bath 1800 years ago made a still more respectable appearance than it does now. . . . I am using my utmost endeavours to teach Poor old Aunt that my name is Louisa, and am in hopes that in due time, she will remember it is not Maria. . . . Adieu.

Lady Webster to Maria Josepha.

Nice: February 11, 1792.

I have been ill and am still Ghostly in my appearance. . . . Indeed I must be very stout for next Sunday, as Il Vescovo di Nizza dines with me and a Score of outlandish Gigs, and I must contrive to render my risible Muscles very pliant, as amongst them is a Descendant of Madame de Sévigny's, who unluckily thinks he must be as celebrated as She was, and attempts every sort of Wit; but particularly the Making of Impromptu Verses, which are sometimes tolerable; he also spouts and expects one to cry or laugh as the Subject requires, and as I am very accommodating, you know I must contrive to comply. . . . I have written a sad deal of nonsense but I am tired of being Wise, for the Bishop has just left me and I promise you I was sententious enough with him, for a week. I am sure he will think me a very learned Dame, as during his Visit there arrived an Electrical Machine, he saw my Telescope, and took from my Table a Book ' L'Electricité des Météores.' I thought by his mode of looking at it that Monseigneur was no great 'Physician' and I tried his knowledge by dashing away about 'La Foudre ascendante et descendante,' Electricity, Comets and the Lord knows what; but though I was very soon 'au bout de mon Latin' yet I found Monseigneur had none to boast of, so I think my Impudence and his Ignorance have established me a fine Reputation. I don't mean to insinuate that he is a Fool, as he is very much otherwise. I shall continue writing, and if none of you answer me, I will positively address myself to the House, Post, or Mr. Barr at Fletching. Don't tell Miss Firth. Adieu.

From Miss Moss to Maria Josepha.

Geneva : May 12, 1792.

Très chère Joséphine,—If a Fortune Teller had told me six months ago that I should on Sunday, May 6, be actually sitting with young de Severy in Mr. Gibbon's Pavillion at Lausanne, I should most certainly have treated her prognostications with derision ; yet such is the fact ; and a most cordial and gracious Reception did I meet with from the Historian. This is only by Way of Preface, but I must now give you a sort of Journal, because the most trivial occurrence is consequential when so prodigious a distance divides two friends.

I sent on a most miserable 'Griffonage' dated from Calais, merely to signify that I had not been made a Toast for Neptune. I shall now proceed to acquaint you, that as we were detained at Calais a day longer than we expected, (it being Sunday, they did not chuse to search

K

the Baggage on that day), I went to Mass, where seeing
a collection of Children of about forty in number, I ask'd
if it was a School ? A Nun told me it was, and that it was
under the inspection of five of her Order, who made it
their business to collect them together on a Sunday, that
they might not be idling about the Streets. This appeared
to me, as if it was in some degree a Sunday School. So
either we have imitated them or they us. I took one of
the Prayer Books out of the Children's Hands, and perceiv-
ing it was all in Latin I said to her, ' Ma chère, je vois
que ces prières sont en Latin, et assurément vous n'enten-
dez pas le Latin,' to which she replied, ' Non, Mademoiselle, mais c'est égal.'

. . . I must tell you that at Calais we enquir'd if it
was necessary to get Passports, but as they said it was
no longer necessary, we set off without applying for any.
However, when we got to St. Omer we were stopped at
the Gates, and as we had none, two Guards attended the
Carriages to the Hôtel de Ville, where I really believe we
were detained two Hours, ' car, imaginez-vous, il y avait
douze portraits à peindre.' At last we were liberated and
after visiting the Cathedral and the Abbey of St. Berthier,
which is indeed a most beautiful Pile of architecture, and
which is now put up for sale, we set off after an Excellent
Breakfast of English Tea, for Sens, where they gave us
wet sheets, and we were obliged to put on our cloaths for
the rest of the Night. . . . From Langres to Gray. Here
was a Scene of a very different nature ; the Patriotism of
its inhabitants has just now turned their brain ; when we
enter'd the Town, the Canaille calling out with great
energy, ' Aristocrates ! Aristocrates ! '

However two officers of the Police came to the Inn, to
assure us that we were in perfect safety, which comforted
our *çi-devant* Fears, but we were soon annoy'd by a prodigious noise in the Street, when on getting up from

Table to see what it was, we saw a long Procession of
Patriots, two by two, headed by violins, Tambour de
Basque, &c.; playing ' Ca Ira.' It was some time before
I understood thoroughly what all this meant ; but as
they approached under our windows we discovered a Lady,
(who it seems had sported Aristocratic Principles), whom
they oblig'd to head the Procession, and to take hold of
the Arms of two nasty, dirty fellows who were to conduct
her to the Grande Place, in the center of which was a
long Pole, at the Top of which was placed a Red Cap.
Round this Pole they made her dance, and kiss the Cap,
and take an Oath never to listen to a Priest, who had not
agreed to the civic Oath. They then put this ' Bonnet de
la Liberté ' on her head, and made her walk round the
Principal Streets. They then serv'd a Priest in the same
way and another Man, which Three Persons I saw myself,
for they led them down to our Hôtel. Seeing this democratic Rage, the Gentlemen of our Party thought it would
be a Security to us, if they shew'd a Spirit of Patriotism,
and therefore took a Bottle of Burgundy and went to our
Windows, and poured out Glasses of Wine which they
drank to ' Ca Ira,' as the Procession advanced. This
pleased them so much ; they all took off their hats, and
clapping their hands, said ' Vive les Anglais ! '

We now thought we might venture out to walk about
the town. When it was moonlight, there was a prodigious number of Gentlemen and Ladies, inhabitants,
dancing round this Pole of Liberty, and our Gentlemen
joining in the dance (called un ' Rond ') and likewise
Kissing the ' Bonnet de la Liberté,' they threw National
cockades at their feet, which when they returned to the
Inn they fix'd to our Hats, so that I shall preserve mine
as a curiosity. From Gray we went to Besançon, the
prettiest Town I saw on the Road . . . thence to Pontarlier

. . . and Lausanne, where I immediately wrote to young De Severy, who came in about an hour's time to the ' Lion D'Or.' We both went immediately to Mr. Gibbon. De Severy went to announce my arrival, and I immediately obtain'd an audience, as well as a most gracious reception. Mr. Gibbon wished me much to dine with him the next day, but I was obliged to set off for Geneva. He took the trouble to show me the House, with which I am delighted, and if I was not afraid of my Reputation, he wish'd I would go to spend two or three nights at his House. After an hour's chat I returned, accompanied by De Severy to the ' Lion D'Or,' and in the evening Monsieur Levade and young Severy came to see me again. . . . If I had been acquainted with Levade for Twenty years, he could not have been more cordial. . . . On Monday morning I left Lausanne for Geneva. . . .

I have made an acquaintance with a Lady who has lived some years in Spain. She says, the manner they have of bringing up those little Tiny Dogs which are not larger than one's Fist is—they dip cloths in Brandy, in which they wrap the poor object ; they give them three Almonds in the Morning, three at Noon, and three at Night. They give them no drink, but what may be held ' dans le creux de la main ; ' and besides this, in order to keep them Squat and broad at the haunches, they put a weight or Bag of Sand to prevent their growing. She had one given her which they were breeding up in this fashion, and which she thought cruel ; she therefore took the liberty of giving it as much food as it could eat, and I see it every day—a most beautiful little fellow.

Miss Moss to Maria Josepha.

Geneva : May 17, 1792.

. . . *A propos* of Lausanne, I desire that you will send me by Pache [the *Voiturier*] or by Letter, the Verses which Lally made on the Sheffield Family.

When you write to Mr. Gibbon, pray tell him that I have broke my Tenth Commandment ever since I have been at his House : 'Car il me faut absolument cette maison.' I had already rais'd my Expectations about it ; but they have fallen short of what I have seen.

It is really a little Paradise. The day I was at Lausanne I sent to inform Mr. Gibbon I was there. He was drinking his Coffee at the time young Severy arriv'd with me. I went into the Pavilion (where I sat down in the *Bergère* which I suppose Mr. G. had occupied in the morning, for there was his Table and reading Desk placed in Form, with a volume of Spencer's Faerie Queen), and there admir'd the Lake, Terrace, &c.

The Room which you told me was to be Paper'd after you left Lausanne, is hung with a very handsome Green and White Sattin, and everything looks pretty and neat. Mr. Gibbon, after we had sat in his Library a considerable time, took the trouble to go over the apartments. I went into your Bedchamber, which I believe is now that which he occupies. There is a sattin Embroidered Bed in it. I saw the other room which he called Miss Louisa's, and which looks on the Ouchy Road ; but he told me you got possession of the room and lock'd it up. The Boudoir which Lady Sheffield had, I admire the view from, but I think I should have lived in the Pavilion. The sopha, chairs, two green Lamps which hang in the middle of it, all this you perfectly recollect, I am sure. In short the situation is charming, tho' I saw it to great disadvantage, for it rain'd the whole day. Young Severy attended me back to the 'Lion d'Or.' . . . I hope however I may take another Peep at Lausanne before I leave the country. I do assure you, I may say, that I have scarcely an hour that I can call my own. I am invited to several *sociétés*, and as I came here to see the men and manners of the country, of course I embrace all opportunities of mixing with the Nations. I have met with two Ladies, French Aristocrates, very interesting and pleasant, Madame de Mirabeau, et Madame de Pras. Their Husbands are now with 'les Princes en Allemagne.' Of course as there have been two or three Skirmishes, they are often out of spirits ; and as they have only been Wives a few Months, one may put some faith in their seeming anxiety.

A propos of Skirmishes, I think the Travellers had a hair-breadth escape when at Douay, as we have since heard that on the next day the engagement took place between Tournay and that place, and where poor Dillon[1] was massacred. You certainly have had the accounts by our Papers. It seems the Soldiers thought he had sold them to the Austrians, and therefore when he perceived the disaffection in his Troops towards him, he made his Escape, and took shelter in a Barn. They pursued him and cut him to pieces, and what is still more cruel, they have been laying Wait for his Wife, who was expected to follow him, but have not succeeded. . . . I have done all I can to avoid playing Cards, for, indeed, I find the Génévois play extremely well ; but as 'Le Reversi' is here fashionable, for Madame de Sévigné's sake, I am learning it. . . .

I am quite astonished at the very fashionable Work of this Place—Knitting of Stockings ! It struck me as a vulgar employment ; but that must be the Effect of my Ignorance, for everybody, Rich and Poor, are with their

---

[1] Theobald Dillon, put to death by his own soldiers. See letter from Comte de Lally, p. 136.

Balls of Thread or Cotton, knitting away. I have seen also a good deal of 'Broderie' in Coloured Cotton and Silk. I send this Scrawl by Pache, *le Voiturier*, who sets off for England the eighteenth of this Month. . . . It is possible that as Hostilities are really begun, I shall be obliged to remain at Geneva, instead of visiting Paris; but that will be better than my running the risk of becoming a Prisoner, and indeed we did run a little during our Journey, as the attacks began while we were actually in the same District.

CHAPTER VII.

MAY TO JULY.

1792.

COMTE DE LALLY'S TIDINGS.

Letter from France—Tragic end of Theobald Dillon—Vicomte de Noailles
transmits news of June 20th—Mob at the Tuileries—Insults to the King
and Queen—Ten hours of agony—Fainting of Louis XVI.—The National
Assembly opens with a ballet-pantomime—Dinner to 500 Sans-culottes
—Stormy deliberations—The procession—The Tables of the Law—
Assault on the Tuileries—Courage of the King and Madame Elisabeth—
' Les tigres adoucis '—The Dauphin plays with the Bonnet rouge—The
Queen's dignity inspires respect—At last the day ends—The decrees—
Pétion—' Go to bed.'

[The following letters are from contemporary copies
made apparently by Miss Firth for Maria Josepha, and
docketed with the names of the writers.]

From the Comte de Lally to Lord Sheffield.

Le 25 mai, 1792.

JE vous écris, my dear Lord, dans une affliction profonde, causée par l'assassinat du malheureux Théobald
Dillon, un peu mon parent, un peu mon ami, et mis en
Morceaux à la Lettre par un peuple furieux, et une infâme
soldatesque, au retour de la première expédition qui signale
cette exécrable guerre.   M. Dumouriez, notre Ministre des
Affaires Etrangères par le titre, et notre principal Ministre
par le fait, mériterait tous les supplices qu'on ait jamais
fait subir aux Traîtres.   Malgré les lettres régistérés de nos
trois Généraux qui tous lui ont mandé que rien n'était
prêt, ni Tentes, ni Chariots, ni Chirurgiens, ni Boulangers,
ni recrues ; il s'est obstiné non seulement à déclarer la

Guerre, non seulement à la vouloir offensive, mais à ordonner aux Généraux d'entrer sur le pays ennemi,prêts ou non prêts, faibles ou forts, à la réception de ses dépêches. M. de Biron devait se porter sur Monsieur de Luckner, je ne sais où, et Mr de la Fayette qu'on veut perdre, sur Namur, comme le point d'attaque le plus difficile. M. Dumouriez promettoit impudemment à tout le monde que le pays était gagné, que les François n'avaient qu'à se montrer et que les Autrichiens, Soldats et Bourgeois, seraient à leur Cou et arboreraient la cocarde Nationale. Le 28, Théobald Dillon, Maréchal de Camp, a reçu ordre de M. de Biron de se porter sur Tournay, avec une petite armée de 5000 hommes. Sorti de Lille à dix heures du soir, il a marché tranquillement jusqu'à deux heures du matin, a fait prendre une réfection à sa troupe, puis a continué son chemin et est entré sur le territoire ennemi.

Quelques poignées d'Autrichiens, garnissant quelques postes en avant, se sont successivement retirés et ont amorcé nos gens par cette retraite. Comme on faisait une seconde halte et que les chevaux étaient débridés pour manger l'avoine, on a vu tout-à-coup paraître sur des hauteurs les Autrichiens, au nombre d'environ dix mille Hommes, et une Batterie de dix Canons a été subitement démasquée—Nous n'en avions que six avec nous. Théobald Dillon a senti la nécessité de faire une retraite. A peine était-elle commencée qu'une Terreur inexprimable s'est emparé de toute l'armée. L'Infanterie jetant armes, havresacs et Bagages, s'est enfuie par vingt routes différentes. La cavalerie, ventre à terre, a passé sur le corps de toute son Infanterie. Général, Officiers, ont fait de vains efforts pour rallier leurs Troupes ; ·M. de Pully, Colonel des Cuirassiers, père de Pauline, a été culbuté deux fois dans les fossés, en voulant se mettre en travers devant ses Cavaliers pour les arrêter. Il est parvenu à rassembler Douze hommes et petit-à-petit jusqu'à cinquante, avec lesquels il est arrivé en bon ordre à Lille. Il y est entré à 2 heures et toute l'armée y était rentrée à neuf, tant elle avait couru.   Les Autrichiens ne nous ont pas poursuivis deux cents pas.   Nous avons perdu un monde énorme, et l'Ennemi ne nous a pas tué 40 hommes.   Le reste s'est entretué en fuyant, et surtout a été écrasé par la Cavalerie.   Cette infâme Cavalerie est rentrée dans la ville en criant, 'à la Trahison,' pour couvrir sa honte.   En un instant les Jacobins de Lille ont dénoncé le pauvre Dillon comme un Traître, le peuple furieux s'est jeté sur lui, l'a mis en pièces ainsi que son Aide-de-Camp, Chaumont, un Officier du génie, homme d'un mérite distingué.   Six Tyroliens faits prisonniers par ces malheureux ont été pendus.   Ces Détails sont sûrs, car je les ai puisés dans une lettre écrite à son frère par le brave père de Pauline qui commandait les Cuirassiers.   Son fils, âgé de seize ans, s'est beaucoup distingué.   Il a vu un Autrichien prêt à pourfendre un de ses Chasseurs, il a couru sur lui, l'a renversé de deux Balles dans la poitrine, et a donné le Cheval du tué au Chasseur qu'il venoit de sauver.   Dans la déroute, le Père, courant partout pour ramasser du monde, et arrêter les fuyards, a eu la consolation de trouver son enfant, qui retenoit les Soldats tant qu'il pouvoit, et qui pleuroit à chaudes larmes de les voir tous fuir.   Ces petites anecdotes sont indifférentes à la grande affaire; mais vous ne serez pas fâché de savoir ce qui intéresse si vivement cette jolie et aimable Pauline, qui s'est trouvée mal au premier mot qu'elle a entendu du combat. La Lettre de son Père, fermée Lundi dernier, étoit terminée par un Postscriptum ainsi conçu.

'On bat la générale : la crainte s'empare de tous les Esprits ; on dit que les Autrichiens marchent sur Lille : tout le monde perd la Tête.' C'est avant-hier qu'on a reçu la nouvelle de ce premier échec. Hier on a appris que M. De Biron, qui d'abord s'étoit emparé de Quinevain, marchant ensuite sur Mons, avoit été attaqué, abandonné par une partie de son armée, poursuivi, et obligé de rentrer dans Valenciennes. Restoit M. de la Fayette qui étoit déjà à Givet et qui manquant de tout, n'ayant pas même des Tentes, ayant pris Chevaux et Chariots à tous les habitués du pays Messin, devoit le trente, (ce mois), marcher sur Namur. On lui a envoyé d'ici un Courier pour suspendre toute attaque et on espère qu'il sera arrivé à temps. Les Jacobins avoient espéré le succès de M. de Rochambeau, Luckner et Biron, et la défaite de M. de la Fayette. Un officier arrivé ici hier, a vu une Lettre écrite de la main de M. Dumouriez à un des hommes principaux de l'armée de Rochambeau, et le Ministre y disoit mot à mot, 'Nous ne pourrons pas nous confier à La Fayette, il faut nous en défaire, et donner le commandement à Biron.' L'Assemblée Nationale est condamnée ; les honnêtes gens fuyent ; on s'occupe d'une Pétition qui doit être présentée à L'Assemblée pour détruire le Club des Jacobins. Il y a déjà vingt mille signatures. Mon cousin, Arthur Dillon, a été hier à L'Assemblée, demandant justice et Vengeance de l'assassinat de Théobald. Il faisoit la consolation d'une sœur qui a pensé devenir folle de chagrin il y a 4 ans, en perdant une fille unique qu'elle adorait. Je voudrais bien, mon cher Lord, que vous eussiez la bonté de faire passer ces nouvelles à Lord Loughborough partout où il est ; tous ces détails sont trop affreux pour pouvoir les écrire deux fois. Je vous envoie un exemplaire d'une seconde Lettre à M. Burke, qui commençoit à avoir beaucoup de succès ici. Mais le moyen aujourd'hui de penser à autre chose qu'aux Gazettes ! Si Lord L. est absent je vous prierais de vouloir bien le délivrer à John Haskett, mon beaufrère. Il demeure au Temple, et l'on sait positivement

son adresse chez Lord L. Ce seroit à lui à suivre officiellement mon affaire auprès de M. Dundas, il me l'a offert
avec sensibilité et je serai enchanté de lui avoir cette
obligation, car je ne veux pas, non plus, mon cher Lord,
abuser de vos bontés. Mais il est extrêmement urgent pour
moi d'être constaté Anglois, pour pouvoir ici toucher mes
revenus comme Étranger et payer mes Créanciers sans une
Résidence de six mois. Qui sait, bon Dieu ! ce qui nous
arrivera d'ici à six mois ? Il me faut aussi cette qualité
D'Etranger, pour conserver ma pauvre petite terre, en
quittant ce maudit pays. Si la question n'était pas
décidée en ma faveur, c'est-à-dire, si le petit fils d'un
sujet Britanique n'est pas reconnu par la loi, sujet
Britanique lui-même, il me reste alors le Moyen de
demander des Lettres de Naturalisation. On dit qu'elles
coûtent beaucoup à Londres, mais qu'en se réunissant
plusieurs pour les obtenir, chacun en est quitte, pour une
centaine de guinées. Alors je ferois encore un bon
Marché, puisque le lendemain de ces lettres de Naturalisation je toucherois ici 30 mille francs. Nous avons, ce
jour ci, des Détails toujours plus affligeants. La Déroute
de Mons a été plus humiliante encore que celle de Tournay.
Une poignée d'Autrichiens a mis en fuite toute notre
armée : tous nos gens se sont mis à crier—' Nous sommes
trahis ! sauve qui peut ! on nous a menés à la Boucherie ! '
M. de Biron, rentré le dernier à Valenciennes, a entendu
autour de lui les mêmes imprécations que ce pauvre Dillon,
et peu s'en faut qu'il n'ait été Victime comme lui. M. de
Rochambeau, déjà indigné que tout son plan de guerre
défensive ait été culbuté par le Conseil, a été au dernier
degré de fureur quand il a vu toutes ses entreprises
désastreuses, dont on lui avoit fait un Mystère. Les ordres
avoient été envoyés directement à M. de Biron, sans passer
par le Maréchal qui commande toute l'Armée. C'est peut-
être la première fois qu'une pareille marche a été

imaginée. Il a envoyé sa Démission qui a été acceptée avant-hier, Mercredi. M. de Biron a écrit de son côté avec fureur, qu'on lui avait promis qu'il n'avoit qu'à se présenter et que tout le pays alloit se déclarer pour nous : qu'au lieu de cela, il n'avoit pas pu trouver un guide parmi les habitans ; n'avoit pas vu venir à lui un seul déserteur Autrichien. Hier—Jeudi—un Courier de M. de la Fayette est venu apporter la nouvelle qu'au moins son Armée n'était pas entourée ; et qu'il avoit reçu à temps le contre-ordre. M. de Grave, Ministre de la Guerre, pleure à chaudes larmes du matin au soir. M. Dumouriez, frappé dans ce premier moment, avoit repris hier toute son impertinence, toute son extravagance, et il a fait décider dans le Conseil qu'on suivroit le système de la guerre offensive. Le Peuple n'est pas dans une grande agitation. Pour jeter du froid dans son indignation et de l'incertitude dans ses opinions, on vend et on crie à la Porte du Palais Royal, une grande relation de la Prise de Mons. On avait écrit avant-hier une Lettre de Mystification au Maire de Paris pour lui annoncer cette conquête—il a donné en plein dans le Panneau, a couru annoncer cette nouvelle à la Municipalité et on s'est moqué de lui. Car tel est le Caractère de cette Nation avilée qu'une moitié jouit des désastres publics, et qu'on oublie qu'il y va désormais du salut de la France. Adieu, mon cher Lord, je vous embrasse de tout mon cœur.

ce Vendredi, le 25 mai 1792.

'*Relation of the Assassination of M. Theobald Dillon, Maréschal de Camp, at Lisle, on April* 29, 1792. *By an Eye Witness.*

'I remained in the street to observe the dispositions of the people. About four o'clock I went towards Fiffe gate (Tournay). In the entrance of the street the agitation

was great, and the howling most terrible.   At last I heard
the cry of "He's coming! he's coming! To the lantern!"
I asked, with a trembling voice, "Who?"   "Dillon,"
they answered, "the traitor, the aristocrate!   We are
going to tear him to pieces, he and all that belong to
him!   Rochambeau must also perish, and all the nobility
in the army.   Dillon is coming in a cabriole; his thigh is
already broken, let's go and finish him!"   The cabriole
soon appeared; the general was in it, without a hat, with
a calm and firm look; he was escorted by four horse-
guards; he had hardly passed through the gate, when
more than a hundred bayonets were thrust into the
cabriole, amidst the most horrible shouts!   The horse-
guards made use of their sabres, it is true, but I don't
know whether it was to defend themselves or to protect
the general.   The man who drove the cabriole disappeared, the horse plunged, and no bayonets had yet been
fatal, when a shot was fired into the carriage, and I think
this killed M. Dillon, for I never saw him move afterwards; he was taken from the carriage and thrown into
the street, when they trampled upon his body and ran
a thousand bayonets through it.   I neither heard from
him complaints or groans.   Between seven and eight
o'clock I went to the market-place, where a great fire was
lighted, in which his body was thrown.   French soldiers
danced round the burning body of their general.   This
barbarous scene was intermixed with the most savage
howlings.'—*Extract from Annual Register*, 1792.

Maria Josepha to Serena.

Sheffield Place: Sunday night, June, 1792.

The Packet came from France to-day, and brings
shocking accounts of the situation of Paris.   Some officers
known to Noailles give the following account.   On Sunday

or Monday last there was some Fermentation among the People at St. Marceaux, St. Antoine, and in the Palais Royal concerning the Three Decrees which the King had refused to sanction. On Wednesday morning the People were collecting in large bodies, and the Commanding officer of the National Guard, M. D'Acloque, being informed of it, doubled the Patrols and marched two Battalions of Infantry and all the Cavalry to the Tuilleries, where he drew them up and ordered them to load. The Guard marched with the greatest regularity, and declared that they would defend the King to the last, for he was a Citoyen entitled to his Freedom as much as any Man in Paris. About one o'clock at Noon, M. Pétion, the Mayor, sent orders to the commanding officer upon no account to prevent the People from approaching the King and delivering their Sentiments.

An immense Mob, consisting of all the 'sans culottes' of Paris, armed with Pikes, guns, etc., and wearing Red Caps, came soon after to the Palace, and in consequence of the Mayor's orders were admitted.

They went to the King's apartment and placed a Cannon at his Door. They then went into the Room and brought the King to the Mouth of the Cannon, when they asked him if he would revoke his Veto. The King declared that he would not; that the Decrees were unconstitutional and injurious to the Constitution, and having sworn to support it, he would never sanction them. Pétion and Santerre, (a Brewer), came to the King while these People were there, (or came with them, I am not sure which,) but they were in the room, and endeavoured to persuade the King to yield.

A Grenadier who came with the Mob then came up to the King with a white cockade in one hand, and a Red Cap in the other. He put the Cockade to the King's heart and asked him if it never beat at the thought of it, and then abusing him in the lowest Paris jargon, he forced the Red Cap on the King's head.   He raised it above his Eyes, upon which the Grenadier forced it down again, and the King fainted.   The Dauphin was taken ill, and the Queen ran off with him, the Mob abusing her, and saying that she might go, for she was not of consequence enough to be noticed.   They then sent for a Bottle of Wine and endeavoured to give the King a glass to restore him ; but his teeth chattering together broke the glass, which put the Grenadier into a great Passion and he forced some down his Throat from the Bottle.   He revived, and they put the Question to him again, but he firmly persisted in his refusal.

At one o'clock in the morning, ten hours after their arrival, Pétion said that they had done enough for one day and the Mob retired.   During this time the Assembly sent twelve Deputations, consisting of Men armed with Pikes, to know whether the King would · revoke his Veto.

The Prince de Poix, the Chevalier de Coigny, and several of the King's old Guards came to the Palace in the Morning ; but the King dismissed them, saying that he would have no people about him who could give the least pretence for suspicion, and it is understood that he took an Oath at the Altar on Sunday last never to sanction these Decrees.   These officers who arrived to-day left Paris on Thursday at eight o'clock.   Paris was in the greatest Consternation.   The Mob had entirely left the Palace.   The Guards were at their Posts.   Many of the Soldiers were so indignant at the Mayor's orders that they took off their Coats, slit them, and threw them away. On Monday or Tuesday the Assembly received a letter from La Fayette, giving an account of the Army, and at the latter end of it he says, that if any attempt were made to force the King to sanction the Decrees in question, he will instantly march with the Army to Paris. . . . The Jacobins have in consequence sent four Men to endeavour to seize La Fayette's person.

From Mons. le Comte de Lally.

21 Juin 1792.

Depuis plusieurs Jours une extrême fermentation, qui était évidemment l'effet d'un complot, annonçait que les factieux allaient frapper un grand coup. La Terreur des Jacobins les portaient au Désespoir, à la fureur. L'expulsion des trois Ministres, leurs favoris, la lettre de l'exécrable Roland, qui était une provocation aux Régicides, envoyée à tous les Départemens : celle de M. de la Fayette arrivée dans l'Intervalle, et à laquelle on a attaché une importance, que malheureusement elle n'avoit pas ; le projet annoncé de la part du Roi de refuser sa sanction aux deux Décrets sur la députation des prêtres, et sur le Camp de vingt mille hommes ; la Démission de Dumouriez ; tout se combinait pour mettre le Trône et le Républicanisme en présence et les forcer à un combat. En arrivant de St-Germain lundi dernier, je mis pied-à-terre aux Tuileries, et me perdis dans les groupes. La Lettre de M. de la Fayette venait d'être lue à l'Assemblée. J'entendais d'un Côté—'Il est devenu fou,' de l'autre, 'C'est un Traître : ' Ici : 'Il va venir avec son Armée,' et je disais tout bas, 'plût à Dieu !' Là—'Il va partir pour Coblentz.' Des femmes s'écriaient, 'Il a violé les Droits : ' des hommes répondaient : 'Il parle en Maître à L'Assemblée : ' Le plus grand nombre cependant, prétendait que la lettre n'était pas de lui, qu'il fallait savoir qui l'avait écrite, et le traiter comme il le méritait. On arrivait ensuite au Roi. J'ai entendu dire de ce Prince si désintéressé, si humain, que c'était un Coquin, un Voleur, un Assassin, et

L

j'ai eu besoin de penser à vous pour ne pas pérorer à mon
tour : on ne peut pas répéter ce qui se vomissait de toute
part contre la Reine : des injures on passait aux menaces :
—' Il fallait créer un autre pouvoir exécutif : il fallait faire
un exemple Terrible de celui qui en ayant été revêtu par
la bonté de la Nation, en avoit fait un abus si coupable :' on
annonçait Mercredi comme le grand jour, comme le jour
décisif où le Faubourg St-Antoine et le Faubourg St-
Marcel auraient raison de la perfidie ' de cet Homme et de
cette Femme ! ' Tel était l'état des choses lundi soir, et
c'est au milieu de tous ces horribles symptômes que les
petits amis de M. de la Fayette avaient à prendre sur
Eux de mutiler sa lettre dans la crainte qu'elle ne fût
trop forte. Le Mardi, les Symptômes se multiplient avec
un caractère plus aggravant encore ; le Roi se hâte
d'envoyer son veto sur les deux décrets, à fin que ce
fût une chose faite pour le lendemain. Une partie du
Bataillon de St-Marceau alla trouver son Chef, St-Prix le
Comédien, et le requit de marcher à sa tête pour accom-
pagner, avec Armes et Canons, les Citoyens du Faubourg,
que ceux de St-Antoine venaient chercher le lendemain,
avec leurs armes, leurs Canons, leur Santerre, et le projet
d'aller tous ensemble, présenter une pétition au Roi et
une à l'Assemblée Nationale. St-Prix répondit qu'il ne
marcherait qu'étant requis ; que la Loi défendait les at-
troupemens en Armes, et que, quant aux Canons, il se
coucherait dessus, s'envelopperait des Drapeaux et atten-
drait ainsi qu'ils le fusillassent. Il y eut un Dîner solennel
à une Auberge appelée ' Le Jardin Royal.' Les convives
principaux étaient Condor, Brissot, et Gensonné, les trois
Ministres populaires renvoyés. En un mot 400 ou 500
couverts, et les Sans-Culottes y recevaient du pain, de la
viande, du vin, de l'argent, et des ordres pour le lendemain.
On alla du Dîner à la Séance de l'Assemblée. Un Secrétaire fit lecture d'une lettre écrite à la Législature par

l'Armée Marseillaise : voici plusieurs phrases de cette lettre. ' Les hommes du Midi sont armés pour la Liberté : Le jour de la colère du Peuple est arrivé. Le peuple est las de parer des coups, il veut en porter, employer la force populaire : Plus de quartier ! Qu'un Décret nous autorise à marcher vers la Capitale : Le Peuple veut absolument finir la Révolution : devez-vous, pouvez-vous l'empêcher ? ' Cris d'approbation, applaudissemens forcenés ; vaine réclamation du Côté droit, Décret qui ordonne l'impression, la mention honorable, et l'envoie aux 83 Départemens. Le Côté droit prit une stérile revanche, encourant les mêmes applaudissemens ; un arrêté sage et ferme par lequel le Directoire du Département avertissait les Citoyens du projet des factieux de se porter à de nouveaux attentats, et enjoignait au Maire, à la Municipalité, au Commandant Général, de prendre sans délai toutes les Mesures qui étaient à leur Disposition pour empêcher tous rassemblemens illégaux, et de faire toutes les dispositions de force publique, nécessaires pour contenir et réprimer les perturbateurs du repos public. Hier matin, Mercredi, 20 Juin, cet arrêté s'est trouvé affiché partout à la pointe du jour, mais l'infâme Pétion et l'imbécile Romainvilliers n'avaient garde de le mettre à Exécution. On s'est moqué du Département, et les deux Faubourgs se sont mis en marche. L'Assemblée a ouvert sa Séance par un Ballet pantomime—que les Femmes, les Garçons et les jeunes Filles de St-Denis, ' formés en groupes fleuris et jolis invités à l'honneur de la Séance,' suivant l'expression d'un Orateur, sont venus danser devant les Législateurs ; arrive ensuite le Directoire du Département. Roederer, obligé de porter son organe à quelque chose de juste, et donnant l'idée du Démon dans un Bénitier, annonce au nom de tous ses Collègues que la Loi est violée, que les Autorités constituées sont désobéies ; qu'un rassemblement d'hommes armés a lieu dans ce moment ;

qu'ils marchent vers l'Assemblée et le Château, voulant appuyer une Pétition par la force des armes. Le Directoire demande que la loi reste intacte et que l'Assemblée n'admette pas en sa présence des Citoyens rebelles. On délibère. M. Vergniaud s'écrie qu'on injurie le Peuple en lui supposant mauvaises intentions, qu'à la vérité une Loi défend de déployer l'appareil des Armes dans le Sanctuaire de la Législation, mais que L'Assemblée a déjà tant de fois enfreint cette Loi par des 'contraventions sans doute bien excusables,' qu'elle peut bien l'enfreindre une fois de plus. Des Commissaires de Police font dire qu'ils ne peuvent pas contenir le Peuple attroupé, armé sur le Boulevard de L'Hôpital. Une lettre de Santerre arrive ; les habitants du Faubourg St-Antoine célèbrent aujourd'hui l'anniversaire du serment fait au jeu de Paume ; ils demandent à défiler devant l'Assemblée. M. Ramond demande qu'ils soient tenus de déposer leurs armes à la porte avant d'entrer. Le Président annonce que la Réunion n'est que de huit mille hommes et qu'ils demandent à entrer. M. Calvet demande qu'on lève la Séance. M. Ramond insiste sur le désarmement ; on met aux voix s'ils entreront ; un Huissier ouvre la Barre ; ils entrent ; les Membres se récrient. L'Huissier dit qu'il a cru le Décret rendu—on le rend en présence des Pétitionnaires et on décrète qu'ils seront admis après qu'ils sont entrés. 'Le Peuple est prêt à se venger,' dit l'Orateur, 'et si le Roi s'écarte de la Constitution il n'est plus rien.' On défile depuis onze heures jusqu'à quatre heures et demie, hommes, femmes, ouvriers, mendicants, visages noircis de Charbon pour se rendre plus hideux ; les uns à moitié ivres, les autres à demi-nus : pour armes—des piques, des fourches, des faulx, des Broches, des tenailles, des Massues, des instruments de la Guillotine ; pour Drapeaux, des Haillons, des Torchons sanglans, des Culottes, excepté les pelotons de Garde Nationale

semés parmi eux, qui avaient des fusils et leurs Drapeaux.
Des Fifes, des Tambours, des Chants, des Cris, des Hurlemens, les Applaudissements continuels de l'Assemblée et
des Tribunes, formaient une Musique digne de cette scène
et de ce Théâtre infernal. Enfin M. Santerre a fini par
offrir à l'Assemblée au nom des deux Faubourgs réunis,
un Drapeau ; l'Assemblée l'a accepté, et le Président a
invité ces Messieurs à respecter la Loi dans leurs plaisirs.
Voilà pour l'Assemblée—passons au Château.

À onze heures le Roi avait ordonné qu'on fermât les
Tuilleries ; à midi-et-demi on est venu de la part du Roi,
ordonner à M. de Champonas de faire ouvrir les portes.
Il ne connaissait pas le porteur de ce prétendu ordre : il
n'a pas imaginé de conçevoir la moindre méfiance, et a
fait ouvrir les Portes entre une et deux heures. J'ai
passé sur la Place de Louis XV, allant voir le Chevalier
de Coigny et M. de Beauvace. J'ai vu peu de monde sur
la Place ; le pont tournant occupé par un fort détachement de la Garde Nationale, des Canons braqués, un
Bataillon de la Troupe Blanche rangé près de la Statue,
et j'ai cru à la tranquillité. Revenant le long du Quay,
j'ai vu la Porte vis-à-vis le Pont-Royal ouverte, et tout le
monde y entrant. Je suis descendu de voiture et me suis
jeté dans la foule, ne doutant pas qu'il n'y eût là beaucoup
d'honnêtes gens, prêts à se jeter dans le Château pour
défendre les jours du Roi s'ils étaient menacés, et en
effet j'en ai trouvé un grand nombre. Ils m'ont dit que
le Roi avait prié tous ceux qui étoient chez lui de se
retirer, ne voulant pas, disait-il, renouveler la scène du
28 Février. J'ai demandé à plusieurs combien ils étaient ;
ils m'ont répondu, environ 600 ou 700. Il y avait quarante
mille Banditti. Au reste, à peine entré dans le Jardin,
je n'ai plus vu l'image du Danger : un triple rang de
Gardes Nationaux, les deux derniers ayant les bayonnettes
au bout du fusil, bordait la Terrasse depuis la Porte du

Pont-Royal jusqu'à celle vis-à-vis St.-Roch. Les Banditti défilaient assez paisiblement : quelques pelotons seulement s'arrêtaient de temps en temps, sous les fenêtres des appartemens royaux, agitant leurs armes, criant 'A bas Veto!' 'Vive la Nation!' Les trois quarts de ceux qui étaient là, y étaient, comme à un Charivari pour se réjouir. J'ai entendu un de ceux qui portait une des armes les plus horribles, et dont la bonne physionomie contrastait singulièrement avec son costume féroce, dire, en voyant les Fenêtres du Roi fermées : 'Mais pourquoi donc ne se montre-t-il pas ? De quoi a-t-il peur, ce pauvre cher homme ? Nous ne voulons pas lui faire du mal.' J'ai entendu répéter ce propos : 'On le trompe.' Un autre répliquait : 'Mais pourquoi croit-il plutôt six hommes que 745 ? on lui a donné un Veto, mais il ne sait pas gouverner.'

Une Machine énorme, taillée comme les Tables de la Loi de Moïse, et sur laquelle étoit écrite en Lettres d'or la Déclamation des droits de l'homme, était la grande Relique de la procession ; à côté des femmes qui portaient des Sabres et des Broches, on voyait des Hommes porter des Branches d'Olivier—les Bonnets rouges étaient par Milliers, et à chaque fusil ou à chaque pique pendait une Banderolle sur laquelle on lisait : 'La Constitution ou la Mort.' Ainsi chacun portait sa Condemnation au-dessus de sa Tête. Enfin, après avoir rôdé depuis deux heures jusqu'à quatre, n'ayant vu que quelques méchans isolés qui ne paraissaient pas devoir être craints, et une masse d'hommes faisant une procession dégoûtable et ridicule, j'ai cru pouvoir aller dîner au Luxembourg, me promettant de revenir encore le soir, mais par curiosité seulement, et sans aucune des idées qui m'y avaient fait descendre le matin. Je dînais avec un Membre de l'Assemblée Nationale, un des bons qui croyait ainsi que moi la journée à sa fin, lorsqu'on est venu nous avertir que l'Élite du Faubourg avait tourné les Tuilleries, s'était présentée du Côté du Carrousel et avait forcé la Porte et le Château. J'ai couru aux Tuilleries—voiçi ce qui s'était passé. Du côté du Jardin, l'ordre n'avait pas été troublé. Du Côté de la Cour, les Officiers Municipaux avaient ordonné à 23 Gardes Nationaux exçellens, qui à eux seuls contenaient toute la Colonne, de laisser passer ce que ces Messieurs appelaient les ' *Pétitionnaires*.' Alors touts les Bandits enragés avaient couru au Château, s'étaient emparé d'une partie du Canon des Gardes Nationaux, et l'avaient braqué contre. le palais, ainsi que celui qu'ils avaient amené avec eux. La Garde Nationale marchait comme mal disposée de la manière qu'elle serait entretenue ; elle avait voulu tirer, et d'ailleurs, ne recevant ni réquisition du Magistrat, ni ordre du Commandant, était devenue spectatrice, les Grenadiers pleurant sur leurs fusils chargés qu'ils n'osaient pas tirer—D'autres indifférens, plusieurs, et beaucoup trop, prenant la main de tous ces gens.

Parvenus à la Porte de l'appartement, un cri universel avait retenti de toute part: 'Enfonçons! Enfonçons !' Le premier coup avait été donné par un Garde National en faction. Un Grenadier avait arrêté le second, en lui disant, ' Malheureux ! tu déshonores l'habit que tu portes ! ' On avait mis un Canon, démonté de son affut à force de bras, dans la salle des Gardes. Le Roi après avoir examiné de chez son Valet-de-Chambre, Septeuil, ce qui se passait dans les cours, entendant les coups redoublés qu'on donnait à la Porte de l'Œil-de-Bœuf, s'était arraché de la Reine, avancé vers la Porte, et accompagné du Maréchal de Mouchy il avait dit: ' Je m'en vais à eux, à mes quatre Grenadiers.' Un Grenadier s'était précipité, criant : 'Avec vous j'irais en Enfer.' Leur avait-il dit, ' Qu'on Ouvre,' on avait ouvert. Un Coup de Bayonnette, dirigé sur la Porte pour l'enfoncer, allait atteindre le Roi; un Grenadier l'avait détourné. Le digne Acloque s'était mis au devant du Roi en leur criant, 'Respectez votre Maître, vous n'arriverez à lui qu'après avoir passé sur mon Corps.' Un autre Grenadier avait dit au Garde National qui avait porté le premier coup à la porte, et qui en entrant ouvrait la bouche pour maudir le Roi, 'Criez Vive le Roi, Malheureux,' et le Malheureux avait crié, 'Vive le Roi!' et ce cri avait été celui de la surprise et du saisissement. Le Maréchal de Mouchy, Acloque, et les quatre Grenadiers avaient entraîné le Roi dans la troisième travée pour qu'il ne pût pas être entouré. Là il était monté sur une chaise, leur demandant ce qu'ils voulaient. Enfin un furibond nommé Legendre s'était avancé, et du milieu d'un groupe d'assassins avait présenté au Roi le Bonnet rouge. Un autre lui avait présenté à boire. Il avait mis le Bonnet rouge; il avait bu! Legendre lui avait enfoncé le Bonnet. Voilà où en était cet horrible événement lorsque je suis entré aux Tuilleries. La Grille du Milieu était fermée. Une députation de l'Assemblée était Chez le Roi, et plusieurs Députés y étaient pour leur propre compte.

Damas avait couru dire à l'Assemblée : 'Le Roi est dans le plus grand Danger—insulté—menacé—il ne peut se faire entendre—ni donner des ordres. Je l'ai vu avili sous un Bonnet de laine rouge!' Plusieurs voix s'étaient écrié : 'Eh Bien ?' M. Thuriot avait demandé qu'on rappelât à l'ordre 'ceux qui insultaient le peuple.' Isnard et Vergniaud criaient dans les appartemens : 'Respectez votre Roi Constitutionnel! fiez-vous à l'Assemblée Nationale!' Le Peuple criait au Roi: 'Vive la Nation!' et le Roi répondait par le même Cri. Mais, lorsqu'on lui demandait la Révocation de son Veto, le Rappel des trois Ministres renvoyés, il les rappelait à la Constitution, professant un attachement inviolable pour elle, et répondant toujours que rien l'empêcherait de se

servir, pour le bien de la Nation, du Pouvoir qu'elle lui
avait confié.   La Députation arrivée jusqu'à lui, lui a
proposé de passer au milieu d'elle dans une Chambre où
l'affluence serait moins grande.   Il y a passé.   Depuis
ce moment le danger a beaucoup diminué ; de demi-heure
en demi-heure les Députations se relevaient auprès de
lui.   J'en ai vu entrer quatre.   Pétion était arrivé pour
jouir de son triomphe : applaudi dans les cours, il avait
dit à tous ces misérables qu'il ' n'avait fait que son devoir,'
qu'il était bien sensible à leur amitié.   Près du Roi il a
harangué, et au milieu de sa harangue il a invité ce
malheureux Prince à ne rien craindre et à être tranquille.
' Tranquille ! ' a repris le Roi ; ' Je le suis; quand on a la
conscience pure, on n'a rien à craindre,' et prenant la
main d'un Grenadier, il lui a dit, en la posant sur son
cœur : ' Ami, sens s'il bat plus vite qu'à l'ordinaire, et
dis-lui si je suis tranquille.'   Ces mots ont produit un
effet merveilleux.   Les Brigands en ont été frappés.
L'Assemblée l'a couvert d'applaudissemens quand il lui
a été rapporté par la seconde Députation, et avec la
seconde, Santerre, dont on a été obligé d'invoquer la protection.   La foule a commencé à s'écouler.

Mais vous ne savez pas encore tout.   Lorsque le Roi
s'était avancé pour faire ouvrir les Portes, Madame Elisabeth s'était seule de sa famille avancée avec lui, et elle
était toujours restée à la première travée, avec son visage
angélique moins effrayé peut-être de cette scène que des
autres, parce que dans ce moment le Roi lui paraissait un
martyr.   Ces Tigres s'étaient adoucis malgré eux en la
voyant, et leur fureur était un peu amortie avant d'arriver
jusqu'au Roi.   Pour la Reine, sept ou huit personnes,
parmi lesquelles le Vicomte de Monteuil, l'avaient envir-
ronnée et malgré ses cris l'avaient entraînée dans la
Chambre des Conseils.   On avait mis la Table en
travers ; des Gardes Nationaux faisaient le fer à Cheval

depuis les deux extrémités de cette Table jusqu'aux deux Portes. La Reine était de l'autre côté de la Table avec ses Dames et quelques serviteurs. Elle ne voit pas son fils près d'elle, elle le demande. Une femme de Chambre accourut et s'écrie, 'M. le Dauphin est enlevé!' La Reine tombe évanouie : une autre lui ramène son fils et l'homme qui l'a défendu. 'Madame,' dit-elle, 'Voilà l'homme à qui vous devez le salut de votre fils.' La Reine se jette aux pieds de cet homme. Les Brigands défilent par la Chambre du Conseil, on jette un Bonnet rouge pour le Dauphin—on demande qu'il soit monté sur la Table avec ce Bonnet, et il y reste pendant une demi-heure ; il se familiarise avec tout ce spectacle, et finit par jouer avec ce Bonnet rouge. La Reine avait un maintien fort digne ; les uns en étaient frappés—les autres restaient insensibles. Ici, on criait, 'Vive la Reine !' Là, on vomissait des horreurs. Les Députés de l'Assemblée sont sortis d'avec Elle, pénétrés de respect et attendris, plusieurs malgré eux. Enfin à 9 heures et demie tout a été dissipé. Le Roi est rentré chez lui, et la Reine est venue se jeter à ses genoux, et l'a prit dans ses bras, non pas en pleurant, mais en criant.   .

Ce matin tout Paris s'est trouvé plongé dans la Consternation ; l'Assemblée dans la honte ; la Garde Nationale dans les remords et dans la Rage. Le Roi à fait venir un Juge de Paix pour constater les traces de violence et de Vols commis dans le Château. On a volé dans les appartemens, des meubles et des serrures ; à un détachement de Gardes Nationaux, 75 fusils ; à d'autres 42. Le Département a fait commencer hier au soir une information : vingt témoins out déposé qu'un certain grand Nègre de M. le Duc D'Orléans, nommé Catalan, était à la tête de ceux qui ont braqué le Canon contre le Château. M. Pétion et un autre municipal nommé Serjent ont été ce matin hués, frappés, lapidés, dans la Cour du Château

par les Gardes Nationaux et par le Peuple. Le Département-
ment songe à suspendre ou même casser la Municipalité.
L'Assemblée a décrété, 1^{ment} qu'aucune troupe armée ne
serait admise à se présenter à la Barre, ni à défiler devant
elle ; 2^{mt} Que les Citoyens ne pourraient se réunir en
armes sous prétexte de présenter des pétitions. Ce gueux
de Merlin, et un je ne sais quel Couthon, ont fait la
Motion de décréter que le Roi ne peut opposer son Veto
sur le décret de circonstances où il n'a seulement pas
voulu les entendre. Il y a encore eu un Ballet Législatif
formé par des jeunes Filles de Versailles, mais leurs Messieurs étaient sans armes. Le Roi à écrit à l'Assemblée
une Lettre très sage et très courageuse, par laquelle se
terminera ma longue narration. 'L'Assemblée Nationale
a déjà connaissance des Evénemens de la Journée d'hier.
Paris est sans doute dans la Consternation, et la France
ne les apprendra pas sans douleur. Je laisse à la prudence
de l'Assemblée à maintenir la Constitution et la Liberté
individuelle du Représentatif Héréditaire du Peuple.' .

J'ai oublié de vous dire que j'ai été hier au soir à l'Assemblée, entendre le rapport de Pétion. Il a passé toute
expression pour l'Audace et la Bêtise. Il ose commettre
des crimes, mais il n'a pas assez d'esprit pour les pallier.
Il avait dit aux Brigands dans les Appartemens, ' Amis et
Amies, Citoyens et Citoyennes, finissez la Journée avec
autant de Dignité que vous l'avez commencée ; vous êtes
montés à la hauteur de la Liberté ! faites comme moi et
allez vous coucher ! '

Demain la Séance doit être intéressante, mais je ne
serais pas instruit à temps pour vous en instruire.

CHAPTER VIII.

1792.

EVIL DAYS. THE PITY OF IT.

Scene in the Champ de Mars and the École Militaire—Fidelity of the Grenadiers—Fortitude of the Royal Family—Ça ira—Seditious cries—Temporary revulsion in favour of the Royal Family—Princesse d'Henin
reports the Manifesto of the Duke of Brunswick—Paris the week pre-
vious to the Massacre of August 10th, 1792—Letter from Berne—Charges
against the Swiss Guards refuted—Arraignment of the King—His digni-
fied Demeanour.

Mons. le Comte de Lally à la Princesse d'Hénin.[1]

LA voilà terminée, ma chère Princesse, cette Journée
qui m'avait causé tant d'inquiétude pour le Roi, et qui
vous avait fait craindre pour vos amis en même temps
que pour Lui. La voilà terminée, non seulement sans
malheur mais encore avec un grand avantage pour le Roi.

Lisez le logographe, et vous verrez avec quelle im-
prudence—quelle tyrannie, le Maire avoit été réintégré
avant-hier ; des placards invitaient les Citoyens et le bon
Peuple à ne pas sortir le lendemain du Champ de Mars,
sans avoir vengé le sang répandu le 17 Mars de l'Année
Dernière ; et l'on voyait dans les Boutiques, des Armes
qu'une imagination féroce s'était plu à inventer et qui
faisaient frémir. Votre neveu, Lametier le bon, un de leurs
amis et Moi, nous sommes partis de front, résolus de
pénétrer à l'Ecole Militaire, et de nous joindre au Défen-
seurs du Roi s'il étoit attaqué. Il était huit heures
du matin. Il y a deux Ans, que dès quatre heures
le Champ de Mars était rempli. Jugez quel a été

---

[1] One of the group of French Emigrés to whom Sheffield Place became
a second home during their exile in England.

notre étonnement de le trouver un désert! Un Champ
vaste, aride et sablonneux tel qu'un Lac, dont les
Eaux auraient trouvé une issue et se seraient entière-
ment retirées. Sur des Monticules de sable étaient placé
circulairement 83 petites Tentes. Devant chaque Tente
un peuplier, mais si petit, si frêle, qu'un souffle paraissait devoir tout renverser, et que chacun avait peine à
résister au jeu de la Banderolle Tricolore dont on les avait
tous chargés. Vous vous doutez bien que cela signifiait
les 83 Départemens, et comme les Départemens n'étaient
pas en faveur je me suis étonné qu'on n'eût pas mis
quarante-quatre mille Peupliers comme signes représenta-
tifs des quarante-quatre mille Muncipalités. Dans le
milieu étaient couchés par Terre quatre Châles de Toile,
peints en gris, qui eussent fait une mauvaise décoration
pour le spectacle de la Foire, et qui devaient former un
Tombeau pour tous ceux qui sont morts, meurent ou
mourant à la Frontière.

On lisait sur un des Côtés—'Tremblez, Tirans! nous
les vengerons!'

Il y avait de quoi s'indigner, en songeant tout-à-la fois
à la prodigalité barbare avec laquelle on dévoûe des
Milliers de victimes au trépas, et à cette ridicule parsi-
monie qui croit consoler leurs Mânes avec une Toile de
Théâtre. L'Autel de la Patrie était où vous l'avez vu,
imperceptible et formé d'une Colonne tronquée sur le haut
de ces gradins innombrables élevés en 1790. Sur les
quatre petits autels angulaires on brûlait des parfums. A
cent toises derrière l'Autel on avait élevé un grand Arbre,
appelé, 'L'Arbre de la Féodalité,' aux branches duquel
étaient suspendus des Ecussons, des Casques, des Cordons
Bleus, entrelacés avec des chaînes, et cet Arbre sortait du
milieu d'un Bûcher, sur lequel étaient amoncelés des
Couronnes, des Tiares, des Chapeaux de Cardinaux, les
Clefs de St. Pierre, des Manteaux d'hermine, des Bonnets
de Docteurs, des Titres de Noblesse, des Sacs de Procès.

Parmi les Couronnes en était une Royale; parmi les Ecussons étaient celui de France, ceux de Provence, d'Artois, de Condé—et l'on devait proposer au Roi de Mettre le Feu au Bûcher. Une figure de la Loi et une autre de la Liberté étaient placées sur des Roulettes à l'aide desquelles on devait faire mouvoir les Divinités. Une grande Tente à droite était destinée à l'Assemblée Nationale et au Roi. Une à gauche aux Corps administratifs de Paris.

Elles s'élevaient de beaucoup au-dessus des autres, ce qui était une infraction à l'Egalité constitutionnelle.

Enfin cinquante-quatre pièces de Canon bordaient le Champ du Côté de la Rivière. Je crois n'avoir rien oublié que le Bonnet Rouge qui couronnait les arbres, et vous qui connaissez la localité, vous devez parfaitement vous représenter sa disposition.

Tout cela était désert—et le petit nombre d'individus errant dans cette enceinte immense, avaient à peine l'air de curieux; jugez s'ils étaient enthousiastes! On vous dit que le Peuple était à la Bastille, voyant poser, par 60 membres de l'Assemblée Nationale la première pierre de la Colonne qui doit être érigée sur les ruines de ce fameux Château. Nous nous sommes hâtés de nous présenter à l'Ecole Militaire.

Admis sans difficulté, nous sommes entrés dans les appartemens qui étaient tous ouverts excepté celui destiné au Roi et à sa famille.

Nous avons bientôt vu arriver le Chevalier de Coigny; M. du Châtelet, D'Haussonville, de Puységur, de Grillon, etc. Aucun Maréchal de France n'est venu, parce que la veille, le Ministre de la Guerre leur avait écrit pour les inviter au nom de la Municipalité à figurer dans la Marche; en les avertissant que les Maréchaux de France étaient destinés à porter l'oriflamme, et qu'il fallait se rendre à six heures du Matin, sur la Place de la Bastille.

Vous figurez-vous votre Oncle Beauvau se levant à six heures pour porter un Drapeau le long des Rues de Paris dans une pareille Mascarade ! Tous s'y sont refusé, comme vous le croyez bien, et par conséquent ont été condamnés à ne pouvoir se montrer du jour—ce qui a bien coûté à M. de Beauvau.

On avait annoncé que le Serment se prêterait à Midi. À onze heures on a dit que le Roi arrivait, nous nous sommes portés du Côté de la Cour. Le Cortège était très imposant. Un Détachement de Cavalerie ouvrait la Marche ; puis un autre d'Infanterie ; des Troupes de Ligne ; les Pages ; les Ecuyers et un grand Nombre de Palefreniers suivaient. Il y avait trois voitures. Dans la première étaient M. de Poix, M. de Brézé, Le jeune Tourzel, M. de St-Priest, etc. ; dans la seconde, les Dames de la Reine—dans la troisième le Roi, toute sa famille et Madame de Lamballe. Cinq cents Grenadiers volontaires nationeaux escortaient les Voitures, et les Ministres étaient à pied aux portières de celle du Roi. Quatre Compagnies de Grenadiers Suisses fermaient la Marche. Les Trompettes, les Tambours et un Salve Générale d'Artillerie ont annoncé la présence du Roi. Nous avons été sur son passage au haut de l'escalier. Il avait l'air calme d'une bonne conscience. La Reine avait la Dignité qu'elle ne perdrait jamais, mais on voyait sur son visage l'empreinte du Malheur que son Courage cherchait à dominer. Elle me faisait penser à une Strophe d'un Poète Anglais que Madame de Biron me faisait traduire dernièrement au Val, et qu'il n'y avait qu'un mot à changer.

> Ô Honte des Français ! dans sa prison obscure
> Elle abreuve en secret sa couche de ses pleurs,
> Tout de son Cœur royal vient aigrir la blessure ;
> Les Grâces sur son front ont fait place aux Malheurs,
> Et, semblable à la fleur que L'Aquilon dévore
>   À sa première Aurore,
> Elle a vu sa beauté naître, s'épanouir,
>   Se faner et mourir.

Madame Elisabeth avait toujours l'air d'une Ange. Madame Royale présentait une tristesse intéressante, et le Dauphin étoit beau comme l'Amour.

Ils ont salué avec sensibilité tout ce qui s'offroit à eux, on a dit qu'ils allaient se renfermer dans leurs appartements et nous nous sommes retirés de l'autre côté. Cependant une des Troupes a traversé l'Ecole Militaire sous le Portique du Milieu, et a été se former en bataille sur le Champ de Mars, tandis que l'autre occupait les avenues du Côté des Boulevards. Je parlais à M. de Choiseul, quand nous étions agréablement distraits de notre conversation par un cri de, ' Vive le Roi ! ' Nous avons couru à la fenêtre. Le Champ de Mars commençait à se garnir. Un groupe nombreux de peuple bien vêtu s'était rassemblé sous le Balcon, le Roi venait de s'y montrer avec toute sa famille—le Cri se prolongeait et on y trouvait l'accent du Cœur.

On est venu dire que les Fédérés n'arriveraient pas avant trois ou quatre heures. Ils s'étaient rendus à six heures au Faubourg St. Antoine, mais L'Assemblée Nationale n'avait député qu'à neuf, les 60 Membres qui devaient poser la première pierre de la fameuse Colonne, et l'on trouvait tout simple et peut-être fort gai, de faire attendre le Roi pendant trois mortelles heures. Du moins elles ont été tranquilles pour Lui, et même Lui ont valu des consolations. On m'a dit que les portes de l'appartement royal étaient ouvertes et qu'on y entrait.

Je vous dirai à vous, une petite anecdote qui peut intéresser particulièrement mes amis, et je la disois même à d'autres, parce qu'elle fait juger de l'excellent esprit qui animait les Grenadiers des Volontaires Nationaux. Ils remplissaient l'Antichambre. A peine y suis-je entré, qu'un d'eux m'a reconnu, a sauté à mon Cou, m'a nommé à son voisin, qui a fait la même chose, et vingt sont venus successivement m'embrasser avec une espèce

de transport.	Un d'eux me disait, ' Je suis un des Grena-
diers qui n'ont pas quitté le Roi le 20 Juin : ' Un autre—
' J'ai couché dans sa chambre.	Il avait été bien calme le
jour ; mais pendant la nuit, quel sommeil ! quelle agita-
tion ! quels bonds il faisait ! '	Un autre a fendu la presse
et s'est écrié : ' M. de Lally doit connaître Cassot ! '
C'était ce Cassot qui, le 20 Juin, avait saisi au Collet un
Malheureux qui demandait, ' Où était le Roi,' pour le tuer,
et lui avait dit, ' Le Voilà ! ton Roi, Misérable ! mets-toi à
genoux et crie, Vive le Roi ! '—et l'assassin avait obéi.
Jugez si j'ai pressé ce Cassot dans mes Bras !	Alors j'ai
été entouré ; ils me disaient tous.—' Ah ! si l'on vous
avait cru !	Ecrivez, encore !	Que Mounier écrive !
Vous nous avez instruits ! Votre troisième lettre à Burke !
Nous avons bien retenu votre cri dans la seconde.	Li-
berté ! Royauté ! Tranquillité !	Ce Cri est le Nôtre ! '

Tout cela s'est fort prolongé, et je n'ai pas besoin de
vous répéter ce que je leur ai dit, pour que vous le sachiez.
Ils me rappellaient l'Exil de M. Necker, mon Apostrophe
aux Communes, mes Discours à l'Hôtel de Ville, des
Phrases entières de mes Ecrits.	Je voyais avec consola-
tion que j'avais fait beaucoup plus de bien que je ne
croyais, et je jouissois surtout de voir de quels sentiments
ils étaient remplis.	' Ne craignez rien pour le Roi,' me
disaient-ils, ' Nous nous y ferons tous hacher !	C'est un
si honnête homme ! '	Le Roi s'est montré, et des cris de
' Vive le Roi ! Vive la Reine ! ' des applaudissements, un
Cliquetis d'Armes universel l'ont accueilli.

La Reine a paru avec le Dauphin en Uniforme National.
' Il n'a pas encore mérité le Bonnet,' a-t-elle dit aux Grena-
diers.	' Madame,' a dit l'un d'eux, ' Il y en a beaucoup ici
à son service,' et les cris d'Enthousiasme ont recommencé.
' Entrez,' me disaient-ils, comme si le Roi ne dût parler
qu'à moi.	Je passe toutes les imprécations contre les
factieux.	Mais ils sont attachés à la liberté comme à la

M

Royauté, et j'ai vu avec peine qu'ils ne soupçonnaient pas encore le Danger de la Guerre. Ils n'admettaient pas même la prise d'une Ville française. Ils disaient que les Autrichiens n'avaient pas de pièces de Campagne, qu'ils arriveraient harassés et hors d'état de rien entreprendre.

Enfin, je suis entré chez le Roi avec votre Neveu, que j'avais perdu et que j'avais retrouvé. Le Roi m'a fait un signe de tête quand il m'a vu ; puis il s'est approché de nous, et nous a parlé à tous deux. J'ai aimé ce qu'il m'a dit.

'M. de Lally, je sais que vous êtes venu ici de bien bonne heure ; on me l'a dit.' Ils mangeaient tous un morceau de pain sec, et l'on avait eu bien de la peine à trouver un Bouillon pour M. le Dauphin. Le Roi a dit à votre Neveu gaiement, 'Vous nous avez donné un Meilleur Dîner que cela il y a deux Ans.' Le Roi était, comme vous voyez, calme et tranquille. Madame Elisabeth souriait—le Dauphin jouait—La Reine était préoccupée—la petite Madame triste—et Madame de Lamballe coquette. Le Canon a annoncé que le Cortège débouchait dans le Champ de la Fédération. Le Roi et sa Famille se sont placés sur le Balcon, qui était couvert d'un riche tapis de velours cramoisi, bordé d'or, et tant que nous étions là, nous l'avons entouré, ou nous sommes rangés à ses Côtés. Ils entraient dans le Champ de Mars par la Grille de la Rue de Grenoble, défilaient sous le Balcon, et se portaient vers l'Autel de la Patrie de droite et de gauche ; on a pu juger ce qu'on allait voir par le Début. A la suite de 50 Gendarmes Nationaux a paru, pour commencer, un Groupe d'hommes, de femmes, d'enfans, armés de piques, de haches, de Bâtons—une musique analogue a joué le fameux air 'Ça ira.' Des Gueux faisaient des gestes et montraient des Ecriteaux insolents au Roi. Les Cris de, 'Vive Pétion ! la Mort ou

Pétion !' ont commencé. Vous n'exigez pas de moi que je vous fasse passer en revue cette dégoûtante Mascarade. Des Bandes tantôt de Chiaulits, tantôt de Mendiants, tantôt d'Assassins, du moins à en juger par leurs armes ; des femmes ivres-mortes, couronnées de fleurs : toute la Canaille des Faubourgs, ayant écrit sur le derrière de son chapeau avec de la Craye 'Vive Pétion !' Les six Légions Parisiennes déshonorées de se trouver là, ayant pêle-mêle dans leurs rangs des femmes, des 'sans-culottes.' Ici des Bonnets rouges, là des pains, ailleurs des Gigots de Mouton au bout de leurs fusils. Des Aumôniers qui dansaient à la tête des Régiments : des Chansons infâmes chantées par des femmes qui s'arrêtaient devant le Balcon royal : Ecriteaux au bout des bâtons, les uns atroces, les autres bêtes, comme celui qui au milieu des Tambours avertissait que c'était des Tambours ; comme celui sur lequel on lisait, ' Vive des Braves Gens Morts au Siège de la Bastille !' Le Mépris de toute honnêteté, de toute pudeur et de toute raison ; la confusion des langues, des hommes et des choses, voilà tout ce que présentait cette auguste Solennité ! On remarquait que les cris de 'Vive Pétion !' cessaient lorsque la troupe armée défilait, surtout les Grenadiers des Légions, surtout les troupes de Ligne. Le 104ième Régiment à succédé à un Groupe formé d'infâmes, et vomissant des infamies—il s'était arrêté sous le Balcon, et sa Musique, au milieu des applaudissements des spectateurs, a joué : 'Où peut-on être mieux, qu'au sein de sa famille ?' le 105ième de même. Jusqu'à une certaine section, qui était, je crois, celle de St-Marceau, il était même aisé de remarquer que les cris séditieux étaient toujours proférés par les mêmes voix et par des Gens apostés.

Le brave Acloque étant venu faire écarter la foule, on a respiré pendant quelques instants ; et à la suite des Tables de la Loi, d'un petit relief de la Bastille, d'une

petite machine que tout le monde prenait pour la Guillotine, et que d'autres soutenaient être une imprimerie,
l'Assemblée Nationale a passé et s'est arrêtée sous le
Balcon pour attendre le Roi.

Vous allez m'en vouloir à la Mort, mais il est onze
heures sonnées. Mieux vaut une Moitié que rien. Le
Reste à l'ordinaire prochain, et sachez seulement que le
Roi a été reconduit jusqu'aux Tuileries avec ivresse, mais
sachez aussi que l'Assemblée effrayée a décrété hier que
toutes les Troupes de Ligne sortiraient de Paris. Tout se
corrompt—les mœurs, la raison, la langue—on écrit dans
le ' Journal des Jacobins : ' ' Un jeune sans-culotte,' comme
on dirait, ' Un jeune Lévite.'   On écrit, ' Un Brigand vertueux,' etc.

Passy. ce Jeudi 19.

J'ai laissé L'Assemblée Nationale arrêtée au bas du
Portique de l'Ecole Militaire, et le Roi descendant pour
les joindre. Tout ce qui était en haut s'est divisé. Ce qui
appartenait au service du Roi l'a suivi, le reste a entouré
la Reine et le Dauphin ; j'étais de ce nombre. Le Président de l'Assemblée, M. du Bayet, honnête homme avec
la tête un peu tournée par la Révolution, a reçu le Roi à sa
gauche avec un maintien respectueux et une tenue dé-
cente. De l'autre côté était le Vice-Président, la Croix—
les cheveux roulés et un digne accoutrement de Jacobin.
Il y a eu une petite altercation pour le service du Roi.
M. du Bayet a insisté pour que tous ceux qui le composaient
allassent en avant : je l'ai vu aussi ranger un huissier pour
qu'il se tînt derrière lui, et non derrière le Roi, et il m'a rap-
pelé ' le Bourgeois Gentilhomme ' disant à ses laquais—
' Tenez-vous bien près de moi, afin qu'on voie que vous
êtes ma livrée.'   Une triple haye de Grenadiers nationaux,
et de Suisses enfermaient le Roi et l'Assemblée : mais le
Roi, les Députés, les Soldats, la Foule, tout se touchoit,
tout se pressait ; il n'y avoit point d'espace vide.   On

voyait une ondulation continuelle, et je n'étais rien moins que tranquille. Jugez la famille royale ! Enfin la Cavalerie se portant en avant, a nettoyé le terrain, et en distinguant le Roi dans une espèce de carré vide, formé par les troupes, on a commencé à respirer. Pendant que le Roi marchait vers l'autel, la cinquième Légion en Section a commencé à défiler. Jusque-là les cris de ' Vive Pétion ! ' avaient paru achetés, ainsi que je crois vous l'avoir mandé, parce que les mêmes voix donnaient toujours le signal et se faisaient souvent entendre très longtemps sans être répétées. Ici ils ont été plus universels. Je ne sais où s'étoit formé ce Ramas, mais les Armes, les Visages, les hurlemens, les costumes, tout était effrayant. Une chose remarquable c'est qu'ils se faisaient justice eux-mêmes, et criaient sans interruption, ' Vivent les Gueux ! Vivent les Brigands ! Vive Pétion ! ' Des Groupes de Coquins enchérissaient encore sur ceux qui les avaient précédés, et chantaient, en les adressant à la Reine, des couplets plus obscènes, plus atroces qu'on ne se permettrait de les imaginer.

On criait, ' A bas l'Autrichienne ! A bas M. et Mme Veto ! Pétion ou la Mort ! ' Enfin le Maire réintégré a paru à la tête de la Municipalité ; les cris, les Blasphèmes ont été au comble ; pour lui, j'ai presque cru dans ce moment qu'il avait une conscience. Embarrassé, pâle. tremblant, la tête baissée, il n'a pas osé lever les yeux· sur le Balcon, il osait à peine les lever sur cette populace en partie soudoyée, en partie enivrée, qui insultait en son honneur la famille royale. Il y a eu un instant quand, malgré moi, les larmes sont tombés de mes yeux. La pauvre Reine était cruellement distraite de ces insolences par la crainte qui l'obsédait quand il n'a pas été possible de suivre le Roi avec les yeux. Elle l'a suivi avec une longue vue, et est restée immobile pendant une heure entière, tenant d'un bras le Dauphin, et l'autre étendu soutenant la lorgnette avec laquelle seule elle découvrait le Roi.   Il y a eu un instant où elle s'est écrié, 'Il a descendu deux Marches,' et ce cri nous a tous fait frissonner. Le Roi n'a pas pu gagner le haut de l'Autel, parce que la foule, et notamment des gens à demi-nus, s'étaient emparé de la partie supérieure.   Il y a eu un mouvement alarmant.   Théodore Lameth, selon les uns, Damas selon les autres, (je crois que c'est le premier) a eu la présence d'esprit de crier: 'Grenadiers! Garde à Vous! Haut les Armes!' et les Sans-Culottes se sont arrêtés et repliés sur la foule.

On dit que l'instant du serment, au bruit des 54 Canons, rangés du côté de la Rivière, a été imposant, pour ceux qui étaient voisins de l'Autel: La 6me Légion n'était pas encore défilée, lorsque nous avons vu la Cavalerie annonçant le retour du Roi.   Cette sixième Légion, marchant au pas redoublé, a été coupée par l'escorte du Roi, et presque culbutée par le Peuple, qui de toute part est entré dans les rangs.   J'oubliais de dire que le Président avait proposé au Roi de descendre de l'Autel du côté de la Rivière, et de mettre le feu à l'Arbre de la Féodalité, auquel pendait l'Ecusson de France.   'Il n'y a point d'Arbres,' avait dit le Roi, et il s'en était retourné par le même chemin par lequel il était venu.   Quand la Reine l'a vu approcher elle s'est levée pour aller au devant de lui, et toute la famille royale, que nous suivions, alla attendre le Roi au bas de l'escalier.

Le Roi, toujours calme, a pris la main de la Reine avec tendresse.   La petite Madame et le Dauphin se sont jetés sur les mains de leur Père, qu'ils ont baisées, l'une en pleurant, l'autre en se jouant.   Alors vous ne pouvez vous faire une idée de l'ivresse qui s'est emparée de tout ce qui était dans la Cour de l'Ecole Militaire; Gardes Nationales; Troupes de Ligne; Suisses; Peuple dans la Cour, aux Fenêtres, aux Balcons, grimpés sur les Grilles;

c'étaient des Cris de 'Vive le Roi !' et 'Vive la Reine !' Des chapeaux jetés en l'air—impossible aux chevaux d'avancer, parce qu'on se jetait dessous—Je vous laisse à penser si votre neveu avec son organe flûté, et votre ami avec son organe ronflant se sont épargnés. On les a suivis ainsi à notre connaissance, jusqu'à l'entrée dans le Château des Tuileries. L'Enthousiasme était encore centuplé, que depuis l'entrée de la Cour Royale jusqu'à celle de l'Escalier, les Troupes, hors d'elles-mêmes de les avoir ramenés sans que le moindre danger les eût approché, avaient l'air d'égarés, dans la crainte que ce court trajet ne leur enlevât toute leur Gloire et tout le fruit de leurs soins, et qu'obligés de laisser passer la voiture seule, par la porte trop étroite, elles s'étaient précipitées avec une fureur d'intérêt et de fidélité pour former la Haye d'une porte à l'autre.

Aux Bénédictions du Roi, se sont jointes les Imprécations contre les Jacobins. Ah ! si le Roi se fût aidé d'un mot, d'un Geste ! mais c'était le Courage sans mouvement, et la Probité en silence.

Le lendemain il y a eu un Décret pour éloigner les Troupes de Ligne, et les Suisses. Projet annoncé de détruire les Grenadiers dans la Garde Nationale—Pétitions pour demander la suspension du Roi—L'accusation de la Fayette—Un Membre a parlé d'accuser toute l'Armée, et il a été applaudi.

Lettre de M^{dme} la Princesse d'Hénin.

Le 3 Août. 1792.

M. de Lally me mande que ce jour même, le troisième, il doit se faire et se signer dans le Champ de Mars une grande Pétition, pour demander la suspension, et peut-être la déchéance du Roi. On doit se porter sur le Champ à l'Assemblée, en foule, quoique sans Armes, demander le

Décret d'un ton impératif, le demander d'Urgence, et séance tenante. On doit se porter à les Violences contre l'Assemblée si elle s'y refuse. Les Marseillois s'étoient réunis la veille au Palais-Royal à l'entrée de la nuit, et chantoient des chansons affreuses contre le Roi, au milieu des hurlements de l'ivresse et de la fureur. Le Roi, la Reine et toute la Famille royale ont Veillé toute la nuit, s'attendant d'un instant à l'autre d'être assiégés, forcés, ou assassinés. On amenoit ce jour même un message du Roi à l'Assemblée sur le Manifeste du Duc de Brunswick, et le Ministre des Affaires Etrangères a dit à quelqu'un, que l'on attendoit d'ici à 3 ou 4 jours, les nouvelles d'une grande affaire entre les Armées. Le Manifeste ne produit aucune sensation dans Paris. Les Aristocrates l'approuvent ; les Modérés en sont mécontents, et les Jacobins ne font qu'en rire.

· La personne qui m'en parle pense qu'il auroit réuni 19 sur 20 de la Nation, s'il se fût borné à demander la liberté du Roi, et sa sortie de Paris, accompagné de sa Garde et d'un nombre de Troupes à lui qu'il choisiroit. Il falloit sans doute y joindre les plus terribles menaces pour toutes les Villes qui arrêteroient son passage et nommément Paris, mais il falloit bien se garder dénoncer aux Gardes Nationaux qu'ils n'étoient en fonction que Provisoirement, et signer qu'on reçoit à Paris une Escorte Autrichienne pour conduire le Roi aux Frontières. Le Duc de Brunswick peut venir enlever le Roi, mais il ne peut pas espérer qu'on lui *amène* le Roi sur un Manifeste, *daté de Coblentz.*

Lettre de M. Gouvernet.

Le 3 Août. 1792.

A aucune autre Epoque de la Révolution nous n'avons été dans une fermentation plus alarmante.

Il est affreux de ne pouvoir deviner quel est le but des factieux ; mais d'être sûr seulement de la Volonté qu'ils ont de commettre beaucoup de crimes, de répandre le sang du Roi, de sa Famille, des Nobles et des Prêtres !

Si le premier coup est porté, ce dont je veux m'obstiner à douter encore, il est certain qu'il sera le signal d'un massacre abominable, né de la fureur, de la crainte, et du désordre de toutes les idées.

A tant de sujets d'horreur et d'effroi, nous n'avons rien à opposer ;—pas une réunion de cent personnes ; et la Garde Nationale, pour avoir voulu le tenter, a été traitée comme le Club Monarchique, et battue par les Marseillais. Cette soirée a été pour moi une des plus désespérantes que j'ai passée. Sur le bruit de l'emeute, j'avais couru au Bataillon des Filles St Thomas, qu'on disoit le plus menacé. Il s'y est réuni plusieurs parties des meilleurs Bataillons de Paris. Nous étions environ Mille—nous avions six pièces de Canon. Les Marseillais étaient au nombre de 500 réunis à quatre pas de nous dans une Caserne.

Je proposais d'aller l'entourer, de les sommer de nous rendre leurs armes, et de les escorter sur le champ hors de Paris, en leur disant que s'ils y rentroient on les assommeroit ; ou bien s'ils faisaient résistance, de les forcer dans leur Caserne.

Eh bien ! on se contenta de se bien retrancher, et mille hommes se crurent très heureux que cinq cents ne vinssent pas les attaquer. Cependant le Courage d'une heure, sauvoit Paris et imprimoit à tous les Brigands une terreur dont ils ne se fussent pas relevés. Au lieu de cela il n'y a aucun doute que s'ils l'osent, les cinq cents Marseillois sont maîtres de Paris, et les Officiers Nationaux y sont aussi en danger que les Gardes du Corps l'étaient à Versailles.

Je ne vous parle que de Paris, parce que cela seul est intéressant. L'armée, vous savez où elle en est. C'est toujours la même chose : les braves gens s'y tuent inutilement. Quand commence à agir le Duc de Brunswick ; voilà ce qu'il faut savoir. On dit que les Chefs Jacobins sont entraînés malgré eux, fort au delà de ce qu'ils veulent.

Jourdan aura tout à l'heure le crédit prépondérant. On ne peut pas se figurer l'état du malheur du Château. Plus la crise est forte, plus elle est près de sa fin. J'avoue que je ne vois pas sans honte et sans horreur la lâcheté avec laquelle nous courons ici d'inutiles dangers. 500 Marseillais dominent dans Paris, et nous avons 4 Batallions Suisses qu'à force de faiblesse on finira par rendre faibles eux-mêmes.

Paris. ce 3 Août.

On the 10th of August the Horrid Massacre was accomplished.

Extracts from a Letter from Berne.

August 28, 1792.

If you happen to meet Bowdler in London, he can give you a full account of our political situation. We are going on working our Ship, as well as we can, in the Storm. I hope we shall weather it ; but it is hard work. It will much depend upon the success of the Prussian and Austrian Armies. The Scoundrels who govern France now are embittered against us more than ever. The horrid murder of the brave Swiss Guards at Paris, and the unhappy fate of the poor King, have raised our hatred and contempt of the Jacobin Gang to the highest pitch, and we would venture anything rather than be guilty of the least concession to their measures. We have a Body of Ten Thousand Men in readiness and under marching orders ; we shall not begin a war with France, but we must attack their Troops, if they break into the Pays de Neufchâtel or into the Munsterthal, which eight days ago they seemed ready to do ; and if we are obliged to march, you may depend upon it we shall fight very soon after. We cannot afford to keep long a large Body of Troops together, and if the French come too near us, it is our interest as well as our inclination to bring, as soon as possible, matters to an issue. An Extraordinary ' Diette ' of the Cantons will be assembled at Aarau on the 10th of next month, (September 1792) ; but I expect little from it. Some of them, led by commercial interest and views, are not inimical to the present system of French Politicks. All of them are kept in awe, by the fear of seeing all the Swiss Regiments in the French Armies used like the Swiss Guards, and the old way of our Forefathers of revenging instantly any national injury, will, I am afraid, be not so readily followed as I could wish.

Our having now got here our Regiment of Ernest, is a lucky circumstance for us. It is encamped three leagues from hence and an excellent body of regular Troops. They wish ardently to march, and our Militia, that of Soleure and Fribourg, are in the same disposition. We live in sad times ; but if anything can extricate us from surrounding Dangers, it is an adequate firmness, and that, I hope, will not be wanting.

I may be short-sighted, but I am intimately convinced that if a Democratical Government in France comes to a Stand, all the other Governments in Europe are unsafe ;

many of them turned topsy turvy, and a long run of civil Broils, of popular Madness, of brutal and depressing Insolence of Mob Leaders, will bring us down again to the level of the Huns and Vandals. Sciences and Arts will be offensive to the Powers in the States : refined Minds will be useless and laughed at. The Talents of a Marius and Clodius will alone receive encouragement, the Sense of Honour will be lost, and even the Vices will not take such a vulgar turn, that the most common minds may grasp at them all. The Pandemonium of Paris has raised such a Fabrick as I maintain to be single in the History of Mankind, and have added such cunning and address to the most audacious measures as to astonish every attentive beholder ; as every Engine to their purpose is lawfull, they work deep and everywhere. The task of the Duke of Brunswick is more difficult than it was supposed to be, and even his successes will increase the difficulties he has to encounter. In Paris and in the Heart of France, with a Victorious Army, he will be like a Man surrounded by the Plague, and it is melancholy to think that nothing but the most relentless severity can perform the business.

We have received the Advice that the French General, Ferrière, had received written orders to take immediately possesion of Pierre Pertuis, the principal Pass into Switzerland. The same night we sent three Hundred Men with Artillery to prevent them. They arrived in good time, and the French, finding our Troops strongly posted, and made acquainted that they were not there for show only, gave up their Project, and the Commissaires of the National Assembly have made a Convention with the City of Bienne, in whose Territory Pierre Pertuis is. By this Act, the French are to evacuate the whole Munsterthal ; we are to evacuate the Territory of Bienne, and the City engages to guard the Passes with her own Militia ;

and has required us in consequence to withdraw the Troops we had sent there. We could not refuse to call them back, as Bienne is part of the Helvetic Body; but we have declared them answerable to the whole Confederacy for any consequence of their Miserable Conduct, and shall set it in its true light at the next 'Diette,' which meets now eight days sooner than we expected, and which I hope will act with vigour, as all the Swiss Regiments in France are dismissed, which will set us at our Ease. The manner of it is as base and treacherous and ungratefull as the rest of the Behaviour of the French to the Swiss Nation.

I see with great pain that your English Papers repeat faithfully the Calumnious Charge that the Swiss Guards at Paris began firing against the People on August 10. Those brave Fellows had strict orders to defend the Palace, and did not fire till the Artillery had fired against them, and it would exceed the length of this letter, if I was to tell you all the villainous treachery made use of against them. One instance only as a sample.

The National Guards upon Duty with them, borrowed great part of their Ammunition, under pretence of being resolved to stand it out with them, and immediately after, in the basest way, joined their Enemies. I hope from the good sense of the English Nation, that they will understand that though Six Hundred Brave Men can defend themselves to the last Breath against Sixty Thousand Assassins, it is not likely that they should be mad enough to attack them first.

Bowdler has a private relation from an Officer, who was in the affair from beginning to end, and I beg you will be at the trouble of reading it.

From a French Emigré to the Princesse d'Hénin,
in England.

Spa. le 14 Octobre, 1792.

Je vous dois, ma chère Tante, la Relation exacte de ce qui nous est arrivé depuis ma dernière Lettre de Verdun, si cependant vous l'avez reçue. La Cavalerie Française est partie de Verdun pour suivre les Armées Combinées qui descendaient la Meuse, pour passer l'Aisne après le Combat de la Croix-aux-Bois, où les Patriotes, forts de leur Position, les avoient attendues et où ils furent forcés.

Ils s'emparaient des Ponts de la Rivière d'Aisne, ce qui nous a retardé de 24 heurs. Les Ponts rétablis, nous marchâmes parallèlement aux trois Colonnes des trois Armées. Le 20, nous fîmes une Marche forcée de 12 lieues, depuis l'Aisne jusqu'à 4 lieues de Châlons, où toutes les Armées se réuniraient. Les Patriotes occupaient un Poste très fort, garni d'une excellente Artillerie ; à 9 heures du Matin, les Armées se rangeaient en Bataille.

Notre Armée, consistant en Cavalerie, formait une ligne de 45 Escadrons et présentait le plus beau Coup-d'Œil. On avait tant bien espéré que les Patriotes seraient forcés dans leurs Lignes. Mais tout-à-coup les Armées s'arrêtèrent et nous gagnâmes un mauvais Village, nommé La Croix-de-Champagne, où l'on établit toute notre Cavalerie, pour laquelle il ne se trouva qu'un seul Puits de 150 pieds de profondeur, et encore dans la nuit y tomba-t-il un Autrichien, de sorte que pendant 36 heures que nous passâmes dans cet endroit, il fallait se passer d'Eau et de Pain.

Le Lendemain on attaqua notre Avant-Garde, qui d'après ses ordres se repliait sur nous. Nous fûmes rangés

en Bataille toute la nuit, mais on laissait les Patriotes
suivre leurs mouvements sans les attaquer. Notre Position n'était pas belle ; aussi fallut-il la quitter, et nous
marchâmes sur l'armée Suisse ; et le Quartier Général
des Princes s'établit à Somme-Jouste, avec l'Aisle gauche,
et l'avant-Garde se logea à Suippes.

Par cette Position nous étions entre Châlons et
Rheims, villes où il n'y avait pas de Garnison. Aussi la
nuit même y fûmes-nous inquiétés ; on nous enleva des
Videttes, et depuis ce jour jusqu'à celui de notre retraite,
nous montâmes à Cheval 2 ou 3 fois par jour.

La Disette se faisait sentir dans l'Armée Prussienne.
Elle ne pouvait tirer de Subsistance que de Verdun.
Encore la grande route de Ham, où était le Roi de Prusse
à Verdun, n'était pas sûr. Les Patriotes occupaient St.-
Ménehould, par où il fallait passer. Ce n'était donc que
par des Chemins de traverse et affreux que les subsistances
arrivaient, et encore que pouvait fournir un Pays déjà
pillé par les Prussiens ? On sentit bientôt la dureté de la
Position des Armées combinées. Celle de Prusse fut trois
jours sans pain. Celle de l'Empereur deux Jours, et la
Nôtre en manquait totalement. C'était à la pointe de
l'épée qu'on pouvait avoir un pain. En vain faisait-on
courir le bruit que les Patriotes étaient cernés, qu'ils
demandaient à se rendre ; les Gens raisonnables s'aperçurent
tout de suite que c'était nous qui l'étions, puisque nous
ne pouvions faire un pas en arrière ou en avant sans
rencontrer l'Ennemi.

On fit aussi courir le bruit qu'il y avait un arrangement sûr, que le Roi de France allait arriver à Verdun.
Enfin tout ce qu'on peut inventer de plus absurde fut
répandu, pour soutenir les esprits déjà affaiblis par le
défaut de Moyen, et l'inquiétude des opérations à venir.
Enfin le Masque tomba, et on reçut l'ordre de faire Retraite. On le colora sur ce qu'il était impossible de vivre

en Champagne. On dit qu'on Marcherait sur Rheims, mais bientôt le bruit tombait ; au lieu de Marcher sur Rheims nous nous retirâmes à Vouziers, sur l'Aisne, où nous l'avions déjà passée, et tandis qu'on assurait que le Roi de Prusse était à Châlons, nous le vîmes arriver à Vouziers et mettre, pendant la nuit, l'Aisne entre lui et les Patriotes.

J'ai toujours pensé qu'on avait voulu nous sacrifier dans ce moment-là. Le Général Clairfait et l'Armée Autrichienne marchoient sur Stenay, et notre petite Armée sans Infanterie restait deux jours au delà de l'Aisne en présence de l'Ennemi. Nous passâmes enfin cette Rivière dans la Nuit, et nous nous retirâmes vers Stenay.

La Garnison de Sedan nous coupa le Chemin, et tentait d'enlever les Princes qui avaient passé la nuit dans le Château de Diez ; mais heureusement notre Corps, qui avait cantonné un prochain village, arrivait sur la Chaussée.

Les Patriotes nous prirent pour le Convoi des Princes, et commencèrent l'Attaque par une vive Canonnade. Nous étions sur une Chaussée revêtue en pierre ; il était impossible d'aller à eux. Leurs Canons étaient soutenus par quelques Escadrons, et leur Infanterie les protégeaient de son feu. A l'abri d'un Bois qui les couvrait nous eûmes cinq Chevaux tués, et heureusement pas un homme de touché. Nous nous mîmes en Bataille devant leur Batterie, et notre arrière s'avançait pour les couper. Ils décampèrent bien vite ; on les atteignit et on les forçait dans le Bois avec grande perte, après quoi on fit la folie de brûler trois Villages : mesure impolitique, et qui peut occasionner de bien cruelles représailles. Arrivés à Menza, près Stenay, nous reçumes l'ordre d'aller où bon nous sembleroit. On nous a ainsi abandonné à la Merci de je ne sais quoi, sans argent, sans Vêtements, car vous vous imaginez bien qu'après une Campagne aussi dure, nous avons usé tout ce que nous avions ; ajoutez, que nos équipages ont été pillés par les Prussiens, ces fameuses Troupes si renommées pour leur Discipline.

Voici, ma chère Tante, le Tableau de notre Misère. Je connois plus de deux mille Emigrés qui vont périr de Faim cet Hiver. Enfin on comprend que la désolation est extrême, on voit comme on a été trompé. Le Roi de Prusse l'a été aussi, et j'imagine que c'est par humeur qu'on nous a traités ainsi. Quoiqu'il en soit, je n'ai pu longtemps être le témoin de la Misère et du Désespoir de nos chers Camarades.

La Bourse de mes Amis est venue à mon Secours, et nos congés en poche, mon Cousin et plusieurs autres nous avons gagné Spa, par des chemins affreux.

Nous partirons demain pour Liège et de là pour Bruxelles, où nous prendrons haleine.

Bulletin.

le 11 Déc. 1792.

Paris a été d'une Tranquillité étonnante. La Voiture dans laquelle étoit le Roi étoit une Voiture de remise, ayant avec lui, le Maire, le Procureur de la Commune et le Secrétaire, Greffier. Les Glaces étoient baissées, ainsi le voyoit-on très distinctement et il ne cherchoit pas à se cacher. Habillé simplement d'une Redingote jaune, et d'un Chapeau rond sur sa Tête : la Tête haute, mais im-mobile, et appuyée contre l'angle de la Voiture. L'œil fixe, mais éteint ; le visage blême et défait ; une longue Barbe ; l'air d'un grand abattement ; tous les déhors d'une douleur concentrée.

Ce Spectacle fendoit le Cœur de ceux qui sentent quelque chose : il a fait une impression profonde sur les moins Royalistes, et a excité beaucoup de pitié dans ceux qui le plaignaient le moins, avant de l'avoir vu. Sous ce

N

rapport cette promenade a été fort utile à sa cause. Le
Peuple en Armes formoit une triple haye tout le long des
Boulevards et de chaque côté. Pas un seul cri, pas la
moindre menace, mais un profond silence, une grande
curiosité pour le voir.

On le trouvoit fort changé. Il l'est en effet, il est
pâle et maigri. Le Peuple qui le croyoit et le disoit bien
coupable, convenoit qu'il étoit bien malheureux, et en
jurant contre lui, accusoit bien plus encore ceux qu'il
prétendoit l'avoir égaré. Tel est le Sentiment qui domi-
noit et non celui de l'indignation. Il seroit possible
qu'il ne fût pas condamné à mort sans souslever Paris, et
la journée d'aujourd'hui pourroit faire penser qu'il n'y
seroit pas condamné, et que l'on se contenteroit d'un
bannissement perpétuel ou d'une Prison. Il est arrivé, à
3 heures, à la Convention et il y est resté jusqu'à 5 et demie
heures, toujours assis.

Les Tribunes et l'Assemblée entière ont été, on ne
sçauroit plus, décentes—pas un murmure—pas une interruption. Le Président lui a parlé avec dignité, mais
sans rien de dur, ni de choquant.

En entrant, il a paru fort interdit, mais pendant qu'on
lui lisoit l'Acte d'Accusation, il s'est remis, s'est rassuré, a
parcouru des yeux l'Assemblée et les Tribunes. Enfin il
a répondu à chaque Grief avec une précision, une justesse,
une fermeté qui ont laissé de lui, la plus haute idée, à ses
plus acharnés ennemis.

Il n'a pas cherché à récuser le Tribunal—il a parfaitement distingué ce qui lui est personnel, et se justifioit de
chaque Grief, et ce qui tient à l'Administration.

Il a toujours dit que cela ne regardoit que ses Ministres
responsables. Ses réponses étoient toutes très courtes
mais très frappantes. On assure que l'Avocat le plus
rusé eût eu peine à mieux répondre.

Il a nié presque toutes les pièces qu'on lui a présentées

à sa charge, après les avoir examinées avec soin.   Enfin, après avoir conservé un présence d'esprit, un sang-froid, et même une fierté admirable, il a demandé un Conseil et s'est retiré.

L'Assemblée, malgré la Montagne, lui a accordé un Conseil qu'il choisira.   On ignore qui il prendra.   Il a laissé dans la Convention un préjugé très favorable ; c'est ce dont tout le monde convient.   Il re-comparoitra Samedi à la Barre avec son Conseil.   Cette affaire va prendre une nouvelle tournure.   Sa fermeté et la Vérité de ses Réponses lui concilieront les esprits.   On croit que l'affaire pouvait tourner en longueur.

CHAPTER IX.

1792.

THE PRIESTS' TALE.

Louisa's letters—Miss Moss's flight—Her journey home from Geneva—
  Lady Webster on Venice and Vienna—The Comte de Lally again at
  Sheffield Place—His imprisonment at L'Abbaye—His release—Arrival
  of eight shipwrecked Priests—Their joy at finding Lally alive—Their
  tale—More Emigrés are received—Subscriptions for the sufferers—
  Letter from Gibbon—Anxiety about Lally—Lady Webster at Naples—
  Louisa's opinion of Mr. Fox.

[From these historic heights a letter from Louisa
brings us back again to the level of ordinary life in
England.]

Louisa to Maria Josepha.

Southampton : Wednesday, August 8, 1792.

. . . You must first know that it is very hot, and now
you shall hear that we left Bath exactly at eight in the
morn. yesterday. The three Ladies of the Bedchamber
in a post-chaise, and five in the Coach. . . . Left Salisbury
half-past five and arrived at Southampton half-past nine.
I really thought the Postillion had made a mistake and
had carried us to a French town instead of an English
one ; after having gone through as nasty, little narrow
streets as I would wish to see, we alighted at the habitation Mrs. Quin had prepared for us . . . very clean, but
smaller than anything I ever saw. . . . There was nobody
in the house, but an old woman who was in great tribula-

tion, as she did not expect us that night; there was not a single thing in the house but chairs and tables, only one candle for a considerable time, all the water must be bought, and what with this old woman and another old woman slower still, we did not get anything whatever till near eleven. By degrees we sent the man out, and got some excellent cheese, bread and butter, beer and two or three more farthing candles. We got to bed half-past eleven, and never waked till seven in the morn; after having once waked, it would be utterly impossible to compose oneself again, for what with cocks crowing, carriages, carts, people's talking, etc., you might as well try to sleep in the street.

Louisa to Maria Josepha.

'Les Rochers de Bognor:' 18ᵐᵉ Aout, 1792.

Friday morn we made our Escape from the noise and bustle, the Hogs and Dragoons of Chichester, and arrived here 'sans obstacle.' Our house will not be ready to receive us till the 22nd; but we have taken up our quarters at the Hotel, which stands by itself close to the Sea. We have not more room than is necessary, to be sure, as the three Balfours sleep in one room, the three maids in one bed, and Aunt and I have another; but the sitting room is large enough for twenty people, a bow at each end with three separate windows, two fire places, two Doors and four Tables, great comforts to independent spirits. . . . I long to hear something about the wretched King and Queen of France. Can anything be more mad than the whole Nation? Surely they cannot escape now from total Destruction. The Sovereign Lords of Berne will not take the Massacre of their subjects very quietly. How interesting it is to have seen Paris now! Are you not sorry for the Statue of Henri IV.? It was so tiresome the other day, when we went to the Coffee Room, there was a party had got the Paper for the Day, and one was reading it out, so we, not being close enough to hear every word, only came in for the most dreadful part, every now and then we heard 'massacres,' 'murder,' 'Death,' etc., when we were all eager to know what it was about.   I have had a nice dip; the machines are very convenient with a curtain all round that nobody can see you; you are not put in as at Brighton, only one woman gives you her hand and in you jump.   Aunt and I went in two machines, but close together, so she had the satisfaction of hearing me flounce in, and I of hearing how she behaved, as the same woman executed us both.

Louisa to Maria Josepha.

Bognor : September 8, 1792.

You do not know that you might not escape some degree of Scandal, if it was known that you receive Letters from the Centre House, Hothampton Place, Bognor.   I assure you it is not at all ascertained in the neighbourhood what sort of Ladies we are.   Sir Richard Hotham enquired of Weller, who lets the houses, if he knew what we were, as he does not like his houses should be let to Ladies who are not so good as they might be. Weller very prudently answered, that it was doubtful, we might be respectable people ; but that he was by no means certain.   I flatter myself they are a little better satisfied now, as the Knight heard our Etymology and Chronology from Mrs. Poole, and after having called on us one morning, with a thousand apologies for not having been before, sent us some fruit out of his garden, and invited us to dinner to clear our characters.   Our Neighbours are the pleasantest, unsociable people in the World, for they never give us the trouble of visiting them.   Every house seems quite independent of the rest: at our right hand are two Miss Hanbury's; fine, fat, jolly, important looking Damsels, rather approaching the Old Maid, each has a footman, a maid and a little Spaniel, the latter every day carried down to the Sea by the former; they are in slight mourning; both dressed exactly the same; keep their dogs in good order, and have a carriage of their own . . . Next to them reside Dr. and Mrs. Bell, a nice, snug little Parson in a full bottom Wig, and she, a tall, sedate, Elderly Woman. Have you heard of the disturbances in Ireland? I am sure I do not envy the Hibernians [the Balfours] their Bog! I should expect every night my house would be burnt, and my throat cut; how can they think themselves safe when the Papists are ten to one, and they preach up to them that all the Estates of the latter belong to them and are theirs by right? indeed, they seem to think it very probable they may be roasted. . . . We hear from a Gentleman, just come from London yesterday, that he had seen letters mentioning the Queen's Trial as coming on that day; if it was true, I suppose she will hardly be alive to-morrow, as they would take care to find her guilty and not delay putting the Sentence in Execution. I was extremely glad to hear of Lally's arrival, and I long to hear whether he will be so obliging as to spend another two or three days at S.P.

Miss Moss to Maria Josepha.

Berne: September 29, 1792.

Before you receive this, the Papers may have inform'd you of the alarm the Genevans received on Sunday, the 23rd, by the News of the French having arrived at Les Marches in Savoy, at which place they were Victorious over the Troops that were there stationed.

They were proceeding to Chamberi about fifteen Leagues. from our little Republick, and the Inhabitants of the Banlieu, that is such places as Plain, Palais, etc., had but just time to fly within the Gates of the Town, to which the Conseil Général advis'd them to repair. I packed up my little all in the Space of Two Hours, and was so fortunate as to get a Bed at a friend's House, for the Sunday night, that I might be ready to leave the Town next morning at Six o'clock. If you had seen the Consternation and Dismay in which every creature was on the Sunday! everybody you met had their arms filled, either with their children, or bundles of cloaths. Carts and Waggons laden with the Goods of those who had flown from the Suburbs, and the Cannons drawing to the Ramparts, were the whole day in motion; while the footways were really block'd with People, who were universally alarm'd and talking over their apprehensions. Madame Barde, in about three hours, pack'd up every article she had in her house, and a cart convey'd the whole of their Goods before three o'clock, as the Gates were to be shut sooner than usual that Night. I had the good Fortune to be permitted to pass Versoix, and the officer never attempted to unstrap a Trunk, because we were, 'Des Anglois,' while I believe thirty carriages were standing in a line for examination, because they were either French or Genevans who occupied them. One Lady had eighty Louis D'ors in her Pocket, which they took from her. Some Ladies escap'd from Savoy across the Lake in a Boat; but were fir'd at from Versoix. In short, I hope never to be a witness to such a Scene of Distress. I slept on the Monday at a Lady's House at Morges, and on Tuesday arriv'd at Lausanne about eleven. I immediately waited on Mr. Gibbon, who promised me to write to Lord Sheffield, for I had no time to write, as I was obliged to pursue my route immediately. He looks.

very well, and has postponed his visit to England for another year.

I heard Mr. Pelham was at Lausanne ; but I had not time to call upon him. Mons. de Sèvery, le Père, is extremely ill, and Mr. Gibbon thinks it is a final Break up of his Health.

I dined 'au Lion d'Or,' where I believe there were upwards of 50 Persons at a Table d'hôte, of all ranks and distinctions, who had just escap'd from Savoy and Geneva. Spanish Knights, Italian Counts, English Baronets, etc., all mixing Higgledy Piggledy. One Lady (a Mrs. Armitage) told me she has nothing but the Cloaths on her Back, for her Carriage with all her Baggage, had been stopped on the Lake in a Boat they had taken, thinking it safer ; in short, you may figure the conversation or ' Jérémiades ' that prevailed during the whole meal. I had Twenty little Articles I meant to purchase, but the hurry of my Escape prevents the Execution. . . . Yesterday I had the pleasure of meeting on the road, between Avranches and Morat, 18 fine Pieces of Cannon, all sent from Berne to the assistance of Geneva, and which were to be sent on the Lake from Vevay, as on Thursday. I heartily wish them success. If I had been the Officer who attended this Artillery, by way of inspiring them with courage, I should have made them Halt ! to look at' the Burgundian Bones, which are in the Chapel on the roadside before you come to Morat. As we dined on Wednesday at Avranche, while the Dinner was getting ready, (which is always to come in a ' petit quart d'heure,') I went to see the Roman Mosaic Pavement, and the Arena and Den, which is in the Bailiff's Garden, and mentioned by Mr. Coxe. It is a great pity it has not been better preserved. . . . On our route to-day we met the troops going to Geneva. I suppose you know Luckner is killed. I supped last night with ten officers, who had no doubt they should give the French a warm reception from the Genevan ramparts.   This is the second time, Ma très chère Joséphine, that I have escaped a detachment of 'Mounseers.'   I must beware of the Third.

I am quite provok'd.   'Imaginez vous,' that after having called in the Swiss to their assistance, the French Resident at Geneva has just signified to Le Grand Conseil that the French mean no Hostilities to the Republick, but if they call in the Swiss, they (the French) will bombard the Town, so now all their defensive Operations are stopped. . . . I believe we go to Schaffhausen instead of Bâle.   We are three in a Post chaise, and very snug. I desire you will never think of calling me 'Old Cat' or 'Old Girl,' for I have been so much flattered and run after, that I must think myself 'dans la première jeunesse.'

I hope you always make proper affectionate respects to Lord and Lady Sheffield. . . .

Adieu, etc.,

C. M.

Miss Moss to Maria Josepha.

Wurtzburg: October 9, 1792.

Ma très chère Joséphine,—I promised to write from Brussels, but as the French have thought proper to enter the Emperor's Dominions, and I am in the heart of Germany, I thought you might like to know what was become of me.   Know then, that I am now safe at Wurtzburg, a strong fortified Place; so much so, that there are several of the neighbouring Princes who have flown here with their Families and Treasures for safety. . . . We went thro' Heilbronn, a very old Town and Cathedral, next morning we set off for Heidelberg and had got to Senzheim, the Second Post from Heilbronn,

and were here told that French, in number 15,000, had
crossed the Rhine and were at Heidelberg ; that their
intended course was to march on to Heilbronn, where
there is a ' Magasin.'   You may imagine the alarm this
put us in, to have this formidable Body at our Heels.
We chang'd Horses and instantly went back to Heilbrunn,
where we arrived at five o'clock.   If you had seen the
confusion that existed at the Inn !   All the Carriages that
were come back, as well as those that were coming to
Heilbronn, made the Company very Numerous, and oblig'd
to be all in one large room.   Italians, French, Germans,
English and Swiss, and of various ranks, formed a Motley
Groupe, as well as a confusion of Tongues.

While we all waited at this Place the arrival of a Courier
who confirm'd the News of the Enemy's March towards
us, and said that they had taken Spires and Mayence, at
which place the Troops who resisted were cut to pieces.
We now had no other Alternative but to fly as fast as
possible, and therefore we set off at Eleven at night, and
travell'd as hard as we could by the Moon, and so arriv'd
at Hall the next day at eight in the morning. . . . A
Courier from France arrived at this House last night :
We had him introduced into our Room.   He said there
was a Truce between the Armies, which I think a bad
thing, as it must be by desire of the Austrians who have
been unsuccessful yesterday.

While we were at dinner, we heard a great tumult in
the Street, and getting up to see what it was, we found it
to be the remaining part of the defeated Austrians in the
recent Battle of Spires.   You cannot imagine how melan-
cholly a sight it was to me to behold all these brave
fellows.   They look'd quite dejected.   I saw one wounded
, officer laying in one of the Baggage waggons : no wonder
they were beat, 15,000 against 3,000.   And to-day, I, who
you know am rather curious, had a little conversation

with one of these defeated soldiers, (by means of an Abbé for an Interpreter). He said that the Bourgeois of Mayence actually fired on the Austrians who came to defend them—a plain proof they wished well to the French.. I really could have cried out of Madness!

The Merchants of Frankfort, have sent their Money to this place as it is a sure one, as the French are expected to attack that next. . . . When we flew from Geneva to avoid the enemy, and determined to come by Germany in order to be secure, I little thought we should fall in their way, and have them at our ' Trousses ' within a post and a half, which was the case at Heidelberg. Oh! when I see you in the winter what a deal I shall have to tell you!

Lady Webster to Lady Sheffield.

Venice : October 10, 1792.

What must you have thought of me for not instantly answering your kind letter? or expressing as I feel, the gratitude for your having made such an Exertion to give me pleasure? But, Inattentive as it may appear, you will acquit me when I tell you it followed me from Vienna hither, and that, at the period I received it I could not acknowledge it, nor till this moment. Accept again, my dearest Lady Sheffield, my Sincerest Thanks for your Goodness, and be assured of my warmest attachment for all your Expressions of Kindness about me.

We have been delayed here near a fortnight on C. Ellis' account, who has been very near dying of a putrid fever. . . . The Physician was for twelve hours uncertain of his Life. He is now recovered, and we quit this Watery Prison to-morrow. Of all the places I have yet seen Venice answers less its Description.

Canaletto's Views raise the Imagination to a Pitch

which the Original does not fulfill. The Rialto is very insignificant and not comparable to the Bridge at Blenheim. The only Things that really deserve Notice are the Place of St. Mark's and some of Palladio's Churches. They undoubtedly are magnificent.

The Ducal Palace by Moonlight always makes me think of the Alhambra at Granada, for tho' the architecture is not Saracenic, yet it strikes me as very like the Views, Swinburne gives of that Noble Vestige of Moorish Dominion. The Gondolas are very Luxurious, and at first I thought, from being tired of the Motion of a Carriage, that I should never weary of them ; but I have had them enough to be ready to exchange for the Jolts of a Carriage, as the way of Sitting, or rather Lying, Fatigues one for a length of Time, and in hot Weather they are dreadful.

We do not see this place to much advantage, as the Canals Stink; the Weather is Bad; and the Venetians are absent. Luckily the Theatres are opening, and we have had two Excellent Operas. This is classic Ground to us English, as every Step reminds one of Shakespeare or Otway. Nor has the character of the ' Super Subtle Venetian ' changed since the Days of Iago, or less deserves that Epithet.

I really did write to Lord Sheffield from Vienna, but I am certain that Letter, with all those I wrote from Germany, is lost ; so I shall forgive him if he accuses me of Idleness. I shall again tell you my Opinion of that charming Place.

You know how I liked Dresden ; but there I was more obliged to our own Island for Amusement. But Vienna ! Dear Vienna ! How can I do justice to its Merits ? It is, I believe, the only place upon the Continent where English Society may be dispensed with. The Women are Lovely, Clever and Obliging. The Men that are in Society are all of a Certain Age, and from having been generally employed either in the Foreign or Military Line, have had an opportunity of seeing other Countries, which has brought them to appreciate the Merits of each. Their Manners are Polished, and their Way of Thinking Liberal. Ceremony and Etiquette do not exist. Frankness and Ease strike me as being the Characteristics of Vienna Manners, which I take to be the result of Purity of Morals and Conduct, as no place was ever more exempted from Corruption or Gallantry; for the Happiness of those I lived with did not extend beyond their own Foyer, and Domestic Comfort, which has fled all Capitals, reigns Triumphantly at Vienna. The Family of Thünn, of whom you must have heard much, possess amongst them every Quality that can Interest or Charm; in Short, I know no place where one might lead a happier or more Rational Life than there.

The Invasion of the French into Savoy has deranged the Plans of all the Lausanne Party, and poor Lady D. is obliged to make the Détour of the Tyrol to get to Pisa. T. P. [Tom Pelham] comes either with her or the Duchess. I am sure you will be happy to hear he passes the winter in Italy, and will be astonished at my being disinterested enough to wish him to make Pisa his Headquarters, on account of the Baths. I am afraid I shall not see him for some weeks, as I am going on to Naples as soon as possible, it being necessary for me to be quiet some months before I am to be confined. I know nothing of our Naples Set; only the Palmerstons, Cholmondeleys and Duchess of Ancaster; but I do know what is of infinite consequence to me, that Dr. Drew will be there. I shall write either to his Lordship or to Maria from Florence. Adieu! I send you a Venetian Ring, also one for Maria.

Maria Josepha to Serena.

Sheffield Place : October 16th, 1792.

Le Cher Comte has been here since Wednesday ; but popped off to town this morning on a summons from Madame D'Henin, on some business, and Mdme. D'H. expects a young lady [1] who she educates and takes care of from France. She is a very pleasing sensible girl and I shall be very glad to see her here. I knew her at Lausanne. Probably they will all come here together.

Lally was confined in the Abbaye, in a small room where there was scarce space sufficient to lay down, with three others—one a young Swiss officer just 18, another Montmorin, Governor of Fontainebleau. I did not hear the name of the third. His (Lally's) spirits are much worse that when he was in England before, and I am not at all surprized. The scenes he has witnessed must make a strong and melancholy impression, and the re-collection that these three unfortunate ' Camarades de Prison ' were all murdered, and by the greatest good fortune he escaped, is enough to make any body ' triste,' and I believe he has more feeling than nine men out of ten. He was confined 5 days, taken out of his bed at the Luxembourg where he lodged, in one of the ' recherches nocturnes ' that are made at Paris ; tried by the Section, and immediately acquitted ; but they did not dare release him directly, as the Mob would suspect a collusion between them and probably murder both parties, Ac-quitted, and Acquitters. Therefore for his own security he was sent to the Abbaye, where he would in all likeli-hood have been left, till the Massacre, if his friends, and particularly a door keeper of the Assembly, who had formerly known him, had not exerted themselves

[1] Pauline, daughter of General De Pully. See Lally's letter, May 25, 1792.

vigourously, to get an order for his release. He left
the Abbaye, at 8 o'clock, Friday evening, and the Massacre
began Sunday at three. He employed himself the two
first days with preparing Montmorin's Defence, and
proved his innocence so clearly, that he was acquitted
and released; but 'les aimables sans culottes' interfered,
and insisted on a New Trial, in consequence of which he
was sent back to the Abbaye, where he met his unfortunate end. The three last Days, Lally made his own
speech for the Scaffold, and intended to hold very high
Language, and to let them hear a little truth. I have
sometimes doubted whether he was not disappointed at
losing the opportunity of delivering his harangue. But
all his friends, and all who know him, must rejoice at his
disappointment.

I really believe he owes his life to himself, that is to
say, to his amiable disposition. I am convinced most, if
not all those who have been murdered, have fallen sacri-
fices to private pique, as Assassination is now an innocent
amusement.

If he had had an enemy in the World, he has been so
well known to have written La Fayette's Manifestoes and
Letters, and to have been so hearty and sincere a friend
to the Royal Family, he must have been in another
world long ago—and it is astonishing the number of
warning letters he has had, to desire him to take care
what he wrote and said, for everything is known as soon
as done, at Paris, as the principal business of the Servants
in every family, is to be spies.

Last Thursday, eight Priests came here from Seaford,
where they landed from an open boat, as wet as if they
had swum over, from incessant rain during an 18 hours
passage. Papa is one of the Committee for the distribu-
tion of the County Collection, and they were sent here to
have assistance to enable them to proceed to London,

as they had not a farthing except in 'Assignats,' and 'Assignats' are only paper in this Country—very little more in France. If you had seen their extasy of delight, when they found Lally was alive, you would have been convinced he was one of a few; for as they were not personally acquainted with him, it must be his general Character that makes him so much beloved.

Two of these Priests had escaped from the number of those who were murdered with the Archbishop of Arles during the Massacre at the beginning of September in a Convent of Carmelites at Paris where they had been imprisoned some days.

The one who related the Events of that Day, was a Man of very sensible appearance and manner, and related them with that unaffected feeling, that convinces every hearer that what is said, is true. I have some scruples in telling you a shocking story, that must affect you very much; but Mama says you will like to have it, and one is so accustomed to horrors since the beginning of the Liberty of France, that a little more or less does not make much difference to our feelings. The idea that the Man who gave this account was an eye-witness and had narrowly escaped being a Victim, added very much to the interest with which we listened to him—and my relation must fall very short of his, being a kind of translation.

They were allowed to walk in the Garden every day at five o'clock. On Sunday, Sept. 2, they went out as usual—they expressed their surprize at some large Pits, that had been digging for three days past, and wondered for what purpose they were designed. They said to one another that the Day was almost over, and yet Manuel had promised on the Friday, that on Sunday following, their imprisonment should end, and that before the Sun had set, not one should remain a Prisoner. All at

once, they heard some Shots fired, a number of National
Guards, some 'Commissaires de Sections,' and some Marseillois rushed into the Garden.   The poor wretches
assembled under the Walls of the Church, not daring to
enter, lest it should be defiled with Blood.   One, who
from Age and Infirmity, was behind the rest, was shot
dead.   One of the Chiefs of the Brigands, called out,
'Point de Coups de Fusil!'—this death was too merciful.
'Les fusiliers' retired to the rear.   'Les Piques, Les
Haches, Les Poignards,' came forward.

They stopped at some distance from the Church,
called loudly for the Archbishop, and insisted that he
should be given up to them.   The Priests crowded round
him, and determined to defend him as much as lay in their
power.   The Assassins threatened to break this 'phalange
sacrée,' and again called for their victim.   'Let me pass!'
said the Archbishop, 'if we must all die, what does it
signify if I am the first killed? And if my blood will
appease them, is it not my duty to preserve your lives at
the expence of my own?'   He desired the oldest of the
Priests to give him Absolution, and the last Benediction.
He knelt down to receive it.   When he rose, he lifted up
his Eyes to Heaven, crossed his arms upon his breast, and
advanced towards the People.   Not one stirred to meet
him.   When he spoke and said, 'Je suis celui que vous
Cherchez,'' they were seized with an involuntary awe and
respect, and amongst those abandoned wretches, not one
had courage to lift his hand against the Venerable Prelate.
They reproached each other with Cowardice, but in vain.
They advanced towards him, but one look made them
tremble and retire.   The Priests who had been prevented
from following him by his express order, and who in their
concern for him had forgot their own danger, began to
hope their Benefactor, their Friend, might escape—for
since the beginning of the Revolution, he had parted with

most of his private fortune, to support the necessitous Clergy of his Diocese. At last, one of the Miscreants struck off the Archbishop's Cap, with the end of his Pike. This served as a Signal, and the Respect they had hitherto felt towards him once violated, their Fury returned.

Another assassin, from behind, with a blow from a Sabre, cut thro' his Scull. The Archbishop only exclaimed, 'Oh ! mon Dieu !' and put up his right hand to his Eyes —a second stroke cut off the hand. He repeated the same exclamation and put up the other hand. He was yet standing ; but another blow flung him down and a fourth extended him lifeless, and thus was murdered the Archbishop of Arles, one of the most amiable Characters of his time, and of all France, and as much a Martyr as any upon record.

The National Guards then made the Priests go into the Church, telling them they were to appear one after another before the ' Commissaires de Sections,' who would try them and determine their Fate.

The Man who related this, was uncertain whether this was a precaution, lest any should escape, or whether it was the last resource of a pusillanimous pity, thinking to tire the patience of the Assassins by prolonging the Executions. They had hardly, however, entered the Church, before the Brigands grew impatient of their delaying to appear before them. They surrounded the door and called out only these two words—' Venez vous ? ' These unfortunate Victims then knelt before the Altar and the Bishop of Beauvais gave them Absolution, after which they were made to pass two by two before a ' Commissaire,' who did not ask them a single Question—only counted them—and enjoyed their torments. They advanced in sight of the heaps of Dead to which they were going to be added, and invoking the Mercy of Heaven for them and for their murderers. 120 Priests of all ranks, amongst whom were the Bishops of Saintes and Beauvais (both of the Rochefoucauld Family) were put to death.

I have an Infinity more to tell you, but I am afraid of tiring you all by my voluminousness. But I must give you the event of our Embassy to Newhaven. The wrecked Passengers were Madame de Belbœuf (whose Husband is in the Army of the Princes), her three little girls, the eldest 8, the youngest 3. M. de la Brisse, Doyen de la Cathédrale de Mens, and two servants, who all joyfully accepted the invitation to come here. They none of them understood a syllable of English, which puzzled Madame de Belbœuf very much, as well as how to express her gratitude to a miller's wife at Newhaven, who had been very attentive and humane in assisting them. The only language they both understood, but which I think must have astonished the Englishwoman a little, was for Madame de B. to 'l'embrasser mille et mille fois,' as she informed us.

She is sister to the Lady whose history I sent you in my last, Madame de Sermaisons. She was then settled at Brighton, and heard of a French family being wrecked on the coast, without the least idea, it could be her sister and relatives. Her little Boy, about eight years old, was very anxious to go and assist them, and it was with difficulty that their Preceptor, could convince him, as he had neither money to give them, nor a Carriage to bring them home in, that he could not be of any use to them. In the evening of the same day he heard it was his Aunt, who had had so much of his compassion. Madame de Belbœuf stayed with us from Sunday to Friday—she was very ill, the two first days, from the fright and agitation of mind, she had suffered, and from a violent blow on her head, which had almost closed one of her eyes, in preserving her youngest girl in the Vessel, (when violently tossed) from being hurt. They are now all lodged at Brighton—the two sisters and their families. They have an Uncle, the Bishop d'Avranches, who is in London, and they hope to persuade him to come and live with them. I am very glad the Subscriptions in London are so well furnished. Our poor eight Priests expressed the greatest gratitude for the attention they met with here, and particularly that Protestants should be so humane to Catholics. They went on in two Post Chaises, after a very comfortable dinner, which they seemed to enjoy very much.

I have just had a letter from Mrs. Moss, who left Geneva with the greatest precipitation. . . . She wrote from Berne, and is travelling with an English Gentleman and his Lady in a Post Chaise. She hopes to be in England the 25th of this month. All the Inhabitants of the suburbs of Geneva were obliged to fly to the Town in a great hurry as the French were very near. I have not patience when I think that those horrid French 'sans culottes' should scare the dear Swiss in their lovely country so much; their system is to be on the defensive and not the offensive. If you like a specimen and figures of speech used in the National Convention, the following is a true and good one. One of their most famous Orators began a speech, ' Mon Âme est sans culottes,' and the next best example is to sign myself,

Ton Egale,

M. J. HOLROYD.

[Writing later, Maria adds, that their two Guests 'miraculously escaped the fate of the other Priests, by climbing trees in the garden and from thence over the tops of the buildings.'

The thrilling story was told in the Library of Sheffield Place, where the family formed a half circle round the fire, M. de Lally and Lord Sheffield occupying the hearth, à l'Angloise, and helping out the narrators by questions.]

Miss Moss to Maria Josepha.

.   Ma très chère et Bièn aimée Joséphine,— . . . I have
so much to say, that I scarce know what to begin with, but
I anticipate the joy I shall have in relating all the Events
of my Life for five months past; though I am sure We
shall both talk at once, and consequently make such a
Noise that the other part of the Family may be distracted.
You may believe me when I say, that although I was
grieved at being oblig'd to quit the Continent, so many
months before the time I meant, yet my sorrow at having
left a most precious collection of Alp Plants behind me is
much the greatest.   The Guide I had on Montanvert and
the Col de Balme had likewise attended a great Botanist
a few days before he went with me, and therefore was
enabled to point out those that were most rare.   We
therefore collected above two Vasculum full, which my
trusty Nina suffered me to hang about her Neck, and
brought safely home, for your sake most likely.   When I
arriv'd at Geneva I sent there some plants to a Gentleman who had promised to dry them for me, and behold!
those miscreant Patriotes galloping to Chamberi, obliged
me to Muddle my Cloaths, Pell Mell in my Trunk, and
fly away, leaving my Herbière behind.   That you may
judge of the round those ‘ Sans Culottes ’ caused us to
take, you must follow me on your Map.   From Würz-
burg to Werneck, Hammelburg, Brückenau, Fulda,
Neuhof, Schlüchtern, Salmünster, Gelnhausen, Hanau,
Frankfurt, from which place I would have brought you a
Muff, if we had not repeatedly been told the French
were at our heels. . . .

Yesterday morning, Saturday, at nine, I enter'd the

Packet, Princess Royal, and by reason of a Calm the greater part of the day, did not arrive Here till two o'clock in the morning; lucky that there was as fine a ' clair de lune' as in Switzerland. We had fifty-seven Passengers on Board, Ten Horses, and Two Carriages; judge of the Cram; it was the only Vessel that could go off for a week, and I had some Inclination to stop at Ostend. I shall steer directly to Downing Street because the rest of my effects are there, and I am in want of some wearing Apparel. Have you got my Keys? If you have I will manage without them. Pray give my Love to all that bear the Name of Sheffield.

The greater Part of my Fellow Travellers were French Emigrès; one Lady of the name of Beringher who is well acquainted with our friend Lally. Poor Woman! she is come on a wild errand, and I think without probability of Success, as the following Decree I have copied from a French Paper is not in their favour.

Décret au 23 Octobre.

La Convention Nationale décrète que les Emigrés Français sont bannis à Perpétuité du Territoire de la République, et que ceux qui, au Mépris de cette Loi, y rentreraient, seront punis de Mort sans néanmoins déroger au Décret précédent, qui condamne à la peine de Mort, les Emigrés français pris les armes à la Main.

While we were at Brussels we saw an English Gentleman that was taken up as a Spy, and conducted out of the City, Guarded very strongly. Our Landlord, à l'Hôtel du Prince de Galles at Brussels, told us on Wednesday that quarters were taken at that Place for Twenty-five thousand Troops; so you see they fear for that City.

Edward Gibbon to Maria Josepha Holroyd.[1]

Lausanne : November 10, 1792.

In despatching the weekly political Journal to Lord S, my conscience (for I have some remains of conscience) most powerfully urges me to salute, with a few lines of friendship and gratitude, the amiable Secretary, who might save herself the trouble of a modest apology. I have not yet forgot our different behaviour after the much lamented separation of October 4, 1791 ; your meritorious punctuality, and my unworthy silence. I have still before me that entertaining narrative, which would have interested me, not only in the progress of the 'carissima famiglia,' but in the motions of a Tartar camp, or the march of a caravan of Arabs ; the mixture of just observation and lively imagery, the strong sense of a man expressed with the easy elegance of a female. I still recollect with pleasure the happy comparison of the Rhine who had heard so much of liberty on both his banks that he wandered with mischievous licentiousness over all the adjacent meadows. The innundation alas! has now spread much wider, and it is sadly to be feared that the Elbe, the Po, and the Danube may imitate the vile example of the Rhine. I shall be content, however, if our own Thames still preserves his fair character of

'Strong without rage, without o'erflowing full.'

These agreeable epistles of the Maria produced only some dumb intentions and some barren remorse ; nor have I deigned except by a brief missive from my Chancellor, to

---

[1] Portions of this letter appeared in the *Memoirs* of Gibbon, which Maria helped her father to arrange. Matters personal to herself were there omitted, and the letter is now printed *in extenso* for the first time from the original.

express how much I loved the Author and how much I was pleased with the composition.

That amiable Author I have known and loved from the first dawning of her life and coquetry, to the present maturity of her talents, and as long as I remain on this planet, I shall pursue, with the same tender and even anxious concern, the future steps of her establishment and life. That establishment must be splendid, that life must be happy, if she will condescend to apply her good sense to restrain some sallies of imagination, to soften some energies of character which are the source of our virtues and talents, but which may sometimes betray us into error and mischance. She is endowed with every gift of Nature and fortune, but the advantage which she will derive from them depends almost entirely on herself. You must not, you shall not, think yourself unworthy to write to any man; there is none whom your correspondence would not amuse and satisfy. I will not undertake a task which my taste would adopt, and which my indolence would too soon relinquish; but I am really curious from the best motives, to have a particular account of your own studies and daily occupations. What books do you read? and how do you employ your time and your pen? Except some professed scholars, I have often observed that women in general read much more than men; but for want of a plan, a method, a fixed object, their reading is of little benefit to themselves or others; if you will inform me of the species of reading to which you have the most propensity, I shall be happy to contribute my share of advice or assistance. I lament that you have not left me some monument of your pencil. Lady Elizabeth Foster has executed a very pretty drawing, taken from the door of the Green-house, where we dined last summer, and including the poor Acacia, (now recovered from the cruel shears of the gardener), the end of the terrace, the front of the Pavilion, and a distant view of the country, lake and mountains. I am almost reconciled to d'Apples' house, which is nearly finished; instead of the monsters which Lord Hercules Sheffield extirpated, the terrace is already shaded with the new Acacias and Plantains; and although the uncertainty of possession restrains me from building,[1] I myself have planted a bosquet at the bottom of the garden, with such admirable skill, that it affords shade without intercepting prospect.

The society of the aforesaid Eliza commonly called Bess, of the Dutchess of D &c. has been very interesting; but they are now flown beyond the Alps, and pass the winter at Pisa.

The Legards, who have long since left this place, should be at present in Italy; but I believe Mrs. Grimstone and her daughter returned to England. The Levades are highly flattered by your remembrance. Since you still retain some attachment to this delightful country, and it is indeed delightful, why should you despair of seeing it once more?

The happy Peer or commoner, whose name you may assume, is still concealed in the book of fate; but whosoever he may be, he will cheerfully obey your commands of leading you from —— Castle to Lausanne, and from Lausanne to Rome and Naples. Before that event takes place, I may possibly see you in Sussex; and whether as a visitor or a fugitive, I hope to be welcomed with a

---

[1] GIBBON'S HOME IN LAUSANNE.—A house of much historical interest to English people is about to disappear from Lausanne. This is the house in which the historian Gibbon passed so many years of his life, and in the garden of which he finished his *Decline and Fall*. The whole terrace to which the house belongs is to be turned into a post office. The particular house in which Gibbon lived is to be a coach-house for the post carts. The work of destruction is to be begun early in the New Year.—December 1895. 'This has been accomplished.'—Private letter from Lausanne, May 1896.

friendly embrace. The delay of this year was truly painful, but it was inevitable; and individuals must submit to those storms, which have overturned the thrones of the Earth. The tragic story of the Archbishop of Arles I have now somewhat a better right to require at your hands. I wish to have it in all its horrid details; and as you are now so much mingled with the French exiles, I am of opinion, that were you to keep a journal of all the Authentic facts which they relate, it would be an agreeable exercise at present, and a future Source of entertainment and instruction. I should be obliged to you, if you would make, or find, some excuse for my not answering a letter from your Aunt, which was presented to me by Mr. Fowler. I shewed him some civilities, but he is now a poor invalid, confined to his room. By her channel and your's I should be glad to have some information of the health, spirits, and situation, of Mrs. Gibbon of Bath, whose alarms (if she has any) you may dispel. She is in my debt. Adieu.

Most truly yours,

E. GIBBON.

Louisa to Maria Josepha.

Bath: October 29, 1792.

I want to know something about Poor Geneva. I suppose you will hear from the Historian. The last I heard was dated the 17th. We see the ' Star ' every day almost now Edward Coxe is here, as he takes it; yesterday I got the 'Moniteur;' if they get Geneva I suppose they will proceed to Lausanne and the Pays de Vaux. O! if an Avalanche would but keep the Demons warm in their way! Mr. Gibbon will not think Papa's Prophecy so ridiculous as he did last year; but they would not do him any harm, being 'un Anglois,' which name he will now probably condescend to make use of, and not talk so

much of ' nous Suisses ' as he did. Is it true that there
is an Idea of Trying and condemning the King and Queen
and then sending them out of the kingdom with 12,000*l.*
a year to live on ?

Serena to Maria Josepha.

Bath : October 29, 1792.

. . . I think it not impossible the Historian may be
driven to England. It is quite dreadful to find those
French Demons overrunning the world as they do. Poor,
innocent, beauteous Switzerland I would have always
free and quiet.

Lady Sheffield to Maria Josepha.

Wednesday, November 14, 1792.

Your welcome Letter is welcome as usual. No news
yet of poor Lally. Where can he be? Will he ever
return in safety to his Patrie? or will he be at last a
Victim to the Furies at Paris—the last time Lally wrote
to me, Monday the 5th November, he said he had sub-
joined his ' Ouvráge ' concerning Fayette, he desired me
not to show it or speak of it, till he had seen what would
be determined as to his property in France. He says :
' Je n'ai point trahi ma conscience, j'ai servi l'amitié, j'ai
dit quelques vérités flatteuses, j'en ai adouçi d'amères ; le
danger de 'confiscation passé, je ne craindrai pas de me
nommer, mais il ne faut pas dans ce moment donner de
prétexte au Brigandage.' . . . After all, he did not send
me his ' Ouvrage ; ' I wish extremely to read it—desire
dear Pa to send it to me. . . . What do you think of the
Capture of Mons, the flight of the poor precious Arch-
Duchess and of her being obliged to fly from Brussels ? I
am sure God fights for the Jacobins to punish all the

world.   Upon no other principle can the unmixed success they meet with be accounted for.

I think you will have your desire, formed some years
since, and that there will be variety ever going on to
amuse even the most unreasonable Person.   I only wish
you may not be driven from Sheffield Place in future.

Perhaps it may last your Father's and my days !

Lady Sheffield to Maria Josepha.

Thursday, November 1792.

We sat down a round dozen of Hudsons and Wood-
cocks yesterday at dinner.   Mr. Greatorex . . . appeareth
to me qualifying himself fast for chanting Hallelujahs.
I never saw such a Spectre as he looked yesterday. . . .
This morning Madame Lally sent a verbal message that
the Count was safely arrived at Paris, and sent likewise a
parcel containing the inclosed note, two copies of his
Letter to Burke, and a Parcel of Papers sealed, and wrote
upon ' A Brûler si je Meurs.'   I dare say the Books, etc.,
were desired to be sent the day he went, but Madame
probably forgot them till he wrote, and I conclude desired
her to let us know he was safe at Paris.   Mr. Nichols
dines here to-day, and I propose going in the evening to
Lord Guilford's. . . .

Lady Webster to Maria Josepha.

Naples : December 3, 1792.

This is the first Letter I have written with any satisfaction since I have been here, as I am sure at least her
Sicilian Majesty will not read it, as it will be put into the
post at Rome.   Whatever the College of Cardinals may
do I cannot say, but if any read it, I beg they will send it
on, as I fear that my dear, sulky Maria has already accused
me of making promises I do not keep, and she is a sort of

Malicious Monkey that I know but too well thinks 'l'absent a toujours tort.' If these Bandit Invaders come, they will not as declared enemies. I was at a Conversazione where the Nations received the Republican Minister for the first time of his being admitted. I hope for the preservation of my Philanthropic Feelings, I shall never witness such a Scene again. Suffice it to say they behaved like Italians, he like an Upstart. Such Servility! Such arrogance. Believe me it beggars description! It is yet uncertain whether the Fleet will come, but most likely not, as they would not appear here after their menaces, but in a manner to awe us, and I hear from Intelligent People, that from the vigourous and judicious preparations that have been made, they must be very formidable to do that; besides they have suffered very much from desertion, as 500 sailors in a body went off at Genoa, complaining bitterly of the hardships they had undergone, both from want of Provisions and ill-usage. The Russian told me, that a considerable force had sailed towards Smyrna, with an intention of going to Constantinople to support Lemoncielle's arguments, either to the Grand Signior or to the People : to the first, by assisting him to attack his old enemy in the Crimea, (where he is very weak), if his Sublime Highness will listen to his proposals, and in case he should be too nice, to excite the People to rebel and overturn the Govt. of Mahomet's Successors. These are Historic Times to be sure, and better for us that Gibbon should narrate, than we experience, as I think these dangerous principles will more or less affect all Europe. Basseville, a Republican Emissary, is very active in his Endeavours to corrupt the people at Rome ; and he seems to have adopted the never failing maxim of gaining, by being ' all things to all men.' He lives in the Churches where he assumes the appearance of most decided piety, and distributes in the shape of·

Alms, Bribes to the people amongst whom he has made many Converts to his Doctrines, 'telles qu'elles sont.' Is it not very extraordinary that all the Artists and Bankers in Italy are furiously Democratic ? as they are the people who would suffer most from the levelling principles being adopted ; but enough of Politics, as I am sure you are bored to death with them. A mind must be cast with a Torpedo's not to be delighted here, but as I told Lord S. I think it an odious place for a Residence ; our set of English is limited, the only Women Lady Plymouth[1] and the Dunmores, the first is the comfort of my life by her Goodness and Attention to me : of men we have few. Lord H. Hamilton whom I never saw, and his son, whom I never desire to see, Lord Bruce,. Mr. Brand, and the Messrs. Fortescue.

To-morrow the Cholmondeleys may come and soon the Palmerstons. I have just got a letter from the Duchess of Devonshire to tell me Pelham has become a hideous monster from the Gnats and could not see to write. My Spouse joins in every kind wish. Adieu.

Louisa to Maria Josepha.

Bath : December, 1792.

Yesterday we went to a most stupid Ball at the upper rooms. I believe it was called a good one, 700 people and the dancers better than common ; the first four minuets, an old officer in regimentals and a beau ; the four next a man with one eye and one of the present diminutive race ; the ladies were in the common course of things. What excellent Christians are the Inhabitants of this place, who make a rule of going twice, if not four times a week, to these meetings !

---

[1] Honourable Sarah Archer, wife of fifth Earl of Plymouth.

Louisa to Maria Josepha.

Bath: December 9, 1792.

Everybody is in great Wrath at Mr. Fox's Speech and wish him all that a good Christian is allowed to wish against anybody.   I should like to put him in La Fayette's Prison of ten feet square and see how he would take to it.

Bath: December 19, 1792.

Indeed you raised my Indignation more than once in your last Epistle. 'I suppose you have heard or read,' &c.   What impertinence to suppose I and all the world had not sent C. Fox to the empty place whence came the National Convention long ago.

f. Downman Delt 1780

Abigail, 1st. Lady Sheffield.
ob. 1793.

Walker & Cockrell Ph. Sc.

CHAPTER X.

1793.

DEATH OF ABIGAIL, LADY SHEFFIELD.

Lady Webster's son—Death of Louis XVI.—English politics—Housekeeping—Gibbon mourns over changes at Lausanne—Lady Webster at
Naples—The Emigrés—Their destitution—Lady Sheffield's exertions on
their behalf—Disquieting foreign rumours—Lady Sheffield's illness—
Her death—Miss Burney—Evelina.

Lady Webster to Lady Sheffield.

Naples : March 5, 1793.

I HAVE not heard from you for months, which tho' dis-
tressing is not alarming, as I hear of you from other
Quarters. . . My child is a Phenomenon, really the most
wonderful Natural Production I ever beheld, so much so
that I think it quite unjust not to Pickle him, to send to
John Hunter's Museum which he would adorn. He is
little beyond belief. He certainly is bigger than a geome-
trical point, and ' c'est tout dire.' When he has learnt the
art of sucking he will live and thrive.

Poor Louis! How hard has been thy Fate! I still
struggle with my reason to believe the Perpetration of so
horrid a Deed ; and can hardly credit the Reality of it.
Events of this dreadful Sort that come immediately within
one's own time are more difficult to believe than those
equally horrible (if such there are) in remote Periods.
None of us doubt the Execution of Charles I. and yet the
Murder of Louis appears Impossible. . . . Nothing can
be quieter than we are here, which makes me fear you
will think my letter sadly stupid ; as one from the Continent without Massacres, Insurrections or Invasions must

P

be the dullest of all dull things. However we have had
our day, for in the course of one Month we might either
have been Bombarded by the French, Smothered by the
Mountain, or Swallowed up in an Earthquake, any of these
three would have been a Fine Catastrophe. I felt two
Shocks of the Earthquake, and a most unpleasant undu-
lating Motion it was; it was slight here, but at Salerno
the Inhabitants quitted their Homes. Poor dear Pelham
is ill, he was recovering so delightfully that I thought
nothing was to be feared; but he is now Confined to
his Bed with an Erysipelas in his Face, you may suppose
how this worries me. . . Say everything kind to dear
Lord S. and Maria, and believe me

faithfully yours,

E. W.

Maria Josepha to Miss Ann Firth.[1]

March 7, 1793.

I have wished to write to you, my dear Miss Huff very
much; but have never been able to find time. I laboured
Day and Night at Louisa's Tail which was despatched on
Tuesday, and I hope she had it in time for Wednesday
evening. It must seem very odd to you, the sudden Darkness in which you exist, after the profusion of Light you
have lately enjoyed. I mean as to Politics. You will
have quite forgot how to call things by their right names
and how and where to apply the words 'infamous Rascals,'
&c., &c. I think you will like to see the Letter from the
Whig Deserters, and will rejoice to see it signed by so
many respectable names. I wish the Duke of Portland
were added to the List. I am quite ashamed to see it
placed before Lord Lauderdale's, Fox, Erskine, Grey, &c.
After a long and anxious suspense, Intelligence arrived

---

[1] Miss Firth had left Sheffield Place to reside with her relations at
Doncaster.

last night of the arrival of the Transports in Holland.
All sorts of unpleasant reports had made People very
uneasy.

I went to Sir Henry Clinton's yesterday evening, just
after I had heard the news. Lady Elgin, who had a
' Corps Diplomatique ' Dinner, sent us the earliest Intelligence, and I had the pleasure of being the first conveyer
of glad tidings to the Portland Place family [1] who had been
almost distracted with apprehensions. . . . The taking of
Breda by the French made little impression on us, we
were so glad to hear of the safety of our Troops. That
place was lost through the treachery of the Governour. It
is a melancholy thing to see these wretches succeeding in
all they undertake.

. . . Mama went on Tuesday to Visit the Dowagers
at Richmond, and took the Princess D'Hénin with her to
hire a house.

Maria Josepha to Miss Ann Firth.

Saturday, March 9, 1793.

. . . The ' Morning Chronicle,' you know, tells all good
news grudgingly ; but this is authentic intelligence, and
the 120 pieces of Canon taken at Aix la Chapelle is a
success of some consequence. You have no Idea how it
raised everybody's spirits yesterday. . . . Many people
have been much alarmed by the arrival of Hope, the great
Banker from Amsterdam with all his family, bag and baggage. It certainly looked as if he had his fears. . .

Papa had a letter at last from Mr. Gibbon yesterday.
Poor Lausanne ! How it must be altered ! so many
principal families banished, and for such trifling offences !
The Poliers [2] he thinks will be included in the number of

---

[1] Sir H. Clinton's.
[2] Colonel et Madame de Polier, residing at Lausanne.

Exiles and it does not appear for what ? that 'aristocrate enragé' says, he almost wishes they were allowed to appear and answer for themselves.

I am very angry with the Historian—in addition to his *almost* wishing People had a fair trial, he says nobody went into mourning for poor Louis; not even the emigrants, and that he, as the only Englishman of any note, was afraid of being singular or would have been tempted to mourn. . . . Lally and the Duc de la Châtre are with Papa at present. Some of the finest Nobility in England wish to raise Companies of their Countrymen and gc over to Holland with them. . . . I heard the Emigrants fought bravely in the last action under the Prince of Cobourg, and that three hundred were killed; but this is not confirmed. The Duke of York went up the river with the Gun Boats certainly. . . .

Maria Josepha to Miss Ann Firth.

Wednesday, March 13, 1793.

There has not been any important event since I wrote last; but when People are in the country it is a satisfaction to hear there is nothing worth hearing. . . . Papa dines next Sunday at the Archbishop of York's to meet Hope the Great Banker. It is said he has brought over with him, and placed in the funds, two million in specie— a pretty little sum. . . . Thro' our dear Mrs. Nicholls we have got acquainted with Lady Mary Duncan, who has such pleasant Dances and Parties, and we are to be asked to them. But the Dance I look forward to with the most pleasure is my Dance into the Country in a fortnight. We have not had any difficulties about housekeeping; but it seemeth to my youth and inexperience as if we eat a Monstrous deal of Meat. The Butcher's Bill comes to 4*l.* a week. I do not like to see and know what the necessaries of life cost, because it makes me uncomfortable to think how it is possible the poor people can buy meat now it is so high.   What a disagreeable thing it is we cannot live without Money.   I envy your primitive style of living exceedingly, all but the early rising. One is so happy when asleep, it is a pity not to have as much of it as one can.   I know you will not agree in my Maxim; but I can't help that. . . . Adieu, my dear Miss Huff.

Ever truly yours,
M. J. H.

Lady Webster to Maria Josepha.

'Naples: March 16, 1793.

Seven Posts from England being due naturally made one conclude that the 'soi disant' Republicans had extended their Brigandage upon the Mails; and we all trembled lest their Depredations on such a valuable Deposit would render the Effusions of Friendship and Fancy a Subject of Criticism for half Europe.   I was discouraged from writing from a wish not to add to the Repertory of Valuable Manuscripts that I supposed would contribute to the Mirth of Mankind when published in the ' Moniteur' or ' Gazette des Sans Culottes; ' but this alarm has ceased since the arrival of our solitary Courier, by which the Stoppage of our Letters was accounted for; but since Religion is out of Vogue, it was natural to impute to the French what in ancient times we should have accused the Devil or his Imps of, for they are his Legal Heirs from their near Relation to all his Deeds !   But, Miss Maria, I charge you not wantonly to suspect me of Idleness, for I must tell you before my Wonderful Production saw the light, I could neither bodily nor mentally even, write. The first you can easily credit; the second, requires your

being informed that I felt such a film over my 'understanding,' that from the dullness of that, I was nearer the
Standard of a Crétin than of any other being of the
human species; nor is that mist as yet thoroughly dispersed; and since the Reason I have given has prevented
all on this side the Apennines from Venturing a line, if
you have any reason or humanity you will amply acquit
me, and withdraw all the Curls of your Lip and Nose,
both of which I suspect are perpendicularly and laterally
twisted, according to the degrees of belief you give to my
assertions. But you are a satirical little Gipsy, unless
you give implicit Credence to all I say. Indeed I think
this Epistle will hardly get to you, as I suspect shortly
all Communication to you 'Tramontanes' will be stopt,
for how amidst Armies, Skirmishes, and Sieges, a letter is
to pass I know not; so set your wits to work and facili-
tate the discovery of a North-West Passage, that you
may hear by way of America of the State of affairs here.
'En attendant,' I will tell you a little—such as that our
Mountain blazes in a Grand Style, and that I mean to
ascend it amidst torrents of red hot lava, and showers of
burning stones, none of which I hope will singe my
Locks, tho' perhaps they would do me a Charitable Service
in extirpating a Colony that has Emigrated from the Noddle
of some Lazzaroni into mine, and who are as naturally
established there as the Principles of Democracy are in
some heads 'chez vous.' All the English excepting the
Palmerstons and those who stay the summer here have
flown. The Gaieties, however, go on merrily. To-morrow
we have a Fête at Portici, which consists of Breakfast,
Dinner, Concert, Ball, and Supper. Of the Day, sufficient is the Evil thereof. I do not mean to attack such
a Phalanx of Pleasures; but only a small share. You will
hardly believe all this is in honour of Lady Templetown's
Beaux Yeux, or know that she is the Belle of Naples;

but those who knew her before are all astonishment, for she is the Gayest of Gay People here. You will soon have another Princess in England, as it is very much believed that Prince Augustus will be tempted or seduced, or betrayed, you shall have the word you like best, into marrying Lady A. Murray. They are now at Rome. What say you to my News? Of Matrimony I must say now Lord Bruce is to be married to Miss Hill, a daughter of Lady Berwick's ; further, the Deponent sayeth not, as there is a wonderful sterility of Matter except the Ignited which the dear Mountain throws up in abundance. I wrote you a very pretty history by M. la Flotte, who carried the account of the Massacre at Rome to the Convention, but he is such an Anthropophage that for want of better food I dare say he eat the Letter.

Tell dear Lady Sheffield how much I love her, and that I shall write in a week. Lord Sheff : is a Dragon and out of the Question. Ask Lally if he remembers his Elizabeth. Pelham is better, but he has lately been very ill again. Adieu! Ever yours as you deserve.

Maria Josepha to Miss Ann Firth.

March 21, 1793.

. . . Papa has got into Guy's Hospital four Frenchmen, Gentlemen and Officers who perhaps you may recollect something of their having been a long time confined on board a ship, and at last escaped by swimming to shore ; I forget the particulars. How melancholy to think that these Gentlemen are most thankful for admittance to the Hospital! but one of them, a very genteel young man, is almost eat up by the ' Itch,' and as it is a very extraordinary complaint, and they had no other proper place to put him into, he is now in the same apartment with the lunatics. They have hardly a

Shirt to their Backs and neither Shoes nor Stockings.
With the greatest difficulty they (four in a Hackney
Coach) collected amongst them two pence to pay the
turnpike.   James went to the Hospital to receive them
and recommend them to the Steward and offered them
money by Papa's desire.   They refused accepting it,
saying they should want for nothing there.   What uncommon generosity of mind! for Men who are not above
entering into an Hospital cannot be accused of false
pride.   Papa has sent Walpole to-day to get a lodging
for the Itchy Man if he finds himself at all incommoded
by his situation among the madmen.   It really makes
one's blood run cold to think what extremities hundreds
are reduced to, and what a number of melancholy stories
there are that come to our ears.

Adieu.   I am in Haste, but ever

yours affectionately,

M. J. H.

Lady Sheffield to Maria Josepha.

Friday, March 29, 1793.

His Lordship having most feloniously embezzled my
' Star' without with my leave, or by my leave, doth not deserve the 'Times' likewise.   But, Sir, I do more than
my Duty, and I send it herewith.

I was most graciously received last night at the
Chancellor's by both Lord and Lady, each discoursed
with me, at least each and separately.   There were many
foreigners, Duc de Luxembourgh, Prince de Léon,
Malouet, &c.   It was not a large party.   I went with
Sir George and Miss Cooper to Lady Cath: Douglas,
where I had a long Flirtation with Sir Archy Macdonald;
he is quite fond of me and so is Mr. Douglas: he and
Lady Cath: were so obliged for my visiting them.

Mr. Batt had dined there and many of the Markhams, a very pleasant party indeed at Lady Cath's.

I heard a most charming sermon at the Asylum this morn, and heavenly singing from the Orphans.   Went no whither after Church, am not going any whither this evening.   Poor dear Horses have got through two Days' hard Duty with me.   Mr. Hervey sat two hours with me after Church.   Young Harrison has been with me, and has answered all my queries written to his father.   Three only of the five French patients, were admitted into the Hospital last Wednesday, why the other two did not get in, young Harrison does not know.   I sent the list of their names to old Harrison.   The apartments for the Itchy ' Galles ' will not be ready till next Wednesday the 3rd of April.

I have wrote to Count O'Haguerty, the needful concerning letting the patients know they need not go to Guy's to-morrow.   I have taken a world of pains about the whole lot, and done my business well and much more to the purpose than it has been done yet, by either English or French undertakers.   I have settled all about the Cloathing for the ' Sans Culottes ' Patients in a very Barber like fashion.   Mr. Hervey saith Lady Bristol hopes to see me whenever I can make it convenient, she is always at home from eight to eleven.

I have a long letter from Lady Webster and a ditto from Lady Auckland.   Lady Webster wrote to you by the Courier that carried Tom's letter to Lord Sheff and the Duke of Richmond.   She says her child is a Phenomenon for littleness.   Tom Pelham confined to his bed with an erisypalus in his Face, very ill indeed ; not a word of his coming to England.   I was rejoiced at the sight of your paw per post this day.   I send t'other half of the French song I sent yesterday.   Mrs. Moss says it is very pretty.   Is Mrs. Ducamel alive ?   If she is, desire dear Sister to carry you to her with a ticket round your neck from me, and to say I sent you to be looked at.

Kindest love to Aunt.

To be sure and I don't write long letters.

A. SHEFFIELD.

[The above was addressed to ' L'Unique Miss Madam.']

Maria Josepha to Miss Ann Firth.

Sheffield Place : April 1, 1793.

You are a very good sort of woman, my dearest Miss Huff, and perhaps flatter yourself that I do not expect to hear from you, as having no particular events to relate. I have not epistolized you for some Days.   But the best people may be mistaken, and this happens to be your case if such are your sentiments.   I want to hear how soon you intend to visit the Bath Dowagers, as when you are once set in motion you will seem to be nearer returning to us at Downing Street.   I am likewise impatient to hear your opinion of Louisa.   At present I have a very indifferent opinion of that young lady, as it is above a week since I heard from her.   I suppose she is settling the Bath Bank, which I hear is broke to pieces.

We came here on Thursday, and we all join in regretting the absence of a friend of ours.   It seems unnatural to come to S. P. for Easter without you.   Mama has been unwell since we left town—Fainting and very Sick. That Fainting trick she has got is very ugly.   I have no opinion of Mr. Farquhar knowing much of her constitution ;   all he understands is sending a quantity of draughts *ad infinitum,* when he has once ordered them, without coming to enquire if they have been of service.

I am infinitely discomfited at all communication being stopped between France and England.   The

English Mail was refused entrance at the Port of Calais last week, and no French ones have arrived since. I cannot tell what this forebodes. But I believe there is a very strong Party beginning to shew itself in favour of the Royal Family. Bretagne is very Royal, and in many places where the National Assembly has sent their Commissioners to examine and report the state of the country, the People had risen and murdered them. Probably it is to prevent things being known that they have stopped the Mails. I heard that Malesherbes had had two Conferences with the Queen in the Temple, and that her confinement is much less strict than formerly. If they do not put them to death, which I think now they will not dare to do, probably a short time will see the Dauphin acknowledged as King, and the Queen, Regent, by the greater part of France. It has been said in many of the Clubs that they cannot go on without a King. It is particularly provoking just now to be ' sans nouvelles,' because we have heard so many flying reports of different kinds without having them positively confirmed or denied. . . .

Tuesday, April 2.—Mama has been very ill. Fever and violent Pain in her Side, with incessant cough. Aunt Way is her Nurse, and writes us word to-day that she is much easier and her cough abated and her Fever lowered ; in short that she is gaining health and strength, but she is very weak still. She has consented to Bleeding and Blistering. . . . I have no opinion of Mr. Farquhar knowing much of her constitution.

[Lady Sheffield died suddenly in London on the 3rd of April, 1793, before her husband or her children could be summoned. The event is noticed by contemporary Journals as follows :—

' At his Lordship's house in Downing Street, after an illness of four days, the Right Honble. Abigail, Lady Sheffield. She was the daughter of Lewis Way, Esq., and sister to Benjamin Way, Esq., Governor of South

Sea Company; and was married to his Lordship in 1767.
There are by this marriage two daughters, who, in default
of male issue, are the heirs of his title. The following
very just character of her Ladyship appeared in the
'Courier de Londres:'—

'La société, les âmes vertueuses, les malheureux surtout, et les indigens, viennent d'éprouver une perte aussi
affreuse qu'imprévue. Lady Sheffield vient d'être enlevée
en quatre jours par une mort prématurée. .

'La plus respectable des femmes, des épouses, des
mères, des amies. Des mœurs aussi douces que pures.
Un esprit aussi modeste que clair. Un cœur également
noble et sensible. Une commisération dont la délicatesse
égaloit la prodigalité : voilà ce que pleurent aujourd'hui
tous ceux qui ont connu Lady Sheffield. Depuis les
désastres qui ont jetté parmi nous tant de victimes du
délire Français, elle a rivalisé avec le généreux Lord
Sheffield, son époux, à qui prendroit le plus les soins
pour adoucir le sort de tant d'infortunés. Prêtres, laïcs,
hommes, femmes de tous états, et de toutes les opinions,
pourvu qu'ils fussent honnêtes et malheureux, ont trouvé
un asyle dans la maison ; des secours dans la liberalité ;
des consolations dans l'amitié de ce couple vertueux. Il
est à craindre que Lady Sheffield n'ait été la victime
de son zèle et de sa bonté. Depuis quelque tems, elle
souffroit d'un point de côté qui la quittoit rarement.
Elle n'en continuoit pas moins ses courses bienfaisantes.
Tantôt elle alloit porter elle-même secours à des Fran-
çoises, dont elle vouloit ménager la délicatesse en même
tems qu'elle pourvoyoit à leurs besoins. Tantôt elle leur
conduisoit des médecins, dont elle ne songeoit pas à se
servir pour elle-même. De concert avec son mari, elle
avoit chargé des amis actifs de découvrir tous les malheureux émigrés malades ; elle donnoit des vêtements à
ceux qui en manquoient. Enfin, elle venoit de faire pré-
parer une salle pour ceux même que des maladies con-
tagieuses éloignoient de tous les lieux de secours. Le
Vendredi Saint, elle a été passer près de deux heures dans
cet Hôpital [1] dont son frère étoit président ; elle en a passé
deux autres à l'église par un froid glacial. Le Samedi
matin, une pleurésie s'est déclarée. Le Mardi, des
symptômes de mort se sont manifestés, et, le lendemain
matin, elle avoit cessé de vivre. La famille est dans le

[1] Guy's Hospital.

désespoir ; ses amis dans la désolation. Tous les malheureux qu'elle a connu la regrettent, et il n'est pas un
émigré François qui ne doive à sa cendre des bénédictions
et des larmes.']

Serena to Maria Josepha.

[Bath] Friday, April 5, 1793.

What shall I say to soothe and comfort you ? That
our poor Louisa has relieved herself by some hours'
crying is all that we could hope. It was the best effect
from such a shock, and I should have been frightened if
she had not. Two kind notes from Mrs. Way received
yesterday was our first Idea of my poor Sister being ill.
I confess they so far prepared me that I was glad my
poor Louisa was not present when I received them, as I
was so agitated and shocked as to be totally unfit to be of
any use to her, and as Mrs. Way with the tender wish
to spare Louisa, desired me not to alarm her, it gave me
a hope which I tried to encourage, and of course did not
speak all my fears. We were, however, very far from
feeling the comfort we tried to give each other. This
morning Mrs. Moss came with the account and put an
end to hopes ; but her being here is of great use, and
Mrs. Dashwood gives her leave to stay the whole day.

Your anxiety for us made me begin with this account,
and now let me give a thousand thanks for your dear and
affect^ate letter. Also let me entreat you to thank Mrs.
Way a thousand times for her kindness. It was an inex-
pressible comfort her letter just received by post. Yours
my dear Maria, tho' dated Wednesday and coming by
the Coach, only reached me this day, which I mention
because you might wonder I did not instantly write had I
received it yesterday. It is only to-day I know the event.
I do not know very well what I write, but I trust it will
make you more easy in regard to us than if I did not

write. As to going to you, you cannot doubt our being ready whenever it can be a comfort to you; but for yours and my Brother's sake I should think it better to wait a little. In this I entreat you to judge, and only settle it as best for my d^r Sheff and yourself. Miss Firth being with you makes me glad. I feel that I cannot express myself so as to the event otherwise than by sharing with you everything you feel. That she was in Town, had the best advice and every care, we must feel the greatest satisfaction. For the rest it must be Time. God Bless you! my ever dear Maria; may you be the consolation and the Blessing of your dear affectionate Father. His good, his feeling Heart will lean on his Children, and they, I trust, will be for ever united in tenderly loving him and gratefully feeling what a blessing he is to them. Louisa's heart is full of you both. Let us hear you are well, for we shall know no other wish, and your letter, ever so short that tells us so, will be comfort. . . . Love a thousand to my poor Brother. The very kindest remembrance to Mrs. Way, whom I truly and affectionately value.

Yours ever and ever,

S. H.

[The sad news was sent to Lausanne both by Sir Henry Clinton and by Monsieur de Lally. Gibbon wrote a broken-hearted letter to Lord Sheffield on the loss of her whom he had ' Known and loved for above twenty-three years, and often styled by the endearing name of sister.' His one wish was to share his friend's solitude, and to sympathize with his grief. 'All the difficulties of the journey,' he wrote, ' which my indolence had probably magnified, have now disappeared before a stronger passion,' and he left Lausanne immediately for Sheffield Place.]

Lady Webster to Maria Josepha.

Naples : May 5.

I will not presume, my dear Maria, to offer you any Consolation for the dreadfull loss you have sustained in your excellent Mother, for you must feel, and will daily more, that it is Irreparable ; for with the most unbounded affection for you, She united the greatest Sensibility of Heart, and the Steadiest Judgement, Such as you can never meet with from your best friends, however solicitous they may be for your welfare, for who can be so proper a Guardian of a Daughter's Happiness as a fond affectionate Mother, and such a one my inestimable Friend was to you.   You, who Know the obligations I had to her, may judge of the Keenness of my Feelings upon this Occasion. Alas ! Dear Woman ! How many plans of Happiness had I planned with You ! They, with Her are no more ! You now, my dear Maria, must supply her place towards your Father ; he will require the fond affection of a Daughter to mitigate the acuteness of his feelings for my Departed Friend.   Be to him what his Love for you exacts, and never let him find his Home less easy and chearfull.   Gratitude demands your attentions, but Independent of that for your own Sake you ought to assimilate your desires to his, else from uneasiness in his own house, Estrangement will ensue, and he may contract habits or connéctions uncongenial to your future Prospects.   Nothing but Love for you and him, would prompt me to expatiate upon a Subject which must awaken all your Sorrows, but your Good Sense will make you see my Motive, for the first Debût in your Stile of Living with him will be decisive of your Mutual Peace.   So, pardon the Warm Expressions of an overflowing Heart and impute them solely to their True Cause, arising from an Excess of anxiety about his Happiness, which is now in your hands, and your own future Welfare. He has deserved everything from you, and that every object around you must testify. Besides him, your Sister must be another object of Consideration. From your Seniority she must in many things be dependent upon you, and the example of your Conduct will be a Guide for hers.

I hope, dearest Maria, the regard I have always borne towards you, and the affection which your dear Mother blessed me with, will render any apology for what I have said unnecessary, as I am conscious I only repeat the Sentiments your Heart dictates already.

If you live alone with your Father, you have the Duties of a Wife to fulfill, and accordingly as you execute them, so will the World judge of your Conduct well, when you are placed in that situation. If your Aunt should live with you, you will, from the many obligations you have to her, know how to treat her as a Second Mother, and the only Substitute Nature can give for my Inestimable Friend.

I never can express how I feel her Loss; but I will say no more; but once again beg you to take in good part all I have said. God Bless you! and may you be Happy and make your dear Father so is the sincere wish of your

Affectionate Friend,

E. W.

Maria Josepha to Miss Ann Firth.

Sheff. Place: July 2, 1793.

Papa desires me to write as he has not time, to say he has agreed to let Government have his House (in Downing Street). They allow him 600*l.* for his repairs, and to keep all the Cellars and Stables and a Garret I believe. I wish I had known this for certain before we left Town, for I dare say they will break all our valuable China and Glasses in moving them.

Edward Hamilton came on Sunday, and I suppose will stay till Milord and the Great Gibbon go to London next Monday. I was very glad at his appearance; for I think both the Peer and the Historian began to grow tired of a Tête à Tête after Dinner which always lasted a considerable time, as Gib. is a mortal enemy to any persons taking a walk; I suppose upon the same principle as Satan disliked the situation of Mr. and Mrs. Adam. Moreover he is so frigid that he makes us sit by a good roasting Christmas fire every evening, which is rather too much, though we should like a warmer summer if the Fates had decreed it. The said Historian and Neddy [1] both desire their Loves to you. . . .

Maria Josepha to Miss Ann Firth.

Sheffield Place : July 11, 1793.

Mrs. Sarah Holroyd calls you by very unseemly names, which still having some regard for you, I will not shock your Ears with. But I am perfectly satisfied that no appellation is too bad for you, you villainous Grimalkin ! I am all Impatience to hear what you think of your House, and in this hot weather Impatience is a bad thing ! . . . Papa is very busy settling the Things in the Garret. The Chairs that were in the best Drawing room are to come down here for the Winter Drawing room. . . . What a D—— of a Cat you are ! When I send you so many interesting particulars about House etc. that you should not express gratitude. Unless indeed it is too great to find utterance. I do begin to be convinced you are gone

---

[1] Edward Hamilton.

Q

to Shades below. I hope your Executors will not be surprized at my Style of writing !

It is too hot to swear any more.

Ever sincerely yrs.

M. J. H.

Maria Josepha to Miss Ann Firth.

Sheff. Place : July 28, 1793.

. . . The week after this a portion of the Camp will be our Guests. Notwithstanding Mr. Gibbon's remonstrances at his folly and weakness, the 'Inn keeper' has pressed all (or very near it) of the General officers to accept Beds here. But I am in hopes the Commander in Chief will be too strict to allow them to sleep out of their Tents. . . . Are you not delighted at the Murder of Marat ? But though I am glad he is removed from the power of doing further Mischief, I am sorry he fell by the hand of an Amazon.

What horrid wretches the French of both Sexes are become ! To what an extraordinary length the Siege of Valenciennes is protracted, and when one looks back, how little has been done this Summer, and the War as unlikely to be near a Conclusion as at the first Stroke. I hope you treat yourself with a Newspaper. The Benedictions of Mrs. Sarah and Miss Louise and mine also, to the Grimalkin,

Yrs much and ever,

M. J. H.

Write, you old Cat ! and don't puzzle your stupid Brains about what you shall say in answer to my last. For if I ever thought twice about anything, I should not have flung away my Ink on that subject to such a tiresome old Maid of a Duenna. I pity you all for being so silly.   Don't return the Compliment.   I should be too much flattered.

Maria Josepha to Miss Ann Firth.

Sheffield Place : July 31st.

I have forwarded your packet for Walpole to Papa. All our Birds are flown but Nick who amuses our solitude during the absence of My lord and the historian. Today the Ferrers and Woodwards dine with us. I thought it was much better to enjoy the company of Mr. F. in the absence of 'le grand Gibbon' who would be apt to make round eyes at him. I suppose you are rejoicing over the capitulation of Mayence. I shall be impatient to hear what great thing, the descendant of Frederic the Great undertakes next, and whether success will be as speedy as in this Siege.

I heard yesterday from Mrs. Hadden who is at Tunbridge with her Brattery, and had the agreeable Intelligence that the Duchess and Miss Le Clerc do not attend the Duke to Ashdown Forest. I do not care how many Generals we invite, because probably they will only dine here and go back to their tents in the Evening. Adieu.   Loves from all.

Maria Josepha to Miss Ann Firth.

August 2, 1798.

I do not think I have much to say to the Old Cat, except that 'le Grand Gibbon' arrived yesterday from Mr. Hayley's,[1] a day sooner than he had intended, which threw him and Mr. F. (Ferrers) in each other's way, contrary to my wishes. You would have been amused

---

[1] William Hayley, poet.

at the scene between them.   Did Aunt tell you yesterday
of the strange Mania that a certain Lord has been seized
with to put it in the power of Chance to bring the P. of
Wales, D. of Richmond, Ld. Chancellor, Ld. Guildford
and Heaven knows who besides at the same time to
Sheff. Place?   Mr. G.'s remark is only that he fears
the New Wing will not be ready aired for their accommodation.   I wish we were well at the end of next
week. . . .

Maria Josepha to Miss Ann Firth.

S. P.: August 8, 1793.

There never was so large a Mountain that brought
forth such a little Mouse, as the Expectations of the
Crowd at S. P. this Week and the Reality. . . .

Behold! after all this alarm . . . the Duke sleeps
every night in Camp, the Prince, Thank my Stars ! does
not visit Ashdown Forest—neither the Ld. Chancellor
nor Ld. Guilford come, and instead of additional Inhabitants, this House never was so compleatly emptied,
a considerable Detachment going every day to the Camp.
We went ourselves yesterday, all except the Great Gib :
who thought himself better at home, in which I perfectly
agreed with him.   I was very much pleased with the
Views of the Incampment, which I might have been had
it had less effect, never having seen one before.   But
every body agrees this is uncommonly picturesque and
beautiful.   It is in a woody part of Ashdown Forest,
about a mile and a half from Netley, between that place
and Tunbridge.   Some of the Tents are pitched among
the trees and the Camp itself, being on uneven ground,
does not look formal in the least.   There were great
numbers of country people, and all the neighbouring
Coaches and Post Chaises, which, mixed with the

Soldiers and among the Trees, had an uncommon pretty and lively Effect. The Day was very fine, and a fresh Breeze prevented our being burnt by the Sun. The Army was all out, but did not perform many manœuvres. . . . The Duke and Miss Le Clerc took us under their protection for the greater part of the story. His Grace more gracious than usual, nobody could be more civil. His Tents are very comfortable and elegant without unnecessary finery. . . . The sight I liked best was the return into Camp, which they did with Musick ; the first part of the day they had None. Lord Fortescue . . . and several others one knows by name were there, and that Miss Burney (the Evelina and Cecilia Miss Burney) who is to be married to a Mons. D'Arblay, a French Emigrant. What is Sense good for ? Nothing at all I am convinced to Women, for it is the sensible Women who do the Most foolish things. Adieu. Aunt sends love.

Yrs. affly.,
M. J. H.

Maria Josepha to Miss Ann Firth.

August, 1798.

Dear Mistress Firth,— . . . . I must desire you to wonder at Miss Burney's marriage if I have not mentioned it before. She met with Monsieur D'Arblay at Mr. Locke's, therefore probably Madame de Staël was in the secret. . . . Mr. Locke has behaved handsomely in giving them a piece of ground, and building a Cottage for them where they must live on Love, or starve. He is even worse off than many other Emigrants, who have at least a futurity of Order in France to look forward to. But this man is disinherited by his father for the part he took in politics, having followed La Fayette and been on his Etât Major. Miss Burney has nothing but the 100*l.*

from the Queen. Should you not have formed a better
opinion of the author of 'Cecilia'? I hope we shall
benefit by her Folly, for I think if she has many Productions of Nature, those of Art must keep pace with
them, to find them in Meat, Drink, and Clothing. . . .
To-morrow the Duke says he shall only bring eight people
with him to sleep here, and to-day arrives Mr. Bowdler [1]
and Mr. N. to stay that Identical Night and no longer.

The Sheffield Inn has not lost its reputation you see.

Sir G. and Lady Webster are just arrived in England.
She came at the desire of her father, who is dying, and
left her Children at Florence with Lady Shelley. So she
will return there I suppose. If she stays the Winter in
London I shall have another Reason for rejoicing at being
in the Country.

Maria Josepha to Miss Ann Firth.

Sheffield Place: August 14, 1793.

On Monday morning between nine and ten the whole
Army, between six and seven thousand men, passed by
the Lodge. We were placed under Lady Cecilia's Fir
Tree with the Duke and his suite, and saw them march
by to great advantage. . . . The Line of March was a
mile and three-quarters in length . . . . and though
there were so many men, and they had been three hours
on their march, there was no Tail, alias, no strag-
glers. You may imagine what a beautiful sight it was to
see the whole Road from the Common to the Lodge
covered entirely with Soldiers, and the Bands of Musick
playing. . . . When they had all passed, we rode in a
jolly Party; Duke, Aides-de-Camps, Secretary, Lewis and
William Way, Louisa and I, through the Park to see
them take their ground at Chailey Common, and there
again we had a most lively scene. It is astonishing how

---

[1] The Expurgator of Shakespeare.

quick the Tents were pitched, and the whole Common, covered with white Tents and red coats, had the most chearful effect I ever saw or could have imagined. . . . We had a pretty considerable Party both to dine and sleep. The House probably never was so full ; we sat down seventeen to dinner. . . . They were all so tired, not having been in Bed the night before, that they retired before ten, and were off next morning by half-past three. . . . We were alarmed with the account of the Queen of France being murdered ; but find she is only tried. However I fear that is a sure forerunner of death with those wretches. Young Arthur Young came on Sunday evening, only stayed one Night. He is in the Church ; but travelling about to pick up farming Intelligence for the ' Society of Agriculture.' Adieu !

Maria Josepha to Miss Ann Firth.

S. P. : August 18, 1793.

Papa returned from the Eternal Exchequer Bills on Friday . . . . you will be glad to hear that they have completely answered the desired Purpose, and that public Credit is quite restored. Everybody who deserves it has credit now. This is my Lord's account of the matter. . . . Lally, the Prince de Poix, Malouet and Madame d'Hénin are at their Villa at Twickenham. Papa has invited the three men any time between this and September 3. We have a great loss in Lally's letters, the newspapers are our only Intelligence. Poor Queen ! there is little chance of her Life being of much longer continuance. But I cannot imagine why they put her in the Conciergerie, they might have spared her that additional cruelty. . . . Canning is in Parliament. . . . Expectation is raised high in his favour. . . .

Yours ever,

M. J. H.

Rev. N. Nichols to Maria Josepha.

Blundeston: August 25, 1793.

I am neither 'too happy, too vain, nor too miserable;' and yet very proud of your approbation; very sensible of your kindness; and very desirous of deserving and preserving your favourable opinion and friendship. . . . I saw nothing too sublime in the beginning of your letter, there is more danger of your finding mine too grand. . . . Yarmouth and Lowestoft are both full of Bathers. At the former I have been twice to dine with General Johnstone, the Commander of our Military Defences on this Coast, whose Camp I have not yet visited, though I pass within a hundred yards of it going to Yarmouth. It consists only of two Regiments of Militia—the Middlesex and the Leicestershire.

The East Yorkshire have a Camp to themselves two miles North of Yarmouth. Their Officers are very respectable Gentlemen. I was obliged to go to one Ball at Yarmouth, at which I lost a few shillings at Casino, and my evening, which could not have been less profitably or pleasantly employed.

At Lowestoft which is only three miles distant, there are of my acquaintance Dr. and Mrs. De Salis, the Bishop of Norwich and Mrs. Manners Sutton, and Major and Mrs. Robinson, Lord Clive's sister.

They and the General, some Officers, and some Neighbours have dined here, divided into two large parties, besides which I dined last Thursday with the Bishop and Twenty Clergymen at Dr. Cooper's, the Minister of Yarmouth; having assisted at the Bishop's Confirmation in the morning. The Bishop is a gentlemanlike, sensible and pleasing man. . . . I am glad for your sake that the Mountain produced a Mouse, for in spite of the partiality for Red Coats which you confess so ingenuously, I think you might have had a surfeit of them if the house had been filled with them for a week.

Mr. Bowdler is such an Achilles in the field of Chess that it is more honourable to be permitted to play with him, than disgraceful to have suffered a Defeat. That string however round the neck of one Victorious Invulnerable and fatal Pawn, is (I remember it well from painful experience) an insupportable Humiliation, which (I return you a thousand thanks) you revenge on me by attributing my masterly moves and deep laid schemes to accident. . . . Now as to my conclusion, I have not the least difficulty in assuring you that I am with very sincere regard,

Faithfully yours,
N. N.

Do me the favour to remember me in the kindest manner 'a tutti quanti.' I think of Mr. Gibbon when I look at my Greek books, and when I do not; often of that best and wisest of Aunts; and of you, sometimes.

CHAPTER XI.

1793.

MARIA JOSEPHA AS CHÂTELAINE.

The Camp at Ashdown Forest—A lull in France—Lady Webster's visit—
  Gibbon grumpy—News of Dunkirk—Tunbridge Wells—Society there—
  Death of Marie Antoinette—Brighton—Home life.

Maria Josepha to Miss Ann Firth.

Sheffield Place : August 25, 17⁻⁻ .

WE have been doing various great things since I wrote
last. . . . I do not expect to be soon again as well
amused as I was last Thursday. The Stanmerites [1] invited
us to dine there on Wednesday, and we accepted their
invitation ; also to sleep there, that we might be nearer the
Camp on Thursday morning, when there was the most
considerable Field Day and Battle that they have had, or
perhaps will have. Nothing could be more pleasant than
the whole family was, and I was surprized at not meeting
any form. Except the Prayers, there was nothing different
to any other House.

On Thursday morning we set out for the Camp at
eight o'clock. The heavy Baggage—two Coaches and a
Phaeton went across the Downs to the Devil's Dyke,
which was to be the scene of action. Papa, Mr. Pelham,
and I went in Mr. Gibbon's Post Chaise to the Camp,
where Wonder of Wonders ! Papa let me mount Mr.
Hadden's Horse and I rode the whole morning, about six
hours, with the Army. . . . I was amazingly happy to be
allowed to ride ; but I had very little hopes that I should

[1] Lord and Lady Pelham.

Painted by Edridge, 1795   Walker & Boutel Ph Sc

have leave.   It was a very good Horse and so accustomed
to such things as Field Days, that all the firing of Cannon
did not make him prick up a single ear.   Papa took Silver
Tail out of the Carriage to ride, and Lord Pelham lent
him a Cart Horse to help to draw the Coach containing
Mrs. Aunt, Miss Louisa, and Mr. Gibbon, who, I believe,
had they not been ashamed, would have thought themselves too happy to be permitted to retire in a much
shorter time than the Chorus above mentioned.   I was so
much entertained and pleased with my lot, that I did not
suppose we had been three Hours. . . . The Prince was
happier than any Being ever was before.   I never saw
anything so busy and alive, and I fancy he commanded
very well.   Once I thought him a little childish in sending after one of the Duke's Aides de Camps, who was
coming towards him, to take him Prisoner, and he was
hunted down such a steep hill that it was a Hundred to
One that he broke his neck.   However, the young Gentleman was in high good humour at this Event, and his
capture of six Pieces of Cannon, which he took from Sir
W. Howe.   There is something unfortunate in the name of
Howe, whether in real or mock engagements I am afraid.
    . . . At three o'clock, when the Army went to dinner,
we retired from the Field of Battle and went home ; that
is, to Stanmer to dinner, and came to S. P. in the evening,
attended by a most lovely Moon, and the Day after to be
sure I was a little stiff or so, but not in the least tired, or
the three Dowagers in the Coach either, tho' they did not
enter into the Spirit of the Entertainment as well as I
did, who was almost one of the Council of War. . . . I
am not sure if you will be amused at my long History, or
think it very tantalizing ; for I am sure you would have
been very much amused if you had been there.   But it is
right you should have some little Idea of our Manœuvres
in this Country.

If the Coast should be attacked in good earnest, the Prince will, I hope, be able to defend it properly. I suppose he would not be sorry to have an opportunity of distinguishing himself, for it is said, he is very jealous of the D. of York's military fame, and does not receive the Congratulations that are made him on his account, in his usual gracious manner. Mr. Pelham was aware of this, and maliciously complimented him ten times as much as he would otherwise have done on the Duke's good conduct. The Prince did not answer a word. We did not go into his Tent; but I understood the magnificence of its Furniture is very much exaggerated in the Papers. You may well suppose that we were a little inconvenienced to find room for the whole Cargo that came here from the Chailey Camp . . . as to the Servants, I believe, they slept two or three in a Bed, but the Gentlefolks had one each to themselves. . . . Mayence and Valenciennes are in a dreadful ruined condition. I am quite grieved for some of my favourite Buildings at Mayence, that are quite destroyed; the Prêvote, which if you recollect, I sent you an account of, as a very elegant Palace and that the Rooms received light from the top, is entirely pulled down; the Elector's country house the same, and part of the beautiful Cathedral. Have you observed in the accounts of the Convention, that they have decreed the Public Worship of the Sun? I more than ever rejoice at being in an Island, for I think, if we joined to them, I should be in great fear of being swallowed up with them, for surely they must meet with their Punishment in one way or other. The poor unfortunate Queen seems to have a respite; at least it is an advantage that her Cause has been taken out of the hands of those who first had the trying of her, and referred to the Committee of Public Safety. But, whether Life is any

favour in the state of Dread she must live in, is a matter
of doubt I think.   Lally is, I believe, coming next
week. . . .

Maria Josepha to Miss Ann Firth.

S. P. : August 28, 1793.

. . . Lally has been prevented coming this week.
Pauline is likewise expected every day, and the day after
she comes she is to be married to the Gentleman I mentioned, 'Un gros Hollandais;' but who has realized
10,000 Pounds in this country, and Lally adds in a
Parenthesis, 'il nous nourrira tous.'   I think it is quite
possible the Dutchman may not come into this way of
thinking.   Louisa has just come into my room, says you
deserve to be hanged for not writing oftener.   I only say
Guillotined. . . . Adieu, little Miss Huff.

Yours ever,

M. J. H.

Maria Josepha to Miss Ann Firth.

Sheffield Place: September 12, 1793.

. . . Not many events have occurred since I wrote
last, tho' it is a great while.   The tiresome Chancellor and
his Party still impend over our heads, and may or may
not come as it suits their Inclinations, Whims, or Caprices,
while Papa will make no engagement or let anybody else
into his House in case the Great People should come.   I
am almost inclined to be a Democrat and wish we were
all equal, and then Lord Loughborough would make as
little commotion in the family as if he was still Mr.
Wedderburne. . . . Lady Webster (or the 'Diavo-
lady'), will be at Stanmer this week, and (hang her !)
next week she will probably do us the honour of a Visit

and I believe Tom (Mr. Pelham) with her.   I had rather
see old Beelzebub a thousand times ! Tom Fool was here
the day before yesterday.   I believe we shall go first to
Tunbridge Wells. . . . But I am afraid there is not company enough there to give a chance of making you happy
in selling either of us.

Maria Josepha to Miss Ann Firth.

S. P.: September 22, 1793.

. . . On Tuesday last Papa was engaged to dine at
Mr. Sneyd's—a large Party was invited to meet him, and
the Carriage was coming to the Door when a letter
arrived from Tom Fool to say Lady Webster meant to
come from Battle to S. P., and that she might arrive
in better trim, begged our horses might meet her at
Uckfield.   The Dismay of the Family may be more easily
imagined than described.   Mr. Gibbon vowed if Papa
went to Jevington he would immediately set off for
Brighton.   I was aghast, for as Aunt can claim the
Privelege of Invalidism, and Louisa never chuses to talk
more than is necessary, I should have all the Weight of
her Ladyship on my Shoulders.   However, after much
pro and con . . . Papa stayed ; the Coachman went to
Uckfield, and the dear Creature, with an Irish Maid-
servant and two Italian men, arrived about five o'clock.
She chose to be very amiable, affectionate and tender, and
for her, as little nonsensical as one could reasonably expect.   She was unfortunately obliged to go away next
morning, and during the short time she was here amused
us very much with her account of the Camp, near Dunkirk and other Foreign Sights, which, tho' we took all
for granted, were rather Poetical than Historical.   She
went to see General Dalton before he was buried, and
talked of the dead bodies on the field of Battle she passed

over, with as much Rapture as any Vulture might be
supposed to do. I do not give her credit for half the
unfeelingness she pretends to, or I should begin to
question if she were not really an Infernal. She seems to
have gone to the Camp for no other purpose than to make
a Bustle, and to be as troublesome as possible from her
own account. Her Ladyship has entirely adopted Foreign
Manners and Customs, and our Family will, I suppose,
never recover from the astonishment they were thrown
into when they discovered André, the Italian, washed his
Lady's feet, when she went to Bed, which upon my word
is a matter of fact, if one may believe that one hears. I
was present at her Toilette before Dinner, and both of
the men walked tame in and out of the Bedroom while
she was undressing, and one dressed her hair, who was as
frowsy as possible, just come off a long ride. But enough
and too much of such a woman; she says she means
to go abroad in ten days, and Heaven grant she may
keep her Resolution! . . . Friday, Fred. North and Mr.
Douglas came. I am glad nothing happened to prevent
Mr. D. coming. The Gib. would have been furious,
and he was rather grumpy that Papa made him stay a
fortnight longer then he intended. You know he is
Clockwork, and to keep him a day after he had determined to go, is to derange one of the Springs or Wheels.
However, Mr Douglas with his Greek and Latin, and
Fred. North with his Islands of Ithaca and Corfu, have
put him quite in good Humour, and they are much more
entertaining, having him to draw them out. . . .

I do not know what to say as to news, because I
cannot tell what you may have already heard; however
the news this morning of the defeat of Castaux, near
Toulon, is very recent, and Ld. Hood says twenty Cas-
tauxs cannot now do him any harm. . . . I have not been
able to digest the very precipitate retreat of our Troops

from Dunkirk. Col. D'Oyley is come to England till his
Wounds are healed. His account of affairs on the other
side of the water is very uncomfortable, that is in respect
of the D. of Y., and I rejoice most heartily that he is
again under the direction of Cobourg. . . . When the
Army took that terrible Pannick, the French were certainly in a numerous Body, 55,000 we knew of, and some
Reports made them 80.

The Duke's common method of stating that any
number of Soldiers have fallen in an Action is that so
many have 'gone to Hell.' Numbers are daily falling sick.
Col. D'Oyley saw St. Leger at Ostend when he was
coming over, and he told him that since the 16th August
when the former left the Army we had lost 6,000 men
from it, killed, wounded, sick and missing. Col. D'Oyley's
Company in the Action, when he was wounded, went in
forty-nine strong, and only came out seventeen. It
was the Company that suffered most. As to the War it
seems as far from a conclusion as when it began, and
further, for then everybody was sanguine and was of
opinion one Campaign would finish it. . . . There
is now no one Event to make one suppose an End
possible, without acknowledging the Republic, for the
Wretches, if they have not Discipline, at least have
numbers, and at present a hearty good disposition among
the Troops to murder all that come in their way.

The Dismission or Resignation of the Duke of Richmond
was much talked of this week from the Ordnance ; but it
certainly has not yet taken place. He says he has been
very ill-used by the Ministry, and by the D. of Y., who
has written very severely against him because the Gun
Boats did not arrive in proper time before Dunkirk. The
D. says in answer to this charge that the Guns were
ready twenty-four hours before the Vessells were arrived
at Woolwich to take them on board. It was always

the intention of the Cabinet to besiege Dunkirk. They wished it to have been the first operation of the Campaign, then why was not everything ready for the Siege? . . . I hear the King is too much inclined to trust to the D. of York, and to be governed by his opinions, and that when the D. fails, he lays all the Blame at the Door of the Ministers. . . .

There was a long letter from Lally to-day, but dated the 10th, what it had been about so long nobody can guess. There was not any news in it, as you may imagine, except an Anecdote concerning the Court of Ham, giving one a perfect Idea of those Princes, and almost a fear of their Cause triumphing. You know Monsieur the Comte d'Artois and all the Princes, except Condé, who is behaving very well in the Army on the Rhine, are living at the Blue Boar, at Ham. Mounier offered his services to them, which offer, as they have nobody of any abilities with them, one should have supposed they would gladly have accepted. The Answer was, that as M. Mounier did not think in all points like the Princes, (as to the Ancien Régime,) they could not accept his services, lest it might be supposed they had any intention of listening to an 'Accommodement.' Are they not delightful Fools? and if they only were concerned, would any one care what became of Monarchy and Nobility in France?

After such a Diplomatic Letter, I can hardly tell how to descend to write of the little interesting events you enquire after, which might have furnished a letter, if I had been in want of subjects. Next time I will send you a Pattern of a Gown I have begun to work for Mrs. Woodward, in the Tambour, by way of Winter Employment.

Yours ever,

M. J. H.

R

Maria Josepha to Miss Ann Firth.

S. P. : October 1, 1793.

Fred North and Mr. Douglas left us on Sunday, after having enlivened us much by their very pleasant conversation. . . . With the addition of Mr. Gib, it was impossible to have selected three Beaux who could have been more agreeable, whether their Conversation was serious or trifling.   Mr. Douglas improves as he grows more acquainted, and Fred North is charming, though a wonderful oddity.   He desired so many tender and handsome things to be said for him to you, as would have made you quite vain to hear.   Indeed, all the Gentlemen do persecute me dreadfully, to say kind things for them. Mr. D. desired his best compliments likewise, but the other spoke a finer Eulogium as a Preface to his message. . . . Mr. Gibbon left us yesterday morning. . . . The Chancellor and his Party, after keeping Papa in hourly expectation of the delight of seeing him, has at last determined not to come at present. . . . Would you think that if he can get it (and both Mr. Gib and Mr. Douglas think it not impossible), Papa would be pleased and satisfied with an English Peerage ?   What advantage can such a thing be to him in comparison of a Place ? at least, in my opinion. Money would be of more use at present.   He seems much disgusted about Politics now, and vows he will not once go to London during the Sitting of Parliament. Who believes that ?   Not me. . . . I have just got a Jewel of a Horse. . . .   It is an excellent size, quiet and gentle, tho' he has a great deal of spirit.   He is quite a Beauty ; since my Memory, Papa has not had such a pretty Horse.   Lord Auckland has made us a present of two little black Ponies, not so young as they have been, but I hope they will contrive to draw the Tib, better than poor Jacky Grey, who grows Stupider than ever. At present, we may sport a Tandem in a greater Stile than you did, while we were abroad, with your Party-coloured Equipage, and Papa says he will have a Pole put to the Tib, that it may be drawn by the two horses, like a Curricle. However, it is rather too late this year for any open Carriages.

Don't you grieve for poor Cowdry, Lord Montacute's House in this County, which was quite burnt to the Ground last week, and nothing saved; there were many Pictures, &c., that can never be replaced, and will be a great loss. Do you remember Mdme. de Brissac, at the dear Bishop d'Avranches's, the younger of the two Ladies, who came with the Gentleman 'sans Perruque'? She has been this Summer on a visit to Mrs. G. Newham at Newtimber, and lately died there. M. de Chambords came down to see her, only the day before she died. They say her Illness was entirely brought on by the state of her mind, so that she may be said to have died of a broken heart. I cannot help rejoicing when I hear a poor Emigrant is at rest in the Grave, for I think they have little chance for happiness on this side of it.

Pauline is arrived and in a few days is to be sacrificed for the nourishment of the Colony at Twickenham. The Dutchman, we all think, will soon be tired of the Number of Relations he will have gained by his Marriage. Pauline brought a Letter in her Shoe, from Paris to Mdme. d'Henin, from some of her friends there, saying that the poor little King is very well treated, even spoilt— that the separation of him from his Mother was a dreadful thing to both—the poor little fellow will never walk any-where but in the places his Mother used to frequent—but he never mentions her Name.

I think the excursion to Tunbridge Wells will be a good thing for Papa because he will be more engaged,

and he will not write, or use his Eyes, which he will do
even by Candle light at home sometimes, tho' we write
for him all the morning almost.   The Nasty ' Star ' of
this Morning tells us of an Action in which the British
have been beat and no more.   It is very wrong to put in
such reports till they have the Details and know them to
be true.   Adieu.   I have written a fearful long letter, but
it is a great while since my last.   All the folks send love.

Ever yours truly,

M. J. H.

Maria Josepha to Miss Ann Firth.

Tunbridge Wells, October 13 : 1793.

My dear Miss Firth,—As the three Gentlemen in the
Parlour, viz., His Lordship and the Doctor, and Judge
Downes have tired me to Death, with forming Triangles
and all sorts of Mathematical Figures in the Parlour, in
plain English, that they are all three walking backwards
and forwards to the great shock of my delicate nerves,
I am trying to amuse myself as well as I can with talking
to you. . . . On our return from Mrs. Leighton's, we
found the Honble. Mr. Justice Downes had arrived in
the Interim, very fat and well-liking.   When they both
accompany us to the Pantiles, it must be acknowledged if
we have not the smartest Beaux in the World, we have
enough stuff in them to make half a dozen.   The Doctor
is cheerful and pleasant. . . . The Judge is an amiable
cypher.   This morning we went to Church and heard a
most excellent Sermon. . . . The Clergyman's name is
Benson and he preaches here constantly, all the season.
I have seldom heard a better Discourse, or delivered in a
pleasanter or more forcible manner. . . . To-morrow, we
go to a Card Party at Lady Peachey's, and on Tuesday to
Mrs. Leighton's and Lady Heron's, so you see, such as
they are, there are still some souls and bodies in this

desolate Place. Louisa pleads with great satisfaction, her fear of the night air, and stays quietly at home as she does not like cards. . . . I, who am a professed Gambler, you know, like these parties very well. I get a game at Casino which is a treat, but I am afraid you will be shocked when I tell you we play half-crowns; however, I have not been a Loser, tho' not much of a winner yet. I cannot help playing tho', unless I took the Alternative of falling Asleep, as everybody plays either Whist or Casino, and I should be left like Q. in the corner. . . . I most heartily wish that he (Papa) was engaged with some political work, because I am sure he never can be contented without being in an active scene, such as the House of Commons. . . . The Waters have been of very great use to Louisa, she is in much better spirits and has a better appetite than she has had for a great while. I hope Papa sees this, and that he will not be in a hurry to move, tho' he still talks of Brighton. . . . Princess Sophia has also found great benefit and is wonderfully recovered. She walks upon the Pantiles in the morning early with Lady Cathcart and Lady C. Bruce who is come. She cannot leave her Royal Friend, even if she had a mind, but she seemed very glad to see us when we met. Adieu.

Ever yours truly,
M. J. H.

Maria Josepha to Miss Ann Firth.

Tunbridge Wells : October 20, 1793.

As I told you such terrible stories of Invasions etc. you will be pleased to hear we are still under the Government of George III. and not under that of the ' sans culottes.' The Camp continues a fortnight longer at Brighton ; but I hope will have no employment. . . Papa dined with

Lord Cremorne upon Turtle. . . . What an unfortunate Man Mr. Gibbon has been! He has raved about Turtle; all the Summer has been desirous that Papa should send for one from London, and behold! as soon as he has gone, our Bristol friends send one to S. P., which Papa sent off to the 'pert prim prater' of the Northern Race, and if he had come here with us, he might have had a second at Lord Cremorne's. . . .

Parliament does not meet before Christmas; this is Lord Auckland's news. . . . Mr. Pelham has entirely thrown up his Commission in the Sussex Militia, owing to some misunderstanding with the D. of Richmond. It is surely a great pity that he should throw himself out of everything Active in a public Line as he is doing; I suppose to have nothing in England that can prevent his going abroad for his health. I do not know if the Divinity is gone. . . .

Maria Josepha to Miss Ann Firth.

Tunbridge Wells: October 25, 1793.

. . . We are in hourly expectation of the D. of Richmond. Mr. Hadden has wrote us word that he would be here for a night yesterday, to-day, to-morrow or Sunday on his way to Brighton. I wish he was come and gone, because Papa talks of going to S. P. for a day or two, and then going to Brighton and not returning here any more. I wish him gone anywhere where he will find amusement.

. : I grieve sincerely that Mr. Gibbon is absent just at this moment. He might have been of great service to him, for I think he is the only person whose counsel he would follow and who would give him the best and most unprejudiced advice.

Have you not been shocked at the Death of the Poor Queen? tho' you must have expected it. How nobly she behaved! and how clear and concise her answers! . . .

Maria Josepha to Miss Ann Firth.

Tunbridge Wells : November 1, 1793.

. . . We have had a Profusion of Creatures this Week. I will not profane the word ' Beau ' by applying it to them all indiscriminately. Part of the Sussex Militia marched thro' this place on their way to their winter quarters, Canterbury, and of course Papa did the honours by asking them to dine here. Next day we had the Surgeon, who took an opportunity of telling us he had been to Paris, and found a striking resemblance between the Pantiles and the Palais Royal. To be sure the Devil and the Jack Daw, that old Resemblance, have as near an affinity! However, there was a real Star of the first Magnitude of Beaux. . . . It is a great pity that he should be one of the ' sans culottes ' of England, for he has a great fortune, very lively, handsome, of good figure, and those who know him say very good-tempered. This would do, would it not ? But alas ! it only appeared for a day or two to shew such things are, and was snatched away again, before I had time to set my Cap in more than one Attitude. If you like an Officer, there will be plenty at Brighton, for the Prince's Regt. stays there all the winter. For the Coast is to be well guarded. I hope we shall not be too fond of the P., and then the Residence will not be unpleasant, if we find any body we know. . . . We have been to two or three Card Parties this week, and if the Play was lower, they would be very pleasant as the Company is on the whole agreeable.

The People desire their Loves and what not. Ever yours sincerely

M. J. H.

Maria Josepha to Miss Ann Firth.

Sheffield Place : November 8, 1793.

I suppose you know we returned home on Sunday, but to give everybody their due, I must say, it was not intended that we should move before Monday, if Tom Fool had not offered to meet us here on Sunday. The said Tom Fool's Witch is still in England but still talking of going out of it. I think she will continue to talk of it, all the Winter. I have so often regretted, you fixed your departure for this year. For if you could have stayed with us another twelvemonth, it would not have appeared to Papa such a thorough change of people as it has now done, and he would have had somebody to grumble at, who like the Eels was used to it and knew his ways. Indeed, as we are to pass this Winter in the Country, it was particularly disagreeable of you. But what signifies regretting what cannot be helped now, and at the time I would not propose it, because I looked upon it as an Impossibility, your House being got and your Sister wishing to be settled. I wish she would take to herself a husband and I declare we would have you back again Neck and Heels. But do not tell her my good wishes.

Maria Josepha to Miss Ann Firth.

Brighton : November 13, 1793.

Papa took a comfortable Lodging, tho' very minute, just opposite the Pavillion and we came on Monday, since when it has rained and Blown incessantly. The House is well-furnished, and including Linnen and Plate, found us for two guineas per week. But it is very provoking to have left Home which is after all the best place in November. Yesterday Papa received a Letter from poor Mr.

Gibbon which obliged him to go to Town immediately and it is of course uncertain when he returns. Mr. G. says he is obliged to consult Physicians on his case. . . . an operation is necessary and he wished Papa to be with him at the time, so I am afraid there is some risk. . . . I hope Papa's letter to-morrow will say that he is out of danger. . . . Poor Lally cannot accept the Invitation to come here, which I should not be sorry for, if his Absence was not caused by such Calamities. Madame D'Hénin has been very much disturbed and agitated by the Queen's Death, and she had hardly recovered that shock, when she heard that Mdme. de Biron was arrested and put in Prison at Paris. Mdme. de Poix who has lost the use of her Limbs and is incapable of moving without assistance, was brought before the Revolutionary Tribunal and underwent a strict Examination ; but some remaining Sparks of Humanity prompted the Wretches to suffer her to return to her own House, guarded however, Day and Night by two Grenadiers. M. Tour du Pin has been seized and they have done all in their power to force him to declare where his son is. The Society at Twickenham know all this, and yet are ignorant when they can hear more of these and many other dear Friends. What a dreadful State of Suspense and Uneasiness ! You have seen, I suppose, in the Papers, the Tryal and Death of the twenty-one Deputies who, less than a twelvemonth ago, led the whole Nation and are now fallen by Men still more sanguinary than themselves. I have some hope that, if Papa should be obliged to stay any time in Town, he may send us back to S. P. In the two days he was here before we came, he discovered that there is but one set, Mrs. Fitz's ; he is fortunately not desirous we should get into that. The Hours are very late and the Rate of Card Playing very high. . . I much prefer a snug evening at home to the company there is here ; yet S. P. would be still more comfortable. In the

meantime I have got a good Pianoforte; we have subscribed to the Library; I have plenty of Work, and a
Pack of Cards; therefore you may imagine with all these
amusements and the help of a little Writing, the time is
filled up; whether well or ill I do not determine.

Adieu! it is late and I have not time for more.   Much
yours

M. J. H.

Maria Josepha to Miss Ann Firth.

Brighton: November 17, 1793.

I have a great mind to swear at not having heard
from you an Age—but I think I will save myself the
trouble in hopes of a Letter next Post. . . . Mr. Gibbon
has been much relieved by the operation. . . . Papa says,
he hopes he will be better now than he has been for a
long while. . . . I hope we shall be at Sheff. Place before
long, as I flatter myself there is not much Society here
that Papa will like even for himself.   The Howes and
Pitts left last week. . . . We have not seen a Soul
except Mrs. and Miss Scott; the latter has left School,
and is grown a fine young Lady with powdered Locks,
short waist, long Petticoats, and all the etc.'s that denote
she has not forsworn the Vanities of this Wicked
World. . . .

Maria Josepha to Miss Ann Firth.

Sheffield Place: December 1, 1793.

Though we returned on Wednesday, I have not recovered from my Ecstacy of Joy to find myself in my
own Room and by my own Fireside again, and should
have written to tell you so before, but that I have been
in a State of Disorganisation since Sunday, from cold I

took coming out of that uncomfortable, exposed Church at Brighton. Mr. Barr boiled me as soon as I came home in the Great Shoe, and I am quite pert again. . . . I shall indeed rejoice to see old Madam Poole,[1] and hear all about you and your Mansion. I expect my Plants with Impatience. I dare say there will be some Novelties. . . . I wish Lord Moira was fairly off. It is such a pity to lose this good weather and wait for a Storm, and it would be worse if any accident happened from the Elements than from an Action, as they would perish without doing much good. It is very odd we hear nothing positive of Lord Howe. It has been now three days strongly reported, that he had had an Advantage, and yet there are no official Accts.

Adieu !   Ever yours,

M. J. H.

Maria Josepha to Miss Ann Firth.

S. P.: December 5, 1793.

. . . I am sorry Mr. Gibbon is not here this week. He does not come till Sunday. If you were to pop in by surprize one Evening, I think you would stare, at seeing his Lordship regularly set down to Cribbage, at a Card Table, like any Dowager. I am glad to see how he interests himself in the Game. His Luck is amazing. As we only play 3d., however, we shall not be ruined. He is not well or in spirits, I think. . . . Mr. Pelham writes word to-day that Ld. Howe has certainly taken 5 Sail of the Line, and his Authority is Sir L. Pepys, who heard the D. of Clarence wish the Queen joy of the news. Parliament meets the 21st January.

Adieu !   Ever yours,

M. J. H.

---

[1] Miss Poole, a frequent guest at Sheffield Place.

Maria Josepha to Miss Ann Firth.

Sheff. Place : December 8, 1793.

The Historian has put off coming here till Tuesday. The Chancellor is grown so fond of him that he insisted upon his returning to him at Hampstead to-day, and then they both go together to Lord Auckland's to-morrow. This looks like a negociation, and Mr. Gibbon is the best person in the world to manage such a thing. . . . I am very sorry my Uncle will depart before the arrival of our Thucydides. He is very entertaining as it is, but if Mr. G. were here to draw him out, he would be still pleasanter. Was there ever anything so extraordinary as the length of time we have been without hearing of Lord Howe's Fleet in an official manner ? Private accounts seem to put the Good News out of doubt. . . . If you can hire a reasonable Air Balloon, do fly over to us in it. How I should like to pop you down in a Chair in the Corner of the Library.

Ever yours,

M. J. Holroyd.

Maria Josepha to Miss Ann Firth.

December 13, 1793.

I cannot send a letter without a word of French politics, or you would hardly believe it came from me. I hope all the horrid things I have heard of the treatment of the poor Madame Elisabeth is not true, and yet I think nothing is impossible for those Wretches. I likewise heard that the young Princess had not found better treatment. As to the Dauphin, he is kept in a constant state of Drunkenness, and brought into every scene of vice that can possibly be thought of, and this is afterwards to be brought against him as a proof of the badness of his disposition. . . .

Maria Josepha to Miss Ann Firth.

S. P.: December 20, 1793.

We rode yesterday to Mr. Poole's, and found the young Travellers in excellent condition. They delivered up their Charge—viz. the Thimbles and Plants. Many thanks for both, and for the first I send the Thanks of the Trio. Louisa has got the white and gold one; I have that with the Purple edge, and Aunt the other. We met Lady Cope and Mr. Jekyll at Hook. The latter comes here to-morrow for a night. He is a great favourite of Mr. G., which is rather surprizing, as the latter does not, in general, shew a predilection for Those who are less qualified for Hearers than Orators. . . . I have worked with my Thimble and like it extremely, independent of its coming from the old Cat. Aunt says, she shall begin to work again for the sake of using hers; Louisa's is put up in Cotton. Only one word for French affairs—What a Dreadful List of Daily Massacres! If Madame de Barry's Fortune had been told in the days of her Power, how it would have been laughed at! Adieu. Every good wish of this season and every other attend you and the younger Grim: from all, including Mrs. Woodward and family.

Rev. N. Nichol to Maria Josepha.

' Blundeston: Dec. 24, 1793.

. . . Because you all seemed to take in good part the Turkey I sent to S. P. last year, I have a project of sending another for the good of the family in general, of

which I think Lord Sheffield ought not to partake, because
his Lordship, whilst he supports, like Atlas, the credit of
the Nation, and circulates the produce of Sussex through
Canals, which cost him sleepless nights and anxious days,
forgets absent friends, and their minute business, thinks
no more of me and the poor Twenty Sheep I requested
him to procure for me from the South Down, than I do
of the Mayor and Corporation of Bristol. . . . Mr. Coke
has been so good as to promise me what I want, from a
large importation he made last year from Sussex. So,
here is an end of the Sheep.

Not so of the Turkey. What I propose to do is to
send it by the Mail Coach to London, directed to S. P.

I have passed three weeks lately as follows—one part
at the Palace, (the Bp.'s, at Norwich) who unites the
elegance and liberality of a well bred Gentleman to all the
proper Decorum of the Episcopal Character, and is besides, a Man of Sense, of amiable disposition and of
sufficient information. Thence I went to Cossey, by
particular invitation of the Lady of the House (Lady
Jerningham). . . . Thence to Raynham, where, except
Colonels Barré and Loftus, we had only (there never was
an only more out of its place) the charming family, the
Mistress of which would make any house delightful.
Lady Ann is very agreeable, reasonable, and accomplished. Lady Charlotte, handsome, and if report says
true, to be married to Lord Brome, Lord Cornwallis's
Eldest Son. So, to Holkham, where we had Twenty-
three in family, and the most magnificent, elegant, and
at the same time, agreeable style of living. Mrs. Coke
does from good nature and an ardent desire of pleasing,
what others do from vanity or politeness. Lord and Lady
Melbourne and three daughters, Mr. and Mrs. Edward
Coke, and Mr. Anson made part of the society. The last
named gentleman is the husband elect and declared of

Miss Ann Coke, at present fifteen.   She is to wait therefore a year to attain the age of sixteen, before she
assumes the Dignity and functions of a matron and
Mistress of a Family.   Mr. Anson is said to have an
Income of 22,000*l.* per annum, and certainly not less than
14 or 15,000.

You flatter me (and the more because it is not a
failing to which you are much addicted) by wishing me
added to such a party as you describe at S. P.   It is
certain that I, for my part, should have been supremely
happy.

CHAPTER XII.

1794.

THE HISTORIAN'S LAST PAGE.

JANUARY TO JULY 3.

Guests at Sheffield Place—Gibbon—Hayley—Mr. Jekyll—Gibbon's failing
health—Gloomy political prospects—Narrow escape—Gibbon's serious
illness—His death—Grief at his loss—His funeral—His manuscripts—
Quiet days—Inoculation—Canning's first speech—Talk of invasion—
Ireland prosperous—The Gibbon Memoirs—Raising a Yeomanry Corps—
Fashions—Politics—The wry-necked Secretary—Gibbon's first love—
His library.

Maria Josepha to Miss Ann Firth.

Sheffield Place: Jan. 1, 1794.

MANY, many happy New Years are wished you by all
here in the double capacity of this being New Year's and
your Birthday. The two or three last Days have produced Events I did not dream of. Mr. Douglas is going
as Secretary to Ireland, and Sir H. Clinton in the room
of O'Hara to Toulon. The news of the appointment we
had from Lord Auckland, and not from himself.

Françillon has just returned from Switz. Came here
last Thursday and like all the rest of our Inmates enquired a good deal after you by description, though he
was not up to your name. He brought me a beautiful
Cup and Saucer from Mdlle. de S.[1] of the Manufacture
of the Pays de Vaud, with my Cypher on it and two
Figures, representing the Costumes of the Peasants of
the Canton de Berne. M. Levade sent Papa two views of

[1] Severy.

Mr. Gib's House and Pavillion. Poor Historian! He has been very indifferent since yesterday se'en night. It is a great effort to him, going up and down stairs. He fears he shall be obliged to go to Town. I hope not before the French people go, or Mr. Hayley comes. Lally and the Princess came on Monday. They contrived to lose their way and came by Ryegate to Cuckfield, and from thence here quite in the dark. As they said they would set out at 8 in the morning, we depended on their arriving in time; but waited Dinner in consequence of this 'petit détour' till 6 o'clock, and they did not arrive till after 7. Lally does not shine in Presence of his Divinity. I wish it had pleased her to remain at Twickenham, for he does not venture on anything like a Joke. . . . The Prince de Poix we expect today. . . . Mr. Jekyll comes to dinner. . . . Miss Poole has had a strong invitation to accompany Mr. Hayley; but she was afraid, having only just recovered from a Bad Cold. I really believe she would have liked much to have accepted the Invitation, as she Idolizes the Conversation and Talents of the Poet and Historian so much, as to find a Great Treat in seeing them together.

Mr. Hayley comes on Sunday or Tuesday, if Mr. Gibbon can stay so long; I wish he may, and yet at the same time, I am very anxious to know he is in London, and within reach of able Physicians and Surgeons. In his case, I am afraid they are very necessary, and with all their Skill I am doubtful of his recovery from what I hear. In Face, he is as well as ever; but in other respects looks much worse.

We have a Bride just arrived in this neighbourhood—Mrs. Rivet at Maresfield. He has the Living, and she is a daughter of Cullen Smith, and sister to the Man who married Miss Eardley. We have not paid our respects there yet. Papa will possibly go to Town sooner than he

S

intended; but I am not quite 'au fait,' only that he had some Idea of going this week, but put it off at Mr. Gibbon's request, who thought it rather rude to leave his Guests to Fate without necessity.

I am sure you will be glad to hear M. Fazy's Brother has escaped and arrived safe at Geneva; that will be some comfort to the Father in his affliction. Mdme. D'Hénin gives melancholy accounts of France and of the numbers of young Men of Fashion and Family who are obliged to enlist against their wills in the ' Sans Culottes' Army, and are afraid to desert lest their Relatives should suffer by it.

Ever yrs.
M. J. H.

H. Way is going to St. Domingo. By the bye, you see one of our Acquisitions in St. D. is retaken by the Republicans. May '94 produce more fortunate Events than '93—but I fear more than I hope.

Maria Josepha to Miss Ann Firth.

Sheffield Place: Jan. 3, 1794.

I despatched an Epistle so lately that I have not much to say; unless it is to lament the Evacuation of Toulon, which has put the finishing stroke to the misfortunes of this Campaign. Lord H. Clinton's Government is something of the same kind as Sancho Panza's in the Island of Barataria—begun and ended in one Day. Lally, but particularly the Princess, spluttered most violently when the news arrived, and I should have pitied them if they had been tolerably reasonable, but Mdme. D'Hénin abused this Nation so vehemently for going to War, as well as for the Conduct of it, that I was quite out of Patience with her. How can they suppose all Nations are to take up the Quarrel and be at an immense expence merely to restore the Emigrants to their Estates, and Louis XVII. to his Throne! Yet, such is their Idea, and Mr. Gib. and Papa both informed them that we did not go to War for the sake of their 'beaux yeux.' Le Prince de Poix did not come. . . . I believe the Truth is that he had no taste for the Country in the month of January. Mr. Jekyll dined here the day before yesterday. Mr. G. made an Effort and came down; but it is quite painful to see with what difficulty he moves, and I wish he was in London. He seems too now to be sensible of the peculiarity of his appearance. I believe he will go to town early next week, and perhaps Papa with him. Milord is all in Rags. I want to know what price the Cloth that makes his Shirts is? and what Linnendraper you have dealt with last? The 8 Shirts you cut out are all he has in a tolerable State. His others are woful bad. You see I must apply to you for a time, or I should be at a loss about these important matters.

Lally reads a Play to us every evening, which is very pleasant. Last night he read 'Alzire,' one of Voltaire's Tragedies. I think he reads it much better than Comedy. The Ranting Manner he has is more suitable to Tragedy. It is entertaining to see the Interest the Princess takes in his Performance. Adieu.

Much yrs.
M. J. H.

Lord Sheffield to Maria Josepha.

Hotel Pall Mall: January 10, 1794.

The Gibbon is better, although he had but a bad night. He took a remedy, therefore I did not see him till near twelve, since which time I have not left him, except to pay a visit to a French Emigrant in Bond Street, who assures me that the Royalists are marched to the coast of Brittany, and are very powerfull. I learn also that Lord Moira is certainly going thither again,

probably to La Hogue. I dined yesterday with the
Royal Philosopher, and this day I have invitations to the
Chancellor and Sir Joseph, and I am to go to the former.
. . . Nobody believes in the Duke of Brunswick's Victory
of the 29th December. Tell Fletcher to avail himself of
the Frost by carrying as much of the wood and faggots
out of Sheffield wood as possible.

Dr Brat, yrs.

S.

Maria Josepha to Miss Ann Firth.

S. P. : January 11, 1794.

. . . Poor Mr. Gibbon left us on Tuesday, and I
wished him to go long before he did, he seemed so very
indifferent. Papa had so much inquietude about him,
that he followed him on Thursday, and from his Acct.
yesterday I suppose if Mr. G. had delayed setting out one
day longer, he might have been too ill to recover. Papa
says, the Surgeons ordered Bark every 6 Hours and 5
Glasses of Madeira at Dinner. His letter to-day says he
is much better and has less Inflammation. Papa will
return in a few days if Mr. Gibbon goes on tolerably
well ; but he intends to go to Town again when Parliament meets. He recd. a Letter from Mr. Pitt to desire
his attendance on the 21st at the House, as particular
Business was expected to come on that Day, and this
Letter tho' a circular one undoubtedly, yet as it ranks
him among the List of the Friends of the Government,
is a good sign. It at least proves that Mr. Pitt wishes to
suppose him friendly. I should not like to be Minister
just at this Moment, and but that there is no other person
to put in his place, I should think Mr. Pitt might totter
and fall this Session. How very gloomy the Prospect is
at present ! I hate to think on the subject, for who can
pretend to guess what the year '94 may produce? and I
cannot help, as I believe I have said before, feeling that

these wretches must be suffered to succeed for some end we cannot understand, or else that with all Europe united against them in some place or other, they must receive a check. . . .

The bad success on the Rhine is terrible news. We have been trying to flatter ourselves with a victory of the D. of Brunswick's since the Defeat of Wurmser; but I am afraid there is no foundation for the report. The History of Genl. Hoche, the Conqueror of Wurmser in this late Affair is a strong Proof of the Impolicy of the Prussian Conduct in regard to La Fayette. Lally was mentioning it here. Hoche's father was Postillion to Louis XVI., and when a Boy the General himself acted in the same Capacity. He afterwards enlisted as a Common Soldier, and Marshal Biron, finding him adroit, made him a Drill Serjeant. He got raised to the Rank of an Officer, which seems to suppose him a Man of some Merit. At the beginning of the Revolution he was a Constitutionalist, and much attached to the Royal Family, to whom he was of considerable service on the 5th October. He was in the Regt. of Picardy and very much attached to La Fayette, and when the General went off, he had by various Intrigues and Management persuaded a large Body of Soldiers and Officers to follow him; but upon hearing La Fayette's Treatment, he vowed vengeance against the Prussians, and has been a thorough 'Sans Culotte' ever since.

I do not think Lally has furnished us with much news or anecdote. Indeed they have so little communication with Paris, they know very little more than we do from the Public Prints. Mdlle. de Poix is still confined, and the wife of Charles de Noailles is likewise at Paris; but at present safe. I hope poor Lally [1] will succeed in getting his Pension thro' the Interest of Mr. Douglas in Ireland.

[1] Comte de Lally Tollendale's father was of Irish extraction.

I fancy Pauline's Dutchman has proved a true Dutchman, from the Manner in which the Princess speaks of him. She says, ' qu'il est bien avare.'

I have been lately reading over again Swift's ' Voyage to the Houynhnms,' and if it were not for some rare instances, I should feel as morose and as great a Misanthrope as Gulliver. . . . I must tell you of a little Frolick of mine this Week which did not amuse and delight the Family as much as might have been expected.

Belcombe is kept in the Stable to make him look handsome, he eats Oats and does not use much violent exercise—so finding himself very frolicksome on Monday last, he thought, as I liked novelties, I should have no Objection to an Expedition à la Johnny Gilpin. And when Louisa and I were riding out upon Chailey Common, after various Capers, Bounds and Frisks, he began running like the wind. I stuck on for a considerable time very well; but the North Wind meeting me full in the face assisted the Velocity of the Motion to take away my Breath; my Hands were so cold that I could hardly feel the Reins, and we were on the point of going dash down hill; all which circumstances combined to spill me, and I fell prostrate on my Nose, which at first I verily thought was broke; but it bled a good deal and that was all the harm I received.

Poor Louisa's fright you may easily imagine. I am afraid I exemplified Papa's Maxim, that Ladies fling themselves off for fear of falling; but I think I did right. . . . The Horse did not stop directly, but soon trotted back to the others. He has been stinted of his Oats ever since and is very peaceable. My Head ached in the evening, and so there was a Conspiracy in the Family to bleed me, which Mr. Barr performed to my great Horror. I did not like the Idea at all, and as it made me Faint, the Reality did not please me a bit better. However, I am now perfectly well, whether Thanks to the Bleeding or not I cannot say. . . . Long as this letter is, (mercy on you!) I shall not close it till the Post arrives to-morrow that I may give you Papa's account of our poor Historian.

Yours affectionately,

M. J. H.

Maria Josepha to Miss Ann Firth.

S. P.: January 17, 1794.

I am rather disappointed at not hearing from you. Papa returned to us on Wednesday evening, leaving Mr. G. much better; but yesterday an Express arrived between 5 and 6 in the evening from Farquhar, to say he was so dangerously ill, that Papa and Aunt set off directly for London, where I much fear they will not find the poor Man alive. It is a terrible state of Expectation we are in. I wished much to have gone with them; but they would not let me; because I have been unwell this week past with an Erysipelas in my Foot, that has pre-vented my moving till the day before yesterday, and they thought I might catch cold.

I will write again on Sunday. Adieu.

Ever yours,

M. J. H.

Serena to Maria Josepha.

Royal Hotel, Pall Mall: Friday Morn. January 17, 1794.

I hope you received the Note I sent by the Coach, though it was but the melancholy confirmation of our worst fears. It was between 12 and one when sent; but Davey paid a watchman sixpence to give it when the people were up. We could do no more. I certainly had prepared to expect what happened, and yet when poor

Dussot came to the door the picture of despair to tell me
he was no more, I felt as if it was new to me.   Indeed I
had somehow hoped it was possible he might be alive
and even like to see me.   An hour after the express was
sent off, he died.   It is supposed some gathering of
matter within, or else Gout in the Stomach, was the
immediate cause of his death.   They are different
(causes) but they cannot say more.   He was not sensible
of his danger.   He suffered a good deal for a short time
and was speechless, making attempts to speak which
shewed he was not insensible. . . . He was in the shell
of his coffin—Alive but a few hours before !   These
things add to one's horror, though in fact nothing.
Françillon, expecting my Brother, stayed till ten at poor
Mr. Gibbon's lodging and then gave him up.   He called
again this Morn before nine.   Elmsley had put seals on
everything.   The Darells are looking for my Brother,
and they are going to meet there.   I felt it was worth
my coming, for my Brother as we came soothed himself
with now and then talking, and indeed the gloom, not to
say horror of coming to this Hotel last night required
somebody to share it, and by mutually thinking of one
another it diverted some of it.   There was not a spark
of fire in the whole house ; nor a maid up.   A man
opened the door and, looking frightened, said no body
was up, but we might have beds.   We were not in a
humour to care much about anything.   We went to my
Brother's bed chamber, and Bull lighted the fire, and in
about an hour we got some tea, which was all we desired.   We sat up talking and writing till after two.
We sent a letter by an early coach to Mrs. Gould[1] to
tell poor Mrs. Gibbon and to ask her permission to
convey poor Mr. Gibbon to the vault at Sheffield Place.
. . . At nine yesterday Morn he cried out ' O ! my God ! '

[1] Mrs. Gibbon's companion.

several times, in great pain and spoke no more; but
lived till a quarter before one at Noon. When the Will
has been read I am to write for my Brother to the poor
Severys. Françillon offered it; but it seems kinder, and
there may be some things for my Brother to say more
properly himself. Severy has indeed lost a second
Father too soon after the first. I shall not go home
tomorrow. My Brother wants me a good deal; but I
think a day more will be enough. Mrs. Mellish invites
us to dinner. I am really perfectly well and, thanks to
your care, was not I assure you the least cold in coming
to town. We did not stop a Moment on the road and
was at the door at 12. The Night was light as day.
The beauty of it was solemn and almost melancholy with
our train of ideas; but it seemed to calm our minds. I
am now alone without even any more paper or a book;
I cannot go out if I wished it, for the moment he returns
from the Miserable scene of the Will, I shall have to
write for him. You will like to hear all we do. I will
Keep this open till he returns. Send all letters to this
House. The Will my Brother had, and which was made
a few days before you left Lausanne, is the only one
that can be found. It leaves my Brother, Mr. L. Darell
and Batt, Executors. I have not time to write his own
words to account for leaving them nothing, though it is
expressed well, and we cannot doubt his regard for my
Brother. He has left 3000 pounds, and all his plate,
furniture, and carriages to De Severy. All the rest to the
Portens, except fifty guineas to you, to Louisa, to Madame
and Mdlle. de Severy, the Chanoinesse de Polier and M. le
Ministre Levade, all named. His not naming Mrs. Gibbon
I impute to his little Idea of her surviving him, for in a
former Will he left her £200 a year. Your Uncle is
here. We are to be at his house to sleep tonight, so you
may direct your letters there. He is all kindness. He

is going to Denham and leaves us possession. I am going to write for my Brother.

God Bless you all.

. Kind compts. to Mrs. Poole.

.S. H.

Serena to Maria Josepha.

London : January 20, 1794.

. . . I have written for my brother a letter to poor Mrs. Gibbon which will soothe her as much as possible ; but I have little idea she will long survive. We had, by the coach yesterday, a letter from Mrs. Gould to say she bore it with as much fortitude as could be ; but that her frame was such she could not answer for the effect. She is gratified with my brother's wish to have poor Mr. Gibbon buried at Fletching, and I suppose he will be carried there by Friday. . . .

Maria Josepha to Miss Ann Firth (enclosing the one from Serena).

S. P. : Jan. 19, 1794.

The enclosed Letter will save me a painful Repetition. We have lost a true and sincere friend indeed, and just now he is a particular loss to Papa . . . there is no other Person who has half the Influence that poor Man had. The best Sense was always guided by the best. Judgement. All my comfort is, that there was no hope of a cure without suffering much pain through terrible operations, and that he is saved many months of suffering perhaps. Aunt comes back tomorrow. I am glad Parliament will employ Papa, it will prevent his thinking. Did ever anything so unfortunate happen as that the sad event should take place in the very short time Papa meant to be absent ? You will excuse a longer Letter at present.

Maria Josepha to Miss Ann Firth.

S. P.: Jan. 26, 1794.

Many thanks for both your Letters. I was sure you would feel for our irreparable loss as you do. I comfort myself with thinking however that if he had lived and returned to Switz: he would have been nearly as much lost to us as now. For in his state of Health and Body it was not probable that he should again visit England; and as for himself I hope he has been spared much pain. Do you not pity his poor Friends at Lausanne, who could not form an Idea that he was in any Danger, as Papa wrote at the poor Man's Desire the Day before he left Town, only two Days before his Death, that he was much better, and had borne the last Operation very well. The Funeral was conducted with the greatest Simplicity at his desire, only his own Servants attending the Hearse, and 8 Men with Fletcher and John to carry the Coffin. Poor Mrs. Gibbon has borne the shock with her usual Firmness of mind. The first Day she desired to be left alone; but afterwards she was anxious to know every particular and to converse on the subject; and her health seems to have received less hurt than might have been expected. Who could have supposed it possible that she would have been the Survivor?

Mr. Gibbon has left some Manuscripts that are very curious and interesting, with leave to publish them, if they are thought sufficiently finished. They are Memoirs of his own Life, but entirely of his private affairs.

Maria Josepha to Miss Ann Firth.

Sheffield Place: Feb. 2, 1794.

If you wish to form an exact Idea of our amusements, you may suppose Mrs. Poole finishing the Sopha for

Aunt, at which she sets with unceasing Industry from Breakfast till it is too dark to see the Stitches.

Aunt and I read Tom Jones by turns; but I am afraid Aunt's turn comes oftenest and lasts longest. This is varied by a little writing and a little Inspection of the Newspapers and a little Walking or riding, and in the Evening when we are so happy as to have Mr. Barr we play at ——. If not Mrs. Poole and Louisa play at Backgammon, and Aunt and I at Cribbage. . . . Poor Mrs. Gibbon is pretty well. Papa talks of coming down to us and bringing the Papers which we should much like to see, I mean Mr. G.'s Manuscripts; but he is engaged for some time to come and probably other engagements will detain him. I have been surprised there has been so little uproar in the House, or business done. Lord Stanhope should certainly be sent as a handsome present to the Convention. His speech, however, has been the only wild one there has been. I do not approve of Mr. Pitt's manner of telling Mr. Sheridan what he could not have said anywhere else, that 'nobody in the House would believe his opinions.' Have you had That in your Paper? or Mr. Fox's attack on the conduct of the War by Sea, on which Mr. Pitt makes a very poor Defence indeed. . . . Adieu.

Yrs. Ever.
M. J. H.

Maria Josepha to Miss Ann Firth.

Sheffield Place: February 16, 1794.

. . . I have amused myself with making acquaintance with all the Cottages in the Neighbourhood to keep myself out of mischief and find myself employment; and if I had but the means I need not lose my labour, as the Misery is on all sides, and were it to be properly assisted, would thoroughly engage any person's Time and thought; and the little I have been able to do in the way of assisting some of the poorest, has been the greatest amusement I have found for some time.

Papa is very pretty behaved and writes every day; though but a few words in general, it is very pleasant to receive them; he says he has not had time to be indisposed, which sounds well, as consequently he has been amused. This is a natural conclusion, at least, knowing as we do he is never amused but when head and ears in business, or something that he is interested about. . . . The loss of that invaluable, sincere and well-judging friend Mr. Gibbon, is most sincerely felt by us for Papa, and I doubt not by Papa himself. Of what unspeakable consequence would his cool and unprejudiced advice have been to him at this critical time—but though I must frequently think on this subject, there is no use in dwelling on a loss that can never be repaired. I am sure you think as I do, even he could not entirely prevent Papa from taking some steps that he thought imprudent; but he had power to restrain him in some of his impetuosities; but this friend gone, who is there who has the least influence over him?

Great part of our family are under Inoculation. It was so general all round us, and everybody was in such danger of catching it, that upon representing the case to Mylord he gave leave for the Virgo children, Dick and the other Stable Boy, Will Virgo and Nanny the Kitchen maid, to be inoculated, at the Farm House. Mr. Barr performed last Monday, but none of them have failed yet. The Gardener's Baby, just turned the month, was inoculated at the same time. Everybody who has not had it, are frightened out of their Senses. At Lewes 2,500 have been inoc. Mr. Lupton's little Girl has been in great danger, and frightened them both out of their wits, but she is now recovered. Mr. L. quite adores her, Mrs. Woodward says, and is the prettiest Nurse in the world. Mary Fleming has been very Ill with it, but is now out of danger. She has had it so bad that she will not be able to leave the Pest House so soon as the others. Things have gone on in the House of Commons quieter than I expected. I had an Idea much more would be said about the Continuance of the War. Mr. Canning, you see, made his First Speech. Papa says it is one of the best First Speeches he ever heard.

My Correspondence with Mrs. Howard is not very vigorous, as she is very lazy, but I had a long Letter lately. How her Religious Principles stand, I know not, but her Political ones, are sadly perverted. Her Letter was chiefly against the War, and in the complete style of a Follower of Fox's.

I have heard nothing of Lady Webster, since her departure, and am quite satisfied with the state of ignorance in which I am, as to her manœuvres. I suppose she has given me up as a Correspondent, and I am resigned.

Maria Josepha to Miss Ann Firth.

Sheffield Place : February 18, 1794.

Papa says Invasion is much talked of in London, and that People are much alarmed by an Order issued from Council, concerning driving the Cattle from the Coast. This is not however new, the same order having been issued in former Wars. In the same paper I see all the Militia men out upon Furlough, are ordered immediately to join their Regiments at Canterbury. I do not feel much alarmed, for I cannot think our Navy is reduced so very low as to suffer the French to land in any number so as to do much damage. It is well there is some subject to amuse the London Campaigners this year, for there does not appear to be anything very lively or gay in the way of Public Amusements. I hear the Operas are very indifferent, and the Ballets worse. Everything in Dress is, I find, 'à la Turque,' in compliment to Yussuf Effendi. If People are so determined to gain his favour, I suppose it will be the fashion to be fat or he will never give them a place in his Seraglio.

. . . Papa had a letter from Mr. Smith sending him a part of his Rents that he had at last got from Nicholls, which gave a very favourable account of the State of Ireland. The discontented and turbulent are much alarmed and quieted by one or two vigorous measures of Government, and particularly by the active Behaviour and Conduct of the Speaker. Mr. Smith's acct. of Papa's affairs is as pleasant as that of the Public, for he says Land is daily rising in Value and that if the present Tenants quit their Farms, they may easily be let at a higher Rent. I think Mr. Smith would not think of raising the Rents unless he were certain the Tenants could afford to pay them at an encreased rate; but I did not think, considering the state things have been in lately, that it was likely the Value of anything in that Country would rise. I wish I could give as good an account of the Premiums given for Shares in the Ouse Navigation; but I fear your Great Nieces only will be the gainers by your Gambling in Canals. Coals are carried as far as Sheff. Bridge, and other things, but I believe not in sufficient quantity for the Tolls even to pay the Interest on the money borrowed. We now burn Coals in all the Bedchambers. Papa has had Stoves put up in all the rooms. My Fire Place looks quite smart. I wish you was at this Moment chusing your Pattern, and saving me all this trouble by chattering as fast as we could instead, at the other corner of my new Grate. Papa talks of coming to us as soon as the Slave Business is decided. Wilberforce has put off a Motion on that Subject that was to have been made some days ago till Friday next, and perhaps it may not be decided even then. . . .

Adieu, yrs ever,

M. J. HOLROYD.

Mrs. Maynard has agreed to come to us (as House-keeper), and Marina—the Sea Nymph—will be at the Lodge with Vine and his wife, who have returned to their old habitation.

Maria Josepha to Miss Ann Firth.

S. P.: February 25, 1794.

I do not think it necessary to inflict you with a long letter, neither have I time, since I have written to his Lordship and one or two others to-day, but I enclose Pap's Letter of to-day, which will show you how the young Gentleman is going to begin the world again as a Military Man. . . . In one way I rejoice. He will have employment; and as he has little chance of any in the Political Line, I am glad the Military offers itself as an Alternative.

Papa has had a long letter from Lausanne; they felt the Stroke, as you may imagine. Poor Mdlle. S. was very low, and the poor Fellow says ' she did not want no more sorrows.' Think how painful it must have been, the news only just received, and therefore his sorrow so fresh, to be obliged to enter into a long Detail about what was to be done with poor Mr. Gibbon's affairs at Lausanne. For he did not know, everything except the Library was his, as the Council refused to open Mr. G.'s Will unless they had an ' Extrait Mortuaire ' to prove his Death. It is the custom of the country for all Wills to be opened by the Council. Adieu.

Ever yours truly,

M. J. H.

Maria Josepha to Miss Ann Firth.

Sheffield Place: March 2, 1794.

On Wed. I walked to Hettdown, eat Beef Pudding
with Mrs. Woodward, and walked home with her in the
evening without feeling the least tired.   Our two Beaux
make an agreeable Variety in our Style of Living.   Papa
has read us several parts of Mr. Gibbon's Memoirs,
written so exactly in the Style of his Conversation that,
while we felt delighted at the Beauty of the Thoughts
and Elegance of the Language, we could not help feeling
a severe Pang at the Idea we should never hear his
instructive and amusing Conversation any more.   Adieu.

Yours ever,

M. J. H.

Maria Josepha to Miss Ann Firth.

Sheffield Place: March 9, 1794.

. . . Our inoculated Folks at the Farm House are
quite recovered, and have had it very slightly.   The little
Porters are likewise got well.   Mr. Barr has had upwards
of 70 Patients, and I believe every one of them have
done exceedingly well.   He will have made quite a Fortune this Winter.   His Terms are half a Guinea apiece.
Several people have died at Lewes, but I believe very
much from the Ignorance and Carelessness of the Doctors
there.

What do you think I have done ?   An amazing Feat
indeed !   Nothing less than cut out a set of Shirts for
Papa, and I am going to make one Shirt myself.   I have
got a new kind of thing for them, that Mrs. Maynard
recommends, called Suffolk Hemp.   It looks very strong,
and she says it will wear well.

The Weather begins to be delightful.   We have had

T

three most delicious Days, as Arthur Young calls them
I have ejaculated your Name very frequently, and wished
you had been here to walk with me.   I should have been
perfectly of Adam's opinion, and could not have enjoyed
Paradise without somebody to enjoy it with me.

. . . I believe I told you in my last scrap that we had
read all the Memoirs, and that they were, as you may
imagine, in the highest Degree interesting.   There are
many Passages that would be very unfit to Publish.   Of
Mrs. Gibbon he speaks in the highest and most flattering
Terms, notwithstanding he says himself that he returned
from abroad with the greatest prejudice against her, in
the light of a Stepmother.   His relation of his Conversion
to Popery is very curious, ahd goes a great way towards
excusing his subsequent disbelief, from having at one
time believed too much.   I wish you could see them, as
I am sure they would amuse and interest you most
extremely.   The Acct. he gives of the Idleness and In-
capability of the Professors and Tutors at Oxford in his
very sarcastic way, has I am afraid a great deal too
much truth in it; but would exasperate the University
still more against him, and if published would produce
many Scribblers and much abuse, now that his ready
Pen is no more there to answer them.   Papa and Mr.
Darrell agree the Memoirs are in much too unfinished a
State for Publication ; but they both think, with the help
of his Letters to Papa, a very curious Book might be
made out of them.   The manner in which he mentions
his First Love, Mdme. Necker, is very flattering; but
even there he cannot help introducing a little Sarcasm.
At least it is in *one* of the Lives, for he has left Four ; the
last coming down no later than his leaving Oxford, and
that which finishes at 1791 is only Heads and Notes, but
infinitely curious.

He mentions first the Aimiable Qualities, good Sense

and improved Understanding of Mdlle. Curchod; his Love for her which she seemed to share; that on his return to England the stern commands of a rigid Father prevented his entertaining any hopes of calling her his. He says: 'I obeyed as a Son, I sighed as a Lover. Time and Reason effected my Cure, which was likewise accelerated by a faithfull Account of the Tranquillity of the Lady.' He says in another Place, 'that His Heart was defended against subsequent serious Attacks of the Passion of Love, by his recollection of that amiable Woman.'

But I should never have done if I were to give you a full account of every part that pleased and amused me. No part is more interesting than the account he gives of his youthfull Studies and those of his Maturer age. Of Mrs. Porten he speaks with the highest Veneration, as the Preserver of his Existence and the Former of his Mind. Indeed he speaks in a higher style of her improved understanding than I thought it had deserved. However, it appears very plainly that if he had not been banished to Switzerland on account of his turning Roman Catholick, and if he had slumbered away the usual time at Magdalen College in the way he began, 'The History of the Decline and Fall of the Roman Empire' could never have been written by him.

I wish I could annihilate about one hundred and fifty miles between Doncaster and Sheff. Place. But if 'Wishes were Horses,' etc. . . . . Lally has got a Pension of 300*l.* per Annum, so he will be able to repay some of his obligations to the Princess. I have some hopes of seeing Bell and my Uncle[1] at Easter. Henry, (Captain Way,) represented us as such sober, well-behaved young Ladies, and me in particular so altered, that my Uncle thinks he may venture the Experiment. As Harriet

[1] Benjamin Way.

Clinton will be here I am afraid I shall find it difficult
to support my new acquired character. The Captain
sailed a few days ago from Bristol. I do not love croak-
ing ; but upon my word, we seem in a perilous position, if
the Wretches on the other side of the Water make any
desperate attempt. I cannot find out from Papa that any
steps are taken or taking to oppose them if they attempt
a Landing. That shabby creature, the K. of Prussia you
see is sneaking off. If he is not base enough to join or
assist the French, I think it may be a good riddance and
that the Austrians will go on better by themselves. This
is a letter of odds and ends just as they came into my
head. . . . I live almost in the Garden.

Maria Josepha to Miss Ann Firth.

Sheff. Place : March 23, 1794.

. . . As you have not tender nerves on those occasions,
you will not moan over the poor Wood which is very
much dislocated. Great part was cut down last year and
more has followed this Spring. I believe it was very
necessary—but for the present the nakedness of the Land
is very shocking. It is some comfort that the said Trees
will produce a little Cash. I hope the ' Sans Culottes '
will not come to finish cutting down what Papa has
spared ; but I declare I cannot help thinking of them now
and then, tho' I cannot persuade myself to be much
afraid of them. Since Old England will deserve a little
punishment if her Navy is so contemptible as to suffer
French folks to land here, and I cannot think she is quite
so bad as that. But Papa says they are collecting in
great numbers on the Coast of Brittany and Normandy.
It is supposed the Threat against Jersey is only a Feint,
and that a landing here or in Ireland is intended. Large
Detachments are marching from the Army of the North,

and the Troops are to assemble along the Coast about the 14th or 15th of next month for the purpose of embarking. Surely if we have such accurate Information of their Proceedings and Intentions, some Steps will be taken to interrupt them in the Execution of their Designs.

Papa has been interesting himself about La Fayette, and in that Debate joined the 46, and furnished Fitzpatrick, the Mover, with information concerning La Fayette given him by Lally, who has written a long Dissertation, not only exculpating him from all blame; but attributing very praiseworthy motives to him. There are some circumstances which Lally mentions, relating to the poor King and La Fayette curious, and if I have patience to copy the Eulogium I will send it to you. Lally's Style is always animated, therefore tho' I do not think his Hero quite as blameless as he represents him, I am interested in the little Treatise. I never can get out of my Head that *Insurrection is a Sacred Duty.* But yet, I do not think he in any way deserved the cruel treatment he has met with. M. Fazy is in hopes his Father's House at Lyons will be opened again. . . . The sale of the Timber is to-day, and it is valued at 1,000*l.* ; it is to be sold by Auction in three Lots at the Inn. Adieu.

Ever yours,

M. J. H.

Maria Josepha to Miss Ann Firth.

Sheff. Place: April 1, 1794.

Poor dear Pap left us on Saturday; he says he feels low, but I never saw him so quietly cheerful and good humoured; perhaps he is more irritable when in better health, and yet that is odd. . . . In a fortnight he will return to us again, and if nothing happens at present unforeseen, I shall be as happy as—I don't know what—for the old Simile of a Queen will not hold good in these Times. Have you by chance got a receipt for the Dry Rot? I should perhaps say against instead of for. Papa wants it for Lord Lansdowne and desires me to look for it. I cannot find it anywhere, and it occurred to me you might possibly have it. If you have, pray send it to him directly. How lucky you are not still at S. P. I suppose you will open your eyes at this. But could you have breathed freely in the atmosphere of Sir Elijah Impey? He has hired Bewick Park and means to live there all the summer and autumn. I hear there is a large family of young Imp——s. . . . .

While Papa was here, he and I were out all day planting and such things. I have got Harry Mitchell to mend and paint all the seats, and I have got a man of my own in the wood, to spread the lumps of earth left in various parts, and to make a new walk across the second Pond Bay to Sylph Place. You really can hardly tell the pleasure there was in having Papa with us last week in the good humour he was in.

I have got poor Mr. Gibbon's Seal with which I am sealing this letter.

Maria Josepha to Miss Ann Firth.

S. P.: May 3, 1794.

Aunt and Louisa set off for Windsor yesterday morning. Papa and I depart to-morrow. Papa went to Lewes on Thursday to attend the County Meeting for raising Yeomanry Corps, and yesterday was the Quarter Sessions; therefore he did not return till Evening. The Meeting was well attended and a much greater subscription than I expected—4,000*l.* upon the spot. The D. of Richmond, Lord Egremont, and Lord Ashburnham, 500*l.* each, Lord Pelham 300. Papa 100, and several other Gentlemen 200,

100, and 50. . . . What will be done next does not appear very clearly, or that when the Corps are raised they will be of any service. However, as I have not the least apprehension of Invasion at present, now the French have so much work on their hands nearer home, I think it is a very harmless amusement for the Country Gentlemen. Henry Clinton is more improved than anything I ever saw, and I think he is one of the finest looking and most pleasing-mannered young men in England. I was wonderfully pleased with his manner of relating the Action which brought him over—map in hand—and the rest of the Party were as much so. There was Clearness and Spirit in the Narrative without the slightest mixture of Conceit or Vanity. He was chased and very near taken by a French Privateer coming over. I am very glad he was out of the way of the last Action, which seems to have been a bloody one, tho' the final success was great and complete. The loss of 57 pieces of cannon must be a very serious one to the French army, tho' their Train of Artillery is so great. . . . On Monday Uncle has asked us to dinner. . . . I have a Ball to attend in the Evening at Lady Langham's, upon the recommendation of Harriet Clinton, so I emerge quickly into the Gulph. I suppose I shall be a Fright in a short time, as I depend upon some charming Ranelaghs and Balls, but I shall return to refit in the country by the beginning of June. You threaten me with finding it all Vanity and Vexation of Spirit; but I think not this time, as my greatest pleasure will be Harriet's Company, and I mean to take the rest as it may happen; at all events I shall be more at Liberty than ever. It does require some Resolution to leave the Country at present. I never saw it in greater Beauty. . . . The Fruit Trees promise very well, and the Grapes are in abundance. Aunt has taken a lodging at Bath for three weeks; she has taken with her the Memoirs to show Mrs.

Gibbon. She is one of those who has a pleasure in talking over lost friends, and I daresay will enjoy much seeing Aunt. The said good old woman (not Mrs. Gibbon, but Mrs. Holroyd) was a great deal better for the little Routation we had in the Family.

I hear the Legards and Miss Grimstons are coming home immediately. Sir John is to bring over the papers of Mr. Gibbon's that were at Lausanne. Severy talked of sending the picture by him, but I should think that is too cumbersome, for a family already probably much loaded, as they are on their return to England after an absence of some years. He asks for a copy of Papa's and another of Mr. G.'s picture, which Papa has promised him.— Adieu.

Remember me kindly to the younger Puss, and believe me ever yours affectionately,

M. J. H.

Poor little Marina has been very ill with Whooping cough, but is getting better. Mrs. Maynard returns with us into the Country. Once more adieu to you and Prolixity, for you will not set Eyes on such a fine Epistle for one while.

Serena to Maria Josepha.

Bath: Wednesday, May 7, 1794.

Tell Sheff that I have seen poor Mrs. Gibbon; carried her the watch and papers; and said all the kind things he desired, with which she seemed sincerely pleased. . . . I am sorry to find she is grieved at not being named in the Will, and does not take it as I hoped she would; but no notice must be taken to her of this confession. She is not angry, but affectionately grieved. I hope to make her change her idea before we part. She is very happy in my Brother being her Trustee, etc. etc., and totally depends on him. . . .

Maria Josepha to Miss Ann Firth.

Portland Place: Wednesday, May 14, 1794.

When this Letter will be finished depends on so many fortuitous circumstances, that I can make no calculation as to its probable termination; but I am determined to begin, which is a great step towards a conclusion. We arrived here on Sunday se'ennight to dinner, and found all the Family well. On Monday I made a good Beginning as we were at three Balls—Lady Elcho's, Mrs. Rawlins', ci devant Miss le Maitre, Baroness Nolcken's Daughter, and Lady Langham's. To the first however we went so early, the Musick had not arrived; at the second we did not dance, as we were prudent and did not like to heat ourselves; therefore in fact we had but one Ball though it sounds well to talk of three. Lady Langham's was a very good Ball—that is, there was a great deal of Company, handsome rooms, and a very elegant Supper. I met there several acquaintances; I danced eight Dances; I did not fatigue them (my Partners) however with much dancing; for after my long Rustication, I found I could not get on at all, and preferred sitting still to skipping about. We came home between four and five. . . . Thursday, Papa and I dined at Lord Aucklands, and Lady A. took me in the Evening to Mr. Weddell's. Nobody dined at the Aucklands but ourselves—all the family was everything kind, and I should never be tired of seeing them 'en famille.' It is a lovely sight and the most pleasing Picture of Domestic Happiness one can conceive. . . . Friday we went to Lady Elcho's and Lady Bassett's Assemblies. . . . Saturday we went to the Play and saw the New Theatre. The first Effect is beautiful; but in my opinion it is rather too much in the French Style, and looks very like Confectionery. . . . The Play

was a new one of Cumberland's, called 'The Jew.' It
did not please me much, because at a Comedy I expect
to laugh, and there was so much sentiment throughout,
that with a very little Pains one might have cried.
Bannister and Miss Farren performed their parts as well
as possible; but I have seen them both appear to greater
advantage. We went afterwards to a Child's Ball at Mrs.
Neave's, but Aunt was tired after her Play, and we soon
left them, otherwise it was a pretty sight to see the children dance. Sunday, we went to Portland Chapel to
hear Mr. Nicholls preach. His Sermon was a good one ;
but I am afraid he had not time to write it out fair ; for he
made a fearfull number of Blunders. . . . I will just
frighten you with a List of our Engagements for a
Week to come, and then I think even if I should not
have time for any more scribbling, this will be a very
decent letter :

To-NIGHT.—We go to an Assembly and a Ball.

To-MORROW.—Ball at Mrs. Bruce.

FRIDAY.—Dine at Lord Pelham's, and in the Evening
        Mrs. Clive's Assembly.

SATURDAY.—Probably the Opera.

SUNDAY.—Concert and Supper at Lady Sykes.

MONDAY.—Concert at Mrs. Lockhart's, and Lady
        Hudson's Ball, which I expect to be very
        pleasant.

TUESDAY.—Unless we go to the Opera again I do not
        know what will become of us.

WEDNESDAY.—Ranelagh.

THURSDAY.—Mrs. Boone's Assembly.

FRIDAY.—Ranelagh again, and I know nothing farther.

However, if we should be doomed to rest a day or two I
think one might be able to bear it.

The Reports of these last two days have been, though

favourable, very unpleasant ; as no official accounts have arrived and no particulars are known. All the reports however say that the French are driven back to the Gates of Lille with considerable loss. The Packet which was bringing over Lady A. Fitzroy and her Brother from Lisbon, where she lately left her Husband, is either taken or lost, but the former is thought probable. I forgot to mention we were at the Shakespeare Gallery and Exhibition last Week. There are some good Paintings of Beechy's and Hoppner's. Lawrence is very much gone off, I think, in his Style of Colouring. There is a Portrait of Lord Auckland by him, very like, though I do not admire the Painting. . . . As to Fashions, I have not seen any Pink Breeches, though I heard of them before I came to town. The Dress at present worn is very elegant and becoming—in moderation. I do not think it is at all the Fashion to Pad this year. Many people look as if they had no Petticoats on, and as the Gowns are mostly Turkish and seem to set loose from the Body, I expect if a foot is set upon a Train, to see the Ladies disrobed.

5 o'clock.

News is at last arrived, good for the Publick ; but poor Henry Clinton having received a slight wound we have not been able to thoroughly enjoy the goodness of it. . . . Dear Harriet was terribly agitated. . . . I do not know any particulars of the Action.

Ever yours,

M. J. H.

Maria Josepha to Miss Ann Firth.

Portland Place : May 27, 1794.

Your friends are quite well and safe at present ; but how long they may remain so, is so uncertain that there is hardly any comfort in knowing they are so now.

Henry's wound kept him out of the Action on the 18th, in which he would have run great risks. The Duke of York and P. Wm. very narrowly escaped being taken, and of course Henry would have been with them, and perhaps sent on to reconnoitre, and he might have fallen into the Enemy's hands. Poor P. Wm. tumbled into a Ditch in getting away, and Wm.[1] extricated him out of his difficulty. I am glad to find the D. of York was not to blame at all in that Business—so far from it, that if he had obeyed the peremptory orders that were sent to him to march on to Linselles, the whole Body of Troops under his Command must have been cut off. By the young Men's letters and Sir H.'s comments upon them, it appears that the Plan of Attack that Day was very good; but the Execution very bad indeed. The D. of York's Division and Genl. Otto's were the only two out of five that succeeded in their attacks, and unless the others had accomplished what they were sent upon, it was impossible that the Duke and Otto could advance. The General gives the Duke great Credit for his conduct that day, which I am glad to find. I wonder the King will persist however in the Duke's commanding the Army in Person, for one trembles to think of the Consequences if he were taken Prisoner, and I should never be surprized if I heard he was, as it seems that the French make an object of taking him. Mr. Pitt, the Duke of Richmond and all the Cabinet, were very much against his going this Campaign, and opposed it all they could; but George was obstinate, as I believe he can be when he has taken a thing into his head. Of Home Plots and Conspiracies I have not heard much lately. I cannot find out the reason of passing the Bill for the Suspension of the Habeas Corpus in such a violent hurry, as no immediate measures have been taken in consequence.

[1] William Clinton.

The Report of the Secret Committee in my opinion contains nothing that was not known long ago, and has been published in many of the newspapers. I fear, however, there are but too many designing persons in this Town, and a few more such bad pieces of Intelligence as we have lately had might make them shew themselves. I will hope better things, however. The last Action ended in our favour, as the French were obliged to fall back, though the loss on the side of the Austrians was considerable ; and it is no comfort to hear of three times the number of Devils killed, as it is what the Convention rather wishes, and numbers more are ready to rise up in their places.

But a truce to Politics.

Lady Hudson's Ball was very pleasant. There were plenty of Beaux, as many more as Ladies almost. . . . We were at the Opera on Tuesday; but I was not much amused. . . . I do not know whether I return with Papa or stay a day or two longer. . . . I am not very anxious about staying here any longer, as I am in great hopes Mrs. Carter and Harriet will soon come down to us at S. P. and pass the summer there. . . .

I have not time for more.

Yours Ever Truly,

M. J. H.

Maria Josepha to Miss Ann Firth.

Sheff. Place : June 7, 1794.

Once more quietly seated in my own room, I write with a degree of tranquillity I have not experienced for some time : for my letters to you have been moments snatched from the Wreck of Time in London ; which expression, tho' not usually made use of in that Sense, may I think be applied to poor Time in that Vile

Metropolis.   Mrs. Adair had a Ball on Monday which I was at till 5 in the morning. . . . We were at the Opera the Thursday before and the Play on Friday.   At the first I heard the famous Banti who is indeed a delightful Singer and I was very much entertained. . . . The Pit was crowded beyond anything I ever saw.   The Play was the 'Pirate,' a musical Thing, and uncommonly pretty.   Horace Bannister, Snett, and Mrs. Crouch, all perform in it and are all charming. . . . Papa had a letter from Lausanne to-day which mentions Madame Necker's Death.   The Papers and Papa's Picture are coming over with Sir J. Legard, who is to be in England the latter end of this month.   It was very obliging in him to take charge of such a ponderous Thing as the Picture.[1]   Nothing is yet done about disposing of the Library.   It is moved out of Mr. Gibbon's House, as M. de Montagny would not suffer it to remain there any longer.   I think he has shown a great deal of haste to take possession. . . .

The wry-necked Secretary is an acquisition lately made, and intended for Country use.   Papa has not had him in Town.   It is a very agreeable circumstance, and will save Aunt and I a great deal of trouble.   He will be particularly usefull, as Papa intends to undertake the Arrangement of Mr. Gibbon's Memoirs and letters for the Public Eye.   The young Man was recommended by Mr. Hayley, who had him from Mr. Cowper, the Author of the 'Task.'   His name is Socket; he is about 16; has had a good education; can read Latin and French; and is to have £20 a year and to live with the Servants.   It would have been very unpleasant to have a Person in that Situation one of us; and yet there might have been a doubt about the disposal of a Secretary if he were older.

[1] Of Lord Sheffield, painted for Mr. Gibbon by Sir Joshua Reynolds.

I hope no unpleasant reports from abroad will happen during the summer to disturb our Pleasure in the Country. Harriet is to bring her own Horse, and we shall have some very pleasant Rides, I hope. Papa was yesterday at Lewes to attend a Meeting upon the Subject of the Troops to be raised in this Country—a Troop of Dragoons and some Artillery Cavalry are to be added to the Militia; but the Offers from People to command Companies of Infantry come in very slow. Young Campion is to have one; but I do not know of any other Hero who steps forth in defence of his King and Country. (Papa) talks of going the Tour of the Camps, and it would be a very agreeable expedition. There is one at Brighton; one at Bexhill; one at Hastings, and I believe another somewhere upon the Coast in this county. The Country looks everything that is pleasant, but feels Winter. It is quite cold enough for a considerable Fire.

Adieu; Love to young Mrs. Grim.

Yours Ever Truly,

M. J. H.

Maria Josepha to Miss Ann Firth.

Sheffield Place: June 17, 1794.

I would Give a good deal that you could be transported from Doncaster and safely deposited in your own Room. I am sure you could not guess where you had got to. I enclose a Pattern of the Bed. It makes up very handsome, and is but 20*d.* the yard. Mrs. Maynard has made it up with full Valences, and has raised the feet, to give it a more modern appearance; and with the assistance of a new Feather Bed it looks almost as smart as any Bed in the House. Your old Cabinet, Louisa has taken into her room as a great Treasure. We have put a Toilette Table and a neat Pembroke Table, and a Scotch carpet

round the Bed. We have another Coachman and a
young Person in the Still Room Maid's place. But what
do you think her name is? Winifred Gap ! ! !

George Coxe came yesterday to stay three weeks—
he is a very pleasant Man when in good spirits. He
is just come from Lady Rivers, who is at the Isle of
Wight, and he was at Portsmouth when Lord Howe
arrived there with his Prizes, and he says, as I can
easily imagine, it was a most glorious sight to see him
enter the Port amidst the acclamations of hundreds,
and the roaring of Cannon. By the bye, what a fortunate and well-timed Victory this has been ! Perhaps,
take all the circumstances together into consideration,
it is the greatest victory this Country ever gained at Sea ;
something was so much wanted to raise the spirits of one
party, and quiet those of the other ; and a Naval Victory
is what John Bull comprehends perfectly well. I am
afraid we want something to counterbalance the state of
Affairs in Flanders, which is not just now very promising..
I thought I had told you that Madame Necker had the
satisfaction of going out of the World with the knowledge of being Mr. Gibbon's First and Only Love. Papa
sent Extracts of the Passages where he mentioned her
and the Severy Family to Severy ; and she had the
pleasure of reading them before her death. She must be
a dreadfull loss to poor Necker, who, I cannot help thinking, meant well, tho' I fear he was the cause of all that
has happened ; at least the second cause ; for the Events
of the last three or four years are of such a wonderful
Nature, that it appears to me as if something uncommon
either in the way of punishment or warning was intended.
Can anything be more shocking than that Robespierre
should make a pretence of his intended Assassination by
a young Woman, to propose and carry a Decree for giving

no quarter to the English and Hanoverians? Did you read the Duke of York's General Orders to the Army in consequence? They are very well written, and with much judgement and humanity, and if anything is capable of making an impression on the French Army I think this Manifesto will. What a dreadfull savage War it is likely to become, if the Decree is really carried into execution ; for it will be impossible to restrain our Troops from retaliation even if it is attempted. Thursday 19th. We expect Fred. North to-morrow and a young Greek, who is his Ward and who he is going to place at Eastbourne, with a clergyman there. Adieu.

Maria Josepha to Miss Ann Firth.

Sheff. Place : June 27, 1794.

. . . How very bad affairs appear on the Continent ! Yprès gone, and the French Army within seven miles of Ostend. We no sooner gain an advantage in one part, than it is made of no avail to us by some superior Advantage gained by the Enemy in another. I shall croak if I write Politicks, so I say no more.

Papa is making great alterations in his room, putting up Bookcases to contain the Law Books and Tracts, which will make room for the New Books in the Library. The French Mémoires are a Library in themselves, between 60 and 70 volumes. I do not hear any more of the Yeomanry Cavalry, and do not suppose it will come to much in this country. To-morrow we expect Sir J. Sinclair and two of his Daughters, school girls, about 12 years old. I wish he was to come without them, as it is very difficult to know how to entertain girls of that age. The Aunts go out in the Tib, which just suits them. The Phæton lost three wheels on three different

U

expeditions, and at last the Body of it broke down ! The
Ponies are Dears, and I wish they had a better carriage.
Adieu.

Ever yours,

M. J. H.

I hope you will be able to decipher the beginning of
this Letter, but I have such pale Ink, 'à la Firth,' that I
fear you will find some difficulty.

Maria Josepha to Miss Ann Firth.

Sheff. Place: July 3, 1794.

I purposely avoided saying anything of public affairs,
till I had told you all the chit chat trifles of what company we had, etc., because I thought, like My lord, I
could not mention them after the others.   Everybody
croaks, and worse than croaks ; they seem almost in
despair of keeping anything in Flanders.   The Duke and
his Army will, I hope, find they can make a safe Retreat
by way of Holland, and so will end this Glorious Campaign probably, if it ends no worse. . . . Harriet had a
joint Letter from her Brothers yesterday ; Wm. was
just setting off to join the Prince of Coburg's Army.   I
hope he would be in no danger where he was sent.
Several of the papers have informed us that Sir H.
Clinton is appointed Govr. of Gibraltar; but this is all
we know about it. . . . I think indeed he will be ill-used
if he has not something given him to make up for the
Sancho Panza's Government at Toulon. That Government
was something like the play of Bob Cherry. Lord Auckland
writes very much out of spirits about foreign affairs, and
says he quite gives up any hopes of our Allies performing
their Engagements properly.   The cause of this War
seems more the cause of the Austrians than of any other

Nation, and as much that of the Prussians as ours, and yet they behave in the most shameful way possible. Lord A. has just lost his second son, which such an affectionate father must feel very deeply. . . . Aunt is very nervous ; the daily bad news she hears is not likely to make her better. . . . H. desires her Love to the ' Old Cat of Miss Holroyd ! ' I assure you, my dear Miss Firth, I am quite shocked at the Impertinence !

CHAPTER XIII.

1794.

OLD FRIENDS AND NEW TIES.

JULY TO DECEMBER.

Ministerial changes—Highland uniform—Papers and picture from Lau-
sanne—Alarming adventure—Neighbours—The camp at Brighton—
The review—Interesting Swiss and German guests—Revising the Gibbon
Memoirs—Marriage of the Prince of Wales—Ingenuity of Fletching
Ringers—Loss of Friends—Lord Sheffield's second marriage—Invitation
to the wedding—Letter from Hayley—A friendly hermit's advice.

Maria Josepha to Miss Ann Firth.

Sheffield Place : July 8, 1794.

WE are enjoying the cool Breezes in the North Hall,
the only place in the house tolerably cool. We have
been in a state of anxious Suspense to know if the
General [Sir H. Clinton] was a Governor or not. At
last, this day has brought us a Confirmation of the news.
. . . The Government is 3,000*l.* in time of Peace, which is
a pretty little addition. Papa goes to Town next week to
assist at the close of the Exchequer Bill Business, which
has fully answered the end designed in every particular.

I wonder what changes are going to take place in the
Ministry. I understand the D. of Portland wishes to
have a place under Government, and that the Foxites are
enraged at his desertion. Lord Spencer is talked of for
Ireland. Lord Fitzwilliam, it is said, told Mr. Pitt he
thought he could be of more use if he supported Govern-

ment without taking any place. If so, he has behaved very handsomely. I am afraid *we* shall be entirely overlooked in these new arrangements, and if so we shall be very sour I am afraid.

Maria Josepha to Miss Ann Firth.

Sheffield Place : July 24, 1794.

Mr. Godley, who came on Saturday leaves us to-day. He has more than once desired me to send his best compliments to you. Our Coz. has left off his Wig and wears his own Grey Locks, which give him a very venerable appearance. Sir J. Sinclair, who has paid us three flying visits within a fortnight, was to have returned to-day ; but is detained in Town. One day he treated us with a sight of him in the Uniform of his Rothesay and Caithness Regiment, and a more curious figure I never saw. The Coat was the only part of his Dress not perfectly outlandish. Scarlet turned up with yellow, a large silk Plaid, partaking of the Nature of a Spanish Cloak crossed before and was flung over one shoulder. Trowsers of the same Silk half way down the Leg and checked Red and White Stockings. He was not quite compleat, as he had not his Scotch bonnet, which would have added a foot or so to his Stature. . . .

All the Papers and the Picture are arrived safe from Lausanne. The Journal Mr. Gibbon kept while at Lausanne the second time, is very curious and entertaining. The other Papers were mostly letters from different People, and it astonished me to find what sort of Letters he kept. There are several Love Letters of Madame Necker's among them. If the Papers had fallen into the hands of a Boswell, what fun the World would have had ! All the papers left at Lausanne were sealed, and directed to Papa ; but I am surprized he did not leave some directions in his Will that they should all be given only to him or some be destroyed. Alas ! I am afraid in a few days I shall lose Harriet. . . .

> Adieu, yours very Sincerely
>
> M. J. H.

Maria Josepha to Serena.

July 30, 1794.

The Clintons will go down to O. P. soon after the Races. I am glad I have Harriet to go with me, but wish she was in better Spirits to enjoy it. . . .

You have had a very narrow escape of hearing from Louisa, as the only survivor of the noble family of Holroyd. We were within an Inch of being drowned last night in the Iron gate Lock, by the oddest Accident that perhaps ever happened in Navigation. The Water was rising very fast, and by inattention, the end of the Boat got hitched under the Bar or Beam that goes across the Gate of the Lock, and Papa could not push it off, consequently as the Water rose, it raised the other end of the Boat, and filled the lower part. Papa very quietly informed us we were going to sink, which was not a very pleasant Idea with ten feet of Water beneath us. I was at the upper part of the Boat, which was within two or three feet of the side, and I skipped out, and Jessy Sinclair, the youngest, after me, by the assistance of my hand. The rest, Aunt, Harriet, and Miss S. instead of following me, clung to Papa who called them to stand upon the Bar of the Lock (that, which is half way) and Aunt and Miss S. were dragged up to the Side by Vine. Poor Harriet while she was upon the Gate of the Lock went into strong Hysterics, and when she was pulled up, fainted away completely ; for, added to the degree of alarm we all felt, the Cord that tows the Boat entangled round her Leg, and if it had sunk, she must have been pulled down with it, and perhaps Papa with her, who had fast hold of her. In short, it was not at all amusing at the time. Jessy and I got out quite dry, but Harriet and Miss S. who were longer on the Gate than Aunt, were wet up to their knees almost. It was astonishing how fast the Boat filled, but when we were out, it floated tho' brimful of Water. It was a great blessing neither Mrs. C. nor Louisa were with us; the latter took a quiet Ride by herself another way, but if she had happened to come along with us, and rode by the side, as she did, in our last Navigating excursion, in her nervous state, she would have been almost frightened to death. The Coachman, who was with us, was so terrified he was of no manner of use, which he acknowledged to the Servants when he came home, saying that he never was so frightened in his Life; he expected to see all the family ' knocked up, at once,' was his expression.

Last week we paid our first visit to the Impeys. If I could forget Nunocomar, (perhaps I have not spelt it right) I should have liked Sir Elijah [1] very well as a good sort of old man. Lady I. has the ' beaux restes ' of a very fine Woman. They have several Children, but I only saw one pretty, fair girl, and a Captain West, who is one of the family; what the name of his employment is, I do not know; but his business seems to be, to ring the Bell; open the Door; remove the Parrot when she squalls too loud; laugh at the good Jokes sported in Company; supply a Chasm by some excellent one of his own, and hand the Visitors into their Carriage.

Maria Josepha to Miss Ann Firth.

Sheffield Place: July 30, 1794.

. . . Papa's Picture [2] looks very well in the Library between the Windows. . . . I cannot write Politicks unless

---

[1] Rajah Nuncomar, aged 70, and head of the Brahmins of Bengal, was hanged 1775, sentence pronounced by Sir Elijah Impey.

[2] That painted by Sir Joshua Reynolds for Gibbon.

I heard something pleasant to relate. Henry Clinton's letter yesterday from Antwerp, of the 23rd, says the Armies are still retreating further. The P. of Cobourg's behaviour is unaccountable. In the moment when he had proposed a General Attack to the Duke of York, he gave orders to his Troops to retire to Maestricht. If Lord Spencer and Mr. Grenville who are gone to Vienna cannot spur up the Austrian Court to make some further exertions, the case is indeed desperate. Landieu has surrendered; everything that we have gained with loss of men, and in a length of time, is gone or going. Harriet will not let me write any more. .

So Adieu, yours ever,

M. J. H.

That plague of all plagues is in Town and wants to fidget them up to him because he finds he is expected to go to Gibraltar in September, but I had set my mind on having Harriet at the Races, and it will be a great disappointment to me if she does not stay for them next week. I have a shadow of Hope that the General may come here instead.

How very bad affairs are going on, on the Continent! What will become of poor England?

Adieu, Yours ever Sincerely

M. J. H.

Maria Josepha to Miss Ann Firth.

Sheffield Place : August 5, 1794.

I have been all impatience to tell you our Lewes history. I should have enjoyed the Olympic Games more than I ever did before if poor Harriet had been quite well; but she did not recover the effects of her fright in the Boat all the time we were at Lewes, and had frequent returns of Hysterics and faintings; however, she was fortunately better at the Balls than I expected, and was well amused, as she had the good fortune to meet a London Acquaintance, a pleasing Man, Mr. Chester,[1] one of General Bruce's Aide-de-Camps, which was much more agreeable than dancing with 'Introductions.'

I was obliged to write a long Letter yesterday to Bell, to congratulate her on Lewis Way having obtained the Fellowship in Merton College, of which he was so desirous, and when I have an excuse for scribbling to Denham I generally take the advantage of sending a Volume, as frequent Correspondence is interdicted. To relate all in order; we left S. P. on Thursday morning and went immediately to the Race Ground. . . . Lady Pelham took charge of us at the Ball, Papa acting as second in command. Tuesday will be a very black day, for Mrs. C. and Har. positively go away to O. P.

Yours ever truly
M. J. H.

Maria Josepha to Miss Ann Firth.

Sheffield Place: August 12, 1794.

Mrs. C. and Har. are just gone. We have been together, with only very short intervals, since the middle of April, and it appears to me as if I had lost one of the family. We have been uneasy about Louisa these three days past. . . . As soon as she is better, Aunt and she go to Tunbridge, so that instead of anything particular pleasant to comfort me for the loss of Har., I shall be particularly lonely and dull; but Mrs. Russell will be here till the 19th.

Mr. Sneyd comes to-morrow; the Judges some time this week; Lord Thurlow and the Paynes talk of coming here, and Hayley, Elmsley and Rose will be here the 26th, for a fortnight I suppose at least.

---

[1] Harriet Clinton afterwards married Captain Chester.

I must tell you of our Expedition to the Camp last Friday. . . . It is two miles and a half from Brighton, and about half a mile from the Sea above Hove. The ground is unequal, and the Sussex Militia has the best position in the Camp, being on the highest part, and commanding a beautiful View of the Sea and the rest of the Encampment. There are six Regiments of Militia ; Lancashire, Warwickshire, Dorsetshire, Suffolk and Sussex, the Prince's Regiment of Cavalry and the Horse Artillery, and though only half the size of last year's Camp, had, I think, a much more beautiful effect. The Men are now in Tents, as large as the Subaltern Officers' Tents ; ten in each, which look much better than the small pointed things they used to have and gave a much more grand appearance to the scene.

I should have liked to have had a Resurrection of Cæsar, Alexander, or even Frederick of Prussia, to see what observations they would have made on the Glass Doors, paved Entrances, and neat Parterres of Flowers round the Tents of some of the officers, and whether they would not have given up the Country for lost where such Effeminacy prevailed. We went to see the Prince's Tent, which is very handsomely furnished ; but not a bit too much so for his Rank ; the Bed, which I had heard was too sumptuous for a Camp, was removed, and quite a Common Tent Bed in its Place. There is a Dining Room in the Centre, with the Bed Chamber and Drawing-room on each side, forming the Wings and communicating with the Dining-room. All hung with different Chintz Patterns. The Drawing-room, particularly beautiful, with a highly glazed chintz which gives it the appearance of a Silk ; two Sophas covered with the same, and Camp chairs and Stools. After we had walked about for some time, we went to Mr. Pelham's Tent, which is a very comfortable one. We stayed there till Dinner was ready in the Mess Tent. . . . On our entrance into the Dinner Tent we were alarmed at first by the numbers of Red Coats awaiting our arrival. I do not think Harriet got the better of her fright during the whole Dinner. For my part I was excessively amused with the Novelty of the Scene, both at dinner and before. We were in all twenty-six at Table, and had a very good dinner, with good Wines and in Ice. The Band played to us, and in a reasonable time we adjourned to Mr. P.'s Tent; but not before we had been called upon for our Toasts, which alarmed Harriet and me most amazingly.

For my part, I had the assurance to give Major Clinton. Harriet, after mature deliberation, gave Lord Moira, and we departed from the Scene of Action before it came to the turn of the Old Ladies to be called on. . . . We drank tea with Mr. Pelham, and sorry we all were to be obliged to leave the Camp at eight. I never was more amused by a Party of that kind and never so little tired.

Wednesday 13th. Louisa is much better this morning. They will go to Tunbridge to-morrow. . . . Henry writes in good spirits about affairs in Holland and Flanders, and says he has no doubt but that they may once more enter Austrian Flanders. Count Mercy D'Argenton who is coming to England in his way here, declared that it was the Emperor's intention to defend Holland, and that he had himself given the necessary instructions to P. Cobourg, who was otherwise about to retreat. The Imperial Army to the number of 60,000 men, cover the Meuse from Liège to Venlo. At Antwerp alone, the French have levyed contributions to the amount of twenty millions of Florins, and the people there and at Ghent begin to be disgusted with their new masters, and will be ready to receive us when we advance.

. . . Adieu, my dear Miss Huff, I am infinitely more agreeable than I was at the beginning of my letter. But at all times sincerely and affectionately yours

M. J. HOLROYD.

Serena to Maria Josepha.

Sion Hill, Tunbridge Wells: Wednesday, August 20, 1794.

. . . . I think Louisa much better. . . therefore we shall, I trust, find it worth coming. . . . She will probably tell you of our intimacy with Lord Stanhope and Lady Hester, his daughter. It was unlucky we were not well enough to go to Mrs. Tyson's Ball with the Duchess of Cumberland. . . . I want to know what you think of the Convention. I cannot be sorry for Robespierre; but I fear it is only another party of Demons, I dread all these Guadaloupe evils. We are going to visit Lady Hester, and I write in a hurry. . . .

Yours Ever S. H.

Maria Josepha to Miss Ann Firth.

Sheffield Place: August 24, 1794.

We paid a Visit yesterday to the dear Invalids at Tunbridge. It is impossible to doubt the good effect of the waters when one sees Louisa, for she has some colour; she complains of being hungry. They have a delightful airy House at the top of Mount Sion, looking directly toward Crowborough, so they have even the advantage of Sheffield air. . . . Papa and I dine at Hook to meet the Pelhams, and bring Miss Poole home with us. At all times she is a very great favourite of mine; but now her society is doubly welcome. . . . Elmsley is alarmed at the Riots in London, and does not like to quit the protection of his house and property. The Riots have been very alarming I believe, and in these times any disturbances are unpleasant ; but particularly when they are on something like just grounds. The practice of kidnapping is certainly a very shocking one, and should not be allowed if it is possible to get Soldiers without. . . . We went with the Pelhams on Monday to a Ball at Brighton given to the Prince by a Club of Gentlemen in honour of his Birthday. There was a great deal of Company—a mixture of course ; but much very good. Lord and Lady Euston, Lord Albemarle, two Lord Spencers, Lady K. and Mr. Douglas, Lady A. North, Lady C. Herbert, the Thrales, &c., besides all the County people. The D. of Clarence was there and danced all the evening. I nominally danced with Mr. Campion, Mr. Courthorpe, and Captain Chester, (for Harriet's sake I suppose he asked me). We supped at the Prince's Table and his Band played all the time. We did not get home till 4 o'clock, for Lady Pelham stayed two dances after supper, contrary to her usual practice. Lady Holderness and Lady Mostyn were of our party. The latter is uncommonly pleasant. Tho' we were so late, Miss Pelham, Mrs. Russell and Papa and I got up at nine to attend a Review of the whole Line near Brighton. The Day was very fine, the View from the Downs beautiful; the Sea covered with Shipping; and a great deal of Company from Brighton attending upon the Soldiers, made the Scene very lively and pleasant. We were out with them till near three, when the Review finished. The whole family of Pelhams were very pleasant and gracious to us.

Once more adieu. Ever truly yours

M. J. H.

I gave Louisa a good scouting for indulging her moralizing turn to such an extreme degree when she wrote to friends a hundred miles off, and I hope she is ashamed of herself.

Maria Josepha to Miss Ann Firth.

Tunbridge News continues to be good, and the house is full again, therefore all these good things make me feel quite alive.   We dined at Hook on Monday, and brought Miss Poole home with us.   Her company could never have been more acceptable than at this moment, as besides her being a pleasing Companion at all times, just now when there was nothing but Gentlemen and so many of them, I should have wished very much for a female companion ; besides this, her Intimacy with Mr. Hayley makes the house pleasanter to him, and brought us acquainted more easily with him.   He and Mr. More arrived here on Tuesday, and Mr. Bowdler to dinner ; the same day brought us two unexpected Visitors—a Swiss Gentleman, M. de Zeerleder, who brought an Introduction from Severy, and a Baron de Stein who travels with him ; but I do not suppose the former is Bear Leader to the latter as I at first supposed.   They are both remarkable Personages.   The Swiss is a Grandson of Haller's, his Mother being his daughter, and the Baron is Son to Werther's Charlotte, which was a true Story, all but the Catastrophe, as Werther is still alive.   Perhaps you may remember in Lavater, a Silhouette of a Man and a Boy of about ten or eleven years old, and another of a Woman with the Bust of a Boy in her hand.   The Bust, and the whole length of the Boy, is the Baron de Stein now here ; the Man, the Author of Werther, and the Woman his Mother, Charlotte.   They are both pleasing, well informed young men, but the Swiss is much the most pleasing.   I speak seriously, without prejudice, because at first, I supposed them both Swiss, and gave the preference to the real Swiss, without knowing the other was a German.   They are making the Tour of

England. You will expect to hear what I think of Mr.
Hayley. I like him exceedingly, and can easily imagine,
when he takes pains to please, he must be very enchanting.
Mr. More was announced by him, as a very sensible young
man ; what he says is certainly sensible and clear, but he
has the pertness and conceit natural to all young lawyers,
which makes his first appearance not so pleasing.

Mr. Hayley, Mr. More, and Miss Poole are closeted
reading Mr. Gibbon's Memoirs, etc., and Mr. Hayley
thinks a great deal must be omitted in publication. I
hope his advice will be taken, for I have a great opinion
of his judgement.

I suppose we shall all have returned from Tunbridge
about the middle of October, therefore it will be delightful
if you can come to us about that time. I cannot tell you
how much pleasure it will give us all to see you here.

Adieu, My dearest Miss Huff,
Ever yours affectionately,
M. J. H.

I am going soon to drive Miss Poole in the little
Phæton, which is a jewel of a Carriage, and I drive like
an Angel !

Maria Josepha to Miss Ann Firth.

Sheffield Place : September 10, 1794.

I cannot say half enough of the impression the Poet
has made upon Papa and me. I was quite happy that
Papa and he agreed in every material point relative to
the Memoirs, etc. They found much to lop off ; but much,
very much, of a most interesting nature will remain, and
by Mr. Hayley's assistance, I think such a work will
appear next Spring as the Publick have not been treated
with for many years, and that all candid Persons will
approve and admire. Mr. More was an excellent person

to attend the Committee. He was as good a Judge as the two others in point of sense and feeling; at the same time that being unprejudicial to Mr. Gibbon as a Friend, he gave the opinion of an impartial person, which frequently furnished the other members of the Committee with useful hints. Ten years of common intercourse would not have brought Papa and Mr. Hayley so well acquainted, or made them like and love each other as the cause and subject of this visit of only ten days has done. They were each and almost equally very warmly interested about the fame and character of a common friend who was very dear to both. As to Mr. Hayley, I never figured to myself, much less saw, any person possessing such an animated mind, such Enthusiasm of friendship, and a heart so wholly and entirely divested of every selfish principle. Grâce au Ciel! he has a Wife and is not twenty years younger! Or else, my poor heart would be in danger. As it is, I think I shall not like the conversation and manner of any man I meet with for six months to come, as well as I should have done were this dear Poet unseen.

Mr. Douglas came on Thursday and slept here that night. He made himself very agreeable, and three hours from tea to supper passed like three minutes, being employed in Conversation of a literary kind, between Mr. Douglas, Mr. Hayley and More. The two former took immediately and much to each other, and Mr. Douglas asked the Bard and his friend to dine with him the next day at Brighton. What do you think of this house being once more in brick and mortar?

The Job now about, however, is I believe a necessary evil, but I hope I have helped to stop another that was certainly not so. They are now pulling down the partition between Papa's bed-chamber and the dressing-room, which, being built of brick and without support, promised to descend speedily into the inferior regions. The superfluous dilapidation is a Project of a Mr. Latrobe's, an architect employed by Mr. Fuller in the house he is building upon the Forest, and brought here by him. It is to open a great window into the Dressing-room, and the Lord knows what vagaries besides.

Reverend Norton Nichol to Maria Josepha.

St. Gluvia's : September 26, 1794.

I read and trembled yesterday and to-day I write and tremble, least no effort of mine should have power to appease the indignation I so much deserve. To Indolence I plead Guilty—to Indifference Not.

. . . I thank you for what you tell me with respect to the publication of Gibbon's Posthumous Works, in which no one can feel a warmer interest than I do. I should have been delighted, (unworthy as I am,) to have assisted at the Consultation and to have enjoyed the Society you mention. I was at College with Hayley, and thought him amiable though I knew little of him, but he has taken great strides towards literary fame since that time. The extract from Gibbon's Journal is not flung away upon me, and bears a just and honourable testimony to the Character of Lord Sheffield.

Maria Josepha to Miss Ann Firth.

Tunbridge Wells : September 27, 1794.

Is it possible you Doncaster people can be so behind hand in the affairs of the World as not to know the Prince of Wales is really and truly going to espouse his Coz. ? Indeed I thought I had mentioned it in one of my Letters. I hear a very high character of her for Beauty as well as amiable qualities. Lord Southampton, it is said, is to bring her over, and I have heard the Duchess of Devon-

X

shire mentioned as one of the Ladies who are to go for her; but the truth of the report I do not know.

I shall be more comfortable after Monday, when Lady Albinia Cumberland leaves the other half of this house. At present, I am obliged to trot home at night with a Candle and a Lanthorn to guide my Steps whether it pours Torrents, or whether Jupiter, Venus and the Great Bear display all their charms to assist me on my way. My nightly Habitation is not a great way off, but far enough to chill the end of my poor Nose these cold frosty nights.

We rode to Hettdown the day before we came here and saw Mr. Woodward. I believe though I told you so in my last. But what I was going to tell you is an instance of the Ingenuity of the Fletching People which almost exceeds Belief. Papa left a Guinea for the Ringers, to ring a rejoicing Peal at their good Vicar's recovery. I heard him tell Beezly, of the Church Farm, apparently a very intelligent Man, what it was for, and he seemed to understand him. Poor Mrs. Page happened to die the Day the Bells were put in activity, and would you suppose, it was reported and believed in Fletching, that Papa had ordered the Bells to ring for Joy at her death, because he wished so much to' have her house!! I thought I had told you that Papa had a letter lately from that D. of a woman, Lady Webster, from Florence. She talks of coming over here as a great proof of condescension; but makes an agreement she is not to be taken to Battle. The account of Battle Abbey falling, has been much exaggerated in the papers.

Maria Josepha to Miss Ann Firth.

Tunbridge Wells: October 7, 1794.

I have nothing very lively to write about to-day, indeed Subjects of a quite different nature engage our

Thoughts, and must engage my Pen. Sunday, we received an account of the death of poor Henry Way, from Mr. Adair, who very kindly wrote to tell Papa of it, that he might communicate the melancholy news to the family, and prevent their having the shock of seeing it first in the Newspapers. He died at St. Nicolas Mole, the 9th of August, of the Yellow Fever that has swept away such numbers. By the same Post, I had a letter from poor Bell, expressing great anxiety about him, and saying they were trying to prepare their minds to hear the worst, as they had had no Letters from him since his departure from Cork Harbour, 6 months ago. It is pleasant to recollect that he spent a very happy week with us before he went, and that thro' Papa's introductions he was much noticed at Bristol, and many civilities shown him there, with which he seemed much pleased. It is likewise a comfort to think he liked his Profession very much and went abroad in great spirits. I think I have no more private misfortunes for your amusement; but what do you think of the D. of York's retreat across the Meuse and his leaving Holland open to the French? who have taken Crèvecœur, and almost all the fortresses that defended Bois le Duc, which will I suppose, soon be surrendered. If the Duke's movement towards the Rhine is with the intention of joining Clairfait, both one's public and private feelings are alarmed lest he should hazard a Battle.

Papa leaves agáin to-morrow to attend the Quarter Sessions at Lewes, and goes on to Stanmer to have a Talk with Mr. Pelham, who has only just returned from the Armies of Clairfait and the D. of York. He must have many interesting subjects to talk of. He writes word that the Mynheers are at last determined to exert themselves, and that the P. of Orange is gone with authority to use every possible means of putting the Country in a state of Defence ; so I suppose if nothing else will do they will try Inundation.   Which way shall I turn to find something chearful to look upon in public affairs ?   Lord Howe is out in one of the most violent winds we have had, and makes one fear for the safety of the Fleet.   The accounts from the West Indies, besides the dreadful ones of the Ravages of Disease, which is almost incredible, are very unpleasant ; mentioning the rapacity of the Commanders, which has been so great as to disgust our new conquered subjects very much ; which added to the reduced State of our Forces there, leaves everything to be apprehended in that Quarter if the French have sent out a considerable Force, as it is said they have.

Adieu, Yours Ever

M. J. H.

Maria Josepha to Miss Ann Firth.

Tunbridge Wells : October 12, 1794.

You will have flattered yourself perhaps, that my last Letter contained melancholy events enough for some time, and I am sure you will be very much concerned at the sad Account I have to give you of poor Mrs. Woodward's death.   What a loss she is to me, nobody who did not know her, can imagine.   She shewed her regard for me in many instances, but nothing pleased me more than her telling me what she thought wrong in me, which she often did, and though she certainly thought more highly of me than I may deserve, she never seemed to flatter me. Nobody can replace her, to me.   To hear of the death of two Relations and one true friend, within four days makes one think, and think seriously ; surely few people have lost more friends within a year and a half than I have. God preserve those that remain !

Maria Josepha to Miss Ann Firth.

Tunbridge Wells: October 19, 1794.

We have very bad accounts of Sir Henry. Mrs.
Carter is extremely anxious about him. The Physicians
advise his going immediately either to Lisbon or Gibraltar
as the best thing he can do. I dread Harriet's and Mrs.
C.'s going with him, which they would certainly do if
he would let them. At this time of Year, and in War
Time likewise, a Sea Voyage for Ladies is a shocking
thing. Lady Shelley and her family have been taken by
the French on their passage from Lisbon lately.

. . . Adieu, yours Ever,

M. J. HOLROYD.

*   *   *   *   *   *

[No allusion whatever is made by Maria to her Father's approaching
Marriage to Lucy, daughter of Lord and Lady Pelham, so possibly the
knowledge came as a surprise.

The Marriage proved a very happy one, and the 'Dear Lady,' by which
name she was always remembered, brought joy and brightness with her to
her new home.

With her affectionate letter to her Step Daughter Maria, the record of
the year 1794 closes.]

*From Lady Pelham, inviting Maria and Louisa Holroyd
to be present at the Marriage of their Father, Lord
Sheffield, with her Daughter Lucy.*

Stratton Street: December 16, 1794.

My dear Miss Holroyd,—We feel that we cannot
trust even to Lord Sheffield, in whom our Confidence is,
it should seem, pretty well established, to enforce
sufficiently to you and Miss Louisa how very earnestly
and cordially, Lord Pelham and I, and Lucy, request and
solicit the pleasure and satisfaction of your Company at
Stanmer at a certain approaching happy Event. We
hope you will have the kindness to come at least the day

before, as much earlier as you please, and remain with us as long as it will be agreeable to you both. Miss Louisa's Dinner is already ordered at two o'clock. Lord Pelham, Lucy and Emily desire their best compliments and kindest love, and the most affectionate regards to Lord Sheffield, who We hope will have arrived safe and well long before You can receive this.

Believe me Ever, my dear Madam,
Your most affectionate and much
Obliged Humble Servant
ANN PELHAM.

From Lord Sheffield to his Daughter Maria Josepha Holroyd on his Wedding Day, Dec. 26, 1794.

Stanmer: 26 December the blessed: 2 o'clock.

The Beatification has taken place without any accident. I do not recollect that any of Mahomet's Heavens are up to mine. If you do not bring with you as many Clintons as possible I shall revile the whole Family of them. The Dear Poll must be quite mistaken if she is not in a hurry to come to Sheffield Place. The 31st, consequently, is the latest day. I send three parcels of cake which have passed through the Ring, and we are this moment to set out for the Weald in a steady Snow.

Mr. Hayley to Maria Josepha.

December 27, 1794.

May the Hermit assure the feeling and accomplished Maria, that he has often thought of her with much tender solicitude on the late important occurrences, and with a cordial wish, that they may conduce to her Happiness as they assuredly afford an ample Field for the display of her many excellent Qualities.

Pauline informs me you are now fluttering on the

wing of pleasure in the Great City; but I trust you will perch again in the South before January 7, when my Lord has kindly intimated a wish to see me at Sheffield Place. If we are not blockaded by the Snow I mean to pay our Devoirs to you all in our way to Town, where I am soon to settle my dear diminutive artist, who begs leave to join with me in kind remembrance to you, and in wishing you as rare a portion of Happiness as you certainly have of engaging sensibility. Adieu.

Poem which Accompanied the Foregoing Letter.

A lovely Form with lively wit
Added to Fortune and to Birth.
What more, the heart and mind to hit
Can dear Maria wish on Earth?

Say! do you want one potent charm
Which few possess or few retain it?
And lest such hints your Pride alarm
Allow Serena [1] to explain it!

Make it your own as Maid or Wife
And tell me while your Smiles confirm it
You learnt one charm, the first in Life
By list'ning to a friendly Hermit.

From Lucy, second Wife of Lord Sheffield, to her Step Daughter Maria Josepha Holroyd.

Sheffield Place: December 28, 1794.

My dearest Maria,—Don't give yourself the trouble of answering this but by word of mouth on Wednesday, at which time I hope most sincerely to see you with Dear Louisa and your valuable Aunt. I do assure you I expect your Arrival with great Impatience, as I am most

---

[1] Allusion to the heroine in the *Triumphs of Temper*, by W. Hayley. Publ. 1781.

anxious to show you by every Attention in my power, how sensible I am of every affectionate Sentiment you have so very kindly expressed towards me, and how earnest I am in hoping that our Affection and Attachment to each other may be such as I wish ; and if you could read my Heart, whilst I write this, I flatter myself you would all be thoroughly persuaded that the preserving and Improving our Mutual Regard and Esteem will ever add very considerably to the Satisfaction and Happiness I now feel in subscribing myself

> your much Obliged and
> Affectionately Attached Friend,
> LUCY SHEFFIELD.

CHAPTER XIV.

1795.

LUCY, LADY SHEFFIELD, 'THE DEAR LADY.'

Lady Sheffield's influence—The Birthday dance—Reception at Carlton
House—East India Company entertain Warren Hastings—Louisa leaves
Bath—Serena's regrets—Wheat and flour—Mr. Jekyll—Effervescence of
wits—Madame d'Arblay—Edridge's portraits—Lady Sheffield to Maria—
The Brighton ball—Attempt on the King's life—'Vie de Madame Roland'
—An old friend's wedding.

Maria Josepha to Miss Ann Firth.

Sheffield Place: January 1, 1795.

I CANNOT any way describe the various sensations and
emotions of my mind in sitting down to write this Letter
to you; but I must hasten to make you understand they
are mostly of a pleasing nature. It is your Birthday, it is
the Birthday of the Year, and I am even so sanguine as to
believe it is the Birthday of the Happiness of this Family.
At this moment I am certain your heart pours out the
most ardent prayers that it may prove so, and you will
feel pleasure in hearing how easy the apprehended
Meeting, and all yesterday Evening passed off. I expected
civility and even affection in the manner and behaviour of
Lady S., but I cannot describe, I can only feel, the many
and nameless instances of delicate attention and Feeling
which I have perceived in her conduct towards us all,
but me in particular, and the kind of attention that could
occur only to an amiable mind, and which in these few
Hours have opened a prospect to me of greater domestic
comfort than I have ever yet known : not the least form

in her manner either, all easy and natural.   Philosophers
may preach and argue against a sanguine way of seeing
things.   But even if I should be ultimately disappointed
I would not wish to have other feelings than those that
now make me believe everything I wish, and that cause
me to do more than hope—to depend (as far as human
felicity can be depended on) that '95 will be of a very
different colour to '94.   At the same time, I am not so
sanguine as to be blind, or so happy as to have no contrary
feelings ; and I think you would have felt just as I did,
therefore I need not say how that was, in seeing him give
her, before us all, among many other things of Mama's,
her Pocketbook with the Gold Instruments and Lock, all
her Rings and the Dew Ring with the Diamonds, altered
to form an S.   It is very plain however to me, that she
has no Idea these things were hers, therefore I restrain
my feelings with great care before her, as I should be
unpardonable to give her a moment's uneasiness, for
circumstances too, that she cannot help were she inclined.
One thing I have suggested which I was sure was right,
and she seems much pleased at having carried the point—
which is, that Going to the Assembly to-morrow before
they had been at Church, would not have a good
appearance in the County ; but this being New Year's
Day was a good Cause for having Service at Fletching,
and Mr. Woodward was sent to yesterday evening, who
answered it was perfectly convenient to him, as there was
to be a Christening, which would form a small Congregation in itself and he would give notice to others.   They
are accordingly all gone.   Do you not agree with me that
this has been a good manœuvre ?   I must say a few
words about our Journey here.   We were two hours going
to Croydon, as the Streets were so slippery.   One of the
Horses fell with the Postillion, but neither were hurt ;
the last stage, with our own horses, we came the quickest.

It was just five when we arrived, and we found the Lady dressed in her wedding garments to receive us. She seemed very much agitated at first. You would love her if you saw her affectionate and warm heart peeping forth without the possibility of supposing it acting. The most suspicious person could not have a doubt, and anyone the most disposed to see things in a rebellious manner must have been disappointed in their intentions by her manner. For my part, I wish I had more merit in my behaviour; but believe me, I have none; for I feel delighted to think when sooner or later troubles come, as we who know the gentleman must fear, that we shall be a mutual comfort to each other, and if those or any other troubles of the kind do not come, we must be as happy as possible. I cannot help repeating much the same as I believe I have said before, but my heart is full of these feelings, and the overflowing of it will not be unpleasant to you, I am certain.

It is a brilliant Day and likely to last so. I am not very superstitious or absurd on these subjects, but I wish no Cloud may appear in the Sky, and I will suppose it an Emblem of the ensuing year. Adieu. I have written a long letter, and it is a great satisfaction to think you will read it with as much pleasure, (Did you suppose I could be so conceited?) as I have had in writing it. Once more Adieu, and Believe me for ever,

Yours most affectionately,

M. J. H.

Aunt and Louisa send their kindest love; but have too just an opinion of themselves to suppose their letters can be worth reading at the same time as mine; therefore defer writing to another day!

Maria Josepha to Miss Ann Firth.

Sheffield Place: January 8, 1795.

. . . I suppose Aunt has told you of our dance on my Birthday. I have not enjoyed dancing so much for a great long while past ; we had seven or eight couples, and danced every dance down twice and very seldom sat down for more than a few minutes. . . . You would be terrified at the disorderly hours we keep . . . the day after the Dance, we did not breakfast till past twelve. In a common way, we do not assemble till near eleven. Dinner nearer to 6 than to 5, and retire between 11 and 12. ' My Lady' improves upon us every day. I do really think I never saw a pleasanter creature. Her Spirits seem to the full as likely to run away with her, as mine can be, and she is all Mimickry and Drollery, that is to say, before Grandpapa and Grandmama[1] came ; for yesterday she was upon her good behaviour. Aunt has determined to go on Tuesday. Papa and she will have a scuffle over it. Louisa and she wish you to look if their Tickets in the Irish Lottery are Blanks or Prizes ; Nos. 21,034, 20,775. Louisa likewise desires me to remind you of the Phosphoric Matches.

Mrs. Maynard and Jacky removed themselves on Monday last. Marina stays here till we go to Town ; there is a call of the House on the 20th, which will oblige Papa to go.

Mr. Hayley and Tom come to-morrow ; he is going to place the Boy with Mr. Flaxman. Adieu—I envy Aunt and Louisa seeing you so soon.

Yoursever

M. J. H.

[1] Lord and Lady Pelham.

Serena to Maria Josepha.

Bath : January 28, 1795.

Thou dear Child. I cannot help venting a little of my delight at your letter received yesterday. You were all my own Maria when you wrote it, and every feeling of your heart was amiable while you were painting the dear and really charming woman with whom you had passed so happy an evening. A Blessing to us all, I do indeed agree with you, she will ever prove, and your sweet prayer that she may herself equally continue happy I most heartily join in, and trust there cannot be a doubt of. She is formed to attach every one to her, and just the Woman my Brother must ever love and esteem ; while you two will enjoy each other as cordial friends, in which there is so much comfort that in truth nothing can equal it. I look forward to more happiness than you have long known, for even to you I may say that she will love you the better the more she knows you. She will find that your ' brusqueries ' are only lip deep and on your sincerity she may now depend. Allow me to say too, my dearest Maria, that she will be of infinite use to you, for her manner, which though lively, is uncommonly playful, never a moment deviates from perfect feminine softness and elegance, will soften your sometimes too wild spirits. Never seeing a sharp angle you will take up the same tone insensibly, and then I may say, without flattery, that you will be a sweet companion and that I shall have little left to wish. . . . You will easily imagine how often Louisa and I wish we could fly to you and how much we talk of you. . . . I shall long to see the dear Lady and you presented. . . . Adieu dearest Maria. Beg of the dear Lady to love me, and to accept Louisa's and my most affect. wishes. Also to dear Sheff.

Yours ever

S. H.

Serena to Maria Josepha.

Bath: Sunday morning, February —, 1795.

I am sorry that Pap. could not make Mr. Pitt sensible about Franking. Not that I perfectly comprehend how far the evil will extend. The powder tax I confess appears a very good one. I only grunt over the wine as I already pay twenty-six shillings a dozen and do not approve of adding six more. Tell me, have you heard that Lord Howe's orders are such as to restrain all his motions? I was told that he and all his Officers were prevented acting when they had such opportunity, as to make them half wild at remaining inactive, and that the account came from an Officer on board one of his Ships. Hannah More, 'entre nous,' my Authority, who is not you know Anti-ministerial, and vouched it as 'pos' truth. . . . Why do you not tell of Sir J. Borlace Warren? We hope he has taken fifteen ships, and we intend that the King of Prussia should have drubbed the French handsomely. Pray confirm it . . . God bless you my child.

Serena to Maria Josepha.

Bath: March —, 1795.

. . . I wish I could persuade you to be very much tired of London at the time that I suppose Louisa to leave me, and that you could get some young friend you like to come with you to me in her place, for I confess I feel a Coward and want you to comfort me. I would do anything on Earth you liked best, or take any excursion, were it to the Antipodes to amuse you. I would seriously try to coax Mrs. Carter to let Harriet Clinton come, and I would pay your journey etc. Think about it and let me know if there is a shadow of hope for me. I rejoice the dear Lady has been out and hope she will soon regain her strength. Adieu, dearest of all Marias.

I am very sincerely yours

S. H.

Serena to Maria Josepha.

Bath : April 10, 1795.

And now before I talk of anything else I will answer about your coming and Louisa's going. Not in the remotest or most jaundiced corner of my heart could I ever take what you say as want of kindness to me. I am very sure if I was in a situation to make you really necessary to me, you would come, and with that belief what can possibly be so pleasant to me as your openness? It is the only thing that can give me ease in proposing schemes at any time and, most assuredly, I could not enjoy your giving up the pleasantest time in London. . . . She (Louisa) is now past eighteen. On the whole I do really wish her to be four or five weeks in London to see her friends, and in short to have some of the advantages of her father's House, and Lady Sheffield's society as well as yours.

Maria Josepha to Serena.

London : May —, 1795.

I am going to make my Début to-night at the Marchioness of Buckingham's which is to be a superb Ball, on the approaching Marriage of Lord Temple and Lady Ann Eliza Bridges, and to which I hear, between 900 and 1,000 people are invited.

I expect to be much amused with the various extraordinary figures I shall see. I have not yet seen a Crop, except walking in the Streets; when, their Hats being on, the full Quizzism of the thing is not displayed. Lady Auckland is so good as to take me; her two eldest girls are just presented and look beautiful.

The West India Fleet at last has had fair winds for its setting out and I hope will have no more obstructions. Adieu till to-morrow. No—one word about the 'Memoirs.' They are hastily drawing to a conclusion. I suppose there cannot be more than twenty pages wanting to finish the second volume. Papa always intended you should have a copy. I am sure it will interest and amuse you, more than anybody, except just ourselves. You will be at home on every page.

Yours most truly,
M. J. H.

Maria Josepha to Miss Ann Firth.

London: Friday morning.

We returned from Lady Buckingham's at five this morning, and I have only time to say it was a very fine Ball, and for a fine one, pleasant, as I met a great number of people I knew. There was a great number of Beauties and a great Crowd. Not a great number without Powder, but almost all with the Hair turned up behind and no Curls at the sides. Adieu.

Yours affectionately
M. J. Holroyd.

Friday.

To-morrow we dine at Sir Joseph Banks, go to the Opera Concert, Lady Galloway's assembly and Almack's. My lady does all but the last. I go with Lady Rothes.[1] I have been frequently to the Opera this year, which is a great treat to me.

I have not time to add much as I did not wake till half past one, and ever since I began dressing I have been interrupted by various and sundry people coming, to whom I appeared in my deshabille ; among the rest my Uncle and Aunt Greg (Gregory Way) whom I had not seen for several years.

[1] Sister of Lucy, Lady Sheffield.

Maria Josepha to Miss Ann Firth.

London: May 12, 1795.

My dear Miss Huff,—I have indeed been as gay as possible this Winter and since Easter, particularly so. I had a delightful pleasant Ball at Sir J. Coghill's on Wednesday where I danced nine dances without stopping a minute, and came home between five and six without feeling tired; tho' I had been in the morning to Carlton House, and we had Company to Dinner, and an Assembly to go to first. I had not been before to Carlton House, as we waited, thinking there would be less crowd the second day than the first. Only a few are admitted at a time into the Room where the Princess is, and when they have been presented, they pass on; therefore, there is no pushing and squeezing as at St. James'; and as the Company move on thro' the Suite of Rooms and none are suffered to return, if the numbers are ever so great, they cannot be as troublesome, as they all move forward the same way. The Presentation is the most formidable business possible, so much so, that neither My Lady nor I had the least idea what the Princess had on, or what the room was like, tho' a slight View showed it very magnificent. Alas! Poor Woman! she has probably too often wished herself in a less splendid dwelling. The P's behaviour is . . . but it would be endless to repeat half the stories that are told. . . .

The East India People are going to give a Great Ball to Mr. Hastings which I hope I shall go to. I was at the Tryal the day sentence was passed and wished much you had been there, having been such a constant and eager attendant at the beginning of it.

Adieu, my dear Miss Huff.

Ever affectionately yours,

M. J. H.

Y

Almacks was a good Ball; but not quite so pleasant as the last, from there being more people. I danced only with the gentleman about whom you make so many enquiries. I am very sorry to inform you that he is an Irishman; in the Law, but without a single Penny; but very pleasant and does vastly well to fill up my time in the flirting way, as he has all the disposition possible for it; but any further I have not considered the matter. You made me laugh with your solicitude about him, and I hope on your return to Bath you three Dowagers will lay your heads together about it and talk wise. Louisa has never honoured me with a single observation on the subject, which has disappointed me very much as I thought she would be sagacious on the occasion.

I must conclude, but I cannot help telling you what a favourite Mr. Tennant is, both in Lord Pelham's family and this. Thank my stars! My Lady has gained the point of having him as the 'Apoth' of the family instead of Mr. Farquhar. Adieu.

Serena to Maria Josepha.

Bath : Tuesday, June 9, 1795.

You are a dear Soul, and are always attentive to me in time of need. Your letter has really done me more good than anything else could, and I love you for the thought. Three years and a quarter never having had dear Louisa out of my sight, and so often requiring care, I may as well confess what you would know without it, that it is like tearing a Polypus out of my heart, root and all, and that I feel like Jacob, bereft. . . . As soon as I recovered my Stupor yesterday I took such an Antipathy to everything round me that I went and shut myself below stairs where I never sit, and I rejoiced sulkily in the rain that nobody might call, tho' I was sorry for the

poor travellers. . . . Bull chose to have everybody uncomfortable and therefore took poor Tuft[1] to be washed.
Then, because I left the drawing-rooms, she took up
carpets, etc., and made a compleat bustle. I thought I
should like it, but it made me worse. I had a letter to-
day from G. Coxe [Rev.] dated just as he landed in Ireland
after a passage of eighteen hours. Tell dear Louisa I
hope to hear she is good and happy the moment she sees
you. Bull says the whole house is dismal. I am sending
her and William Foley to the Play to-night to comfort
them.

Serena to Maria Josepha.

Bath: July —, 1795.

I had a letter from Ireland yesterday from G. Coxe,
who says that in one day he had rode forty miles, travelled
in a coach twelve, and afterwards danced from eight
o'clock till Four. If I did not suspect him of ' Zigzag,' I
should suppose him crazy as he has just sense enough to
imagine I may do. He is living gaily at other people's
houses, tho' attending his Church, where the Congregation
daily encreases and the people all civil, etc. He says
that in the neighbourhood of Kelly, about ten miles from
him, the ' Defenders' are again very daring; burning
houses; laming cattle and roasting people alive; harrassing
the Military who are night and day out; but do not seem
in their hearts much against them. I beg leave to write
' Zig ' under the roasting part of his story, though he says it
is literal fact. I dare say he was told it.[2] We want to
make a subscription here to enable the Bakers to give
bread cheap to the Labourers' families and the poor
industrious, but it is not easy to prevent impositions.

Adieu, dearest of Marias.

[1] Lady Sheffield's dog, adopted after her death by Serena.
[2] Witch-burning having taken place in 1895 in Ireland, this story may
be true.

Y 2

Serena Holroyd to Maria Josepha.

Bath: July —, 1795.

Though I have taken no notice of it, I was not in-sensible to Sheff's motions in Parliament. I approved Mr. Pitt's coincidence. Also of the Honourable mention and recourse to last year's Exchequer bill business, of which he was Chief. Sheff may well hold me cheap as to Politics in general, but I don't allow him to suppose me torpid where he is interested.

My great Garden is, I assure you, full of sweet roses of various kinds, though I am actually cold over a large fire. There is a most unpleasant sharp dry air that shrivels my poor old flesh and freezes my blood. You will all be warmer in the good house at S. P., which is now no small advantage. Adieu, dear good thing. Love to all.

Yours Ever,

S. H.

Maria Josepha to Serena.

[Fragment concerning Wheat and Flour.]

July 5, 1795.

He, Papa, gave each of the Workmen a 6d. loaf of it, at first, and they all agreed that it was very good—indeed, I prefer it to the white. The Parish pays all above 8s. a Bushell; and Papa has sent the Millers everywhere they could think of, and given them money for the purpose as the Farmers would take only ready money. It is really a pleasant idea that he may have preserved a considerable district around us from the probable dangers of famine in that article at least, and of riot in consequence. I expect some of the considerable people in the adjoining parishes will be indignant at his interfering; but they were asleep till he roused them; the essential good he will have done makes that of little consequence.

Maria Josepha to Serena.

Sheffield Place: July 8, 1795.

. . . It is such a sudden transition from the bustle of a crowd to the total retirement of Trees and Crows. Perhaps you will swear at me for this, and perhaps you would swear still more if I acknowledged the total change I feel in myself as to the interest and affection I always had for this place.   Indeed, it is the only different sensation I have since the Event, and it is much better it should be so considering what may happen.   I love the dear woman too well to feel anything disagreeable towards her for being the cause, and I am sure I shall love her Monkeys when they come; but I cannot delight in my walks as I used to do.

Don't scold or grumble.   Indoors I bless the change, for we do not know what it is to be out of humour, or to stamp like a sheep.   Therefore I am more than satisfied, but when I write to you I cannot help turning myself inside out, and telling everything as it comes into my head. . . . I do not mean to make you a compliment, but I must say I know no one but you, who go round about and round about and coax me first into a good opinion of oneself, and then always end with making one sensible (though God forbid! I, for one, should ever acknowledge it, at the time) that one has not common sense.   It is very disagreeable that you would not come to us this summer.   I should have liked to talk to you every now and then, and Bounce thinks it right too, for he very often stops at your door to enquire if I am going in.

You will repent, I am afraid, of poking me up to write to you, for now I have begun you see there is no end of it.   I rather thought as how we should have had a bit of an Epistle to-day, so I write out of spite to bore you.

Adieu, dear old Aunt. I wish I was with you now by means of a Balloon, and then Papa would bring me back in August.

Yours ever affectionately,

M. J. H.

Maria Josepha to Miss Ann Firth.

Sheffield Place: July 9, 1795.

. . . There is now with us, a Mr. Van Couver[1] who would entertain you very much. He is making an agricultural Tour through Sussex, and seems a very sensible, well-informed Man. He has a considerable tract of Land in America, where he has lived several years and has visited several other Countries, from whence he seems to have brought away in his memory many curious and entertaining circumstances.

The Emigrants you see, are safely and easily landed on the Coast of Brittany; to have succeeded in their debarkation, they must have friends in the Country, but whether in sufficient force to enable them, when joined, to do anything of consequence, remains to be seen. I shall be impatient for further accounts from thence.

The Pelhams propose us a visit on Monday, and Mylord and Mylady mean to return it on Thursday, which is the day of the Quarter Sessions at Lewes, but leave us and Theresa Parker[2] and Miss M. etc. in possession of the house. Our Races this year are very late—not to begin till August 6. My time is expired.

Yours most sincerely,

M. J. H.

[1] Of Vancouver's Island.

[2] Sister to Lord Boringdon. One of the brightest and wittiest of M. J. H.'s girl friends.

Maria Josepha to Miss Ann Firth.

Sheffield Place: July 19, 1795.

My lord and My lady went to Stanmer last Thursday and returned on Sunday. He went for the Quarter Sessions at Lewes. The Prince sent to ask the Pelhams to the Pavilion one of the evenings, and hearing of our people being there, sent a second messenger to invite them; and accordingly they all went. They did not meet anybody but those belonging to the Household; played at Cards; and were amused by the Musick in which the Prince bore a part. She, poor little Creature, is, I am afraid, a most unhappy Woman; her lively spirits, which she brought over with her, are all gone, and they say the melancholy and anxiety in her countenance is quite affecting.

There is a prospect of a Curacy for William Way,[1] which if he can get will be delightful; he is hardly of age to be ordained, but he hopes it is possible to persuade some kind Bishop to look over that defect and ordain him, in which case he would be quite happy. . . . The Gibbonian Memoirs go on swimmingly. I really think one sees Daylight, and that they will appear before the Extinction of Arts and Sciences in this Country. If they do, there can be no doubt of the Pleasure and Instruction they will give all sorts of readers. Adieu. Louisa is writing.

Serena to Maria Josepha.

Cheltenham : August 1, 1795.

Yesterday, between the hours of four and five, Mrs. Holroyd, Miss Bull and Mr. Tuft arrived at Cheltenham

---

[1] 'Mr. William Way played Backgammon for twenty-four hours at a sitting, rising a loser of 10,000*l.*' See memorandum on Downman's portrait of W. Way.

where they were most kindly welcomed by Aunt and Harry (Mrs. Carter and Miss Harriet Clinton). The country most beautiful the whole way and perfectly new the last two stages—ergo, a great treat to my sight. The corn looking remarkably fine and strong, though I am afraid last night's heavy constant rain must subdue it. Just after I got out of the Chaise at Rodborough Inn, I had the pleasure of seeing the springs compleatly break down, and felt what an escape I had. Had I just then broke my neck and wakened in the next world I should have gone out of this with my mind in a transport at the beauties of Nature, for indeed within some miles of Rodborough it is enchanting, and the eighteen miles on this side seem a continual fine wood, &c. Miss Mellish passed the evening with us and looked quite pretty without powder, in one of the new little cap bonnets. I should have slept well last night, but that those poor creatures the Emigrants at Quiberon, and all our disasters got so into my head that I could not help being uncomfortable. I dread the event at Quiberon may have other consequences, for those traitors may betray things here, that might as well not be known perhaps. I long to know what the future designs will be, or if all must not now be given up for the Royalists. Also the State of the West Indies terrifies me; but I will say no more on such subjects. Hannah More's last Ballad is an excellent one, 'The Riot, or half a loaf better than None.' I rejoice you are all going to Lewes; but I hope dear Lady will not do too much. I do not admire her squeezing six in a Coach. Love to all dear Sheffs.

Ever truly yours,
S. H.

Maria Josepha to Serena.

Sheffield Place : August 2, 1795.

The Banks family came on Sunday. The Ladies, as usual, visited Mrs. Newton, and Sir Joseph and Papa the Wool Fair at Lewes on Monday. . . . The Red Ribbon has made no alteration in Sir Jo. in any other respect than that there is a red ribbon across his waistcoat. He sprawls upon the Grass, kisses Toads, and is just as good humoured a nondescript of an Otaheitan as ever. . . .

I assure you Mr. Jekyll is too great a favourite here, to be mentioned in that very contemptuous manner with impunity. I do really think him one of the pleasantest and most entertaining companions I ever met with. For an Acquaintance he is inferior to none for pleasantness, and as far removed from a vulgar Irish Wit as anybody I know. You cannot think how he won even Lady Pelham to like him. I wish you had been here last Tuesday, you would have acknowledged yourself entertained.

Papa had a little bit of a letter from the Governor of Dominica to-day, but written before his Deed was done I suppose, as he does not mention it. You will see from the Papers he has repulsed the French from his Island. . . . I wish he may be safe from further attacks ; but with such a Ministry as ours, never sending out succours till everything almost is lost, there is more to be feared than hoped.

Theresa Parker to Maria Josepha.

Deans Year : September 1795.

. . . I flatter myself that Counsellor Jonquill [Jekyll] will not revisit you till after the Stanmer family have left. . . . You know one might as well attempt to analyze an acid and an alkali in effervescence as to tranquillize

you in his company.   I hope that said Counsellor will not
go to Sheffield Place, as I should really feel *too* envious.

H. Hamilton, Governor of Bermuda, to Maria Josepha.

My dear Lasses,—My Directress is very much bent
on going to England, her health and mine require a
change of Climate.   Know ye that she was born in
England (Bath) and is not of the Gingerbread hue of a
Creole.   The kind letters she has received from my
kindred are a strong inducement.   I have sollicited leave
at a Peace, for I am still enough of the ' Vieux Militaire '
not to consult my own ease only.   D—— the French !   I
have been so over-enraged at the execrable deeds of those
Satanic people, that almost they persuade me to be no
Christian.   That infernal wretch our Neighbour Victor
Hugues has lately given some specimens of the sweetness
of his disposition, which place the Savages of America in
a very fair point of view.   But I won't sicken you with a
detail of his many infamies—two I select—and the last I
think less odious and cruel than the first.   He ordered
two Ladies, Whites, of Guadaloupe, to be chained with
black slaves and worked with them.   An old woman near
80 having been denounced to him for saying her prayers,
he sent for her and questioned her if the report was true.
She answered that from her youth up she had been in the
practice of addressing her Adoration to the Creator ; that
she continued to do her duty in the same manner; that
at her advanced age it would ill become her to swerve
from the service of her God.   ' À la Guillotine ! ' and she
was executed.   Is Hell warm enough for such a Miscreant ?
People tell me I am to be transferred to Guadaloupe if it
should be conquered.   Well ! I have been a rolling stone
for forty-one years, perhaps I may rest and rust there.
Let me have some months at least to pass with my

friends and then I will resign all thoughts of Europe. Such a resolution may appear to you young people too gloomy, but you forget your Father and I are contemporaries : he is a year only younger than I am, and yet the fellow has had (like me) the audacity to marry.

Yours while you behave well,
H. HAMILTON.

Serena to Maria Josepha.

Bath : September 3, 1795.

When you left me I retired to my sopha for an hour to meditate and compose myself for a walk. Tell dear Louisa that we shall get tipsy drinking her health, this being her birthday. Mrs. Bull's first salutation to me was a remembrance of her. William Foley gave me to understand that being in a livery was unbecoming his future hopes of being raised in the World by some fair one falling in love with him . . . so we have agreed to part when I get one to suit me. I think I give no bad wages in giving sixteen guineas besides cloaths.

Serena to Maria Josepha.

Bath : September 6, 1795.

I last night heard of Charette having destroyed eleven Thousand and having himself lost sixteen hundred. Miss Hunt got the letter from Honiton. It was written by a young officer on board 'Lord Bridport' and could not yet be officially known. It was added that the War was carried on in the most savage way on both sides. . . .

Serena to Maria Josepha.

Bath : September —, 1795.

Miss Cambridge and many Honorables are to subscribe for Madame D'Arblay's, *alias*, Miss Burney's new Novel for her and her Husband's and Son's support. I must give my Guinea. Will you send a few from your house. To be paid on subscription. It would be pretty, though I confess I am more disposed to buy Bread.

Mrs. Lyon has just now written to tell her son of the friend she would be united to if he has no objection, and she thinks it very generous for a Man to allow his hopes to rest on a Boy's decision. There can be no answer to this in less than three months, but if there are good accounts of her son sooner I do not suppose her lover will stay abroad so long.

Love to dear Lady S. and so God bless my dear loves of every sort. Amen.

Yours ever and ever.

S. H.

Maria Josepha to Serena.

Sheffield Place : September 20, 1795.

. . . I wish you had not been the most ill-tempered of all Bath Dowagers, for it would have been so delightful to have had you done by Mr. Edridge. I wish you could contrive to be miniatured. I hope you will like Louisa's. Everybody as yet who have seen it quite squall at the resemblance. I own I did not expect anything near so like. . . . He has copied Sir Joshua's Picture of Papa for Miladi very well indeed. I am sure his Image will be scattered over the Land, few people have been more frequently depicted. . . .

At Stanmer, in Tom's Room, I met with a compleat Edition of Rousseau, by which means I had an opportunity of gratifying my curiosity about several of his works I had never seen. A Volume of Letters is delightful. I wish you could get it, and read four Letters of his to M. de Malesherbes containing an Apology for his Style of Life etc., much of which is in the 'Confessions,' but some new and all I think much better told : and likewise two letters to M. de Luxembourg written from Molier Travers, near Neufchâtel, giving such an account of the Country, as is enough to make one distracted, ' on peu s'en faut.' As you are a sort of tamed Enthusiast, I think you are quite fit to read these Letters. The weight of Years and Wisdom upon you will prevent the sad effect above alluded to, and yet the native phrensical imagination you are possessed of, will enable you to taste the Description and Style. Ask Orontes if he has ever read the two last mentioned Letters. I should think they would make his Eyes come quite out of his head with opening them so wide, for I believe as how he has a Soul and· Heart, (which I think helps the Soul upon these occasions very much) to enter thoroughly into the remembered beauties of Switzerland. Adieu.

Yours ever and ever.

M. J. H.

Maria Josepha to Miss Ann Firth.

Sheffield Place: September 22, 1795.

. . . Louisa and I returned home from Stanmer the Tuesday after I wrote last, and we passed our time very pleasantly ; though I still think S. P. a more agreeable place of abode, I am much more at home at Stanmer than I was, both with the place and people, which is natural it should be so, now we are more acquainted ; and likewise, the stronger my affection becomes for the dear Lady, which indeed every day must increase, the more I feel disposed for her sake to like her friends and Relations, and to be pleased in their company. . . . Louisa and I remain here during Milady's confinement. Mr. and Mrs. G. Pelham passed a few days here last week. Mr. Stanley, of the Cheshire Militia, likewise Mr. Jekyll dined and slept here, one night, and we expect him again to-day to dinner ;

he was in one of his most entertaining humours when last here.

Tommy Partingdon and Mr. West came last Friday; the latter left us next day, but little Tommy is here still and I really think he must have some design upon Louisa or me, by his long visit, but I cannot at present inform you which. All the Stanmerites came on Saturday, Mr. Sec. Pelham with them, who was very pleasant, and meant to stay here till next Friday, when alas! on Sunday night arrived an express from Lord Grenville, to inform him his Majesty required his services to go to Vienna, and he left us early yesterday morning.

Mr. Edridge who painted me for Harriet and began a Drawing of Miladi in Town, has been here, near a fortnight. He has finished the drawing and it is certainly like, though not as pleasing a resemblance as some he has taken. He has copied Sir Joshua's Milord, very well indeed, and made a miniature of Louisa, so like, it is impossible to look at it without laughing, not having omitted her stoop, which in a painting is more picturesque than if she was more erect. I hope Aunt will be satisfied with it; we are all much pleased. My turn is to come next. Miss Pelham is sitting at present for a drawing as a companion to that of Mr. P. which you saw, and which has been copied for Milady. She, (the latter) is likewise sitting for a Miniature, which she means for Emily. Mrs. Lyon is at Bath and so is G. Coxe and the Trio seem to be constantly together.

Aunt has not been so well, I think, since I was with her, as she was at that time. She talks of not sleeping and not being able to walk far, but she rides double, which I hope will be of service to her. Mrs. Gibbon, from her account, appears to be growing so much weaker, that if it is possible for her to die I should think it must happen soon. I saw her three times while I was there, and never was in any person's company I thought more entertaining and cheerful than her.

The Harvest has been got in without a drop of Rain, and the Crop of Oats, which from being sown later, did not suffer from the cold and wet of last Winter, so much as the Wheat, is so considerable about us, that Papa has found difficulty in putting it all in his Barns. One field of twelve Acres in Coleham, and another at the bottom of the Lane going to Fletching produced four Load per Acre, which is nearly double the usual quantity. I hope the Wheat being got in without the least Injury, will compensate for the Crop not being so great, as might be hoped for, and I think people are pretty well disposed to make use of substitutes. Potatoes come in aid extremely well; our bread is one third made of them, and there cannot be better bread when pains is taken about it. Adieu.

Yours ever affectionately
M. J. HOLROYD.

Maria Josepha to Miss Ann Firth.

Sheffield Place : September 30, 1795.

To my very great satisfaction and pleasure, Emily[1] got an unexpected leave to accompany Milady (her sister) to Town. I wish them all home again, though to do our powers of amusing ourselves and one another justice, the two days that have passed since they went, have flown away so quick, every hour that struck and every Meal that came before us appeared to be premature.

Mr. Pelham declined the Post I mentioned, and is to return to Ireland, which all his friends wished him to do, as if he once engaged in the Embassy line, a man of his Abilities never would be suffered to remain quietly at home, and he would be eternally sent about from Court

---

[1] Pelham.

to Court.   Lord Camden likewise begged him to continue with him so earnestly, another winter at least, that he could not quit him, at present.

I am surprised we have no accounts of the landing of the Comte d'Artois.   Henry Clinton sent us an account of the only news that has arrived from General Doyle, which was dated the 18th, and they were next day to attempt landing on the Island of Noirmontier, which they expected to be very easy as the French force there was very small.   Puiṣaye had deserted from us; his friends gave out he was only going to rouse the Chouans in la Vendée.   This is the man who had chiefly the command of the last Expedition.   They are a sad set of Vagabonds, Emigrants and Republicans, to be sure, it must be allowed.

Mr. Edridge left us on Monday, having finished the drawing of Mylady begun in London, the figure of which was better than the face; made a drawing of Miss Pelham excessively like; copied that you saw of Mr. P.; copied Sir Joshua's picture of Papa in miniature for Milady; painted an excellent Miniature of her for Emily, which he is to copy for me, and painted Louisa's and my Picture for Aunt—so that he carried off a good many Guineas.   I like the Style both of his Drawings and Miniatures very much, and shall be impatient to know how Aunt approves them.

Our Butler, Mr. Foy, seems a very civil, well-behaved Man, though an Irishman.   Don't you remember attacking his Lordship for his prejudices about the poor man's Country?   The Housekeeper, who is a high-spirited Dame, has plagued poor Milady with quarrelling most vehemently with Mr. Foy, but I think at present she is a little calmed.

The Memoirs are in a progressive state, and I should hope Papa's being in Town may help to forward the

Publication, as Printers are people who want much spurring.

Milady has taken nobody to Town with her but Mrs. Quin and the Kitchen Maid. Mrs. Q. I think will not stay long; and I am sure I hope not, she is as idle in the way of work, as it is possible—even the gentle Lady is frequently finding fault with her, which she does not take good humouredly; and she is much too pretty in my opinion, and knows it too well. Adieu.

Yours ever affectionately,
M. J. H.

Lady Sheffield to Maria Josepha.

Privy Gardens: Tuesday, October 20, 1795.

. . . I send you some Gloves. Your Clogs and your Satin are likewise sent. And now, My dearest Puss, I am going to ask a favour, which if you grant you will doubly encrease every comfort you have already so tenderly assisted in procuring for me; and add very much to the satisfaction and pleasure the Dearest of Fathers feels in your sweet and constant attention to me. It was my Idea, from thinking it an attention I owed to Dearest Aunty that she should be sollicited to answer for my poor little dear Babe if it should live to become a Christian (jointly with Mama), as there is nothing uncommon now in having Four whether a Boy or a Girl. I find by what I have endeavoured to collect, that Dearest Aunt and the Good Dear Man will be both as well, and the latter better, pleased if you would undertake it. I had a sweet and dear letter from Bath on receipt of the Pictures, and from what she says I think it would be more gratifying to her not to be answerable the first, but stand the chance of a second opportunity rather than that I should not have the comfort of your being one of them. My intention therefore is that if it is a Lord Herbert, the Sponsors

should be my Father, Yourself, and another Man and
Aunty. The Gentleman seems to think Uncle Way
would not like the office. If a Queen Mab, my Brother,
Mama and you. Both ways I hope to have the Dearest
Puss, so let me know what you like about it now I have
told you what we shall be delighted with. I have not
seen Lady Shelley, as I am positively forbid the Streets,
they have not been new paved, and some Carriages have
been actually overturned from the badness of the Pavement. What a Shame! Bless you, Dearest. Once more
Adieu. The Dearest Dear Man desires his Love and
Blessing to the Dear Bratts, and wishes they would let
him know how the Weir looks, and whether the Water
falls over the Bay properly.

Good night, and love me as your sincerely and truly
affectionate

LUCY SHEFFIELD.

Maria Josepha to Serena.

Sheffield Place : October 23, 1795.

Harriet and I dined, dressed and slept at Mrs. Luther's
on Tuesday for the convenience of going to the Ball at
Brighton with less Trouble. Lady C. Strutt took us, and
I found it an uncommon pleasant evening, partly I
believe because I had not formed any great Expectations
of pleasure. The D. of York and his Suite left
Brighton the morning before the Ball, of course none of
them were there. I danced before Supper with Mr.
Stanley of whom I think you have heard before. He was
here for a couple of days not long ago and I had the Good
Fortune to have him as my Supper Partner. His conversation is of such a different sort to that of young men
in general, and we conversed upon such a variety of
subjects, that I never passed two or three hours at a Ball
more pleasantly, and my ci-devant Flirt Mr. Miller with

whom I danced afterwards seemed considerably lessened in my eyes by comparison. We returned home at five o'clock.

My lady has expressed her wish that I should be one of the Sponsors for her Babe be it Male or Female, as it is no uncommon thing to have four, Lady Pelham the other. She desires it as if she were requesting such a favour that I am rather pleased she sees it in that light, as it gives me an opportunity of obliging her ; but it was my wish before she mentioned it, though I thought it was not the thing, to offer myself, or at least was doubtful about it : but if I had not thought about it, I should like it, from both her and Pap wishing it. I expect a long letter soon. Your last to Louisa was received in my absence and committed to the care of Vulcan before my return ; because I suppose there was some moralizing in it.

Yours ever truly
M. J. Holroyd.

Serena to Maria Josepha.

Bath : October 25, 1795.

The soldiers are all manœuvring and firing at such a rate in the field just behind my Garden, that I am jumping and shaking all over every moment. I wish they would spare their powder. As to the subject on which you reason rationally, I am not sure I quite agree with you. I do not think it a fair trial of a man's understanding his talking in a trifling manner situated as he was at the Coach Door before such witnesses. . . . You have never heard any unfavourable account of him from anybody. He is also in manners a Gentleman. He may rise in his profession, and I think dear H. has many disadvantages for so sweet a girl, which makes me wish her settled if it can be with tolerable prudence. You are a dear sort of a thing after all, and know yourself very humbly, but I would not give you the same Advice, for you would make a D—— of a Wife to a Man you could not look up to as high as a Steeple. It would require uncommon Sense and Temper to make a right impression on you, for which I humbly hope if you marry you will not be the Guide, because you could not be happy without preferring his judgment to yours. I give free consent to Mr. S. and a great deal more than consent for I would love him. If you meet again I wish I could be your invisible Sylph to check some things. You should have all your own powers of pleasing without your impetuosity and thoughtlessness. You should be animated without losing softness or delicacy, you should never show feelings you ought not to express. The Man who thinks of a Wife is, believe me, a very strict observer, however he may seem enamoured. Could I but make you quiet and above fluttering at the notice of an agreeable Man, you would be as near my wishes as you well could be. Dearest of dear Marias, do love me enough to think seriously of conquering these points in yourself. Believe me, near as you are to me I have not escaped being told of these faults as being so far against you as to prevent Men being more than partners for a time. What pity with all Nature has done for you! God bless you! Your happiness is very essential to making me like this little Globe I assure you. Give love to dear Louisa and Miss P.

Ever and ever yours
S. H.

Lady Sheffield to Maria Josepha.

Privy Gardens : October 24, 1795.

The Trio in Privy Gardens are still in good Preservation. . . . .

I suppose you have seen in the Gazette that the Title

of Loughborough is granted to all the Erskine Family. Be so good as to say we desire if all the Turkeys and Geese are not eat, that Mrs. Harrison will sometimes send them up to us, as we cannot live upon the half Sheep she sends once a week, and as to the Pheasants they do nothing towards keeping the Family. Veal in London is 10d. a pound. They must send things by the Coach as judiciously as possible, as they have just doubled the Carriage from 1sh. to 2sh. this year. The Coach waits to take us out an Airing, so must say Good-bye. God Bless the Dear Good Babes. Adio.

My Lord desires that pretty Poll will send up Five yards of the New Blue Cloth and he hopes Miss Harriet and the two Misses behave themselves perfectly well. He begs it may be announced to Fletcher that Hay is six Guineas a load in London and that he should not sell for less than 5l. or four Guineas and a Half.

Lord Sheffield to Maria Josepha.

Privy Gardens : Half-past twelve, Wednesday morning, Oct. 28, 1795. .

The most precious Woman is said to be safe. . . . The Doctor and all the Women declare they never observed such an Instance of fortitude and Patience in all their experience or a more painful case. The mother and son could not both be saved. I am perfectly satisfied that the dear Woman is safe. I only fear that she will be still more uneasy when she recovers strength. . . .

She now talks with great cheerfulness, but Brush will not allow her to talk even a minute with the dear Emily, who has proved herself as amiable as might be imagined on the occasion. The Coachman must return, but I send orders for John Joyney to carry a note to Stanmer, which should be there at half past eight as Lord Pelham is to come to Town this day to attend the reading of the King's Speech.

It is now half past one o'clock.

Serena to Maria Josepha.

Bath: October 30, 1795.

One little line in my Louisa's letter was a comfort you did not think of, because you did not know I had terrified myself about William Clinton, having been told that he and Genl. Doyle and L'Isle Dieu were fallen into the Devils' hands, and I believed it for a whole evening and night. Next morn it was contradicted, but I still felt anxious, so that your saying William was daily expected, gave the security I wanted. Oh dear ! Oh dear ! when will all fears cease of these Hydra Headed Monsters ? We are comforting ourselves with the hope that the Austrians at least will revenge themselves on the paltry King of Prussia. Poor Austrians ! they have acted bravely and suffered enough. I do wish them some compensation.

I had written quietly thus far, when some lines from dear Sheff, which it was truly good in him to send, have agitated me and will end my other subjects.

That the good amiable Woman is safe seems compleatly to comfort my Brother for the Death of the Babe, and he thinks of nothing but her Patience and her not being disappointed. I love him for it, as it is often the contrary in Men. Her life is truly precious to us all. . . . Mrs. Lyon got the most delightful Letter from her Son, dated Sept. 8, not only saying he was well, but giving the most perfect happy approbation to her intended Marriage, so that I hope soon to tell you all my secrets, tho' I am earnestly requested to be silent a little longer.

Maria Josepha to Serena.

Sheffield Place : November 1, 1795.

The King was at the Play on Friday, and most graciously received. 'God Save the King' called for and played three times. What a Situation the Country might have been in, if that Infernal Plot had succeeded, and as it is, the disposition of many people is very unpleasant. He was pelted returning from the House, and his Coach pulled to pieces on its return to the Mews.

The Isle Dieu Colonel has reason to be proud, so many hearts trembled for him last Sunday. Mr. Jekyll came here to Church, and told us the news with great satisfaction. He thought Opposition would meet Mr. Pitt with something to fling in his Teeth, and only think how disagreeable to have Blank Monday without a Post follow this information! What wretches Politicians are!

Serena to Maria Josepha.

Bath : Sunday morning, November 1, 1795.
Raining torrents.

Yesterday we exchanged letters, by which you will find that the news from Privy Gds. was sent me directly, and the next day was followed by a bulletin from Miss Pelham saying the Doctor found the dear Lady's pulse as well as if nothing had happened, which comfortable account was I hope the reason of my not hearing again yesterday.

This is the only subject almost that could take the place of the horrid attack upon the King. I can scarce yet recover the idea. I think nothing is clearer than the intention to murder him, and that it was to be the beginning of a General Revolution. Conceive the Confusion we might now be in had he not been providentially

saved, almost indeed miraculously. I must think that
the late Conventional Meetings were preparatory to this,
and in spite of Lord Lansdowne's Diabolical Surmises,
that it is a most serious business, but I hope it will be
taken up in such a manner in Parlt. as to make us more
secure than if it had not happened. I see my Brother
is one of the Committee on this business. How very
strange that the King should be left with only two
Servants after what passed, on going and coming from
Parlt. If he takes no precautions, others should. It is
so like the French Devils that all their horrors rise
into my mind and make me tremble. I take it for
granted you read the Debates, for they are even to me
now the most interesting, and I think Pitt's speech
beyond anything I ever read. I went thro' Sheridan and
Fox. Wit and abilities without a grain of worth or
reasoning. . . . This moment the post brings me two
delightful bulletins from Miss Pelham, that the dear
Lady was to rise to have her Bed made, eat chicken, etc.
Thank God! I now hope all danger over. I went to
the Post from Impetuosity. The man asked Five Pence,
and I gave it without observing my letters were franked.
What sense and Courage in the King to go to the Play,
and yet I feel frightened when I reflect on their tearing his Coach to pieces even after he was safe. I am
glad Sheff carries the Address. I wish all respectable
People to show loyalty at this critical moment. It makes
one wish for Military Government or even Despotism in
preference to such Liberty. We have had Rain enough
for a Deluge, and I have stayed two whole Evenings at
Home.   Yours Ever,
                                              S. H.

Maria Josepha to Miss Ann Firth.

Sheffield Place : November 8, 1795.

Did you not tremble for the probable consequences that would have followed, if the King's Life had fallen a sacrifice to the Diabolical Villains who attacked it? and don't you think he had shewn wonderful courage and coolness in pursuing his usual way of Life, going to the Play etc. as before. I heard that some of his Attendants wished to dissuade him from going to the Play the day after the first Attack, and that he answered that they might propose and expect, but that there was a Supreme Disposer of all things in whom he trusted for his preservation. I cannot think how the King can have any private enemies, as his private Character is excellent. . . .

Adieu. I have not time for more.

From Lady Sheffield.

Privy Gardens : November —, 1795.

My dear Dear Babes may be well assured that She who feels the Affection of a Mother for them will do all she can to hasten her return to them, but she must remember she has a good deal of strength to get up. The first time I have used a Pen is to say that I am

Most cordially and sincerely

The dearest Maria and Louisa's

Ever Tenderly Affectionate

LUCY SHEFFIELD.

Maria Josepha to Serena.

Sheffield Place : November 11, 1795.

What a comical Animal a good-natured Friend is, and what a propensity human creatures have to communicate bad news, are the two observations that occurred upon reading your letter. As Charity begins at home, I must wish your Friends and Acquaintances to employ you with a little Misery, because from my observations that you go plunging on, out of one, into another uncomfortable scene, I am perfectly convinced, if your Mrs. Lyons, Mrs. Byams, &c., were happy and so forth, that we S. P. folks should do something disagreeable to fill up the vacuum of your mind, and to furnish the supply of sorrowful food that is necessary to the support of your frame. But setting these excellent reasonings aside, I do feel very much for the poor Woman, and still more from thinking that Henry is so soon to run all these risks, and still more than that, for the dear old Aunt who is obliged to undergo comforting the Beastess, at the same time dreading the worst. I hope you will soon know what to hope or fear, as a state of uncertainty or suspense is of all situations the most horrid, and if in future the wicked ones are kept in a State of Purgatory, uncertain what is to become of them, I think the aid of the Great Prince will not be wanted to torment them further; and now we are flown from the subject I began with so far as the Nether Regions, we will return if you please.

Quick! as fast as you can, turn Heaven and Earth to get la 'Vie de Madame Roland.' We have just got it, and some Passages are Rousseau-like and find their way perpendicularly to one's heart. The strength of mind she shews is wonderful, and in every way, even in those parts to which you will not assent and in others in which you will be shocked, still I am certain you will find great entertainment and pleasure. After having said you will be shocked, I hope I shall not shock you, in telling you it is partly the recommendation and principally the subject of discourse of my dear Mr. Stanley at the Ball. It is true however that he said, if I read it, (when he found from what he had mentioned I was very near setting off from the Ball

room to get it) I had better get Lord Sheffield to point
out the Passages worth reading. Thinks I, if I wait till
then, Lord have mercy upon me! but I did not say so.
I stated very prettily that Milord had many avocations
both public and private, and that Milord instead of
reading, particularly as his eyes were not very good, liked
to be read to, etc. etc. So, at last, my gentleman came
honestly to confession, that if I was his sister, he should
say, 'Read the book and no harm will come to you ; but
that it would not sound the thing to talk of the work and
quote Mr. Stanley for the person who recommended it.'
So I have read it, do not feel much corrupted, and only
mention my recommender to you in confidence. I should
tell you there is nothing against 'les Mœurs'—tho' a
Frenchwoman, she never had an intrigue, at least 'avoué'
—but she gives a minute account of all her feelings, and
the dawning and progress of her opening mind. As she
is thoroughly 'naïve,' her descriptions may be of such a
nature as a gentleman would not exactly chuse to put
into a Lady's hand, at the same time that the mind and
heart will remain as pure as before the perusal. Now do
get it if you possibly can. There are four Pamphlet
Volumes. The 1st and 2nd are very curious, but more
political, the 3rd and 4th are her private Life and what I
particularly wish you to read and give me your opinion of.
I should like you also to read Mrs. Woolstencroff's
'Vindication of the Rights of Women.' There are
many sensible and just observations.

Maria Josepha to Serena.

Sheffield Place : Tuesday, — 15th, 1795.

I stand up Champion for Madame Roland's Purity
and Mr. Stanley's Propriety, so cruelly attacked by the
Venerable Bede in her last epistle. . . . I do not allow

there are any strong contradictions in her character. . . .
Have you got the two first parts of the work? though
they are political they are full as interesting, particularly
the account of her being arrested and her confinement
first in l'Abbaye, afterwards in St. Pélagie. . . . We are
now reading another publication of the same kind, 'Le
Recit de mes Périls,' par Louvet, who was 'mis hors la
Loi,' and pursued at the same time as Madame Roland
was, but had the good fortune to hide himself till the
overthrow of Robespierre. . . . Adieu, dear old Aunt.

Yours ever,

M. J. H.

Serena to Maria Josepha.

Bath : November 19, 1795.

Will you like to be told I have a blister on my back
which I put there last night for the whizzing which came
yesterday with as much violence as the first time at S.P.
I grew quite deaf with the noise. In the night I had a
real pleasant feel from fever. The blister pain gave me
spirits and made me rather delirious, and I was uncommonly happy singing the Easter Hymn and 104th
Psalm, and my want of voice was no impediment. It
shows the delight of a drunken Man. Adieu, dearest
Girls.

Yours Ever and Ever,

S. H.

Maria Josepha to Serena.

Hook [1] : Friday, November 21.

If ever I write again to the Dearest of all Aunts till I
have said my Alphabet in every Language I know, and
drank a Quart of Water, I will consent to feel as queer
as at this moment, because I shall deserve it. What can
I say, not to apologize, but to express what I would do or

[1] Mr. Poole's house.

give to recall yesterday's letter, or to erase it from your
Memory? I will only throw myself upon your Heart,
which knows mine under all its rubbish for the rough
Precious stone (am I much too vain?) that the Cock was
scratching for in the Dunghill. I have a great mind to
promise—I hardly dare write the word perform—that with
a little more scratching it shall appear in native Lustre.
At least at this moment I feel as if this Lesson would
remain in my mind. Indeed I shall be miserable till I
hear from you again. I am not afraid you will be angry,
but I dread your foolish head being so ridiculous as to be
vexed. I wish it was not in my power to vex you. But
I will add no more on this subject. Pray forget it easier
than I can.

[The naughty letter which caused Maria such remorse cannot be found,
and the burnt edges of the original of this one suggest the measures that
Serena took to close the episode.]

I have just received a dear letter from Lady Cremorne,
supposing me in London with Milady, and asking if I
have any Commands or Messages for Bath, where she is
going in a day or two. I must thank her myself for her
kind attention, though as she will see you I can have
nothing to tell her.

When you first mentioned a Domestic Worry I feared
Mrs. Bull was in it, as I thought you were not sufficiently
interested in the others to be worried by them. I am
very sorry upon her own account, and hope the Match is
not a very bad one, as her Health and spirits are not
calculated to struggle against difficulties.

Maria Josepha to Serena.

November 24, 1795.

I am quite delighted Mrs. Lyon has had so much
happiness at once, not that I ever doubted her Son

would do otherwise than give his hearty approbation ; yet it is pleasant all suspense is over. As to your weighty secret, it must either regard the confirmation of your Marriage, which you know I have suspected, or else something wonderful in regard to the Gentleman of Mrs. Lyon's choice. As you must know him now, why did you not tell me who it is, and whether it is anybody I ever heard of ? But you and Louisa are fond of Secrets where there is no occasion, at least in my idea. She is as impenetrable upon all subjects as an old experienced Lady of eighty, and I wish I had some secret of my own ; I would do my best to keep it from you both as a punishment for your various ' Cacheries.'

Never any astonishment equalled that of Mine, Louisa's, and Fanny's (but I cannot keep suspecting hers acted) as I think she must have seen it beginning, when we found who Mrs. Bull's Husband was. Poor woman ! what can happen to her but Misery, and perhaps Beggary, with such a Man, and how prettily she used to join in laughing at him and his Coxcombries. Well ! nothing is wonderful in the way of Marriages—and so I have said a hundred times, and yet I still wonder every day almost. What becomes of Mrs. ' Fooley ' ? [1]

We have just received Intelligence that Milord and Mr. Pelham are coming to dinner to-day in order to attend the County Meeting to-morrow at Lewes. . . . I shall postpone finishing this till to-morrow, in case the people from Town furnish me with anything to say.

Wednesday morning.

Oh ! what a delight to have two men in the House ! Seriously, it is so long since we have seen any person

---

[1] Serena's Housekeeper, Bull, passed into Maria Josepha's service in 1797. Her imprudent marriage to Foley was succeeded by two others. In spite of these interruptions she remained the devoted nurse of the family under the name of ' Moomie ' till her death, more than half a century later.

mixed in the world, that we had Fifty Thousand questions
to ask, and information without end to gain, since Emily's
letters are only bulletins and not chit-chat ones. I do
hope the dear Woman will be able to come soon now.
Doyle is not coming home, since he could not evacuate
the Island, (Isle Dieu) without leaving all his Stores
behind him, and Mr. Pelham, who has heard what is
settled at home in the Cabinet, says they are to remain
where they are, but are perfectly safe. It is possible
William may leave them, but I don't think probable.
'Uncle' Tom was uncommonly pleasant yesterday
evening, and they have so much 'égayéd' us that we
shall get our healths the better for a week to come.
They have just left us to attend the County Meeting and
prepare their Address.

Lady Webster has another boy, fortunate it is not a
girl. They talk of coming over in the spring. I daresay
I have a great deal more to say, but it does not occur in
the hurry and confusion of having had company.

Yours ever and ever,

M. J. H.

Serena to Maria Josepha.

Bath : Friday, November 27, 1795.

Well, you vile impatient Creature, I will tell you the
secret even before I am permitted, and all I lament is
that I cannot be in a corner to look at your Phiz, to hear
you scream your surprise etc., when I tell you that the
Rev. George Coxe is the Man. But I will suppose you
roaring, and will go on to tell you that I believe to-morrow
se'en night the Deed will be done. That no Soul save
his sister Harriet Bowdler, and myself know it at Bath.
That probably Hippogriffe will give her away, and after
breakfast she and her happy Husband will go to Bremerton,
which house is lent them for a week or ten days, and it is
reported that a certain Dowager who has carried on this

love business will be of the party.   Possibly to be met there by Lady Rivers. . . . The present scheme is to live at Bath in Church Street (with Miss Coxe of the party) till he fixes at some Living.   In the meantime he must go back and forward to Ireland.   I have been at Mrs. Gibbon's, and just as I came home first entered Lord Cremorne, and we talked politics, tête-à-tête, for half an hour.   Then came Sydney Smith, and talked sentimental till he was interrupted by Lady Cremorne, Lady and Miss Wake, and the Dawsons. . . . God bless you, dear Girls.   Many here send love.

Yours Ever,
S. H.

[The Rev. George Coxe married Mrs. Lyon, December 1795.]

Serena to Maria Josepha.

Bath : November —, 1795.

I allow you to be angry about my secret if you please, but I don't allow myself to be in the wrong.   It was not my own secret.   I will tell you whenever I am to be hanged or married.   I believe there are none but the Bowdlers in Bath that know of our intended wedding. It is to be next Saturday.   They breakfast with me; we then set out for Bremerton, my maid and his man in another carriage, Lady Rivers to meet us at Bremerton.

Serena to Maria Josepha.

Bremerton : Thursday, December 17, 1795.

We went one morn to look at Salisbury Cathedral and to Lord Radnor's for the sake of some fine pictures.   There are two Claudes reckoned the very best in the World, and some other beautiful Pictures.   As to the Claudes, I could have looked a year at least at them.   I never saw anything the least to be compared to them.   The place itself flat and ugly.   The House old, and nothing at the same time of the beauty of Antiquity about it. A very extraordinary steel chair of exquisite workmanship. Adieu, my precious Girls.

Dieu les Bénisse,

S. H.

Maria Josepha to Serena.

Sheffield Place : December 11, 1795.

Your letter was a very interesting account of Things, and notwithstanding all the affronts I have received, I do sincerely rejoice in the prospect of happiness that is before your ' bien aimé.' I wish I knew her, but indeed I feel as if I did know her. I have heard so much ' sur son sujet.' Your expedient of the Candle hint was excellent and very like yourself. I would not wish for any better contriver than you are, upon all intricate and delicate points.

And now for Madame Roland. I am delighted you have got her, and I hope you will not be disappointed in the pleasure I have promised you from her conversation.

Do tell me your opinion of the Book as you go on.

Have you heard Lady Audley's first Husband, Mr. Moorhouse, is risen from the Dead and returned to claim his Wife? or at least his Money, and as Lord A. married her for that, probably he will beg leave to part with both at once. Instead of being killed in the East Indies, he was taken prisoner by Tippoo, or some of those good folk, and has been exchanged or made his escape lately. At least, this is the story; I do not vouch for the truth of a single Syllable of it; not even the gentleman's return ! Adieu, dear old Aunt,

Yours Ever,

M. J. H.

Papa lives in the Board of Agriculture House of Commons and Corn Committee. I say nothing of politics,

A A

because they would be an endless Subject. But I suppose you have read the Bill against Seditious Meetings, and wondered how sensible Men could talk so much and say so little.

I have had a few lines from the dear old woman herself this morning, the first she has written. She says she is equally impatient to return as we are to have her, but she has a great deal of strength to recover.

Serena to Maria Josepha.

Bremerton, Salisbury : December 11, 1795.

Lady Rivers and Miss Coxe came as we expected on Monday. The latter goes on Tuesday to Bath to prepare for the Married Couple. We stay till Monday se'en night, and I believe if G. Coxe had his will we should stay a month longer. We are in truth all as happy as possible. That amiable woman seems most unaffectedly to accord in likings, dispositions, etc., with the family into which she has entered. All the family are pouring in presents to George and his wife. Aunt D'Aranda sends Twenty pounds to be laid out in Plate. Mr. Rivers 25*l.* for ditto. Lady Rivers brought a dozen teaspoons and tea-tongs new, costing four pounds, as a little keepsake. Sir Peter sends two dozen silver forks, and so on.

God bless you Both. Yours,

S. H.

Serena to Maria Josepha.

December 21, 1795.

We left Bremerton on Friday and went to Standerwick, a very sweet spot within nine miles of Bath—Mr. Edgells, old friends of Mrs. G. Coxe. When I got home I found a dear packet from my Children. Our Duchess of York (Crown Princess of Prussia), in spite of Dr.

Randolph's Oratory and his being Chaplain and favourite,
prefers the Queen Square Chapel because it is more like
going to Church and so quiet. She was so pleased with
Mr. Brisbane's Sermon that she asked to have it. She
paddles about the Streets sometimes alone in all the dirt
to seek out some poor that have been recommended, and
does good as privately as possible, and no less sensibly.
The Duke and she, arm in arm, go into shops together
and are not known, and are diverted making bargains.
A chairman heard her say she had no pin, or would pin
up her petticoat, and he took one out of his Coat and gave
her. She accepted it with a Courtesy, and used it
directly.

Maria Josepha to Miss Firth.

Sheffield Place : December 22, 1795.

What in the name of wonder is become of you ? It is
almost three weeks since we heard anything of you, and
a great deal more, since my own self had a Letter. I hope
there is one taking the Tour of England, or else I should
be afraid something was the matter with you. The dear
people arrived safe and well on Sunday, which I am sure
you will be glad to hear ; they left Town on Saturday
and slept that night at Mr. Snow's, about a Mile on this
side Godstone, and got to S.P. about four the next day ;
the dear Lady was not near so much fatigued with the
Journey, as I was afraid she would have been, and upon
the whole is better than I expected to see her. Thank
God ! she is here and I hope a few weeks will restore her
to her former strength. Papa says, and upon my word,
I believe sincerely at present, that he hopes she will never
have another child. I don't say so ; we allow her to have
a little girl, you know, and indeed I should be very sorry
if she should not. . . .

Sir Jonathan and Lady Cope dined twice at Hook

A A 2

the last time we were there. Her Ladyship is very agreeable and I don't wonder she should like Mr. Jekyll better than her clod of a good man.

Mr. Tennant is very well, but amazingly fat, Milady says. Mrs. Chapman, her nurse, who has seen the ways of a good many in his Line, says she never saw such attention and exactness in the manner of his sending out his medicines. I am very glad any relation of yours should be the substitute, but at any rate, I bless my stars that Mr. Farquhar is routed.

Yours very sincerely
M. J. HOLROYD.

Maria Josepha to Serena.

Sheffield Place : December 25, 1795.

I suppose you have been written to from Portland Place ? I would have written yesterday but I thought you would certainly have received information of the event, and when I had the melancholy Task of writing to poor Harriet I did not feel much disposed for any more. . . .

We are going on very nicely here. Dear Lady looks very well, and is tolerable. Mr. Woodward, Philip and George dine here to-day ; the Pooles to-morrow, and possibly the Rivetts, but we have not had an answer from them.

One little word for Madame Roland. I do not think you very prudish in general, but I do in this instance, because though it is indelicate and therefore would raise a blush if read in mixed company, I do not think it can have any bad influence on the mind and heart. At least I could not see anything seducive in her descriptions, merely laughable, but I perfectly agree with you, they had much better have been left out and that the Book, with a few omissions, might have been made unexceptionable. You do acknowledge, however, that you have been interested and amused which I am glad of. I cannot think what has become of Miss Firth. It is almost a Month since I heard from her.

Serena to Maria Josepha.

Bath : 1795.

It blew a Hurricane yesterday, so not being as strong as a Lioness I could not go to Mrs. Gibbon, but I sent dear Sheff.'s scrap which was *multum in parvo* and will I daresay have given the most perfect satisfaction.

Many many thanks for the kind thought of the dear Lady Sheffield intending to send me her hair which J shall value very highly indeed, as Louisa does the delicate little ring. You have sent Louisa's Lally play instead of mine, but I image I may suppose it mine.

The accounts of poor old Mother are not what I had any curiosity about. I meant those in Ireland of really forty years ago. *These* since she came to England can have nothing curious, tho' I am obliged for the intention. May I not burn them ?

Yours ever,

S. H.

Maria Josepha to Miss Firth.

December 31, 1795.

. . . I suppose that you have seen in the Paper Sir H. Clinton is dead. He is to be buried at Windsor in a family Vault, where the Duke of Newcastle was buried, and it is to take place to-day. He has appointed Papa as one of his Executors. . . .

CHAPTER XV.

1796.

'THAT SOMETHING MAY COME OF SOMETHING.'

JANUARY—APRIL,

Duke and Duchess of York—Brown bread and pottage—French guests—
Anxious times—Narrow escape of George III.—Publication of Gibbon's
Memoirs—London life—Mr. Stanley.

Serena to Maria Josepha.

Bath : January 1, 1796.

I **MUST** not wait till the post comes in, and will not
let this day pass without blessing my beloved Girls as
well as my dear Sheff and his Sweet wife.

How long are we to Mourn for Sir Henry ? I would
do as my Brother wishes. It used to be six weeks for
a first Cousin ; but I believe now not above half the time.
You, dear Child will receive this on your birthday, so that
it has to convey to you a double Blessing, and I trust to
dear Lady S. for giving you a Kiss, and a remembrance
from me with all the affectionate wishes my heart can
bestow. More indeed than I can find words for.

Maria Josepha to Serena.

Sheffield Place : January 3, 1796.

Your sweet ambassadress hastened her rising and
dressing this morning, to come herself to my room with
your dear present and performed all you would have said
and done, to a miracle. You are a dear old Mrs. Aunt,
and unless you could have given them to me your own

self, no substitute could have been more pleasant. I am very melancholic to-day, between Happiness and Sorrow. Something between the sentimental and sad; for myself I have nothing to wish but to preserve the Blessings I enjoy, and a few little, wise &cs. that will occur to you as necessary to my perfection. But I want the dear woman to be as well as she deserves to be; and endless wishes for those dear souls in Portland Place, the Clintons.

Serena to Maria Josepha.

Bath : January 6, 1796.

. . . I went yester morn into public, my first appearance. A concert for the benefit of Sunday Schools Industry, etc. It was requested that we of consequence should honour it with our Presence. The Duke, Duchess, and I of course went there at twelve, and stayed till three, listening to Catches and Glees of the prettiest sort; but beyond all things execrable singers, and I never saw anything so good humoured as the Duke and Duchess were the whole time. She is the sweetest little Woman, doing good everywhere. Giving no trouble or offence. Modest and yet not losing Dignity. Delighted with the privilege of walking with her Husband in all the dirt, and totally unattended except by five Dogs. They leave us next Saturday I understand; but I daresay they will come again as they like us, and are much liked.

Ever yours,

S. H.

Maria Josepha to Serena.

Sheffield Place : January 7, 1796.

Yesterday some people were not forgotten, dear old Mrs. Aunt, your health was drank, and many sentiments, if you understand that kind of toast, given on the occasion; and we were wondrous Merry, as the Song says.

Some hearts thought some comical things about you, too tedious to relate.

I hope no more of your friends have been ' fitty ' or anything like it.

The Fullers dined and slept here on Monday, and we played Pope Joan, Whist, and drank Punch, and such celebrities.

Serena to Maria Josepha.

Bath, Sunday Morn.: January 10, 1796.

Yesterday with great regret we lost our Duke and Duchess of York. Would she had a nice little girl like the Princess of Wales. In other respects, I believe her as happy as if she was not Royal, and her Husband truly fond of her. Sydney Smith asked me yesterday what I had done to gain Lewis Way's heart, for that there was no bounds to his partiality, and said that after enumerating my many virtues, he finished by saying, ' in short She is amongst Women, what the Dean of C. Church is amongst Men.' Louisa, who knows Sydney Smith will imagine how he looked in repeating this amongst us all. I am sure I am not conscious of your cousin's doing me so much honour, tho' I like to be thought well of by all your connections. . . . This evening we are to celebrate Mr. Pepys' Birthday with a Supper at Mrs. Hartley's, because it was he that made us all (Coxes, etc.) acquainted with her.

Adieu dearest Maria, Yours Ever,

S. H.

Maria Josepha to Miss Firth.

January 17, 1796.

Catherine Fanshawe, who gave Aunt a great alarm some time ago, is again relapsed, and very ill. Aunt is always getting into one Melancholy scene or other.

Mrs. Bull, alias Foley, after all the trouble and vexation Aunt had about getting her out of Bath to avoid her husband, has returned there, I suppose, to him.

We were in hopes Colonel Way and Parson Way would have been here at Christmas ; but the former could not get leave of absence from Portsmouth, and the latter, who had just cut off his Tail and taken orders, has been doing duty at Denham and Hedgerley, and was not allowed to stir. We passed the time very pleasantly while the Clives were here. We took fine long walks, she, I and her brothers ; indoors we play Battledore, Chess, and amused ourselves so well, that I had no time for anything else.

We talk and hear of nothing but Corn. Papa made a long and sagacious Speech at the Quarter Sessions on Friday upon the subject of scarcity, and the measures to be taken in consequence ; adding a little abuse of the Millers who refuse grinding and selling the whole Flour except to Gentlemen's Families, who particularly order it—by which means all the Gentlefolks eat Brown Bread and Mixtures, while the Poor feed upon the Whitest Flour, and can get no other. There has been a great alarm in this neighbourhood lately that all the Corn was going upwards. Some people have come down and bought all they could get from the little Farmers, giving three Guineas p^r Load more than the Millers here offer ; and then carry it to London, which is a bad business ; and there is no means of preventing it, but by giving an immoderate price. Papa is selling all his Wheat at the rate of 16 P^{ds} to all the Poor who he puts upon his List. It would never hold out for all the Inhabitants of this Parish. We have got some Receipts for Making Pottage of Bones and the coarsest pieces of Meat, which is very nourishing and excellent, the Goodness depends upon the length of Time it is Stewing. Yours Ever,

M. J. H.

Maria Josepha to Serena.

Sheff. Place : January 25, 1796.

In as much as there are two Letters waiting to go to you, I must write to-day, otherwise, as I have not time for a long letter, I would have waited a little. Mr. and Mrs. H. Foster and the two girls came last Sat., and they stay till Monday next. The French folk, Lally, Malouet and the Prince de Poix, came on Monday, not having comprehended we expected them on the Thursday and Friday preceding. They made a little Tour of it by taking Cuckfield in their way, and of course from thence they explored some of the worst roads in the county. They narrowly escaped going round by Brighton, which as Lally has been here so often was rather stupid. Poor creatures ! They had not eat anything from 11 to 10 at night when they arrived here, and of course eat most voraciously at Supper. They all seem in tolerable good spirits, and I am sure in excellent Voice, for I never heard such a noise as they made last night after Supper, Lally and the Prince de Poix supporting the right of the Young Princess to the Crown, in case of the King and Prince's death, against Malouet and Mr. Foster, who Maintained the right of the Duke of York. It is wonderful to me there can be two opinions about it, as there is no law to the exclusion of Females from the Crown in England, and of course the Inheritance is belonging to the oldest Branch. But I have met with several people who have made it a doubt, therefore I hope the case will never happen, least the whole Kingdom should be divided in opinion. Papa had a letter from one of his Constituents begging to be informed of the Law relative to the case which he stated as I mentioned. I believe we shall not go to Town yet, and I should not wonder if we stayed till Easter. Papa may possibly go up next week for two or three days, and if he does I am hoping to go with him to see Harriet before she goes to Mrs. Dawkins. If I succeed in that, I shall be very glad to remain late in the country, as I am sure it will be of great service to My lady who mends very fast, and it will be a saving to the purses of both Milord and Myself.

They talk very much of a Dissolution of Parliament in the Spring or beginning of Summer; I wish it was well over; but I hope and believe Papa has no thoughts of Bristol or of any place if he is to be at expence about it. I broke off to correct the Press, and it is too late to add more at present.

Adieu. Yrs. ever,
M. J. H.

Serena to Maria Josepha.

Bath : 29 January, 1796.

Thou dearest of all Rigmaroles. You are more delightful in your Medley than the Wisest, and I interpret your misteries better than a Sybil. I comprehend the various movements of mind which you are playing off and I enter into the spirit and essence of every line. 'Cela suffit.' Would it do you any harm were I to confess for once a dawn of something like a hope, or a wish that something would come of something. Comprenez vous? Don't run wild now and suppose more than necessary, so as to make a disappointment, if it should prove otherwise, but do remember like a dear thing, that all you have to do is to be quiet and prudent, and I suppose the whole of your conduct to be watched. It is indeed most really natural to suppose any rational Man will do so before he ventures to speak. Let him not then see you are to be too easily won. Believe me it is the medium between coldness and the reverse that must gain men. If possible not to let them see their power. To be calm, easy,

natural, but more quiet and gentle than you naturally
are. I almost defy any sensible man not to like you when
you are chearful and yet quiet. Exclusive of all partiality
you are at such times most really pleasant, and when you
suppress little Demons of passion and let the best parts of
your heart appear, one certainly must love you. In the
last year of your life you have made your character known
so much to your advantage, that very few girls have been
more favourably mentioned, or more generally known,
which by the way may have its good effect, so that
nothing can be against you but yourself. Command your
impetuosity, your little whims and hurry of temper. Do
not indulge the moment at the hazard of your comfort or
advantage. This is all you have to do, to be a happy
woman, and at all events it is your only means of obtaining everything you wish. This is the burden of my Song,
and, believe me, not merely said as an incentive to follow
my advice, but it is my real opinion. The good accounts
of dear Lady Sheff rejoice me. . . . I hope you are right
as to our Fleet, but letters from Plymouth quite tor-
mented me about our Ships. God Preserve them! Never
sure was such weather for so long a continuance. Oh
Mirabile Dictu—Maria an Æconomist! Without powder
to save it! Observe my words that the times will do good
and teach people to think. Don't imagine I suspect you
of too much thought, but in some points people will take
the opportunity of an honourable retreat from expences.
Never, however, was there remembered a more shockingly
extravagant winter known at Bath. It is really shame-
full to hear of the Private Balls given with everything
brought from Town, etc. One was very excellent. The
fruit, confectionery, and most expensive part did not come
till next day when the Ball was over. They sat up till
nine in the morning. Adieu, Dearest Maria. Tell Louisa
that I give her great credit for her advance in dress, and

set it down to myself. What will be said in future of a sage old Aunt preaching coquetry and dissipation? As my two children are opposites my advice must be (like a Lawyer) calculated for both sides of the question.

Maria Josepha to Miss Ann Firth.

Sheff. Place: Monday, Feb. 1, 1796.

You will have seen in the papers Admiral Christian's Fleet is returned to Portsmouth. What an unfortunate business it has been. . . . The French Folk left us this morning. They have been very entertaining tho' as noisy as I expected. Lally and the Prince de Poix have sung a great deal, and the former read Zaïre last night and repeated in a preceding evening some scenes from a new Tragedy he is writing, founded on the Polish Revolution, called Kosciusko, the name of the General. They were all in good French Spirits, that is, one minute crying over the Letters they received from France, and the next laughing, singing, and talking Nonsense.

The 1st vol. of the Gibbonian Memoirs is quite printed off and the 2nd so far advanced that I now begin to hope, with some confidence, the work may come out soon after Easter. Milady and I are excellent Devils, and corrected yesterday 3 sheets of 16 pages each.

Tomorrow there is a Navigation Meeting. Alas! the poor Navigation!

Adieu. All here desire to be Kindly remembered.

Yrs Ever,

M. J. H.

I should not wonder if we go to London very soon. Papa says he will not again go up without My Lady, and the Corn business is very likely, I think, to call him up, and as that is a subject on which he is so well informed and may be of great use; we all wish him to go on with it.

Serena to Maria Josepha.

Bath : February 5, 1796.

I am not quite easy about dear Lady Sheff. I am convinced those spasms in her throat happen from relaxation and weakness. . . . How shocking the attack again upon the King. I am terrified lest it should affect his spirits, or lest at last some Devil may succeed in these attempts. It seems to me as if they were encouraged by finding that there is no punishment for it. I wish a few were hanged directly in Terrorism, for I am convinced these are not days for too much mildness.

Lord Sandwich told Mrs. Fanshawe of an intention of proroguing Parliament, which seemed a preliminary to a dissolution and put me in a tremor, and yet I should suppose it could not be a worse period for Government.

Tell me all you know, and if Sheff has any plan as to Bristol, etc. A contest seems to be too wild to suppose him to undertake, but I fear being led by fair promises, etc. . . . Bath is intolerable. All Nations of the Earth come to visit us.

Once more, dear vile little Demon, may Heaven preserve you in the right way.

SERENA.

Maria Josepha to Serena.

February 7, 1796.

. . . It is surprising how little anybody in London troubled themselves about the Stone flung into the King's Carriage. These enormities are really becoming so common they will cease to create astonishment or horror. It was a smooth flint cut into sharp corners that was flung. It touched the Queen's cheek. The King caught it in his hand and gave it to Lord Harrington, who was in the Carriage, to 'keep for his sake.' The Duchess of Newcastle mentioned this.

Maria Josepha to Miss Firth.

Sheffield Place: February 13, 1796.

Now that all the Trunks and Boxes are ready to lock and nail down, I can set down comfortably to write to you my last letter from the Country. We go on Monday. The dear Lady has quite recovered, and is, I think, quite as well as before. I hope the moving to Town will not give her Cold again; but at all events she must keep quite quiet there—which is a respite for Louisa till after Easter probably.

. . . Papa thought he was in hopes that he should not be wanted in Town for some time: but if he did he found himself mistaken, and I think he was mistaken in imagining he did not wish to go. The Corn Committee cannot go on without him, and I believe he is one of the most active, usefull members of it; and as this is not a mere political business, but of general Utility, I am very glad he does not give it up. James has at last got a place of 70*l.* a year. It is as Collector of Window Tax at Bristol. He must reside there three or four months in the year, and the rest of the time will be at his own disposal. There was some difficulty about his age, which Mr. Irvine very kindly settled for him. We saw him the evening we got to Town, and for a wonder he, Mrs. Irvine and the little girl are all well. . . . They are removed into Scotland Yard, so are still nearer neighbours to us than they were. We had a good dish of Corn between him and Papa.

Miss C. Fanshawe is mending, and they hope will recover at last. She has had a hard struggle for her life. I forget if I told you Mrs. Bull came back to her husband, and is living at Bath upon what she can get by washing. She never had courage to see Aunt.

Serena to Maria Josepha.

In the first place, I likes your history of your own dear self. It seems to me as if you were more happy and comfortable than ever I knew you. . . . I am glad you have had some excursions into the riot of London. It mixes very well with your pleasant parties at home. I chuse to know all your Beaux. Tell me something of Mr. Stanley. I approve of being told of Books. I never saw Madame de Genlis' 'Cygne,' but have heard it abused as really unfit, as you say, to be read. Have you read Diane de Polignac's Essays? Have you seen a little Thing called 'Leonore'?

Maria Josepha to Serena.

Privy Gardens: Monday, February 22, 1796.

. . . I have not read Mdme. de Polignac's Essays. Do you like them? I have seen the little thing called 'Leonora,' and have got it of my own from the Author, alias Translator, Mr. Stanley; for I suppose you mean a Tale in Verse from the German. I cannot say I am delighted with it. The best parts are the Lines at the End, his own addition. Another Translation is coming out soon by Mr. Spencer which is likely to be better, but Mr. Stanley was very ill used about it. He lent his Translation to Lady D. Beauclerc, who took advantage of it to make beautiful drawings from it, and Mr. Spencer, her Nephew, I think, undertook to improve the Translation, and meant to publish it with Engravings from Lady Diana's Drawings. Mr. Stanley did not intend to publish, but hearing of this he was affronted, and had his translation printed in hot haste.

Maria Josepha to Miss Ann Firth.

Privy Gardens: February 25, 1796.

We received the account of poor Mrs. Gibbon's death yesterday. For three or four days she has been expected to die hourly. She has gone off without pain. Papa and Mrs. Gould are her joint executors and residuary legatees. He wishes very much to avoid going down to Bath—on many accounts, but particularly because the Bristol people would expect him to pay them a visit . . . an honour he is not ambitious of at present.

Mrs. Gibbon's papers are in such confusion that Aunt wishes him to come down if he can. Aunt writes in great hurry of spirits. Besides not being well and being hurried with looking over the papers, she did not like the poor old woman's death when it came to the point. Papa has not an idea what he will get. She had a very generous mind, and has proved it by her Will ; saying she would not avail herself of Papa's active friendship without leaving him a mark of esteem and gratitude. This will was made a short time after Mr. G.'s death. There was a former one in which she had left everything to him and only a 20*l.* legacy to Mrs. Gould.

I have not been out in an evening since we came to town, we have had constant pleasant parties every evening at home, really one enjoys society much more in that way than in any other. Milady mentions to all our friends that she never goes out. Theresa Parker and her Aunt Miss Robinson have been here almost every day. William Clinton [1] has likewise been a great deal with us and has got over much of his apprehension and does not seem afraid we should bite him. He is a dear amiable creature and that's the truth of it.

[1] William, son of the late Sir Henry Clinton, K.B., married Louisa Holroyd in 1797.

B B

Serena to Maria Josepha.

March —, 1796.

You must know that rather wishing to soften matters, I had only told my Brother what Mrs. Gould's situation was. . . . Had Mr. Gibbon survived his Step Mother there is a Will in which Mrs. Gould has but 20*l.* and a few keep sakes, so that she could not long have expected more. My brother, of course, was not named in that Will. . . . All I thought could be expected from him was to give her the furniture as being scarce worth dividing . . . He keeping his Share of Plate, wine and books and Pictures. I shall know to-morrow what he says to her.

. To be sure if I read the Newspapers I must know that the Gib. Memoirs are going to appear. As poor Mrs. Gibbon determined not to like them I do not regret her not seeing them, and I trust she is better employed, but I long to see them. Tell dear Sheff. I have got the large Bible in the nicest oblique way possible. Indeed after I had sent off my letter yesterday, I had a note from Mrs. Gould full of his goodness about the Plate, and well she might, for the Urn and the very large Coffee pot besides spoons, Sugar things etc. she has a noble Share. In short it was a genteel way of giving her the whole, and she considers it so. The tea pot is just sent me with the tiny coffee pot and Candlestick. The tea pot is hideously old, made out of a Canister for a Tea Chest. I never saw it before. I am however very glad Sheff. has been so genteel. It gives more pleasure and speaks more for him, than the taking all he could. I am afraid these large Jars etc., cased and sent to him will cost a great deal. I will send the little coins by the first friend going to town. I hope the watch was received. There is much of the Ancestry ready to go. The poor Oval Mama over the

Chimney was rubbed in the forehead, which I observe that it may not be supposed owing to package.

Adieu, dear Animal, with love to all around you.

Yours,

S. H.

Maria Josepha to Miss Firth.

Privy Gardens : March 18, 1796.

Milady has got a fresh Cold and coughs dreadfully ; she was so well before that it is very provoking, she has not eat a bit of meat or been out even in the carriage for four days.

The Memoirs must now be out in a few days, Papa and Messrs. Cadell and Strahan have got into a little dispute about a part of the preface they did not like to publish, but I hope it is amicably adjusted ; very spirited Notes passed between them.

Serena to Maria Josepha.

Bath : March 20, 1796.

The night before last I went to Lady Northlands' tea-drinking in honour of her Son's Wedding, as he married a Hesketh, niece to Lady H. It was uncommonly genteel. Not too hot, very gay and fine. But it had the advantage of convincing me how very much I should dislike routs, etc. I do not love cards and if I did would not throw away my money. The Lowest is half-crown Casino, and scarce any other game played. Three or four guineas a night so spent if I could afford it, I could not forgive myself for doing it, and without playing, an Old Woman not only passes her time unpleasantly, but looks awkward.

. . . Lady Jane Long was a curious Guillotine figure. Not only her head made perfectly easy to cut off without obstruction of any kind, but her body dress seemed calculated for it. I am told she is as violent as her Brother, Lord Lauderdale. . . . Yours ever and aye

S. H.

B B 2

Serena to Maria Josepha.

Bath : Saturday, April 1, 1796.

To be sure I did get the Memoirs on Wednesday, and in spite of my degree of Fore knowledge they interest and amuse me more than anything I could have, and I think they will do Sheff. credit.   I like the arrangement etc., etc. ' cela suffit.'   I wish we could send them to Mrs. Gibbon, for as now all her little prejudices are removed I think she would be much pleased · with them. . . . They make me feel affectionate to Mr. Gibbon, as you certainly see the most amiable parts of his character in these accounts and in his letters.   Only that he must not be proud (where I hope he is) and it would cost him more grinding down to purifie him, I should think he would be vain of this publication, and I am sure no Friend has done so much honour to the Memory of another as my brother has done to his.

Maria Josepha to Miss Ann Firth.

Privy Gardens: Friday April 15, 1796.

I have been very Gibbonian lately, i.e. very lazy in my correspondence.

You will be very glad to hear that the Ceremony of Presentation is over with Louisa, and that she acquitted herself extremely well ; managed her Hoop. very well and nothing could be better than her manner when presented, as if she had been at Court all her life.   The next best thing to hear is that neither she nor Mylady are much tired to-day, or feel any bad effect from their grand beginning yesterday ; for they went to an immense squeeze at the D. of Leeds at night besides Court.   Louisa's Train was a demi-Saison striped Apple-green and White, narrow stripes about half an Inch wide.   The Petticoat a rich Sattin striped Gauze, with a very beautiful pattern of yellow flowers between the Stripes, a broad Silver Fringe at the Bottom, Silver Gauze, two Ostrich and one Silver feather on her Head. Milady wore the same Train she had last year, a Gold Tissue with a very elegant Petticoat, white crape and gold. Mine was the same in every respect as last year at the Birthday. The Drawing-room was very full, which is less formidable and more agreeable than a very thin one, and considering it was so full, we did not stand a great while. All the Royal Family was present in all its branches. We were at the Duke of Leeds from ten to half-past twelve, so Louisa had an opportunity of seeing many of the Belles of the day, of whom she has so frequently heard. You would be surprised to see how she resigns herself to fate both in going out and buying what is necessary. I want a long Letter with all your remarks on the Memoirs.

Maria Josepha to Serena.

Monday, April 18, 1796.

. . . I have not told you we passed three hours at Mr. Stanley's on Friday morning, most supremely entertained with the sight of a large collection of drawings chiefly by Pocock from Mr. S.'s own sketches done in Iceland, Switzerland and Scotland, and a Series of drawings by Pocock expressing the History of a Ship from her first sailing out of Port to being wrecked. We were shown many other curious things in the way of Books and Prints, and were treated with a Concert by a Nightingale that did sing sweetly indeed. . . .

Yesterday Pap. dined at Lord Fife's, Theresa Parker,[1] Miss Clive and her Brother, and Mr. Jekyll came in the evening. I will not give you the fatigue of hearing of all

[1] Theresa Parker married (1798) Hon. G. Villiers, third son of the first Earl of Clarendon, and was mother of the fourth Earl.

our engagements for this week. You shall have information of them as they take place. . . . I think I must conclude this Letter tho' it is shorter than I like. But now,
I recollect, I will not finish till I have scolded you, which
I have always forgot, for your Indignation about 'Les
Chevaliers du Cygne.' Have I not told you fifty times
(more or less) that I had never heard the character of the
Book before I read it; but took it for granted, as her
former works were unexceptionable, this must be so, particularly as it was professedly written for youth! and
when I had read it, I only mentioned it to you with surprise Madame de Genlis could have composed it. At the
same time I do not agree with you that the whole is
uninteresting and improbable. Armoflé, entirely omitted,
I think there are many beauties remaining, but not the
slightest excuse can be made for her character in any
respect.

To make a great Skip to a very different book : Have
you read the Bishop of Llandaff's 'Apology for the Bible,'
in answer to Thomas Paine's 'Age of Reason.' What I
have read pleases me extremely. The Language is clear
and strong, and more satisfactory than those things in
general are, for I think the more that is said upon those
subjects, the more the case is puzzled, nine times in ten.

Adieu, dear Old Aunt,
M. J. H.

John Thomas Stanley.
(1st Lord Stanley of Alderley.)

CHAPTER XVI.

1796.

THE WORD 'OBEY' IS SAID.

MAY TO OCTOBER.

Éclaircissement—Universal sunshine—Serena's home truths—Wedding cloaths—Tiresome lawyers—'Sheffield for Ever'—Count Rumford on chimneys—Obstacles overcome—The 'Dear Lady's' illness—The marriage—The bride.

Maria Josepha to Serena.

Thursday, May 5, 1796.

DEAREST of all dear Aunts,—I must compose myself by talking to you a little. How glad I am I wrote my last letter to you, but it was very unfortunate Papa did not come home in time to direct it till the next day, otherwise I might have had an answer this morning before I told you any more, much more than I thought at least so soon, I should have had to tell you. I wish I could fly to you, and stroke you, and beg you not be put out of your way, for your dear maternal heart will feel a mixture of sensations when I tell you Mr. Stanley came to an Éclaircissement with that Angel of a Woman, Milady, yesterday evening. She is delighted with the extreme delicacy and honour of all his sentiments and has long ago been convinced of the warmth of his attachment to me. This morning, but a short time since, she told me all she was commissioned to say. My ideas are not yet sufficiently settled to say more upon the subject. The only thing I could do, is to write to you. But as far as I can see, I think I may be a most happy woman—too happy, when the prospect is so good, I cannot check apprehensions. I cannot deserve the happiness I enjoy and have enjoyed at home, with the addition of such expectations as I may indulge. Imagine with what anxious impatience I shall expect your answer. I will write more fully in a day or two certainly, but at present I cannot. Tuesday we were at a Ball at Sir J. Coghill's where he was, and where he was on the point of speaking all night without being able to get courage. He is so intolerably diffident, that he would not suppose it possible he could be loved as he must be for his happiness. How anxious I shall be when you first know him to see your opinion. Adieu my dear best old Aunt. Imagine the most affectionate hug I can give you and pray don't yet mention it to any living soul—it is such early days. Yours ever and for ever.

M. J. H.

Maria Josepha to Miss Ann Firth.

May —, 1796.

One of my oldest and sincerest friends such as you, will I know receive this letter with a warmth of heart and affectionate feeling towards me, such as I have experienced so much of lately that I am completely overcome by it; therefore measure your expressions, I entreat you, more by what I can bear, than by what you will feel on the very serious occasion of my happy prospects, which may at first seem a contradiction.

I have not before mentioned much about Mr. Stanley because I knew your friendly wishes would lead you on very fast and therefore though certain myself, I would say nothing to raise your expectations. I believe I may say with the most perfect assurance of not being deceived, that the most amiable and feeling heart in the world is entirely mine, and what so much encreases my

happiness that all those I love are as pleased as possible with my prospects. That Angel—Lady S.—my Pen
cannot do justice to. I am only convinced (but for what
merit of ours I cannot say) that she was sent into our
Family as a Blessing from Heaven. Papa and Louisa
are all you can imagine them and dear Aunt's letter this
Morning is all herself. I cannot enter into any particulars at present. You may suppose me agitated; but
indeed I am much more so than is rational. However
I cannot help it. Sorrow is more easily to be borne with
fortitude than joy beyond all the hopes I ever had
formed. I have written to nobody about this but you.
I wish you not to mention it—but knew it would give
you too much satisfaction for me to keep it from you,
and it is not everybody, who would give me credit for
the happiness I form to myself in the idea of being
settled with a man I can love, honour and obey, without
putting their ridiculous ideas to it and laughing at me.
You will not laugh.

Believe me that I am and ever shall be your most
truly affectionate   M. J. HOLROYD.

Serena Holroyd to Maria Josepha.

Bath: May 5, 1796.

As I think you are a dear impetuous Animal I will
not wait till tomorrow, though too late and too tired to
say all my say at once, and yet as I can say from my
heart that I approve, I think that will be worth sending.
I have for some time past exactly hoped what I still
hope, not merely in regard to him as being so unexceptionable, but as thinking I saw you coming rationally
round some deliriums that made me tremble for your
peace of mind, and in constant fear of some Sillygisms.
You need never fear my severity. I can very sincerely
suppose the state of your Mind what you describe, and I

see more chance of happiness in such a situation than in what you first preferred, because as I trust you have no real levity, as I also trust your principles are generous and virtuous, you surely would not accept what you did not resolve to deserve, and I can trust your real good sense on great occasions; that you will cease to trifle, and that in fact were you to change your state, you would feel the consequence of preserving the Esteem of the person you chose, and seek his happiness as your own. I have ever said, even when most angry with you, and I still think it, that if united to a Man you could not help esteeming, it would reform you into a rational Being. That having no other pursuit you would be tranquil, and that you would have too much principle to be seriously wrong; all I ever fear is temper, because of all conquests over one's self that, every hour, is the hardest to change; but even in that respect your being happy may do a great deal. You will think me premature in all these observations, but my reason is, that I would entreat you to reflect impartially, (before you accept), what you ought to be, and whether you can do your duty, in which believe me, dearest Maria, I include all tolerable chance of happiness. From all I have heard of his disposition I own it did not seem to me as if you were congenial souls . . . but possibly he is the more likely to make you right than if you married a wild Animal like yourself. You are however too rational when you chuse it, not to give me the most sanguine hopes. Who could read for example this candid sensible letter of yours and not take to you. I feel for you more affectionate hopes and wishes than a folio would express. Tell me all that interests me that I may spare myself thinking of any one else.

God bless you ever.

S. H.

Maria Josepha to Serena.

Saturday.

I begin by saying, don't mind anything I say—if, for instance, I should say I long to see you, because you could be of no real use to any of us, unless Parliament should be dissolved before June, in which case we all hope you will come to us as Milady will accompany Papa to Bristol. But I must be anxious for you to help me to bear being happy. It is so beyond all my hopes and expectations that I should have a prospect of being settled with an amiable man, to the satisfaction of all belonging to me, without any difficulties likely to occur, that I am as perfectly overcome as if under affliction ; and with a heart overflowing with gratitude, I may say, as well as joy, I have a countenance of perfect sadness, and only delight in an opportunity of a hearty cry. And this Man, with his affectionate and tender expressions only makes me so much the worse. How can one feel at the same moment so humble and so proud? I feel as if I could never deserve the kindness I meet from all, but by being totally different; and yet I am more vain than I can express, that, such as I am, I should have so thoroughly gained such a heart as his. . . . I am sure I shall affect you, but I cannot help it. Tho' Louisa laughs at me for saying so, yet I must repeat it, as I say, for ever, I have not been used to such affection, and it is sweet to be loved. May I be worthy of it ! and I cannot help hoping I shall, for the change taking place hourly in my sentiments makes me join with you in hoping all will be well. I would be all I should.

.   .   .   .

I will balance all this with a little on the opposite side of the scale, though not personal—and yet I think when

very happy oneself, one is more apt to feel for those in
sorrow, though the contrary has been said by great philosophers. The poor Aucklands, for whom we thought of
our Balls with most pleasure, are losing one of their little
girls, I much fear, after an illness of about three weeks.
Poor Mrs. Streatfield is in town, and is very little likely
ever to leave it alive. Lady Abergavenny is dying at
Bristol. . . . Emily [Pelham] is much better, and going
on very well, but . . . will not be at any of our Balls, I
am much afraid, which is a sad disappointment.

Adieu, my dearest of Aunts and Friends, anybody else
might think it very strange if I say, I feel a pleasure more
than I can express in the idea you are made happy by all
this. You will understand me—and indeed would much
wrong me if you suspected one improperly vain or conceited idea, dwelt in my mind. Once more, Adieu.

For ever affec^r. Yours,

M. J. H.

Serena to Maria Josepha.

Bath : Sunday Morn., May 8, 1796.

And what think you, my beloved Maria, was the effect
of that dear letter of yours and the few expressive lines
of Louisa received today. Absolutely a burst of tears
till I sobbed, and which are still running down my
Cheeks, and yet believe me, in looking back my whole
life past, I cannot recollect a moment of such unmixed
sincere heartfelt happiness as I feel at this instant. It
is so compleat and so almost beyond idea that every con-
curring circumstance should so combine for us all, that I
cannot compose myself sufficiently to be certain it is not
a dream.

And now my dearest Maria, do pray talk for me to
Mr. Stanley. Tell him I hope for a large interest in his

heart. That I long to know personally the Man whose character you made me love, even before I had an idea of being interested so nearly in it, and that I expect to owe to him a great deal of my future happiness, in which expectation I have the most perfect confidence—therefore I will now conclude with blessing you a thousand times as I feel my heart too full to say more.

Yrs. Ever and ever,

S. H.

Maria Josepha to Serena.

Undated.

I should have liked the pleasure of telling you of the unexpectedly happy news of yesterday myself, but I was so very late in getting up, and obliged to go out almost as soon as I had done breakfast, that it was not in my power. It made the Ball go off so much better than I could have expected, for the best they had allowed me to hope was that Sir John would not positively say No! That he should freely give consent was much beyond my ideas. Mr. S. did not intend going to him at first, but he took courage and went. Sir John met him and wished him happiness, and he came immediately here to tell us his reception, which tho' to be sure it did not assist me in eating my breakfast, was much better than Meat and Drink. I believe to those who know Sir John thoroughly, this has been a matter of triumph indeed. I do not know when he will wish to see me, or to meet Papa to talk about it, but about that I am not at all anxious or impatient. Papa has been. talking to me this morning of his intentions. He wished to have written to you and asked your opinion about what he meant to do in regard to me, but will not have time. However, I told him I had mentioned it.

And now I must tell you something of the Ball, which,

independent of my etcs. went off extremely well.   The
supper was very elegant and plentiful without any superfluous ornament, 146 sat down; they kept up the dancing
till half-past five.   I was *ordered* to go to bed at four,
and, would you believe it, I *obeyed*.   He was so extremely
anxious about my being fatigued—and I had gone through
a great deal, and felt ill a little at the beginning of the
evening—that I could not refuse taking myself away, or
else I had picked up a little by that time, and could have
stayed longer.   I danced eight dances.   I did not like the
appearance of beginning with him, and kept him for
Supper which was better.   My other partners were Mr.
Cockbourne, Mr. Wilson, Sir Thomas Wilson's son, and
Colonel Campbell, a very intimate friend of Mr. S.'s, as
much so as William Clinton. . . .

You do not seem to have attended to a part in one of
my letters relating to your coming to us, in case of a dissolution of Parliament, which I believe will certainly take
place within a fortnight.   Milady would be so miserable
not to go with Papa,—and there really is no reason why
she should not if she wishes it—that I cannot wish her to
stay behind him, and indeed I do not think anything but
his insisting upon it, would persuade her to do so.

Serena to Maria Josepha.

Bath : May —, 1796.

No indeed !

My dear Child I never comprehended your idea in
case of dear Sheff's coming to Bristol.   My invitation
to her dear Ladyship might tell you I only thought of
having them here ; and I was a little thinking about your
being in an awkward state and yet it never once entered
my Pate how it might be removed ; but you precious
poor thing, how can you doubt my going to you if you
wish it, even though Mr. Tuft might take time to be

washed, or my house might take cold or any such grand
objections? Let me only know as soon as you can that
I may be ready to set off. Answer my query about
taking my man servant. I rejoice that dear Sheff has
acted so kindly. . . ..Adieu my dearest Maria. I do so
long to see this Mr. Stanley, though perfectly acquainted
with him.

Yrs. Ever,
S. H.

Serena to Maria Josepha.

Bath: Sunday, before breakfast, May —, 1796.

I have just heard that Lally is here and asked if I
was at Bath. Your letter somehow seemed to draw
nearer conclusions to-day, because things not spoken of
before are talked of, and since you have said so much, I
desire to know where the word *obey* is to be said. I
suppose London, and then to escape to S. P. Perhaps
when we meet you may answer a question in vain asked
before a dozen times. The Country or Place of Abode?
You seem to have no doubt of Bristol. I long to know
how that is. I had a letter this morning from Lord
Worcester requesting my interest as he means to set up
for Gloucester—the County. It was the first I knew of
his giving up Bristol. . . . Against I go to town you are
to think of a smart hat or bonnet for dress for me to look
handsome in. Also if Dowagers wear summer silks buy
me one. The Hat must be fitted to my nose so you need
only think of it. How I long to tell Mr. Stanley what
an Espiègle he has, poor man, taken to. Adieu, dear
thing. God bless you for Ever and Ever,

S. H.

Maria Josepha to Miss Ann Firth.

He is eldest Son to Sir John Stanley, Bart., of Cheshire, has been in Iceland, published an account thereof, has translated a Poem from the German called Leonora—with considerable additions of his own, is, for anything I know to the contrary, an F.R.S., and what is more, has the most amiable feeling heart I believe a Man can be possessed of, and what is still more, if faith is to be put in Words, Actions and Looks—loves me with the most perfect Love. But I must not give way to my Pen which is inclined to run on about my Happiness. . . . Papa has been more kind than anything you can imagine, and has determined from the first that the affair should not be stopped or delayed by the want of anything in his power to forward it. Mr. Stanley's father is as generous on his side, and the general kindness of everybody is to me very overcoming. I don't know how I have deserved such good fortune, for I looked upon difficulties as a necessary part of the business, and we have had none. It is not yet determined whether we accept the place in Cheshire to live at or not. He has a house of his own furnished, in Lower Brook Street, which is a very nice part of the Town. As to present destination, our going to the Country depends upon Parliament or rather Bristol. Papa will wait to be invited there, of which however we have very little doubt, and likewise he is certain to be returned without expense, but of that ' Mum.'

You may talk of it (the marriage) now to anybody you please; it is so publicly known that it would be absurd to attempt keeping it a secret. As to a description of the outside of the Man you perhaps would not be enchanted with his first appearance. He is very dark, black eyebrows [1] that meet, and very near-sighted, but he has a sensible and good-humoured countenance, at least I think so, because I know he is both, but all that is of so little consequence I should have forgot to mention whether he was fair or dark, if you had not asked among your other enquiries.

I have been introduced to his Mother and seen her three times. She is perfectly agreeable to the Match. There are three Sisters and one Brother, all very amiable and pleasing—one sister lives with the Mother, the other two with Sir John.

Two of our Balls are over, and went off with general satisfaction. The last is to-morrow. I have not enjoyed the dancing as I should have done with a more indifferent heart, yet I am glad there has been an opportunity of returning some civilities and pleasing some of our acquaintance . . .

Adieu once more.

Yours most affectionately,
M. J. H.

Maria Josepha to Serena.

May 17.

This morning Sir John Stanley has been here for the first time. Nothing was said on the subject of his meeting, but it seemed as much as he was able to do to come and talk upon indifferent matters. He is so extremely nervous that he has frequently great difficulty in making up his mind to see an intimate friend that he has not seen for some time.

Yesterday and this morning we have been making a great Progress in buying Apparell, and you may imagine there is sufficient employment for our Time. I think

---

[1] This characteristic gave rise to various familiar appellations, such as Crow, Maître Corbeau, etc.

C C

you must have been amused at receiving an empty cover
this Morning. It was left on the table for Louisa, and
Davy, without looking, sent it to the Post. I suppose
you thought my Brains were Wool gathering! How I
long for your arrival! What a Summer we shall have!
We shall not move for two months at least after 'Obey'
has been said.

Maria Josepha to Serena.

Privy Gardens, May 19.

Tiresome Boring old Woman,—How can one descend
to such minute particulars? and how can you ask
such forgetful questions? for how could he frank if he
was not in Parliament! 'Pour cela,' however, it is of
no great consequence, as he does not intend to come in
again, which I am very glad of, as he is so warm in
Politics when engaged, and on the Liberty side too,
which may lead to anything bad, with the best original
intentions, that it is much better and safer for the
Domestic Happiness of both, that he should give up the
pursuit entirely, not having the least ambitious turn of
mind. To proceed—his name is John Thomas, he is
Captain in the Cheshire Militia, and as to Abode, of that
I could tell you more to-morrow, because it is to be
decided to-day, whether his Father gives up one of his
Estates to him in Cheshire or not.

He, the Father, is very desirous of his having it; and
as there is much to be said for and against, I hold my
mind in a state of equilibrium as much as possible, determined to forget all the possible reasons against whatever
is decided. Mr. Stanley himself leaves Sir John to determine without attempting to byass him; but I think he
rather wishes to have it. . . . I must tell you the name
of the place is Alderley, and that it is not far from Man-
chester, in a beautiful Country. I am very glad you

have been so civil to poor Lally. Papa Makes you a Bow
for it. I had an outcry from Miss Huff for detail, and I
wrote her a long history the day before yesterday ; she
was as bad as you about minutiæ.

Many thanks, dearest old Woman, for the Muslin you
mention. I will get nothing like it, and I am sure I
shall condescend to admire your taste. I think I had
better do nothing about your Hat or Gown till you come
to Town as you had better look and see what is to be got.

Adieu, I must scribble no more. Do you want to hear
from me when Franking ceases ? ? ? ?

Yours ever and ever,
M. J. H.

I am surprised to find you know nothing of Miss
Mellish's Match. It has been going on some time. Mr.
Gurdon, Major in the Norfolk Militia I think, at least he
is a Norfolk Man. I would not change with her, but I
do think Mine is no common lot. You will be happy
when you hear how everybody speaks of him, and how
delighted every soul of our acquaintance seems with it. I
have met with much real kindness from numbers. Once
more adieu. . . . The Fanshawes were here last night.
Cat. looks amazingly well. Lady Hesketh is much better.
Deuce take my pen ! I must have another half sheet !
Louisa did dance a little last night. Emily Pelham was
not able to come to us.

Serena to Maria Josepha.

Bath : May 20, 1796.

Lally dined with me yesterday, and I could not help
telling him, and he flew into a rapture and laughed and
exclaimed and so on. You can guess how. He asked if
he might write, and I said by all means an Epithalamium.
I dare say he will. I did not know his Princess was here,

c c 2

and I told him so, else I should have done myself the honour, etc. He informed me she was not well, and they went this morning to Clifton.

Adieu, dear little Stanley elect.

Maria Josepha to Miss Ann Firth.

London: May 30, 1796.

I began a letter to you on Saturday, thinking it was long since I had written and that you would not grudge a few pence, but I was interrupted, which I now rejoice at, as the delay has enabled me to tell you ' Sheffield For Ever ' is the cry of Bristol and that this day he is Chaired with his Colleague Mr. Bragg, who comes in Lord Worcester's place who stands for the County of Gloucester. To take up my History a little further back. Papa went to Bath on Saturday se'en night, not to offer himself, but to be ready if he was invited, an *if* of which there was hardly a doubt. On Monday the Mayor and 3 principal Citizens came to invite him to take up his Residence at the Mansion House and to stand perfectly free of expense. It was thought by some it would be a good Measure if he subscribed 500*l.* ; but he was firm as a Rock in the contrary opinion and if the Contest had continued ever so violent he would have been freed of expense. A Mr. Hobhouse was his Antagonist, a man of most violent Democratic and Republican Principles, supported by all the Mob very vehemently ; but not by one respectable person. . . . We received the delightful and unexpected news at Lord Pelham's on Sat. evening by Express. In short the Election has been as flattering as possible. . . . Mr. Stanley does not come in this Parliament. He was in for Wootton Bassett ; but I am rejoiced to say he does not continue a Politician, for he is not at all calculated for one. He would be too Violent and he has too much

Roman Virtue to make either a good Government Tool or
a decided Oppositionist, and yet in these desperate Times,
a man must chuse his Party and stick to it. Voting and
acting according to Conscience will not do. . . . As for
ourselves, Sir John does not give up his Country House
to us at present. We do not talk even about a Summer
residence, because a round year must elapse before we
can want one. In Septr. we must join the Cheshire
Militia. We must probably go into Winter Quarters;
but if possible I shall hope to pass the Christmas at S. P.
The second Week in July is, I believe, the time fixed—
the business being done—and we shall come up to Town
for the Meeting of Parliament, which will make it very
little awkward for us. We shall go back to S. P. when
married, and the rest of the Family will follow in a few
days. As I have Diamonds and Pearls no more are given
me at present. But the Man seldom comes empty-
handed, and if we do not marry soon, he will ruin himself
first by the handsome presents he makes me. My Watch
is beautiful and the Chain the most elegant I have seen.
Neither of them ornamented with Diamonds; but as
handsome as possible without, and as it is not the fashion
to show Watch or Chain, I like it much better than if it
were finer. I have not time to particularise all my fine
things. I hope to shew you some day those that do not
wear out. Milady has bought all my Cloaths, very handsome and sufficient of everything without any superfluous
expence or extravagance.

The Man is sitting for his Picture to Edridge who
painted us all in the Summer, and I think it will be very
like. I suppose I must have the trouble of sitting again.
Adieu. I cannot write any more at present. The Pelham
interest is very high in our County at present. They
have brought in both the Seaford Members, George and
Charles Ellis, and Mr. John Crosse Pelham for Lewes in

the place of Harry Pelham. But that was a hard fought point and nearly lost by them. Mr. Pelham of course comes in for the County, I have not heard of any opposition.

Yours ever affectly,

M. J. H.

Maria Josepha to Miss Ann Firth.

Sheffield Place : June 10, 1796.

Friday Count Rumford[1] came, and has been turning all the Chimneys and Fireplaces in the House topsy turvy ever since, till this morning when he took his departure. Have you by any Chance seen his Essays which are lately published? I dare say you have not forgotten him as Sir Benjamin Thompson 13 years ago, and that you remember he was an uncommon Genius and very pleasant Man. He has lived the last 20 years of his life at Munich, as Prime Minister to the Elector of Bavaria. What raises him even more than his Talents in my mind is the really philanthropic benevolent motives that urge him to attempt doing all the good he has done. Bavaria owes much indeed to him. He came over to England in hopes of being of some service, and went to Ireland with the same intention, where I believe he has been of much use, and if they follow up the schemes he set them going upon, the state of the poor in that country will be wonderfully improved.

. . . So Lady Webster has ended with *éclat* as I alway thought she would. . . . Milord had just written a pressing invitation to come here the day before she eloped. I am sorry for Lord H. . . .

---

[1] Many fireplaces were reconstructed at this period under Count Rumford's superintendence. His principle for building them proved an infallible remedy against smoky chimneys.

Adieu. Hang these Lawyers! They will not let me go to the Races unless it is as Miss Holroyd, and that I will not do.

Yrs Ever affectly,
M. J. H.

Maria Josepha to Miss Ann Firth.

Sheffield Place : June 23, 1796.

Anything more comfortable than we are you cannot imagine, but if you can imagine a state of perfect felicity, it is that in which we now exist. Everybody happy and pleased with themselves and one another.

It is not merely being in love and beloved that is the agreeable part of the story, for that might be and other things not be as they are; but the society is harmony in all its parts. We came here on Saturday and the days have been as hours since.

How fortunate, how providential every event of late has turned out for me! This dear Woman who has made us all happy, by making me so for one, has, in some degree, harmonised my temper and disposition, and I am sure I am more equal to being a good Wife now than I should have been two years ago. Alas! if I am not one I have no excuse, which is a melancholy reflection; the sin must all rest on my Shoulders, for this Man would make the Devil love him and behave well to him. The House in Cheshire is to be ours, which we were very desirous of as I find it is a small house, the old one having been burnt down some years ago; therefore suitable to our Income, and it is desirable to have a Home and that that Home should be upon what will be our own Estate, as he has a great wish to be a country Gentleman.

We do not go to London to be married as I believe I told you I thought we should, but it will take place here and at Church, which I like much better than a House, unless there was some good reason for preferring the latter.

Adieu—this letter shall be devoted to Egotism and Happiness. I will not write chit-chat news, especially as I know none very interesting.

Yours ever affec^y,

M. J. HOLROYD.

Maria Josepha to Miss Ann Firth.

Indeed I will behave much better when I am married, for I have been very naughty indeed lately; only comfort yourself that every one of my correspondents has been treated still worse. I am sure that must be a satisfaction. I have lately delayed from day to day hoping I could tell you by waiting a little, when the event was with certainty to take place, and till to-day that has been quite impossible. This morning we had a letter from Cotes to say the Deeds were quite completed, and that they are ready to send into Cheshire for Sir John to execute. As he is at High Lake, a bathing place on the very extremity of the county, it will be a week before they can be returned here for us to sign. Monday or Tuesday in the week after this must be the day. I think it cannot be longer. I really cannot be Maidenly enough to help being heartily rejoiced things are drawing to a conclusion. It is a very tiresome state to be in, especially expecting for so long past as we have that a fortnight would conclude, and always finding another and another fortnight tacked on. We mean to go to Town for a week when we are married. I don't know any place we can be more snug and incog. in and as the business has been put off so long, we have some necessary arrangements to make in London before we go to the North. . . .

Now that I have taken up my Pen I have not any pleasant subject for you, excepting the grand one of my Happiness. I am very seriously uneasy for poor Milady's health, which is very bad indeed. She looks miserably, coughs much and sleeps very little. Mr. Tennant came a few days ago by chance, on his way from Brighton, and found her so indifferent that he bled her, and it was very fortunate that he did so for her blood was in a dreadful bad state. . . . I dread to think of her not recovering. She would be such a loss to Papa and indeed to us all, tho' we are leaving home, it is not for ever. I hope a few days in consequence of the bleeding and other discipline she is undergoing, will restore her in some degree; but it must be a work of time, a perfect recovery.

Having a circumstance to mark my ill treatment of you brings it very home to me, and makes me blush indeed, if you could see. Only think! that you have never had a word from me since William and Louisa were allowed to think of each other, and I am not sure if that might not be one reason to prevent my writing.

[Louisa Holroyd was now engaged to her cousin William Clinton.]

Maria Josepha to Miss Ann Firth.

Sheffield Place : October 7, 1796.

At last I can write to you with the power of giving certain intelligence of our motions. The Deeds arrived yesterday and were signed in the evening. Mr. Woodcock brought them and left us in the evening. There cannot be anything more ridiculous than the quantity of writing these Lawyers chuse to perform on these occasions. There were nearly 100 Skins of Parchment, and as many of the Deeds were triplicates, and others duplicates, you may imagine what a sight of Sheep skins there were.

Tuesday is the day we have fixed, and it must be

some very unforseen event indeed, that can any more delay us. Last week we were so much alarmed for our dear Milady, that I really was anxious to have our Union completed lest a melancholy stop might be put to it for some time; but within these three days she is mending, and tho' my hopes are very faint, yet I cannot help encouraging some especially if she continues a few days longer getting better. However at all events we have determined not to return here again. It could only be for a few days, and as she is not able to speak to us or even to see us but for a very short time in the day, and that Papa is almost always shut up with her, (for his attention is affectionate and unremitting to a degree beyond what I could have imagined) we could not give or receive pleasure by returning here equal to the pain of a second parting. Orders have been received by all Officers to join immediately, but Wm. Clinton who went to Town on Wed. applied to the D. of York for leave of absence for us, and he has gained 6 weeks, which time, or at least nearly all, we shall pass probably in London. Newcastle is to continue the quarters of the Regt. all the winter. I have not time at present to add more than that I do hope with some reason I shall no more sign myself,

Your affectionate

MARIA JOS. HOLROYD.

Theresa Parker to Maria Josepha.

Saltram : September 26, 1796.

. . . I long for Wednesday, when I flatter myself I shall receive a letter from a new correspondent, viz. Mrs. Stanley, who, though she may have changed her name, will, I hope, (I could venture to say I am sure) never forget her friendship for me, as 'tis one I value most highly. I often think with pleasure on what you promised me in

London, that instead of losing one friend I should gain two. Pray remind Mr. Stanley of this with my love (the expression may now be allowed). . . . And, now my dearest Mrs. Stanley (I must call you so for the first time but you shall be Jacky Dandy again soon) Adieu, Ever yours with truest affection, Tippy.

I like your assurance in talking of the Leslies[1] making such a Clatter ! ! ! I suppose you are grown such a poor, quiet thing that you would be quite subdued now with the Charivari that used to be made at S.P. by the Honble. Miss Holroyds.

Lord Sheffield to Mr. Stanley the day after his Marriage.

Sheffield Place: October 12, 1796.

Dearest of Crows,—Quod felix faustumque sit, multum et felices—and everything that can be said, suppose said, most heartily, by yours most fatherly,

SHEFFIELD.

I suppose an account of the very dear Lady has been sent you. The last night was not so good as the three preceeding, and this morning she is lower than usual and does not appear as well as she was.[2] Tennant imputes it to your departure yesterday.

Serena to the Bride.

Sheffield Place: October 12, 1796.

Our dearest Maria will have other hearts addressing her from hence this morning ; but I cannot let it pass without adding my little million of blessings which have

---

[1] The nieces of Lady Sheffield.

[2] Lucy, Lady Sheffield died on January 18, 1797.

Lord Sheffield married thirdly, 1798, Lady Anne North, daughter of the second Earl of Guildford, by whom he had a son and a daughter.

indeed never ceased following you since you left us. You will easily imagine you were our sole Theme yesterday. I shut myself up in my room vis à vis to my fire, without being able for a full hour to do any one thing but think of the Event of the Day. I built dear Castles which I hope are on a foundation not likely to be shaken. I traced the characters of my two children. My new one and yourself. I saw that even the difference of shades were such as would be advantageous to both. The essential qualities the same. The mutual confidence in the real worth of each other with the fond attachment already so fixed, seems to make all easy. The calm firmness, the command of temper which I so admire in one whose natural warmth gives it double merit, is your dear Husband's best security of being ever loved and respected by you. His good sense and affectionate heart secures you his kind indulgence, because he will know how to prize every conquest you make over yourself for his sake, and he will see in your errors, the faults only of education. He will look in your heart for the qualities which overbalance all the rest, and he will find you affectionate, faithful and sincere. Too generous to take advantage of indulgence, and only the more complying for it. Happiness never seemed more in the power of Mortals than in yours. God grant it then as I now forsee it! It is one of the first prayers of your

S. HOLROYD.

Theresa Parker to Maria Josepha.

Saltram : October 11, 1796.

. . . The fine weather is gone and we have now a few Equinoctial Gales, which, in days of yore, when the Seasons came regularly, used to happen in September, but probably the equinoxes like variety (a very natural thing)

and perhaps in a year or two they may happen at Xmas.
and Midsummer. . . .

I shall write often from London to you. There are
not many things I like better. I have scarcely recovered
my breath since you talked of not coming to town next
year. How I wish the odious Major and his Regiment,
and all that belongs to him at present, at Old Nick's. I
never will wish any of my friends to marry again—'tis
much too disinterested ; they might as well be dead.
'Tis so provoking that when we had just got to live a
great deal together in such a comfortable way, this *Man*
comes and spoils it all. Give my love to him and tell him
I hate him. (Could *you* say a more Irish thing ?) Adieu.
No room for affection. I can hardly insinuate.—T. P.

Maria Josepha to Miss Ann Firth.

Bolton Row : Oct. 17, 1796.

That I have intended writing every day since that
most dear Tuesday last, is I assure you perfectly true,
and not merely a civil speech thought of to commence
my letter prettily. You will readily likewise, I have no
doubt, think it possible that the first week of Marriage, a
Lady, without having lost affection for her friends, may
appear to neglect them ; and you will now receive the
assurance of my happiness having been secured, with the
most lively satisfaction. I say secured, because it began
five months ago and except in having put it out of the
power of anything but Death to divide us, and having
bid Adieu to anxiety, I have been as perfectly happy all
that time as I am now or ever can be. The little you
will see of my Beloved in our visit to you, I think will .
give you some Idea I have spoke the truth of him, but
he must be thoroughly known to have all his excellencies
of heart and mind properly estimated—but on that

subject you have already heard all that I can say, though I should never be tired of repeating it and therefore I will spare you more at present.

I suppose Louisa has written to you since we left S. P. and I hope she told you I went through the Ceremony very boldly—that is—did not leave out the word 'Obey.' I pronounced it indeed with as much satisfaction, as much certainty of having a pleasure in Keeping the Vow, as the word Love. And one of us must alter very much before I find it difficult to keep that promise. I cannot say it was pleasant taking leave of all those dear friends I am not again to see for so long, or to leave Milady so indifferent; but we parted with them all with much lighter hearts than we should have done a fortnight ago, when our alarms were much greater on that dear Woman's account. My fears are stronger than my grounds of hope, but I had no hopes at all till this sudden change. I know few people who would prove a greater loss to everybody with whom she is connected than this amiable woman. I, for one, should be very ungrateful not to be anxious for her, at the moment I am enjoying the felicity which she was undoubtedly the means of promoting. . . . Of one thing I think you may be certain, no Vicissitude can happen to *us* but from Sickness, Death, or *the Arrival of the French.* I feel perfectly bold in respect to all other possible events, which could in any way affect the perfect harmony we enjoy. . . .

I suppose a Cottage would be almost comfortable enough for us at present, but though we might be content with such an Habitation, yet it certainly adds to my happiness finding myself in the most comfortable house you can imagine, surrounded by every comfort of life and every source of amusement, such as Books of all Kinds, Drawings, etc. etc. with the help of which I could contrive

to find the days short if I was, I by myself I·—and then
the pleasure it gives him to see me take an interest in
all his possessions encreases the value I feel for them a
hundred-fold.   Newcastle, I find is to be our Winter
quarter—we have a month's leave of absence.

Adieu, my dearest Miss F.

Believe me for ever

Yrs. affectly,
MARIA JOSEPHA STANLEY.

INDEX AND BIOGRAPHICAL DETAILS.

D D

E E

PRINTED BY
SPOTTISWOODE AND CO., NEW-STREET SQUARE
LONDON

www.ingramcontent.com/pod-product-compliance
Lightning Source LLC
Chambersburg PA
CBHW030937110726
47900CB00004B/1031